Praise for
HEALER *of* CART...

"*Healer of Carthage* held me captive from the first page to the last. Lynne Gentry's authentic voice and rich detail in this breathtaking time-travel adventure delight with every twist. Gladiator games, plagues, romance, and high-stakes political intrigue carried me from the filthy streets of ancient Tunisia to its lavish palaces with a cast of characters I won't soon forget. Highly recommended!"

—Carla Stewart, award-winning author of
Chasing Lilacs and *Sweet Dreams*

"Until recently, I didn't think there could be a time-travel book that was also Christian. This book blew that idea right out of my head. Lynne Gentry has written a wonderful time-travel story that has elements of medical suspense as well, one of my favorite genres. Her characters leaped off the page, grabbed my heart, and pulled me through the portal. I lived every minute with them. The only problem is that I will have to wait awhile before the next installment comes. Write faster, Lynne!"

—Lena Nelson Dooley, award-winning author of
*Love Finds You in Golden, New Mexico; Maggie's Journey;
Mary's Blessing;* and *Catherine's Pursuit*

"With her debut novel, Ms. Gentry has proven to be a masterful storyteller. *Healer of Carthage* is full of depth and emotion, twists and turns that carry the reader away to ancient Rome. From the first page to the last, the reader is instantly taken into a world of emotion, secrets, and political intrigue. Ultimately, this is a story about healing past wounds and discovering love . . . in its many varied forms. I highly recommend accepting this author's invitation to fall into another world. A wonderful trip awaits."

—Kellie Coates Gilbert, author of *Mother of Pearl*

"What a wonderful premise! *Healer of Carthage* follows Lisbeth, a modern-day doctor, as she's transported through time to ancient Carthage. I found it fascinating to watch Lisbeth apply her knowledge of medicine to a group of very early Christians. This novel is rich in detail and drama. A unique and terrific debut by talented author Lynne Gentry!"

—Becky Wade, author of *Undeniably Yours*

"Lynne Gentry's debut novel pulls you in from page one and never lets you come up for air as you follow Lisbeth Hastings into the turbulent world of third-century Carthage in a gripping tale of mercy, passion, sacrifice, and deceit."

—Lisa Harris, author of *Dangerous Passage*

"From a modern-day emergency room to third-century back alleys, *Healer of Carthage* pulls readers into a riveting story that will keep pulses racing and hearts twisting. Beautiful writing. Compelling story. Enough twists and turns to keep you on your toes every step of the way. Kudos to author Lynn Gentry for this remarkable, haunting story line. Highly recommended!"

—Janice Thompson, author of *Queen of the Waves*

"Extraordinary writing. Exceptional story. I've just discovered my new favorite author in Lynne Gentry. With an incredible, compelling new voice she weaves the past and present together in a fascinating tale that I couldn't put down. I can't wait to read more from her, and while I'm waiting, I think I'll read *Healer of Carthage* again!"

—Elizabeth Goddard, Carol Award–winning author of *Treacherous Skies*, *Riptide*, and *Wilderness Peril*

Praise for
RETURN *to* EXILE

"Compelling. *Return to Exile* took me to a time period that I had never been that interested in and built a sympathetic heart in me for the horrific things Christians had to face in that area and time. Because Lynne Gentry's characters are so well-developed, they took up residence in my thoughts and have lingered there for over a week after I finished reading the book. Of course, I can hardly wait until the next book comes out. I believe every Christian should read these books to give them an awareness of how blessed we are to be able to live our beliefs without fearing for our lives."

—Lena Nelson Dooley, author of the double-award-winning
Catherine's Pursuit

"*Return to Exile*, Lynne Gentry's sweeping saga of lost dreams, epic struggles, sinister passions, and unrequited love—all playing out against the stunning backdrop of third-century Rome—returns to enthrall readers of her earlier *Healer of Carthage*. With surprising twists readers won't see coming, Gentry has created an inspiring story few will be able to put down until the final page. I am a huge fan of the Carthage Chronicles series, and of author Lynne Gentry. Can hardly wait for the final installment to see how everything turns out for Dr. Lisbeth Hastings!"

—Kellie Coates Gilbert, author of *A Woman of Fortune*

"Gentry has done it again! Book two in the Carthage Chronicles had me weeping and cheering right along with the main characters, Lisbeth and Cyprian. Their struggle to forge a life from the ashes of Carthage's diseased city made my heart pound, and as the peril facing them ratcheted, so did my pulse rate. Add Gentry's enviable talent for wordsmithing, and *Return to Exile* makes for an incredibly entertaining read."

—Elizabeth Ludwig, author of *Tide and Tempest*

"In *Return to Exile*, Lynne Gentry takes readers on another breathtaking journey as they are transported with Lisbeth from the twenty-first century back to third-century Carthage. But this time, while Lisbeth thinks she's prepared for what awaits her on the other side of the Cave of the Swimmers, there's no way for her to anticipate the frightening reality, as she is thrown into an impossible situation that will leave readers begging for more."

—Lisa Harris, author of the Christy Award–winning novel
Dangerous Passage

"Author Lynne Gentry has done it again! *Return to Exile* is a high-stakes adventure filled with unforgettable characters and amazing historical details. Gentry doesn't just write with boldness and authenticity but delivers powerful messages in the midst of the plot twists and turns. Turn the page to return to ancient Carthage and join Dr. Lisbeth Hastings in this time-traveling journey!"

—Elizabeth Byler Younts, author of *Promise to Return*

More from Lynne Gentry

THE CARTHAGE CHRONICLES

A Perfect Fit: An eShort Prequel to Healer of Carthage

Healer of Carthage

Shades of Surrender: An eShort Prequel to Return to Exile

Return to Exile

Valley of Decision

VALLEY

of

DECISION

A NOVEL

Lynne Gentry

HOWARD BOOKS
AN IMPRINT OF SIMON & SCHUSTER, INC.
New York Nashville London Toronto Sydney New Delhi

Howard Books
An Imprint of Simon & Schuster, Inc.
1230 Avenue of the Americas
New York, NY 10020

Scripture quotations marked NLT are taken from the Holy Bible, New Living Translation, copyright © 1996, 2004, 2007 by Tyndale House Foundation. Used by permission of Tyndale House Publishers, Inc., Carol Stream, Illinois 60188. All rights reserved.

First Howard Books trade paperback edition September 2015

HOWARD and colophon are trademarks of Simon & Schuster, Inc.

For information about special discounts for bulk purchases, please contact Simon & Schuster Special Sales at 1-866-506-1949 or business@simonandschuster.com.

The Simon & Schuster Speakers Bureau can bring authors to your live event. For more information or to book an event contact the Simon & Schuster Speakers Bureau at 1-866-248-3049 or visit our website at www.simonspeakers.com.

Manufactured in the United States of America

10 9 8 7 6 5 4 3 2 1

Library of Congress Control Number: 2015002897

ISBN 978-1-4767-4641-8 (pbk)
ISBN 978-1-4767-4642-5 (ebook)

For my grandchildren.
The cost of true courage is great.
The day will come when you are called to pay the price.
Remember those brave souls who went before you
and sacrificed out of love.

Love never gives up, never loses faith, is always hopeful, and endures through every circumstance. Love will last forever . . . even when the end comes.

—1 Corinthians 13:7 NLT

VALLEY
of
DECISION

1

WHEN UNATTENDED WOUNDS SUCCUMB to infection"—Dr. Lisbeth Hastings advanced the slide in the PowerPoint presentation, and the raw end of a severed leg appeared on the screen—"amputation of the gangrenous extremity may be the only way to stop a deadly pathogen from progressing to the body's core." She was not surprised by the hand that shot up.

The ambitious resident with thick glasses and freshly pressed scrubs was always looking for an opportunity to prove his brilliance. Debating whether to give him an excuse to derail her lecture, Lisbeth took a deep breath. "Your question, Dr. Gingrich?"

The surgical resident pressed his glasses to his nose. "What about IV Vancomycin or Zosyn?"

Lisbeth kept her expression neutral, but inside she was cringing. Looking at Dr. Gingrich was like looking at herself nearly twenty years ago. Self-serving. Terrified. And determined to control everyone and every outcome. What a waste of precious time and energy. Oh, the things she would tell that desperate girl if she ever got the chance to go back in time again.

She suppressed her desire to take the kid aside and shake some sense into him. Her job was not to coddle young doctors but to make them into quick-thinking surgeons able to face anything the operating room threw at them.

"Vigorous rounds of antibiotics are always the first line of defense. But if modern medicine fails, the ancient practice of amputation is the better decision." Her phone vibrated in the pocket of her white coat. Lisbeth ignored the summons and kept her gaze squarely on the young surgical resident. Maybe if he'd watched his mother amputate a man's leg with nothing more than a serrated saw and a mandrake root for pain, he too would want assurances that he'd done the right thing. "For the treating physician, the decision is never easy. Everything must be considered. Age, overall health, postsurgery quality of life." The phone vibrations ceased, then immediately began again. She hated being interrupted during grand rounds. Seizing the opportunity to equip a surgeon with the ability to make hard choices was the best part of her job. Lisbeth fished her buzzing phone from her pocket and glanced at the caller ID. "Excuse me, I have to take this. You're dismissed." She exited the conference room. "Papa, everything okay?"

"Maggie's gone!" he blurted.

"What?" Lisbeth hurried across the hall, ducked into her office, and closed the door.

"That fancy art college of hers called." Panic made his voice tremble. "She's not been to a single class since we hauled her fanny to Rhode Island."

"I talked to her yesterday on her birthday." Lisbeth's focus shot to the framed photo of Maggie standing outside her freshman dorm. The vivacious young woman waving good-bye was beyond beautiful. Features perfect as sculpted marble. Sea-blue eyes that rippled with a restlessness that was equally becoming and unsettling. Whenever Maggie walked into a room, she commanded attention without even trying, like the aristocrat she was. Lisbeth had been such a tomboy at that age, climbing dunes and digging for buried treasure with her father until he sent her to the States for college. Maggie, on the other hand, possessed a sense of feminine confidence Lisbeth still struggled to grasp.

Leaving her daughter in a city fifteen hundred miles away had been harder on her than it had been on Maggie. Papa had said letting go was a natural part of parenting, but nothing about telling her daughter good-bye felt natural to Lisbeth. She'd loved being a mother. Motherhood had saved her. Given her a place to deposit all the love she still had for Maggie's father.

"What did she say?" Papa's anxious voice jerked Lisbeth back to the present.

She rubbed her temple, trying to recall her conversation with Maggie. "She was excited about turning eighteen and being able to make her own decisions."

"What did *you* say?" Papa's question held a tiny edge of accusation.

What didn't I say? Hairs on the back of Lisbeth's neck bristled as the discussion replayed in her mind. It was the same fight they always had: what Maggie could and could not do; where she could and could not go; and why it was in her daughter's best interest to leave the past in the past and move forward.

Lisbeth's stomach churned at her own hypocrisy. Had she not gambled on what mattered most and taken Maggie to the third century, her failure to reunite her family would not be a wound that refused to heal. Infection, yellow and foul, had seeped into her relationship with her daughter. If she could not stop the deterioration, eventually one of them would be forced to cut the other off. And she knew exactly who would wield the serrated saw. A braid of guilt, regret, and animosity thick as the blond plait that hugged Maggie's neck squeezed Lisbeth's heart.

"I said"—she cleared the lump in her throat—"when you start paying your own bills, kiddo, you can go anywhere you want." She could almost feel Maggie rolling her eyes the moment this statement came out of her mouth . . . again.

"And she said?"

"Whatever, Mom." Loosely translated: *I'm going to do whatever I want.*

"Could she have possibly gained access to the inheritance your grandfather left for both of you?"

"She knew when she turned eighteen I'd set her up with an account that automatically transfers money each month." Lisbeth could feel her heart rate increasing. "Give me a second." A few furious clicks on the computer and Maggie's account transactions appeared.

$1,279.00. TunisAir. Charged at 12:02 a.m. Yesterday. The day Maggie turned eighteen.

Lisbeth's skin went cold. This time the future had gone in search of the past. Fear skipped up Lisbeth's spine. She loved her daughter, but her hopes and dreams for Maggie did not include having her torn between two worlds for the rest of her life. Lisbeth's body prepared to run. "Grab my emergency bag and passport. I'll meet you at DFW."

"Where is she?"

"Where do you think? The very place I told her never to go."

Tunis, Tunisia

LISBETH'S COMMERCIAL flight made the slow descent through the clouds. She watched out the window as they circled the ancient ruins of Carthage's harbor. On about the third pass over the stunning turquoise waters of the Mediterranean port city, the ugly terror swirling in her belly was near eruption. What if she failed again? She removed the barf bag from the seat in front of her, held it to her nose, and breathed in and out.

"You okay?" Papa rubbed her back.

All she could do was nod and pray, bracing herself for the moment the plane's wheels set her down on African soil for the first time in thirteen years.

As they taxied to the terminal, Lisbeth slid her courage back into place and powered on her phone.

She dialed the same number she'd been trying to reach since bolting from her office. "Maybe we can find Maggie before she finds Nigel." She threaded her arm through her father's as they exited the plane. None of her arguments had convinced him to stay behind, and this time she was grateful. "I'm going to keep calling that Irish bush pilot until he answers me."

Inside the stuffy cinderblock terminal a cacophony of French, Arabic, German, and heavy British drowned out the live Berber drums, sitars, and flutes. In the gray haze of cigarette smoke, Lisbeth rotated like a weather vane, listening to her call go to Nigel's voice mail while she sorted dialects in search of the sugary Texas twang of one strong-willed blond teenager in big trouble.

She clicked off her phone. "You don't think he took her to the cave, do you?"

"Maggie can be mighty persuasive, and Nigel's a softie."

"But she's just a kid."

"He took *you* there, didn't he?"

"I was twenty-eight, and it was an emergency." Lisbeth crammed the phone into the bag with the shiny new Kelly forceps she'd packed for Mama just in case they did have to go all the way back to the third century. "This would not be happening if I'd taken your advice and brought Maggie to Carthage the moment she started pressing for some answers." Allowing the past to inform the present was a bridge she hadn't wanted to cross. Lisbeth hefted her bag onto the customs inspection counter. "You were right. There. I said it."

"I'm still living with the consequences of my decisions. You won't hear me judging yours. You're the best mother I know."

"I should have walked her through the ruins. Helped her find closure. Put the past to bed once and for all." Her inability to give Maggie what she wanted—no, what she *needed*—was a constant tug on her heart.

"You can't ask her to do something you haven't done yourself." Papa's blue eyes drilled her. "It's forgiveness that girl craves. And I don't mean from you."

The impatient customs official asked for their passports. "Coming into the country for business or pleasure?"

"Business." Papa presented their passports for stamping. "Very delicate business." He took Lisbeth's elbow and led her around a group of retired Americans on vacation. Flowered shirts, straw hats, and sensible shoes gave away their plans to spend their vacation tramping the sunbaked remains of a forgotten civilization.

The presence of so many tourists shamed her. Carthage was not the volatile hotbed she'd claimed every time Maggie broached the subject of saving her father. Truth squeezed Lisbeth's conscience tighter than the crowds pressing in from all sides. Political unrest wasn't the real source of her reluctance to bring her daughter here.

She'd made a promise.

Until the costs versus the gains of breaking that promise were settled in her mind, she kept her desire to break that promise buried in a tangled web of excuses.

"This way." Papa pushed past the luxury shops, cafés, and beauty salons. "I arranged our ride ahead of time."

Intrusive taxi drivers rushed them the moment they stepped

into air thick with dust blowing in from the Sahara. The nearness of the desert choked her.

A snaggle-toothed man leaped in front of her. "Thirty dinars to Old Carthage."

"Twenty to the Bardo." Another driver hugged her left side. "Much better deal."

A man who smelled like a goat moved in on the right. "Fifteen and a guided tour of the Tophet."

"Camel rides, only ten dinar, pretty lady!" shouted a young Bedouin elbowing into the cluster, the reins of two bored-looking beasts of burden clutched in his hands.

"How did Maggie navigate this on her own?" Lisbeth raised her scarf over her nose.

"She's a smart girl." Papa squeezed her elbow tighter. "Like her mother."

"That's what scares me."

"Doctor Hastings!" Across the parking lot Aisa, her father's faithful camp fry cook, paced the wind-sanded hood of an old Land Rover. His cream-colored tunic stood out against the black smoke pouring from the exhaust pipe of a nearby bus. He waved his hands. "Come!"

They hurriedly wove their way through the honking cars and heavy foot traffic. Aisa scrambled down from the vehicle with surprising agility for a man she guessed to be nearly seventy. Lisbeth threw her arms around the wiry-thin Arab. "Aisa!" The comforting scent of lamb roasted over an open fire accompanied his embrace. She reluctantly released him and allowed Papa a moment to greet one of his dearest friends before she asked, "New glasses?"

"And new teeth." Shiny white dentures peered out from beneath the bush of Aisa's graying facial hair.

"Nice." She pointed at his shiny frames. "I kinda miss the duct tape."

"Nothing stays the same."

His statement was a defibrillating bolt to her heart. Last time she'd traveled into the third century everything had changed. Her husband had returned from exile and married her best friend. Maggie could have stumbled into . . . No, she couldn't let her mind go there. "Please tell me you've got my daughter safely tucked away."

Aisa shook his head and took Lisbeth's bag. "Come. We'll get some food into your bellies and a plan into our heads for what we should do next."

"We?"

"Isn't that what friends are for?" He loaded their gear into the SUV, then hopped in and floored the gas pedal.

The Rover shot into traffic. Lisbeth gripped the dash but still felt she was shaking apart at the seams. Their chauffeur dodged parked cars and bicycles that clogged the streets leading away from the airport. Windows down, they flew along the paved coastal road connecting Tunis and Old Carthage. The salty breeze kinked Lisbeth's hair into knots almost as big as the ones in her stomach.

As they neared the older part of the city, the crowded, narrow avenues forced Aisa to slow down. Street vendors hawked aromatic oils, brightly colored fabrics, and pottery in every imaginable shade of blue. Lisbeth's mind traveled back to the days when this city was new. The days when the love of her life walked these streets. His kiss. The warmth of his touch. The strength in his resolve. She stuck her hand out the window and let the breeze slip through her fingers. How could someone be so close and yet so far away?

Aisa laid on the horn and shook his fist. "Hang on."

At a huge clock tower, their aggressive cabbie abruptly turned east. He zipped through quiet residential streets lined with whitewashed houses trimmed in the same cobalt blue of the pottery.

Leafy trees heavy with ripening oranges filled the yards. Here and there ancient stone columns converted into streetlamps embellished the neighborhoods only the very rich could afford. Grand estates like the one her mother's father had left to Lisbeth when he died.

Aisa whipped into a drive blocked by a massive wrought-iron gate. "Here we are."

"Here?" Lisbeth stared at the familiar gate. "This house belonged to my grandfather." She'd sold Jiddo's estate through a third-party transaction to finance Maggie's steep college tuition. She had no idea the buyer had been her father's camp cook. "You live *here*?"

"Yes." Aisa's toothy grin showed his delight at her surprise. "The good professor is not the only one who knows how to turn sand into treasure."

Lisbeth shifted in her seat. "You sold recovered artifacts?"

Aisa lifted his chin proudly. "My recipe for fried dough."

"To whom?"

"An American food chain." He pressed the remote control attached to his visor, and the gate swung open.

In the distance, Lisbeth could see the hill where the Roman acropolis had been replaced by a huge French cathedral. All around her grandfather's estate the palm trees had grown bigger and had acquired multiple rings of thick bark. Beside her sat a newly wealthy souk vendor who used to just barely eke out a living frying bread dough on an oil drum.

Nothing stays the same.

The power of time had tugged at her since the moment she'd set foot back in Tunisia. The port that had once been the spear pointed at the rest of the world was now an accusing dagger aimed at her. She'd abandoned Carthage in its hour of need. She could take no credit for its survival.

Aisa settled Lisbeth into the room she'd stayed in the few times Papa brought her to visit on their rare supply runs to Carthage. She and Papa didn't come often, because things were always so tense between Jiddo and her father. The two men had never had a good relationship, but after Mama's disappearance it became even easier to beat each other up rather than themselves.

Lisbeth showered quickly, slipped into the simple tunic she found laid out on the massive burled mahogany bed, then followed the enticing smell of roasting meat to the large, wrap-around terrace with a stunning view of the port. Laughter drew her attention to the fire pit. Aisa and Papa were one-upping each other with camp stories. But something about the scene wasn't right. Papa was dressed in a woolen tunic that hit him midcalf. His fry cook was whacking fist-size dough balls with a tire iron and wearing Papa's faded chambray shirt and favorite dungarees.

"It's like old times seeing you two together." Lisbeth kissed both of their cheeks. "But why have you switched clothes?"

Her father handed Aisa a dough ball. "I thought I'd better dress appropriately for our journey into the third century."

"Oh, no, you don't. I let you come to Carthage, but I did *not* agree to let you go back in time. Plus, Maggie may still be in the twenty-first century."

"You haven't been able to get Nigel on the phone. If he's not dead, then he took Maggie to the desert. And we both know he's not dead." Papa eyed Lisbeth as if he could see the ripple of goose-flesh raising the hair on her arms. "I'm current on all my shots."

"That's the least of my worries."

"Well, then. If things are as bad back there as you've always said, you'll need my help. I can tell you right now, it's going to take both of us to wrestle Maggie Hastings back down the rabbit hole."

"I don't suppose your willingness to fling yourself into a

time-altering waterslide has anything to do with finding my mother?"

A sly smile lifted the corners of his lips. "I intend to bring my wife home along with the rest of my family."

How could she argue? Truth be known, she'd always wanted to do the same. Lisbeth held up her palms. "We'll have to hire a jeep."

"I've checked with customs, and the borders into Egypt are closed to vehicular travel," Papa said.

Lisbeth studied the strange expression on her father's face. "So as of right now, neither one of us has a way to get to that cave."

"The bald Irishman is not the only one with a plane." Aisa glowed like his sparkly new teeth at her shock. "Came with the estate."

After a quick meal of lamb and fried dough, they prepared for Lisbeth and Papa's entrance into the past.

What if she couldn't find her daughter? What if she was too late? Losing Maggie forever would be her worst fear come true. Panic, sharper and more frantic than what she'd experienced on the plane, clawed Lisbeth's insides as she checked her medical bag one more time.

A familiar arm, long and sinewy, wrapped around her shoulders. "You okay, Beetle Bug?"

Lisbeth leaned into Papa and forced air into her lungs. Oxygen cleared the panic from her thinking. She turned to Aisa. "I don't suppose you could find a local doc who'd write some antibiotic scripts and set me up with twenty to thirty typhoid blister packs?"

Aisa's whole body seemed to smile. "Easier than frying bread."

2

IRON WRISTCUFFS PINCHED THE tender flesh above Magdalena's rapid pulse. Blood dripped into her eyes from the beating the soldiers had given her before they'd dragged her from the proconsul's palace. She knew choosing to stay behind had risks, but she could never have predicted what had happened. One moment she was a surgeon performing an emergency amputation. The next, she was a slave charged with the crime of murdering the ruler of Carthage and being hauled through town.

Chains rattled behind her. Magdalena glanced over her shoulder. Iltani, her Mesopotamian friend who'd had her tongue removed by the proconsul's bounty hunters after a failed escape attempt, raised her strong chin in silent protest. Following close behind was Tabari. The small, dark-skinned waif from the African desert tribes had become Iltani's voice. Next was Kardide, oldest of Magdalena's fellow slaves. The hook-nosed Turkish wench would swallow hot coals before she would admit she struggled to keep up on this forced march through the city. Magdalena choked back the lump in her throat. Their suffering was her fault. She was the one who'd put them in jeopardy by asking them to stand guard so her daughter could escape through a secret passage in the library wall.

The law required the torture of any slave suspected of a crime.

She feared the blows to her face were just the beginning. Who knew what tortures awaited their arrival at the holding cells beneath the Hippodrome. She'd tended prisoners who'd been beaten with glass-studded whips and kicked with hobnailed soldier boots. If prisoners didn't bleed to death or die from punctured lungs, starvation and poor sanitary conditions would often kill them before their case ever went before the judge. Thank goodness she'd managed to grab her medical bag. Whether she'd be allowed to carry it with her inside the prison remained to be seen.

How have things come to this?

As Magdalena stumbled along, her mind slogged through the blur of the past two days. She'd been hiding out and secretly working at the little hospital Lisbeth had created in Cyprian's home when Aspasius's soldiers found her and dragged her back to her bedridden master. The stench of his bedchamber tipped her off to the putrefaction of his leg. She'd sent Tabari to Cyprian's home to fetch Lisbeth's modern tools, never intending her fellow slave to return with Lisbeth. But she shouldn't have been surprised that her stubborn daughter had insisted on bringing the tools personally and staying to assist.

Lisbeth had argued against the surgery, citing the many risk factors: unsanitary operating conditions; lack of intravenous antibiotics; and, most important, Aspasius's overall poor health due to diabetes and his compromised immune system. In the end, Magdalena had convinced her that doing nothing would guarantee the proconsul's demise. Magdalena had felt she had no choice but to take the gamble, and if she had it to do all over, she'd make the same decision.

Removing the rotten limb had required a great deal of her physical strength. Secretly, she'd been grateful Lisbeth had been there.

But before the proconsul awakened, Magdalena had insisted

that Lisbeth slip through the library's secret door and escape through the underground tunnels. As Aspasius became more and more restless upon the mahogany operating table, Magdalena knew forcing her daughter to go had been the right choice. Aspasius was experiencing complications. The odds of saving him were not in her favor. She'd placed a calming hand upon his chest. Heart palpitations thumped beneath his cool, clammy skin. "Try to breathe deeply, Aspasius. Hyperventilating won't help."

"What's wrong with him?" Pytros, the scrawny, troublemaking scribe, had demanded.

"Septic shock." She'd tried to hide her alarm. "He's been through a lot, Pytros. Why don't you step out and let him rest?"

Aspasius started thrashing uncontrollably, mumbling senseless things. The raw end of his new stump hit the makeshift operating table with so much force that his neatly tied sutures burst open. Blood spurted everywhere. In an instant, a minor crisis turned into a major medical emergency.

Pytros ran from the library, screaming, "Help! She's killing my master!"

Magdalena remembered ripping a strip of cloth and was in the process of securing a second tourniquet just above the knee when she noticed her patient's chest. His sternum rose and fell in the short, labored movements of a man in respiratory distress. Within seconds, Aspasius's eyes rolled back into his head, and his shaking stilled.

When soldiers burst into the room, they'd found Magdalena covered in blood and frantically performing CPR on a lifeless man. Strong arms pulled her away from Aspasius's blue-tinged body. It didn't take but a second for the young soldier in charge to figure out that the proconsul was dead. "What happened?" he'd demanded.

What had *happened?* It could have been a number of things.

Blood clot. Heart attack. Her patient's age and general poor health.

"Keep up." The pimple-faced boy who'd smacked her several times jerked Magdalena back to the present. Aspasius's loyal guard wouldn't have believed her story if she'd had a chance to tell him. That she was here, in the third century, was difficult for even her to grasp. Some days she couldn't believe that a silly argument she'd had with her husband years ago had led to her falling into this nightmare. That's how she'd come to be at the wrong place at the wrong time. A stupid, ridiculous fight. Who would believe such a tale?

Magdalena's toe caught on an uneven paver. She stumbled and skinned her knees on the cobblestones. She waved off Kardide's rush to help and scrambled to her feet. "I'm fine."

"Oh, no," Tabari said with a gasp. "Perpetua's prison."

Magdalena's gaze followed the direction of her friend's horrified stare. Rose-tinted Ketel limestone had been fashioned into a massive arena that dominated the city's skyline.

Legend had it that the pink tinge of the stones came from the blood of the young noblewoman who'd refused to denounce her faith. Perpetua had been led to the arena. There, before thousands of people, a novice executioner botched her execution. In the end, Perpetua had to slit her own throat.

Magdalena choked down rising bile and brushed the dust from her hands. If the Lord intended her to suffer a martyr's death, then no matter how gruesome it might be, he would give her the strength. Soldiers hooked her under the arms and dragged her to an iron door guarded by one uniformed man.

"This one murdered the proconsul!" the redheaded soldier yelled. "Open the locks!"

"Aspasius is dead?" The guard fumbled with the keys. "How? When?"

"We'll ask the questions. You do the guarding," the redheaded soldier said. "Wait." He ripped her bag from her shoulder. "Where did you get this?"

"It's my medical supplies."

"There was a woman who brought it. I saw her fill this bag." He grabbed Magdalena's cheeks. "Where is she?"

If God had answered her prayer, Lisbeth was home. Safe in her proper time. "I don't know."

He peeked inside. "Saws. Knives." He extracted a bone drill she'd purchased from a Greek healer who was going out of business. "I didn't see her put this in here."

"They're mine, I tell you."

Suspicion raised his brows. "I don't even want to know what you do with this."

Hastily tossing everything back into her satchel, he smirked. "How long do you think my superior would let me live if you escaped because you hacked off a leg to get free of those shackles?" The contents of the bag clanked and rattled as he chucked it to the jailer. "These blades are evidence. Put them someplace safe."

"Yes, sir." The guard tugged on the handle, and the prison door creaked open. A musky stench rushed at Magdalena. Unwashed bodies. Dirty hair. Rancid mutton grease. A dark space fouled by human waste. The soldiers shoved Magdalena and her friends into a hallway that stretched into total blackness. The four women huddled in the darkness.

"Do not be afraid," Magdalena said boldly, despite the fear pulsing through her veins. "They can kill our bodies, but they cannot touch our souls."

"Torch," ordered the soldier squeezing her arm.

In the moments it took for someone to appear with a fiery bundle of twigs dipped in tar, Magdalena squinted, letting her eyes adjust.

A tunnel.

She almost laughed out loud. Tunnels didn't scare her.

Twenty-five years ago, God had found her beaten, pregnant, and enslaved in the dankest subterranean passage in the world . . . the tunnel beneath the palace of Aspasius Paternus, proconsul of Carthage.

God would find her again.

3

BAREK AWOKE FACEDOWN IN a coagulating puddle that stank of rusty iron and sweat. Dazed and uncertain of where he was or what had happened, he brought his left hand to his head to investigate the throbbing near his temple. It came away sticky with blood. A painful haze clouded his vision. He pushed himself upright and blinked. Hot, thick waves of air fanned the open door back and forth on creaky hinges. In the fading light, the terrifying events that had rendered him totally ineffective rushed in, sharp as the blade he clutched in his right hand.

Soldiers had come to Cyprian's villa. Searching for the exiled solicitor of Carthage and those who harbored him. Barek remembered grabbing his knife from his belt to defend the innocent, but he was no match for the heartless killing machine of Rome.

Oh, God!

Barek pushed himself upright. Everything hurt, but there was only one way to assess the damage and that was to get to his feet. Excruciating pain stabbed his lungs. Hobnailed boots must have broken a few of his ribs. His legs buckled and sent his body to the floor with an agonizing thud.

"Lisbeth? Maggie?" His unanswered pleas scraped his raw throat.

Had he embarrassed himself and screamed like a girl when

the soldiers began running their swords through the patients who filled Cyprian's home? The shame of his possible cowardice paled in comparison to the shame his betrayal had brought upon this house. Thank God his parents' earlier deaths had spared them the humiliation of seeing their son destroy the church they'd worked so hard to build, as well as the man they'd chosen to lead in their absence.

Barek refused to curl around his injuries. He deserved to feel every bit of pain. What a failure he was compared to his godly father, the former bishop of Carthage. Helping the slave trader Felicissimus sell the evil writs of *libellus* was a mistake. How many people would die because of those worthless pieces of paper? It wouldn't take the Romans long to figure out that true Christians would never give the Roman gods genuine allegiance. If only he could take back his part in this horrible fiasco.

He raised a shaky hand to his lips and called, "Cyprian?"

The house was silent.

No coughing. No crying out for relief from fevers. No sign of the soldiers. All that remained of Lisbeth's little hospital were the motionless bodies of the people he'd failed to protect.

He no longer had to worry about his lack of faith. His sin would never again allow him to boldly approach the one God of his father, but he had nowhere else to turn. Barek squeezed his eyes tight and dared to commit one last sacrilege. "God, please do not make Cyprian pay for my disloyalty."

Struggling for breath, Barek searched the carnage in the atrium. The patients were dead. What about everyone else? Those he loved who had been caring for the sick. If they had been spared, he would dedicate his life to their protection.

Barek grabbed hold of a nearby bench to steady himself. "Laurentius?" His desperation echoed in the frescoed arches. "Naomi?"

Pain accompanied every jarring step. He skirted bodies and hurried to the quarantine hall. The secluded space had been assigned to keep the Cicero family away from those with measles after Lisbeth discovered their daughter carried an even more deadly kind of sickness: typhoid.

"Titus? Vivia?" The bed where the wealthy patrician's daughter had been recovering from surgery to repair her damaged bowels was empty, and her parents were gone.

Barek scanned the destruction in the hall for their bodies.

Nothing.

Behind him a faint rustle was followed by the slightest of whispers. He strained to listen, to nail down the location of what he hoped was a survivor, but his own heart was thudding so loudly in his ears he couldn't trace the sounds.

"Barek?" The female voice came from behind.

He wheeled. "Naomi?" Relief pumped strength into his legs. He rushed to the servant girl and grabbed her outstretched hands. "Are you hurt?"

She shook her head, her eyes wet with tears. "But you are."

Her concern was more than he deserved. More than he wanted. "Where are Laurentius and Junia?"

She tugged him toward the back door. "Come with me before the soldiers return."

4

$\underline{}$

BREATHLESS AND EMPTY INSIDE, Cyprian returned to his villa with great haste. His wife and daughter deserved a chance to be a family. That he would never join them was a sadness he could not let stop him from his promise to locate Lisbeth's mother and half brother. At the earliest opportunity he would send them sailing through the time portal after her.

"Barek!" he called as he burst through the door. Overturned mats, smashed pottery, broken vaporizer tents, and the still bodies of Lisbeth's patients littered the atrium. "Barek!" His anxiety growing, Cyprian picked his way through the mess and sprinted to the gardener's cottage.

The door stood ajar.

He slowly pushed back the weathered wood. "Barek!" Ruth's son stood beside Pontius. Both had their daggers drawn. Barek's eyes were wide, and his ghostly pale face was smeared with blood. Cyprian held up his palms. "Barek, it's me. Where are Junia and Laurentius?"

Barek shook his head as if he didn't understand Cyprian's question.

"Pontius, where are they?"

Cyprian's faithful friend stepped aside. Laurentius had his face buried in the shoulder of the young girl Lisbeth had saved and

Ruth had adopted. Junia's arms were wrapped tightly around Laurentius and Naomi.

"Is everyone all right?" Cyprian rushed to the little huddle. "What about the Ciceros?"

Barek pointed, and Cyprian turned to see them hiding behind the door.

Junia was the first to snap from their terrified trance. "Aspasius is dead."

Cyprian whirled. "What? How? When?"

"Aspasius is dead," Barek repeated.

"Magdalena has been arrested for his murder," Pontius added.

Cyprian dropped to his knees. What had he done? Had he sent Lisbeth home for no reason? Of course not. That was selfish thinking. The medicine Maggie needed was in the future. His place was in the past. Cold swept through his core and rattled his fears. He lifted his eyes. The silent faces surrounding him begged for his action.

Cyprian forced himself to his feet. "We must do what we can for the dead, and then I will find where they've taken our healer." He armed the remorseful Barek with a sword. "We'll deal with what you did later," he told the boy. "Pontius, I'll need your help in the atrium."

Flies buzzed over the crusting blood pools left by plague victims too weak to defend themselves. Cyprian and Pontius set to work removing the bodies.

Pontius lifted the limp body of a small boy not much older than Maggie. "When did life become of so little value to Rome?"

"I'm just grateful Lisbeth isn't here to see what has become of those she worked so hard to heal." Fury burned inside. Cyprian had to put an end to the madness. How? He wasn't sure. The installation of a new proconsul could alter the rules in their favor. He pushed away his doubts. Come what may with the governance of the province, until Rome's heart softened toward Christians, his calling would remain the same: stop the plague and bring an end to the senseless killing of innocent people.

He inhaled slowly, drawing in the sharp scent of eucalyptus. Irreplaceable loss stung his nostrils. The last time he'd made love to his wife, traces of camphor lingered in her hair.

Pontius started to draw the bolt to lock the front door.

"You waste your effort, friend." Cyprian picked up a eucalyptus leaf, held it briefly to his nose, and then tucked it inside his belt. "A flimsy piece of iron will not stop Rome from taking whatever it wants."

The contents of Cyprian's library had suffered extensive damage. Most of his law scrolls had been destroyed. Sadder still, his copies of the Scriptures were in tatters. He dug through the rubble until he found a few usable scraps of parchment and a sharpened piece of writing charcoal. Once he found Magdalena, he would need her to record anything she could about what had happened in the proconsul's palace. Moving on to the kitchen, he and Pontius rummaged through what was left in the larder: a few rounds of yesterday's bread, a jug of water, a small skin of wine. Not much, but hopefully enough to keep Magdalena from starving before her trial.

He peered out the door. Convinced the coast was clear, he and Pontius hurried back to the gardener's cottage. Cyprian paused before the shed and checked to make certain they were not being watched. Then he and Pontius slipped inside.

"What's going on out there?" Titus Cicero, one of the city's wealthiest landowners, was not used to hiding in an outbuilding meant to house slaves, and his displeasure at the humiliating experience showed on his long face.

"It's quiet for now, but I think it would be safer for everyone to move to your home. Did the soldiers see you flee my house?"

"No," Titus assured him. "We managed to slip out after you left with Lisbeth and Maggie."

"Are your wife and daughter safe?" Vivia asked hopefully.

Cyprian wasn't sure how much the Ciceros had figured out about his time-traveling wife, daughter, and mother-in-law. He hoped they'd attributed his family's strange ways to the ever-expanding borders of Rome and not to the fact that the women he loved more than his own life arrived and left Carthage via a deep well. "As far as I know."

"When it is safe, you shall bring them to us," Vivia insisted. "We can't begin to repay Lisbeth and Magdalena for all they've done, but we will die trying." She looked up at him. "And what about you?" Vivia had a supportive arm wrapped around her daughter, Diona, who was still too weak from typhoid to be up and about. "Are you coming too?"

Cyprian swallowed. He fastened his cloak at his throat and raised the hood. "I cannot let Lisbeth's mother die. Pontius will see you and the children to your home."

"I can get them there," Barek offered, color slowly returning to his face.

The young man had put himself between Lisbeth and a soldier's blade, but he'd also had a part in bringing this calamity upon them in the first place by joining Felicissimus in his betrayal. "Now is not the time to argue the merit of having an extra sword along. Pontius will go with you." Cyprian could see Barek shrink at his failure to regain Cyprian's trust, but he had neither the time nor the patience to deal lovingly with the discipline Ruth's son deserved.

"Let *me* go see about Magdalena," Titus begged.

Cyprian shook his head. "I need you to care for what is left of my family."

"But there's a price on *your* head," Titus argued. "Magdalena has been charged with the murder of the most important official in the province. How do you plan to stop her execution on your own?"

"I'll defend her against these ridiculous charges."

"You?" Titus laughed. "Just because Aspasius is no longer the ruler, do not think that guarantees you an amicable welcome by the Senate, or the immediate reinstatement of your solicitor's title. Patricians are not quick to forgive a man they've condemned, let alone forget that this same man has been successfully hiding beneath their noses for months."

Cyprian clasped the wealthy man's thin arms. "All I'm asking is that you take my family to safety. Can I count on your help?"

Titus's face clouded with a mixture of angst and disagreement. "You run a fool's errand. What if Aspasius is still alive and this is a trap?"

Aspasius was dead. Cyprian could feel the relief in his bones, as if the desert winds had blown away the cloud of evil that had hung over Carthage far too long. But the proconsul's death did not assure that justice would once again prevail if someone did not dare rise to the occasion. "I will not leave Magdalena without a defender."

"You're assuming the healer will survive incarceration. I've seen many accused walk into the tunnels beneath the Hippodrome, but in the end, few prisoners live long enough to walk out and stand before their executioner, no matter how swift their hearing. What if it takes several weeks for the newly appointed proconsul to assume his place in the curule seat?"

"All the more reason to do what we can to see that Magdalena stays alive." Cyprian hid his supplies beneath his cloak. "Pontius goes with you."

When Titus could see his arguments had hit a wall, he gave a reluctant sigh. "Had you not given my family refuge, my daughter would have died. I owe you and that dear woman held in Roman chains more than my life." Titus removed a dagger from his belt and pressed the warm handle into Cyprian's hands. "I'll do what I can to find out whom Valerian will send to assume the office of proconsul."

"Pray the new ruler is a man of reason," Cyprian said. "Who is currently acting as praetor?"

"Xystus."

"My father's generous loans once saved the olive groves of Xystus."

"May his memory be better than his oil."

Titus's lack of enthusiasm spoke to the treacherous waters Cyprian was entering. His chest tightened as he kissed Junia and Laurentius, perhaps for the last time. When he came to Barek, the young man lowered his eyes and stepped back. "I don't deserve your kind farewell."

If losing Lisbeth had taught Cyprian anything, it was that he could not allow his anger to cause him to leave things unsaid. Not when there was a chance his decision to make his presence known in Carthage could bring about his own demise. He trained his eyes upon Ruth's son. "Barek, look at me."

Barek slowly raised his head.

"I cared deeply for your mother. She was a good wife and an even better friend." He pulled Barek to him and felt him crumble beneath his forgiving grasp. "You will always be my son."

"I'm so sorry, Cyprian. I shouldn't have helped Felicissimus betray you. I never meant for any of this to happen."

He clasped Barek's face. "I'm counting on you to step up in my place. Understand?" The Senate could refuse to consider his exile the desperate move it really was. If the senators decided to continue Aspasius's legacy of hatred against the house of Thascius, it was important that Barek understood Magdalena wouldn't be the only one fighting for her life. He waited for the young man's agreement. Barek managed a tortured nod. "Very good. Now be the man your mother wanted you to be."

In the silvery glow of moonlight, Cyprian helped the small group exit via the back gate. The fear on their faces put an extra heaviness upon his shoulders.

Lord, help me. He pressed his torn loyalties to the far recesses of his mind, thanked Titus for the use of his home, then turned in the opposite direction and raced toward the prison.

He could not dispute Titus's pessimism. Saving Magdalena would require him to present her case before the local magistrate. Word of his presence in Carthage would spread quickly. It would be foolish to assume that the death of Aspasius had freed Cyprian of his enemies. He could very likely find himself chained beside his mother-in-law. And then who would see to her return? Titus was right. His impromptu plan was fraught with risks, but doing nothing was out of the question.

Cyprian made his way toward the arena, near the southwestern edge of the city. Massive travertine arches several stories high rose from the iron-rich soil. He slipped through the trees that shaded the venue's bloody history with a sense of serenity it did not deserve. The angry roar of wildcats halted his step. His heart thumped, slowing once he realized the sounds were coming from the cages kept somewhere in the maze of tunnels beneath the arena floor.

Uneasiness prickled Cyprian's skin. He swallowed the urge to flee and made his way to the narrow stairs leading down to the most dangerous tunnel in the city.

A small torch flickered above the uniformed guard who slept slumped against the stone wall where he'd propped his heavy thrusting spear. His head was tilted back, eyes closed, and mouth agape. Loud snores rattled his thick lips.

Cyprian drew his hood to shadow his face and tossed a small stone. It pinged off the soldier's breastplate.

The guard roused, arms and legs flailing like a startled bird. "Who? What?" Not fully alert, he clumsily reached for the *gladius* holstered on his belt. "Halt!" He pawed at his scabbard. "Proceed at your peril."

Cyprian waited until the befuddled man had freed his weapon, then he held out the small bag of provisions to show himself unarmed. "I've brought food to a prisoner."

"Which one?"

"The one accused of murdering the proconsul."

"Don't waste your bread." The guard spit, then wiped his mouth with the back of his hand. "They're to be executed in the morning."

"They?"

"Took four of them to do in the proconsul."

"Did any of them confess to the charges?"

"Do they ever?" The guard burst into gravelly laughter, obviously pleased at his joke.

Cyprian pretended to appreciate his crass humor, chuckling along with him. "Then I guess that means they must stand trial."

"Their trial will be a wooden cross. If the lunch crowd is lucky, the condemned will even be set aflame."

Alarm punched Cyprian's gut. "By whose orders will they be denied due process?"

The guard shrugged. "Don't matter to me. I just do as I'm told."

Cyprian reached into his sack and ripped off a corner of bread and offered it to the guard. Feigning nonchalance, he said, "I would not want to be in your boots . . . uh . . . What's your name?"

The soldier glanced around to make sure a superior wouldn't catch him chatting with a civilian while on duty. "Brutus." He took the bread, crammed it in his mouth, and proceeded to talk and chew at the same time. "What do you mean?"

"Allowing prisoners accused of killing a proconsul to be executed before the new proconsul arrives might not sit well, Brutus."

"With who?"

"I mean, if I were the new ruler"—Cyprian moved in closer— "I'd prefer to have them taken to the arena as my first order of royal business. Demonstrate what becomes of those who conspire to commit such a heinous crime against the empire. Put an end to any chance of having someone plunge a knife in *my* back."

Brutus swallowed hard. "I hadn't thought of that."

"When would you find the time, my good man?" Cyprian clapped his hand upon the guard's metal-clad shoulders. "People have no idea how taxing this post can be."

"No. No, they don't."

"Probably not even your commander."

"Especially him. That man stood beside me in this very spot nigh on ten years before our superior retired and *he* got the promotion."

"And you two are still close?"

Brutus shook his head in disgust. "My *captain's* too good to even share a mug of beer."

"See what I mean? The higher ranks move on with nary a thought to how the lower half lives. He probably doesn't care a whit what happens to you. Let me save you a terrible mistake, my friend." Cyprian raised the food bag to the light. "Let me help you keep these accused murderers alive at least until things get sorted out."

"There's not much I can do to stop the wheels of justice."

"But when the new proconsul demands an accounting of what happened, which he will, you can say you did everything you could."

The guard toyed with the ring of keys hanging from his belt and then holstered his blade. "Well, I guess it wouldn't hurt for them to have a meal."

"And if it's their last, it won't be because of you."

Brutus put his shoulder to the metal door and pushed. Despair weighted the rush of cool air fouled by human waste. If typhoid wasn't in this dungeon, it would be soon. Cyprian took the torch from the holder. He drew a deep breath, ducked beneath the doorway's low stone lintel, and descended into the depths of the earth. When he lifted his head, it nearly scraped the ceiling. Rats skittered into the shadows as he waved the flame.

"Mercy," someone begged in the darkness. "Have mercy."

"Sure they're worth it?" Brutus asked.

"I'm sure."

The door clanked behind Cyprian, and the key turned in the lock. Cyprian calmed the intense desire to pound on the thick metal and ask to be released. "Magdalena!"

"Here," she croaked. "I'm over here."

Keeping his torch in front of him, Cyprian saw the entire length of the narrow tunnel come into view. A low-sloped ceiling pressed apart walls made of thick stone blocks by only a mere twenty to thirty feet. To his left, three chained men sat on the floor, their heads resting upon their bent knees. They looked up, and then lifted thin arms to shield their eyes from the glare of the light. Their matted hair indicated they'd survived here longer than most. Which meant they were most likely debtors with families who brought scraps of bread whenever they could.

"Mercy, master. Please."

Knowing anything he shared with these men would take away from the immediate help he could offer Magdalena, Cyprian kept moving. His next visit he would bring extra, but for now he could not afford to be sidetracked. He dodged the men's attempts to reach for him and searched in the direction of his mother-in-law's voice.

"Here, Cyprian."

"Magdalena?" He found her sitting on the floor. Battered and bloody. One leg chained to a wall. "What have they done to you?" He crammed the torch into a holder and knelt beside her.

"You shouldn't have come. It's too dangerous for you."

"Don't worry about me." He checked her for broken bones. "Are you hurt?"

"Nothing mortal. But I'm worried about Kardide." She pointed across the aisle. "She fell, and I'm worried she could have a concussion."

Cyprian swiveled on his heels. Against the opposite wall, three women huddled together. He took them bread and water. "Go easy. I'll bring more tomorrow." Magdalena was right. Kardide had a large gash on her head, but he was able to rouse her. "You'll need bandages for your wounds."

"We won't be here tomorrow." Magdalena's voice was weary, yet peacefully resigned.

"I won't let it come to that." Cyprian frowned at the doubt he saw on her face. "You will not face the judge without representation."

"There will be no judge."

"I won't let that happen. I'll argue—"

"I can't allow you to risk your life for mine. The church needs you. Now more than ever."

"Let me and God worry about my life." Cyprian pulled parchment and charcoal from the bag. "Write down everything that happened. No detail is too small."

She waved off the paper. "Tell me of my children."

One of the chained men coughed, reminding Cyprian that whatever was said here could easily be reported to the guards and twisted for gain. "Your son is with those who can keep him safe."

"My daughter and granddaughter?"

He swallowed. "Home."

"Good." A pleased smile softened the knife scars Aspasius had carved in the corners of her mouth. "Now I am ready to meet my Maker face-to-face." She let her head rest against the wall, her eyes focused on the ceiling, as if she could see straight into heaven.

"You did not murder the proconsul, Magdalena."

"He's dead." Was that remorse he heard in her voice? "I'm the surgeon of record. Who else shall we blame? God?"

"Give me something to work with."

The dungeon's only door creaked open. A sliver of moonlight sliced the darkness. "Time's up!" Brutus shouted from the entrance.

"Please, Magdalena," Cyprian begged. "Anything you can remember."

She lifted her head slowly. The effort seemed to require the last of her strength. She eyed him carefully, weighing whether to speak. Finally she sighed. "Everything you need is in the note I asked Lisbeth to deliver to you."

5

MAGGIE BURST THROUGH THE water's surface, dizzy and desperate to take a breath. She ripped off her nose plugs and sucked in big gulps of rank air. "Whoa! Way worse than I remembered." *Remembered* echoed loudly in the watery chamber.

Fearing her noisy entrance may have alerted someone to her arrival, Maggie's gaze shot to the orange glow above. She treaded water quietly, listening for signs she'd been discovered before she could finish what God had started when he'd sent her and her mother to the third century thirteen years ago. If she hadn't screwed up and gotten sick, her father wouldn't have had to die. She was here to make it up to her dad before that happened and, more important, to her God.

Maggie's eyes adjusted to the dimness. Stone walls formed a circle less than ten feet across. Tighter space than she remembered. No place for a girl with severe claustrophobia. The rapid thumping of her heart meant she was well on her way to hyperventilating. If she didn't want to pass out and drown in this murky water, she couldn't wait for her head to stop spinning from that crazy water ride through the time portal. She needed to get out of this well and fast. Her gaze returned to the faint source of light dancing on the water's surface. There was only one way out: straight up. Jaw clenched, she closed her eyes for a brief moment and sent the fear away.

Maggie kicked to one of the random ledges that jutted from the walls like some kind of prehistoric climbing wall. She wiggled free of the pack strapped to her back and threw it upon the outcropping. She hoisted herself onto the jagged stone. Teeth chattering, she inspected the backpack the cute salesman at a sporting goods store had promised was indestructible and waterproof. Not a single knick or tear. Everything inside bone-dry. Including her cell phone and the expensive camera Mom had given her to take to college. The all-weather pack her g-pa had given her had proven to be worth every penny she'd talked him into spending. Guilt prickled Maggie's skin. She shouldn't have left her new school and set out for Africa without telling her mother, but she felt especially bad that she hadn't at least texted her grandfather.

She clicked on her phone. Blue light pressed back the darkness, but the blank screen was a reality check that cut off her breathing.

No service.

Hopefully this meant she'd arrived in the third century and hadn't simply dropped out of range. Either way, without her phone she was totally and completely alone. With no way to summon help. Fear flickered in her chest.

Maggie turned the phone face to the walls. Light traveled up the trowel marks in the cement plaster, creating interesting patterns of shadow and light. Hard to know if this was the same well she and her mother had surfaced in thirteen years ago. Mom wasn't exactly the sentimental type who would have taken the time to carve their initials or anything. Until she climbed out of here and took a look around, she couldn't be certain.

And then what?

Maggie forced air into her constricting lungs and strapped on the bag stuffed with a tunic and a pearl-handled knife she'd purchased from one of the souvenir vendors outside the Tunis airport. *Insurance*, she'd told herself, but she wasn't taking any chances that a knife was enough. So she'd had her Arab cabbie take her to an Internet café, where she downloaded some ancient manumission papers she hadn't had time to print before she left. She didn't know how many copies of these slave-freedom-granting documents she would need, so she printed several sets on dusty paper. One set was for her grandmother. One for her. The others were backups in case she talked Junia or Naomi into coming home with her. No way would she let herself end up on the slave block.

And Mom thought I couldn't make a plan.

Maggie held out her phone and took a selfie. If she never made it back to the twenty-first century, at least there'd be a record if her grandfather discovered her shriveled remains two thousand years from now. The photographic record wouldn't give a full explanation of her decision to purchase a round-trip ticket to Tunisia, but maybe it would help her mom understand that sometimes a girl's gotta do what a girl was born to do . . . even if she's scared to death.

Maggie clicked off her phone and slid it into her pack. "Ready or not, here I come, Daddy."

She secured her pack to her back and started climbing. The hours she'd spent at the gym paid off. Her arms were strong, and a sense of control was returning. Nearing the top, she stretched for the rocky lip, pulled up, and threw her leg over. She tumbled onto the cobblestones.

Scrambling to her feet, Maggie felt her heart racing as she checked to see if anyone had witnessed her clumsy entrance. The place was dark and deserted. *Thank goodness.* She ducked behind the well. A wind, hot as Texas and moist as a rain shower, kinked her curls.

She dug out the tunic, changed as quickly as she could, then covered her head with a handwoven scarf. A pair of simple leather sandals completed what she hoped looked traditional third-century plebeian. Unwilling to leave her Citizen jeans behind, she stuffed her wet clothes inside the gallon-size Ziplocs she'd packed in her backpack.

Maggie glanced around. She was surrounded by several tall buildings, all of them plastered with the same kind of stucco that was inside the well. Streets no wider than sidewalks fanned out like bicycle spokes.

"Now what?" she muttered. Swapping out her modern clothes was the extent of her reentry plan.

Without access to the Internet maps on her phone, how was she supposed to know which alley would take her out of the slums? Maggie spotted a set of outside stairs on a building that looked eerily similar to their old apartment near the county hospital where her mom had practically lived since she'd decided to become a surgeon.

Taking the narrow steps two at a time, Maggie raced up six flights. A big orange moon, reminiscent of that deadly night she'd talked Junia into going to the tenements to retrieve a doll, illuminated rooftops in every direction. For a second, the haunting sound of oxen hooves thundered in her ears. Tears stung her eyes. She hadn't meant for Ruth to die.

Maggie quickly pushed those bloody memories from her mind and focused on the one thing she knew for sure: her father's villa overlooked the doughnut-shaped harbor. Find the water and she would find him.

"There it is." She took out her camera and clicked off a few shots of the ship silhouettes etched into the indigo sky. "G-Pa is going to die when he sees these."

Pleased with herself, Maggie climbed down and headed in the direction of the harbor's big stone circle. Navigating the same streets she and her mother had once traveled kicked wide open the rusty door to her mind. Memories she didn't even know she had of that terrifying trip flooded back.

People were dying then, and from the walking dead staggering the streets or lying in the gutters now it looked as if they were still dying. Maybe she'd hit closer to her target than she'd first thought. Goose bumps raised the hairs on her arms. Looming large in her swirl of recollections was the vivid image of her mother and grandmother working like crazy women trying to help the sick who poured into her father's huge house.

What was she thinking? She had no medical expertise. She hadn't even brought Tylenol. Maybe this *was* the day her failure to think things through would bite her in the butt, just as Mom had warned a million times.

Too late to worry about it now. She was here. And she wasn't going home without her father.

Maggie drew her scarf across her nose and stepped over the blood trails that led to corpses stacked three to four high on either side of the street. She hustled until she reached the area of town where the houses stood alone and climbing plants circled balcony pillars. As she crested a steep hill, her surroundings started looking vaguely familiar.

Which house belonged to her father? None of the lampposts that lined the deserted avenue had been lit, and the moon wasn't bright enough for her to be certain. A noise drew her attention to the eerie shadows. "Who's there?"

A thin, mangy dog, more of a ghost really, rooted through the bodies stacked along the curb. He raised his head and growled. Maggie froze. Ghosts didn't bare yellow teeth or advance with hot, red eyes. She prayed the stink of dead bodies would override the smell of her fear. She wasn't going to be the first to cave in this standoff. Her father lived around here, and nothing was going to

run her off. Slowly she unlocked her gaze and canvassed her surroundings for a stick.

Deciding she wasn't worth the effort, the dog wheeled and
went back to foraging. He nosed through the rotting heap and then
tore a piece of flesh from a stiff arm.

"Hey! Leave that alone."

The dog trotted off with his spoils. Maggie folded at the waist
and threw up all over her new sandals.

6

"THESE WALLS HAVE EARS." Cyprian removed his cloak and wrapped Magdalena's shoulders. "Say no more."

"Time's up!" Brutus shouted again from the doorway.

Rather than jeopardize future admittance into the prison, Cyprian kissed Magdalena's cheek and heeded the evacuation order. "I'll be back," he whispered.

"Please don't risk it."

"Let someone take care of you for a change, Magdalena." He exited the filthy hole beneath the arena and slid a silver coin into the soldier's open palm. "Remember, Brutus, the new proconsul will be counting on you to keep the healer alive."

"No one listens to me much, but I swear on Jupiter's stone I'll do my best."

"Your word is good enough for me." Cyprian clasped him on the shoulder and then set a brisk pace for home.

The sun would be up soon. He would have to hurry to avoid an encounter with the increased number of patrols. He couldn't risk being incarcerated before he had an opportunity to retrieve the note that could save Magdalena. His boots pounded the cobblestones leading to the heart of the city.

Cyprian rounded a corner. The market was deserted. A piece of paper fluttered from a lamppost—a notice of some sort. Hungry for the latest news, he ripped it down. Breathing hard, Cyprian held the sheaf to the moonlight. His face was sketched at the top of the page. Beneath his picture was penned a proclamation declaring Cyprianus Thascius a cursed man, with a handsome reward offered for information leading to his immediate arrest. He gulped air trying to counter the collapse of his lungs. Lisbeth had been right. Aspasius had been coming for him.

Vivid images of Lisbeth thrusting several papers into his hands upon her return from the proconsul's palace flashed in his mind. She'd brought him a stack of these posters, saying, "He lied. Aspasius lied." Cyprian wished he'd taken a moment to read one, or at the very least understand what Lisbeth had been trying to tell him.

Cyprian slowed his racing thoughts in an effort to sort through the chaos of those last frantic moments with his wife. An expensive piece of paper had been stuck in with the cheap posters. What had he done with it? He'd been so intent on saving the lives of his family that he'd failed to notice Magdalena's note or the blood that must have covered Lisbeth's tunic from helping her mother perform surgery. Bloody evidence that would have landed his beloved wife in prison right alongside her mother had he not sent her back to her time.

Magdalena's sacrifice in all of this was not lost on him. That dear woman had stayed behind so Lisbeth could escape the palace. The cost had been great, and yet when Cyprian told her he hadn't seen the note, he'd felt nothing but peace in her presence. If there was a note, some kind of deathbed proclamation signed by Aspasius, it might negate Cyprian's trouble with the law and make it possible for him to help Magdalena. But where was it?

Trudging up the broad avenue that led to his home, Cyprian noticed someone sitting by his front gate. His steps stuttered to a stop. Had a guard been posted to watch for him? He squinted. *No. Too small to be a soldier.* Who then? The predawn light made it impossible to identify this trespasser with any certainty. Firm hand on the dagger tucked in his sash, Cyprian advanced cautiously. As he neared, the sobs of a woman reached his ears. A young woman. Face buried in her hands. Blond curls spilled out from under her scarf. Probably a plague victim disappointed to learn his deserted home was no longer a place of refuge and healing. How he wished Lisbeth were here to handle this situation.

Cyprian released his dagger. Weariness weighted his advance and made his approach less than stealthy, but the girl seemed too distraught to notice the scuff of his boots. He stopped a few paces from her and called out cautiously, "Hello?"

Her head shot up. "Who's there?"

"Easy." He raised his hands and tried to speak in a soothing tone. "Are you hurt, woman?"

"Daddy?"

Cyprian gave a slight shake of his head. "Has fever addled your thinking?" He hated the suspicion his choices had seeded in his soul, but with his face plastered all over town this could be a trap. "There's no help to be found here."

"Daddy!" She scrambled to her feet. "It's me. Maggie." She threw her arms around his neck.

"Woman, please." He peeled her loose.

She stepped back. "Aren't you glad to see me?"

He'd just put his child down the time portal a few hours ago. This fully grown woman was not his little girl. Yet her greeting was strangely reminiscent of the small girl who'd burst in a few weeks ago and changed his life with those very same words. A daughter he didn't even know he'd had. He'd mishandled the whole ordeal. What he wouldn't give to take back the pain his reluctance had inflicted upon everyone.

"Maggie?" Cyprian wished for better lighting. "How can this be?"

"Don't freak out."

"Freak out?"

"You know, like, go crazy. Mom does it every time things don't go according to her plan."

"Maggie?" He repeated her name slowly, choosing his next words carefully. "How did you get here?" He really wanted to ask, *How have you aged ten years in the blink of an eye?*

"It's a bizarre combination of luck and physics—which I'm really hoping you don't make me explain, because that's one thing Mom *is* right about. Math and science aren't my strong suits."

"But you're all grown up."

"I wish Mom could hear you say that. She still thinks I'm a kid who needs full-time supervision." She crammed her balled fists onto her slender hips, an action that mimicked the five-year-old who used to stomp around the gardener's cottage in Ruth's heels. "You should have seen her when she took me to college. All of the other mothers helped their daughters unpack, and then they left." She hoisted a bag that looked similar to the one Lisbeth had had on her last visit. "Not Mom. She stayed the *entire* weekend. Insisted that she and G-Pa get a hotel room, so they could help me find a church on Sunday, like she didn't trust me to go on my own." She grabbed a quick breath and continued, "I know this sounds bad, but I chose a college on the other side of the country because she hovers so much I can't breathe."

G-Pa. Only one person used that term. But how could Maggie possibly be here now? And perfectly healthy. In the time it had taken him to run from the well to his villa, send the rest of his family to safety, and then visit Magdalena in prison, his little daughter had recovered from typhoid and matured into a beautiful young woman. This was a miracle he would never have believed if Maggie and her mother hadn't reappeared out of thin air just weeks ago.

Wild heartbeats thrashed Cyprian's ears. Maggie's return

meant Lisbeth wouldn't be far behind. He couldn't contain his smile. "Where's your mother?" His gaze searched the empty street behind Maggie.

Maggie shook her head. "She's not coming."

"She let you travel the portal without her?" His raised voice roused the neighbor's dog. "Why would she allow you to face such danger alone?"

A flame flickered to life in the house across the street. Cyprian took Maggie by the elbow. "We can't stay out here." He led her inside and bolted the door. "Don't move." When he returned with a lit lamp she was holding a small pink box in front of her face. Light flashed, and for a second he couldn't see anything. "What is that?"

"Camera phone." She clicked a button, and the light flashed again. She held out the box. "See? It's a picture. Of you." Her finger traced his captured image. "It was getting harder to remember what you looked like." She slid the box into her bag. "Need to save the battery."

Cyprian's eyes and ears told him what his heart already knew. This woman *was* Maggie. Even more disconcerting: she'd somehow managed to find her way to his door. If she could locate him so easily, so could anyone else who'd seen him at the prison or happened to gaze upon those blasted posters.

"Maggie." Hands trembling, Cyprian reached for a rogue curl that had fallen across her face. "What were you thinking, coming here again?"

Her round eyes filled with hope. "That my father needed me."

It was his need to save his child that had sent him rushing to the portal with her feverish body less than twenty-four hours ago. Never in his wildest dreams could he have imagined that a glimpse of his grown daughter would increase his protective desires tenfold. "You can't stay here."

"Who's going to help you clean this up? Barek?" She looked around the room. "Where is he?"

"Safe for now."

"What about Uncle Larry, and Junia, and—"

"All are safe."

She released a jagged sigh. "Good. I was afraid . . . well, the door was open, so I came in earlier. No one was here, but I could see something awful had happened while I was away." Tears rimmed her lashes. "It scared me. I thought I was too late and that everybody I loved had, you know . . . died."

Cyprian clasped her shoulders. "Listen to me. It's very danger-ous here, Maggie. You can't stay."

"I may have been just a kid, but I remember a lot." She wiped the wet trails from her cheeks. "I Googled third-century Carthage. Things are going to get worse. That's why I came for you, Daddy."

For a moment, Cyprian let himself feel a rush of fatherly pride. Maggie had grown into a young woman every bit as stubborn and courageous as her mother. He took her hand and brought it to his lips. "In a perfect world, we could all be together, but I'm going to have to send you back to your mother."

She jerked her hand free. "There's only one way to keep Mom from killing me when I get home, and that's to have you with me."

Cyprian's blood ran through the veins of this exquisite crea-ture, and yet he'd missed so much of her life. How could he bear to miss a minute more? "That can't happen, Maggie."

"Why?" she demanded.

"Because God has called me to *this* place and *this* time."

"I swear, you sound just like Mom."

"Your mother's a wise woman."

"If she's so smart, why didn't she make you come with us? She knew what was going to happen."

"I chose to stay." He could see his admission was a verbal slap to her face, for she took a step back.

"Why would you do that?"

"God has called me to do what I can for the people of Carthage. Your mother didn't like it, but she understood." He couldn't bear the disappointment swimming in his daughter's eyes. "As soon as I find what I came for tonight, I'm marching you right back to that well."

"If you've got everyone else stashed someplace safe, then why can't I stay with them? Please."

"Your grandmother doesn't have time for me to stand here and argue with you."

"What's happened to Jaddah?"

Cyprian instantly regretted his slip. "Right after I sent you and your mother home, I found out Aspasius was dead."

"Aspasius?" She wrinkled her nose. "The guy who sent you away and carved up my Jaddah's face?"

"Yes."

"If he's dead, doesn't that mean you're safe now?"

Cyprian scowled. "No." He hesitated, not sure how much to tell her. "Your grandmother has been accused of his murder. I am going to defend her."

Maggie's mouth fell open. "My Jaddah saves lives. She wouldn't know how to take one." She hoisted the strap of her bag to her shoulder. "Where is she?"

"Prison."

"Then we'll have to bust her out and then—"

"Not *we*," Cyprian said. "Defending Magdalena will require me to present myself before any enemies I still have in Carthage. I can't do my best job for your grandmother if I'm worrying about you."

"I can help."

He shook his head.

Maggie crossed her arms. "Well, I'm not letting you do this alone. You can push me down that hole, but I'll just come right back." Her lips were pursed, and she lifted her chin in defiance.

"You are your mother's daughter."

"Funny, whenever I stand up for myself she says I'm just like you," she countered.

"My house is not safe."

"You're here."

"I only risked coming back to get a piece of paper that will prove your grandmother's innocence."

"You're going to need help to find it in this mess." Maggie lowered her bag.

"Maggie—"

"Light another lamp. I'll search the hall where Mom kept the typhoid patients." She shrugged off his protest. "The doctor promised my shots would be a lot more effective this time."

Before Cyprian could stop her, she disappeared down the hall. Maggie returned a few moments later, paper in hand and a big smile on her face. "See. You need me." She held the paper to the light. "You won't believe what my Jaddah got Aspasius to agree to."

"You can read Latin?"

She rolled her eyes. "Obviously you've never met my grand-father."

Cyprian held out his hand. "Give me the note."

"I'll make you a deal." Maggie whipped her hand behind her back. "I'll give you the note, we save my grandmother, and then you come home with us."

"Absolutely not." He didn't have time for a standoff and from the set of her shoulders she was prepared to dig in. He let out an exhausted sigh. "I'll let you say good-bye to everyone."

"It's better than nothing." She slowly held out the note.

He'd won. Why didn't he feel relieved? Because this was the same girl who'd agreed to let him work out the logistics of retrieving a doll from the slums, then took matters into her own hands. If the stubborn child he'd known a few hours ago had simply grown taller and even more beautiful, this wasn't over. He tucked the note into his pocket. Voices outside snapped their heads toward the door. "Quick. The lamp." He clamped her arm.

"My bag."

"Hush." He dragged her out the back door.

7

CLOAKED IN THE SAFETY of a predawn fog, Barek padded barefoot along the private fishing pier of Titus Cicero. The salty air weighed as heavily as his new responsibilities. If Cyprian's visit to Magdalena's prison resulted in Cyprian's arrest, the care and protection of Laurentius, Junia, and Naomi would fall to him. He would labor to keep them housed and fed. If it took the rest of his life, he would work to earn their trust.

Barek hoisted the heavy net that he'd found in one of Titus's many stables. He'd hastily repaired the frayed hemp by tying the knots he and his friend Natalis had learned from prowling the docks. Would guilty bile always accompany his memories of his friend?

Barek stood on the dock and searched for the small skiff Titus Cicero's stable boys had said he could borrow. The boat was an odd assembly of rough planks scavenged from the aqueduct building projects and lashed together with strips of cured animal hides. A seal of sticky black pitch kept the crude vessel afloat. Pushing aside his worries that a boat constructed by stable boys might not be seaworthy, Barek tossed the net into the bobbing boat.

Launching the skiff in darkness would make it easier to avoid the 25 percent *tetarte* Rome levied upon fish poached from its waters. As an added precaution, come daylight he'd check his catch and discard any shellfish or eel. Those delicacies would fetch an exorbitant price at the kitchen doors of the wealthy, but they would also draw attention he couldn't afford.

Barek freed the rope from the concrete post and shoved off from the pier. When he and Natalis used to fish these waters, they usually stayed close to the shore, but the sailing season was nearing its close. Once the harbor gates were officially closed for the winter, no one would have access to the open waters. He needed to cram in as many nights of serious fishing as possible.

Across the water, he could hear the rattle of heavy chains. Seamen were preparing the military triremes to lift anchor. Lisbeth had wanted the port closed until the plague burned out, but she had been forced to leave before Cyprian could anger the senators by insisting they pursue such a financially disastrous course of action. At sunup, the narrow channel would be clogged with the comings and goings of vessels in the emperor's charge. Barek clamped his hands upon the oars and rowed faster.

The slap of his oars churned the glassy surface. His shoulder muscles began to burn, and cramps tugged at his curled hands. He maneuvered the skiff past the massive stone pillars holding a portion of the Mediterranean waters captive and pressed on through the chilly mist, determined to steer clear of the harbor by sunrise. What was left of the wind would rise with the sun. Once he had enough breeze, he would hoist the tattered sail made of spun flax and let the forces of nature carry him far from his troubles.

His little boat began to rock, gentle as a baby's cradle. He felt his body relax for the first time in days. He needed sleep. What would it hurt to close his eyes for a few moments? Just as his head lolled to his chest, the skiff shuddered beneath him, jerking him instantly alert. Had he hit something? He scrambled to correct his course . . . but which way? Squinting into the drizzle for clues was pointless. The sky and sea had melded together and swirled him in a bowl of black soup. He couldn't tell where heaven left off and earth began.

Barek plunged the right oar into the water. Before he could add the left oar, an enormous swell lifted his boat high above the surface, held him suspended for a second, then cast him down hard between two walls of water that immediately tumbled in upon him. He clawed frantically against the skiff's slick animal skin sides that rolled seaward. The boat took on water at a rapid pace, swamping his feet and then his ankles. The blasted scrap heap was sinking beneath him.

Hands cupped, Barek began to bail. Had he been caught in one of those unexpected early fall squalls that made sea travel so dangerous during the winter months? Or had he crossed paths with the Illyrian pirates who prowled the coast? At any rate, he'd once again proven himself a fool by venturing into deep waters with an untested vessel. It would serve him right to die in a watery grave.

A large swell hit him from behind and flung him across the skiff like the rag doll Maggie had insisted they retrieve from the slums, the rag doll that had gotten his mother killed. His ribs smacked into the protruding oar handle, and he felt as if he'd been stabbed. Air whooshed from his lungs. Gasping for breath, he worked to drag his battered body to the plank bench.

Shouts sounded above him. Threats and protests. A struggle of some sort. The rhythmic slap of hundreds of oars hitting the water in perfect unison told him he was trapped in the passing wake of one of the empire's larger vessels. He stood and scrambled for his oars. Something solid whizzed past his ear. Before he could duck, a giant oar caught him hard in the chest and sent him flying overboard.

Foamy turbulence sucked him under. His mouth filled with water. Barek kicked and clawed against the pull of the deep. Just as he broke through the surface a large object sailed through the air and hit the water only three strokes to his left. He strained to make out what had been tossed overboard, but whatever the sailors had discarded had quickly disappeared in the ship's wake. Ten good strokes to his right he spotted the skiff. Comfortingly, it had remained afloat. Treading water, Barek tried to gauge his ability to make it back to his boat before he was spotted by one of the imperial henchmen who lent their swords to the protection of Rome's commerce.

He searched the settling waves. Something bobbed to the surface. An empty grain barrel? A broken shield? Or was it just a rusty shinguard? Perhaps it was something that would fetch a good price in the market and make up for his lack of fishing success. Barek swam toward the lump.

"Help! I can't swim!" A hand reached for him.

Barek stopped in midstroke.

"Please . . ." The young man slipped beneath the surface.

Barek dove after him. He snagged a hand, then kicked hard for the surface. Gasping for breath, Barek hooked an arm under the man's chin and hauled him to the skiff. By the time Barek had both of them safely aboard, the sky had turned pink. They were surrounded by two hundred imperial vessels.

Barek propped the slumped fellow against the stern. Streaks of dawn peeked through the fog and struck his passenger's face. Red splotches like the ones he'd had when he and his mother suffered from measles. No wonder this fellow had been thrown overboard. What should he do? If he took a contagious man to the home of Titus, the sickness could be passed on to the land merchant's family. And Barek couldn't take him to Cyprian's, because the hospital his mother and Lisbeth had set up in those wide halls had been destroyed. No matter where he took him, there wasn't really anyone left to care for him. Magdalena was in prison. And Lisbeth was . . .

wherever it was she went when she disappeared. Whatever he decided would have to wait until he got to shore because he couldn't stay here.

The young man lurched forward and began to cough up water. When he finally caught a good breath, he said, "Thank you."

Barek dropped onto the plank seat and began to row. "Stay quiet and keep your head down." The man fell back, too exhausted to argue.

Barek took the long way back to the quay berth where the skiff had been moored. Across the harbor he could see deckhands lowering the anchor of the *Syracousia*. It was rumored the enormous fishing vessel was equipped with a lead-lined saltwater tank that made it possible for the ship to harvest live parrotfish from the Black Sea and deliver the delicacy fresh to the bellies of the rich in ports as far away as the Neapolitan coast.

Barek surveyed his passenger as he rowed them past the last of the imperial freighters. About his age. Seventeen. Maybe eighteen. Broad forehead. Patches of pale skin beneath the inflamed pustules. Fire-colored hair the breeze was whipping into a blaze. Sitting square in the center of the man's swollen face was the classical nose of someone with a northern heritage.

When they were out of earshot, Barek whispered, "What's your name?"

"Eg . . . Eggie."

"Well, *Eggie*, what were you doing aboard the *Syracousia*?"

Eyes gray as a summer storm drilled Barek without wavering. "Deckhand."

Barek glanced at his passenger's limp hands. Pink and smooth as a newly shorn lamb. "I don't think you've bailed much bilge water."

"You calling me a liar, sir?"

"I'm saying those hands lack the rope burns of someone who's swabbed decks and wrestled sail riggings across the Mediterranean."

Eggie crossed his arms over his chest and tucked his hands into his armpits. "Maybe I fed the fish in the large onboard tanks. Sea bass can be very demanding, you know." He started coughing and struggled for breath.

Barek glanced around to make sure the racket hadn't given them away. "Looked more like the *Syracousia*'s crew intended to feed *you* to the fish."

Eggie shrugged and held up his hands in surrender. "I am a stowaway with plague. Going to turn me in?"

Barek eased the skiff along the dock. "First I'm going to try to keep you alive."

8

Cave of the Swimmers

LISBETH POKED THE CAMPFIRE she and Aisa had built from brittle tinder scavenged in a dry wadi not far from the Cave of the Swimmers. Sparks popped into the chilly night air. Lisbeth's gaze followed the fiery bits of ash until they disappeared into the vast emptiness like taillights on a getaway car. On the surface, the arid expanse looked lifeless. No shade. No water. Scorching days. Freezing nights. Yet, beneath the windswept sand lay a secret treasure trove, a labyrinth of underground waterways. Dark. Full of life. Her only connection to the past.

And somewhere in that dark, infinite continuum of time her daughter was all alone.

Not since Ruth's tragic death had Lisbeth felt so small. So absolutely helpless.

She'd given Nigel the tongue-lashing he deserved after she discovered him at the cave, kicking at the tires of his plane and cursing his folly for believing Maggie's story that Lisbeth had sent for him. Losing her temper with such a good man hadn't done anything but make him feel responsible, and heaven knew the responsibility for this mess belonged solely on her shoulders.

Just being back in the shadow of the cave and all that had happened in this place confirmed what Lisbeth already knew: pursuing her daughter and bringing her back from the third century was the best course of action. Maggie was a hopeless romantic who remembered Carthage through a five-year-old's eyes. The girl's memories were skewed by the thrill of discovering her father, grandmother, and uncle. The Carthage Maggie remembered no longer existed. Were it not for the scar on Lisbeth's wrist and her beautiful fair-haired daughter, she might believe that it never had.

Lisbeth zipped her jacket to keep her racing heart from galloping right out of her chest. What if she couldn't find Maggie before trouble found her daughter? "Tomorrow, I want to leave at the exact time of day Nigel said Maggie dropped through the portal," she announced to the small rescue party gathered around the crackling flames.

Her father sat cross-legged on the sand, calmly smoking his Meerschaum pipe. "I can go through the portal tonight." A smoke ring floated toward the blanket of stars. "I won't break, you know."

Papa, although spry for seventy-two, had no idea how physically taxing it would be to time-travel through the Sahara's underground aquifers. Riding a waterslide into the past was comparable to being hit with a fire hose for hours. And the physical toll paled in comparison to the emotional roller coaster of stepping into a bygone era. The tears Lisbeth had seen in Papa's eyes when the pilot set Aisa's plane down near this cone of granite told her his emotions were already taxed.

Lisbeth poked the fire again. "We're all exhausted." This cave had changed their lives in so many ways. She couldn't take it if she lost her father in the portal. "To have the best shot at landing at the same time and place as Maggie, I want to repeat her steps exactly."

"But it won't be the same day," Papa pointed out.

"It's all we've got."

* * *

AFTER A restless night, Lisbeth rose before the sun, and strapped on one of the backpacks filled with supplies, including several rounds of antibiotics and her mother's stethoscope. She helped Papa do the same, and then to reduce the risk of getting separated from her father, she strapped their wrists together with a strong cord. Together they ducked inside the cave.

"If we're not back in a week, Aisa, you and Nigel fly out of here and never come back." Lisbeth turned to her father. Despite the alarms going off in her head, she smiled and said, "Ready?"

"Been ready for over forty years." Excitement danced in his eyes, and every muscle in his body seemed taut. He clamped his nose plugs in place. "Let's do this."

Lisbeth placed her hand upon the wall painting of the child with the outstretched arms and let the bottom fall out from beneath the life she'd so carefully guarded. After spinning for what seemed like an eternity in a washing machine, Lisbeth's head broke the water's surface. She took in huge gulps of air. The saccharine stench of death assaulted her nostrils. "Papa!" She tugged at the reassuring weight on her wrist and Papa surfaced, sputtering and eyes shining.

"Amazing!" His exuberance echoed in the well's chamber. "What a rush." *Rush. Rush.*

"Shhh. We don't know who could be up there." Their necks instantly jackknifed toward the moonlight.

"No rope," Papa whispered. "And no one to pull us out."

"Time travel is not an exact science." What else had she miscalculated? What if she couldn't find Maggie? She quelled the fear that had followed her through the portal. "Hang on to this ledge. I'll climb up and throw you a rope." Unstrapping her pack, she hoisted it to the ledge.

Several painful minutes later her arms were burning from her assent. With a bit more effort than it took the night Barek had hauled her and Maggie out of the cistern, she flung herself over the lip of the well. A hollow gourd dangled from a long rope tied to the crossbeam. She untied the gourd and dropped the rope down to Papa. It took about thirty minutes and every ounce of her strength to haul their gear to safety and raise Papa up the slick walls.

"Did you notice the trowel marks in the cement?" He swung one of his long legs over the lip. "Excellent craftsmanship."

"Papa, this isn't an archaeological expedition." This trip Lisbeth had thought to bring the appropriate clothing. She handed him Aisa's tunic. "Try to stay focused."

"Sorry. You're right."

They took turns standing guard while the other slipped behind the well and did a quick change. When Lisbeth emerged clad in her tunic, Papa was standing at the edge of the street staring into the distance like a Bedouin sheepherder come to town for the first time.

"The reconstructed Phoenician metropolis is even more breathtaking than I imagined." Awe radiated from his expression. "Not a fragment of a faded fresco. Not an artist rendition based on estimated measurements, but real brick and mortar." He ran his fingers lightly over the stones of the tenement building. "Being here"—he turned to her, tears in his eyes—"puts flesh upon what I have only known as bones."

He hesitated and then said, "Your mother will want to see me, right?"

She kissed his leathery cheek. "More than anything."

They wove through the alleys that led toward the wealthier part of the city. Streets that once bustled with life were somber as a tomb and just as noxious. Corpses were stacked two and three high at every intersection. Lisbeth clutched the bag of medical supplies slung over her shoulder and kept focused on reaching her goal. These people and their medical needs were not her problem.

According to history, the plagues eventually flamed out. Eradicating measles and typhoid sooner would require that she put herself out there again, invest in changing the past. She'd tried that. Twice. And both times the past had resolutely refused to budge from its destructive course. She couldn't go through the pain of thinking she could save Cyprian and the church again. This trip was her last. She intended to get in, gather her family, and get out before she lost another piece of her heart.

Pale streaks of light showed Byrsa Hill. Papa halted, his eyes wide. "Look, over there. Something's happened." Papa started toward the scores of scarecrow-thin pedestrians, hunched and shuffling en masse along the broad avenue leading to the Forum. Each person had a cloth tied over his or her nose.

"Wait," she called after him.

He ignored her and kept going. "Someone may have seen Maggie."

"So much for keeping our heads down." Lisbeth hurried across the street and caught up with him. "Let me do the talking." She stopped the first person, an old woman with fresh scabs on her face. "What's going on?" Her rusty Latin must have frightened the woman because she backed away. Lisbeth turned to summon her father, but he was right behind her.

Papa stepped in and rephrased the question. The woman nodded in the direction of the proconsul's palace high atop the Acropolis and mumbled something Papa translated. "She says Aspasius is dead."

"What? When?"

"Yesterday."

"That can't be." Was her timing off? The sickening possibility she'd overshot their desired entry time slammed Lisbeth's gut. "Let's check it out, Papa."

"I thought we weren't sightseeing."

"This is one sight I'm not going to miss."

Arm in arm, they approached the line that snaked around the palace grounds. Lisbeth strained to make out the circulating whispers.

"Murdered," Papa whispered. "They're saying the proconsul was murdered."

"By whom?" Lisbeth's pulse quickened. "When?" Did the person who killed the proconsul kill her mother? Had Cyprian already been executed? Was she too late? Where was Maggie? Lisbeth's gaze raced over the crowd. *God, help me find my strong-willed runaway.*

"They're saying Aspasius died at the hand of his personal healer," Papa said.

"Mama?" She and Papa exchanged terrified looks. "That's impossible."

"Well, impossible or not, he's dead." Papa pointed to the cypress branch hanging over the open doors of the palace and the group of women throwing themselves upon the ground and wailing in a mournful rhythm. "I don't think we want to be here. This is the line to view his body." He tried to pull her away, but Lisbeth strained in the direction of the body. "Wait, where are we going?"

"To spit upon the face of the tyrant who tortured my mother." Lisbeth dragged Papa to the end of a long procession of men, women, and children filing past the pale body laid out in the atrium. Different accounts of how the proconsul died reached Lisbeth's ears. One version stopped her heart.

"When he refused to marry his lover, she sawed off his leg and kept it as a memento."

"That's not true," Lisbeth whispered to Papa. "Mama loves you. Not that coward who hid in his bedroom with his gangrenous foot and weasel-eyed scribe."

What she didn't go on to say was that she'd begged her mother not to nurse the man who'd abused her for nearly a quarter of a century. She'd pleaded with Mama to come with her. To come back to Papa. Lisbeth didn't say it, because she didn't want her father to misconstrue the truth. Mama had chosen to remain in the past. Not because of Aspasius but because of his son.

Lisbeth inched forward. She wouldn't believe the man who'd exiled her husband and made her mother's life miserable was dead until she saw his body. She shifted from foot to foot, trying to see around the tall oil merchant blocking her view. When the man in front of her had finally seen enough and moved on in a greasy swirl, Lisbeth gasped.

The bloated corpse of Aspasius lay in repose upon a marble table. The slight tilt of his head had permanently pressed his lips into that wicked, twisted grin he'd given her right before she'd administered the mandrake that put him under for surgery.

In life, the proconsul of Carthage had seemed invincible. His massive girth had filled a room with fear. People cowered when his mercurial red sandals clicked upon the marble tiles of the governing hall. They quivered in the wake of his purple-trimmed cloak and that ridiculous golden wreath he wore to conceal his baldness.

In death, diabetic-induced weight loss and a raging infection had reduced Aspasius Paternus to mere mortal status. His decaying body was no safer from the ravaging effects of a deadly disease than those of the plebeians struggling to survive in the crowded tenements.

Lisbeth averted her gaze, unwilling to allow this man a permanent place in her thoughts. His decades of evil had destroyed the lives of so many good people. People she loved. He'd killed her friend Caecilianus. He'd exiled her husband. He'd inflicted atrocities upon her mother. And quite possibly he'd have removed her husband's head before some postoperative complication had removed him. Dwelling upon her hatred of the former ruler of Carthage would destroy her, and as long as her child was alive, she couldn't let that happen.

"Let's get out of here." Lisbeth clasped Papa's arm and spun out of line.

"Where are we going?"

"The only place Maggie would know to look for her father." Lisbeth set a brisk pace toward Cyprian's villa. When they reached the magnificent structures of the rich, she rushed ahead. "This is it." She burst through the doors. "Cyprian! Maggie!" Her feet went out from under her and she fell hard in a pool of blood. Drying her hands on her tunic, she scrambled to get her legs under her again.

Tossed mats, spilled water gourds, and tumped oil lamps littered the beautiful mosaic floor. "Cyprian!"

"Whoa!" Papa surveyed the mess. "What happened here?"

"When I left, soldiers were destroying the hospital. I can still hear the screams from that day." She couldn't bring herself to say that Cyprian may have sent her down the well and returned to the point of a sword. "The bodies are gone—maybe that means Cyprian is alive." She found a lamp. "It's still warm. Someone may be hiding and too frightened to come out." For better or worse, she had to know. "If it's the family I told you about, maybe they can tell us if Maggie showed up." She started down the typhoid hall.

Something sharp pierced the sole of Lisbeth's sandal and punctured the tender flesh of her heel. Her cry echoed in the empty hall.

"Are you all right?" Papa helped her limp to Diona's deserted recovery bed.

Lisbeth dug sterile gauze from her bag and then pulled a piece of broken pottery from her foot. "I don't think I need stitches." Pressure did little to slow her hemorrhaging emotions. "Maybe everyone's in the cottage out back."

"Or maybe—"

"Don't say it." Lisbeth quickly wrapped her foot. "I'll check the estate grounds. You check the other halls." She then tested her weight. Painful. "I think I can still walk." When her father didn't answer, she noticed he hadn't left the atrium. "Papa?" He stood before a statue of a woman, his eyes fixed on her face. "Papa! What's wrong?"

He struggled to get the words out. "It's one of the Women of Victory."

"Cyprian has lots of art."

"Not like this."

"What do you mean?"

"I unearthed this statue the summer you were born. I had promised your mother I would not go to England to dig but would find a project site near Tunis, one that would allow me to stay within driving distance of the hospital where she worked. So I joined a team excavating in what was believed to be the destroyed wealthy residential area of Old Carthage."

"Destroyed? When?"

He gave a pained nod. "We could never pinpoint the date of destruction."

Of course Cyprian's home hadn't lasted forever. She'd explored modern Carthage before she and Maggie returned to the States after Maggie's typhoid recovery in a Tunisian hospital. Cyprian's villa was not among the visible ruins. When had these walls that had sheltered so many tumbled in upon themselves?

Papa's trembling fingers skimmed to the statue's slender arms. "I had to move mounds of rubble before I found this headless woman and the other two statues buried with her. A coup that made me famous. After news of my discoveries hit archaeological circles, it was easy to raise the financing to do what I'd wanted to do since your mother dug that potshard from my backside: explore the Cave of the Swimmers." He paused, as if whatever was stuck deep inside him would rip him apart should he utter it. He turned to face Lisbeth. "Your mother didn't want me to go on such a dangerous dig."

"Then why did you?"

"I was ambitious."

"Why did she go with you and take me?"

"She wanted her family together as much as I wanted my picture on the cover of every archaeological journal. She insisted on accompanying me to the desert, and since she rarely let you out of her sight, you came along. I knew it wasn't a good idea, but I took the easy way out and agreed. I often wonder what would have happened had I never discovered the Women of Victory." Papa's eyes were damp. "I guess you could say, in a horrible, morbid way, this hunk of stone is the reason your mother and I have been separated all these years."

Lisbeth had never heard this part of their family's story, the dirty underbelly of her father's ambition and how it changed all of their lives. Knees rubbery, she asked, "Are you sure it's the same statue?"

"I brushed away every grain of sand from her stola. Memorized every stroke of the sculptor's hand. I imagined the shape of the statue's face, the line of her nose, even the look in her eyes. I was so obsessed with this particular Woman of Victory and what she could mean to my career that I had a large glass display case built and had her placed in the Carthage National Museum for safekeeping."

Papa shook his head, but Lisbeth could tell the memory was burned so deeply into his soul he would never slough it off. "To see this statue, whole and intact, her face far different than I imagined . . . it is . . ." He swallowed and sadly looked Lisbeth square in the eyes. "A painful reminder that I took better care of an ancient artifact than I did of your beautiful mother."

Lisbeth threaded her fingers through his and squeezed. For so many years she'd blamed herself for what had happened that cold desert night. She thought she was the reason her mother had left the safety of the camp and ventured into the Cave of the Swimmers and fell through the time portal. It wasn't until she found her mother that those distorted memories and wrong assumptions were cleared up. She wanted her father to have that same opportunity.

"We'll find her, Papa. I promise." Lisbeth kissed his cheek, then stepped into the garden, as determined to reunite her parents as she was to find her daughter. "Maggie!" The wind whistled a lonely tune through the pillars of the colonnade. She limped to the gardener's cottage. Cold and dark. Where was everybody? Maybe she'd missed a clue in the house.

"Lisbeth," Papa called from the doorway, his face pale. He held out the waterproof backpack Maggie had talked him into buying. "Her camera's still in the bag."

Terror drove Lisbeth across the garden. "She would never leave her camera." She pawed through the bag. "Or her phone." She clicked on the cell and went to the camera roll. "A selfie in the well." She stared at the girl with wet hair and a wide-eyed mixture of terror and determination in her face. "Oh, Maggie. What have you done?" Lisbeth scrolled to the next picture, hoping for a clue as to where she'd gone. A startled, handsome face stared back at her. "Thank God."

"What is it?"

She thrust the phone at him. "Cyprian is still alive."

9

MAGGIE HURRIED UP THE hill. "Dad, wait! I forgot my backpack!"

"Shhh." He stopped at a massive gate. Looming above the fence was the upper story of a villa twice the size of her father's. "Your life is worth more than whatever was in that bag." He made a fist and rapped out what sounded like some sort of secret code signal.

The gate cracked open and they quickly squeezed inside.

Glass mosaics of charioteers driving elaborate, golden, horse-drawn vehicles glittered in the amber light of morning. Maggie felt a bit like Dorothy in *The Wizard of Oz*: out of place. And lost without her camera or her phone. Her father nodded to the servant who'd let them in, and then grabbed Maggie's wrist. "Hurry."

They followed the beautiful sidewalk scenes to the stoop. Her father planted his sandals upon the heads of two dueling gladiators and lifted the iron ring knocker.

"So who are we running from?"

His brows scrunched. "Probably just looters, but I couldn't risk our discovery."

"I hope they enjoy my camera," she muttered. "So where are we?"

"The home of Titus Cicero."

"I remember the senator. And his daughter, Diona. They weren't all that nice."

"Titus is a very influential man and he's putting the life of his family in jeopardy to help mine."

"He's on our side now?"

A muscle twitched in her father's jaw. "I have to trust that he is." He banged the iron ring against the huge front door three times.

Minutes passed. Maggie couldn't help but steal glances at her father. He paced the threshold with one hand on the dagger in his belt, and both eyes peeled for danger. Near as she could tell, thirteen years had passed for her in the twenty-first century but very little time had passed in this century. She'd popped back in almost exactly where she'd dropped out on the time line of history. Which was more than a little disconcerting. As near as she could calculate, she and her mother had left the third century in the late summer of AD 258. According to most historical accounts, her father was beheaded in the fall of that same year. She had no more than a few weeks to figure out a way to save him.

Maggie studied his profile. She'd have to commit the exact angles to memory and sketch them later. He was still the handsome man of her memory, only now she had the maturity to notice that the weight of the world had carved a few little trenches in his brow. Convincing him to leave before he had everything settled would take some doing on her part.

"So when can I see my Jaddah?"

"It's not going to be that simple, Maggie."

"Well, we can't go home without her."

A wooden peephole opened. A man sporting a bad case of bedhead peered out. The man's sleepy eyes widened. "Cyprian?" The door flew open and they were immediately ushered in. Maggie recognized the man as her father's friend. He clasped her father's shoulders. "I'm sorry. I must have fallen asleep."

"It's all right, Pontius. I trust you've had no trouble."

"Quiet so far." He looked at Maggie. "Who's the woman?"

"Pontius, it's me—"

Her father cut her off. "Fetch Titus and food. I have the strength to explain this only once."

"Very well." Pontius spun on his heel and disappeared down a dark hall.

"Let's sit." Her father sank wearily onto one of the golden benches.

"Why didn't you let me tell him who I was?"

"Pontius has believed my explanations of your mother's comings and goings, but I'm certain your sudden return as a full-grown woman will be a little more difficult to understand . . . for everyone. Best to do it all at once."

Maggie so wanted to snuggle in beside this kind man, to close the gap her years away from him had put in their relationship. But physical embraces sent her claustrophobia into overdrive. Besides, trying to fit into this world is where her mother made her mistake. Maggie reminded herself that her mission was to take her father back to her world. All she needed was a few days with him. Once he got to know her, he could never send her home alone. Maggie took a breath and sat on the opposite end of the seat, working out in her mind where to start.

The ornate Corinthian pillars and elegant arches that framed the large skylight above the entryway fountain inspired her to give her father a peek into her passion. "The lighting in here is amazing." Intricate mosaics decorated the floors, and brilliant-colored frescoes covered the walls. "What I wouldn't give to follow one of these third-century artists around for a few weeks."

He smiled in a way that attempted to apologize for the years they'd lost. "I remember how much you loved to draw."

He remembered! A giddy grin danced across Maggie's face. No wonder history portrayed Cyprianus Thascius as one of the smartest lawyers Carthage had ever seen. Oh, how she wanted to know more about this man, more than the scant details she'd pieced together from fragmented memories or read online. But she needed to play this cool. Not pressure him into choosing between her and his destiny. Mom had tried that, and it hadn't worked out so well. Maggie worked to keep her voice nonchalant. "G-Pa would salivate if he were sitting in the atrium of a real Roman senator."

"Does your grandfather know where you are?"

For a second, Maggie felt a little guilty. How could she explain that telling her grandfather was the same as telling her mother? She couldn't. Not without sounding like a spoiled brat. And she didn't want anything to ruin this perfect moment. Time to change the subject. "I don't think Mom knows about Jaddah's legal troubles."

"How could she? All of this happened after I sent you and your mother . . . home."

"You can find anything on the Internet."

His brow scrunched. "Internet?"

"It's how I found out about you and well, you know . . . all the bad stuff that's going to happen."

He felt her watching and cocked his head to one side. "So you know the future?"

"Not all of it."

A dark cloud dulled her father's eyes, and he gave a slight nod of his head. "Knowing the future is a double-edged sword. Good and bad."

"You know about the . . . bad?"

"Your mother told me." He reached for her hand. "It's why she came. To change things."

Maggie could scarcely imagine how anyone could sit so calmly upon a bench if he knew he was scheduled to die a horrible death. "If you know, then why aren't you jumping at the chance to grab up the rest of the family and get the heck out of Dodge? I don't get it."

Before he could answer, Pontius returned with a tray of big green olives, two kinds of cheese, and a disheveled man. Titus Cicero was palming his Friar Tuck bangs into a smooth, straight line as he hurried toward them. Missing from his face were the pinched lips and haughty expression of her memory. A genuinely relieved smile had taken over his face.

His long arms flew open. "Cyprian! Tell me Magdalena is well."

Her father rose and gave Titus a hearty embrace. "As well as can be expected, considering Aspasius's men roughed her up, along with three other helpless women."

"Women?"

Her father gave a curt nod. "Servants of Aspasius who've been charged in aiding Magdalena in the proconsul's murder."

"Oh, dear." Titus finally noticed Maggie staring at him. "Who is this?"

Her father clasped her hand. "This is my daughter."

The land merchant scowled. "I don't understand."

Her father released her hand and launched into a shaky explanation of her presence. Though she was starving and the olives on the breakfast tray were tempting, Maggie couldn't take her eyes off their host's puzzled face.

Titus rubbed his eyes, fastened them squarely upon Maggie, and then verbalized his doubt. "Let me see if I can sort through what you're *not* telling me. You left your villa with a five-year-old just a few hours ago." His disbelief volleyed between her and her father. "And now you want me to believe this young woman is that same impetuous girl who caused Ruth's . . ." His sharp gaze slid over her. "It pains me even to say it."

"Ruth's death," Maggie said around the lump that always formed in her throat whenever she was forced to remember that night. "Ruth would be alive today if I hadn't insisted on retrieving a stupid doll from the tenements."

The tall man gasped. "How could she know that story?"

"Only one way," Pontius said. "She must have been there."

"Impossible," Titus said.

"Titus, you're going to have to trust me when I say that this girl *is* my daughter." Cyprian placed his hand on the man's shoulder. "Just as I am trusting you with the safety of my family."

For whatever reason, her father was leaving out the time travel part and she could see that Titus wasn't going to fall for any of this without that vital piece of the puzzle.

"I say this girl is my daughter. Wasting efforts that should be directed toward preparing for Magdalena's day in court will serve no good purpose."

Heavy footsteps in the courtyard were quickly followed by frantic pounding at the door. Everyone stopped talking.

Titus put a finger to his lips. Pontius leaped to one side of the door, his sword drawn.

Maggie's father grabbed her arm and shoved her behind one of the columns. "Stay put," he whispered in her ear. He drew the knife from his belt and rushed to a column closer to the entrance. Once he was set to spring upon the intruder, he gave a nod and Titus opened the peephole.

"Barek?" He closed the peephole and opened the door.

"Stand back, Titus." Barek lurched inside with a body draped over his shoulder. "This one has measles."

Titus backpedaled with his hands in the air. "Why have you brought him here?"

Pontius and Maggie's father sprang from their hiding places in the same instant and rushed to Barek's aid. Her father draped the man's limp arm over his own shoulder and Pontius took the other. "Who is this?" They lowered the sick man upon the bench. Maggie eased out from behind the pillar.

"He says his name is Eggie," Barek said, rubbing his own neck. "That's all he'll tell me."

"Where did you get him?" Maggie peered into the face that might have been handsome were his cheeks and jaws not distorted with red boils.

"Who are you?" Barek eyed her suspiciously.

The sick man opened his eyes and reached for Maggie's hand. "She's a goddess." His wink pumped heat from his hand directly to hers. "I have died and gone to live in celestial realms." A thousand secrets lurked in the depths of those bloodshot eyes. Danger clung to him like his wet clothes.

Maggie rolled her eyes. "Has a girl ever fallen for those lame lines?" She tugged at her hand, but the guy with the Roman numeral III tattooed above his wrist had a tight grip for someone supposedly dying. "You smell like a corpse."

Her father removed the sick man's hand from hers. "Release my daughter, young man."

Barek's eyes snapped to hers, then quickly diverted, traveling the length of her, as if measuring her changes from toe to head. As he stood sizing her up, she couldn't help doing the same. She may have grown up, but Barek was exactly as she remembered him: dark and surly. His brooding face, which had nothing in common with the angelic glow of his mother's, was framed by a wet mane of ebony curls. It was all she could do not to brush them from his forehead, but touching him could easily make her say good-bye to the last of her good judgment, assuming she hadn't already used up what little she ever had by jumping into the time portal. Even from this distance, Barek's familiar scent of sun and sea rustled among her senses like an untamed wind in the dune grasses.

He'd paused. "What did you call her?" The instant Barek's eyes met hers, she knew giving him a chance to figure out who she was had been a mistake.

"My daughter," her father repeated. "Both of you boys will do well to remember that and treat Maggie with respect."

A tiny pulse beat in Barek's set jaw. "Maggie?" His shoulders stiffened.

She locked eyes with his and braced for the usual string of insults he loved to hurl her way.

The pencil-thin line of his lips was not what made him look so menacing. It was the coldness in his eyes. As if he would rather she'd died of typhoid than come back to bug him again. He offered no berating, no greeting, no acknowledgment of her changed appearance.

But she wasn't afraid. No, she was not. Because she knew something no one else in this room knew. Beneath Barek's ominous frown and steely armor beat the heart of a guy who'd carried her to safety . . . twice.

Maybe she wasn't in such a hurry to go home after all.

Maggie summoned her most charming smile and said, "Miss me?"

"You are *not* Maggie," Barek declared. "I'd know that little chit anywhere."

"And *you* obviously still need a nap." The old accusation she used to hurl to defend herself against his crankiness unhinged Barek as easily as it did when she was five.

He stumbled back two steps. "I don't know who you are, but you need to go home."

Maggie stepped forward and kissed him square on the lips, then stepped back to secretly enjoy the heat she knew her boldness would bring to his cheeks. "And you're still not my boss."

10

THE MOMENT THE GIRL'S bewitching blue eyes met his, Barek felt his strained connection to the impish daughter of Cyprian resurface, as if she were the one he'd hauled from the well only weeks ago. Which was impossible.

A bratty child was in Lisbeth's sling when he'd shinnied down into the dark depths of a cistern in the poorest part of the city. He believed he'd found these two misfits there because the crowded tenements offered the perfect place for a runaway slave and her illegitimate child to hide from Aspasius.

His mother, however, swore Lisbeth had disappeared back into the time from which she had come, claiming she'd witnessed with her own eyes Magdalena pushing her daughter into the miraculous cistern.

When Barek had questioned his mother as to why anyone would shove her daughter down a well, she'd challenged his skepticism: "Some things are like faith. They cannot be explained."

But this accounting had come from the same woman who'd also told him Jesus arose from the grave and that one day she would do the same. To believe such tall tales required a faith he no longer possessed . . . maybe never had.

Not even a full day had passed since Barek had placed his life in harm's way so Cyprian could carry his small, feverish daughter to safety. He thought Cyprian had taken Lisbeth and Maggie to his country estate. He hadn't asked because he didn't think Cyprian would ever again trust him with the truth. But it had never occurred to him that an intelligent man like Cyprian would push the two people he loved the most in this world through some magical time portal.

No, this alarming beauty standing before him was most likely an impostor sent to aid the followers of Aspasius in Cyprian's capture.

Barek retreated a safe distance from her reach, his lips on fire where she'd kissed him. "This isn't funny," he stuttered. "Maggie was dying."

She raised her chin with the same cocky slant of that child who could ignite his temper with a word. A curtain of blond curls fell across her shoulders. "Sorry to disappoint you, Barek, but I lived." Her eyes, turbulent as the sea in winter, dared him to think her anything other than the small child he'd carried through the Tophet.

"I never meant for her to get sick."

From the arch of her brow, Barek could see she didn't believe for a minute he was sorry for anything that had happened. "I don't blame you for the days I spent in the hospital, so there's no need to be so cranky."

Only one person had ever called him on his foul mood, and that was the daughter of the healer he'd fished out of the well. Barek couldn't explain it, but in that instant he knew . . . this girl with the curves of a full-grown woman was the same child who'd changed everything. How different his life might have been had he let her drown. "I will never understand the pleasure you take in taunting me."

A wry smile fluttered across her perfect lips. "Then you believe it's me?"

Barek ran a hand through his wet hair, suddenly aware that he reeked of fish. "Or Maggie's evil twin."

"Enough." Cyprian wedged between them. "Where shall we make this boy's sickbed, Titus?"

"We can't keep him here." Titus again raised his palms and backed away. "We're not set up to handle measles, and without Lisbeth or Magdalena we have no healer."

"I'll take care of him," Maggie volunteered.

"You?" Barek scoffed. "What do *you* know of measles?"

"I watched my mother build the vaporizer tents."

"So did I, but that doesn't make us healers," Barek said with a snarl. "Keeping him alive will be hard work."

"Then I suspect we will both need a nap by the time he has recovered, because I expect *you* to help." Maggie took several steps toward Titus, balled her fists, and crammed them onto her slender hips. "I seemed to remember that you promised my mother you would do whatever you could to repay the care she and my grandmother gave your daughter."

"Yes, but that was before—"

"Good." She smiled. "It seems to me it's settled."

"It's Maggie, all right," Barek muttered.

Titus rubbed his brow. "My servants will do what they can, but no one in this house has had the rash. We'll need help from your Christian friends, Cyprian."

"There're not many of them left."

"I helped split the church," Barek said. "I should be the one to put it back together."

11

GALERIUS MAXIMUS LAY BOARD-STRAIGHT upon the thick carpet of his bedchamber. He squeezed his eyes shut so his daily elocution exercises would not be spoiled by the ridiculous fresco painted on his ceiling. The artists his mother-in-law commissioned to redecorate his quarters had given the goddess of fertility such a shrewish look. Maximus knew the rendering was Hortensia's subtle way of saying her eyes were always upon him. Especially on the rare opportunities she allowed him to bed his own wife.

In one corner of the spacious room a slave waved a plumed fan. In another corner his faithful bodyguard stacked heavy stone pavers. Under cover of darkness, he and Kaeso had stolen the stones from one of his mother-in-law's extensive garden paths. Oh, how he hated that his father's gambling debts had forced him to forfeit his family's home and move in with his wife's mother.

Maximus inhaled deeply, pressed his back to the floor, and then bent his knees. "Place the stones here, Kaeso." He patted his chest at the indentation just below his breastbone. "I must work on strengthening my projection."

His bodyguard's eyes flitted between him and the stack of pavers. "These stones are heavier than they look, master." Muscles rippled beneath the sheen of Kaeso's soot-colored skin. "If you are crushed to death and I am forced to serve Mistress Hortensia, I shall follow you into the depths of Hades and make certain you are unable to recite a single word in your next life."

The tall, broad-shouldered, shiny piece of marble scowling down at him had been with Maximus since his mother killed herself after his noble birth. When Maximus reached the age of needing a playmate, Kaeso had been purchased to become the young master's personal slave and companion. Thirty-five years later faint traces of the slave's North African heritage remained in his accent. Maximus had learned that Kaeso had been cut from his mother's womb by a raiding Roman war party and forced to serve the imperial troops patrolling the southern frontier until he was ten. Poor Kaeso had been angry about the injustice ever since.

Maximus found it easy to forgive Kaeso's ill temper, for he too suffered from a life of forced service. Had he been master of his own life, he would have joined a theater troupe years ago and traveled the world with his beautiful wife. Instead, his marriage had saddled him with an ambitious mother-in-law intent on his rise in public office. He prayed to the gods that Hortensia would not live forever. Then he and his lovely Aeliana could do as they pleased.

Maximus waved his servant forward and patted his bare chest again. "The stones, Kaeso. Add one at a time if you fear me so fragile, but if I'm to be heard by those watching from the theater's cheap seats I must strengthen my voice."

"Here's to your last breath." Kaeso straddled his chest, and then slowly lowered the paver.

Air whooshed from Maximus's lungs. "Oh." He fought the idiotic tremors of panic and quickly set to work enunciating the drills his acting teacher had given him. Executing the last run of rhyming words had limbered his tongue to perfection when he heard the distinctive click of a woman's heels upon the marbled hallway. He waved his hands. "The stone, Kaeso. Quickly."

"Galerius Maximus." Hortensia breezed into the room, a foul

wind that singed the fine hairs upon his chest. She strode to his side and peered down her nose. "Whatever are you doing casting about on my fine carpets like some sort of plebeian?" She snapped her fingers. "Aeliana, come talk sense to your husband before he exposes himself as an utter fool and shames my house."

Maximus scrambled to stand, intent on impressing Aeliana to root for him in these regular duels with her mother. "I'm quite capable of standing on my own two feet." He smoothed his loincloth.

"That remains to be seen." Hortensia's gaze traveled from his hairless chest to the stone in Kaeso's hands and then on to the pile in the corner. "Are those the new garden pavers I had imported from Egypt?"

Heat flushed Maximus's cheeks. "We'll put them back when I've completed my exercises. I promise."

She was not amused. "Does your foolish behavior have anything to do with that despicable actor . . . ?" She snapped her fingers as if to jar her memory. "What's his name?"

"Cato," Aeliana whispered.

Hortensia cast a glare at her daughter. "What do you know of the theater?"

Aeliana became suddenly very interested in her shoes, dainty silk affairs adorned with expensive seed pearls. "No more than you, Mother."

Hortensia would never lower herself by attending the theater, but Maximus guessed his mother-in-law's sudden interest in the impressive stage artist meant she already knew what he'd been up to. "Well, does it, Maximus?"

"No," he proclaimed boldly, though the lie twisted his tongue and his chest felt as if he still supported a garden paver.

"You were never a good liar, son-in-law." Hortensia turned to her daughter. "Which could be a good thing for you, Aeliana. Unlike me, you shall know when your husband decides to take his physical comfort in the bed of a harlot."

Maximus hated how his beautiful, pregnant wife always melded into the draperies rather than stand up to her mother. "Surely you have not come to my quarters simply to check on my fidelity to your daughter." He hadn't meant for his gaze to sweep the ceiling, but it had. And before he could take the motion back, Hortensia had caught a glimpse of his disapproval of her constant intrusion.

A slow smile spread across his mother-in-law's lips. Then, like a buzzard circling carrion, she swooped in and began to peck him apart. "For someone who comes from such a noble bloodline, you are a scrawny, insignificant disappointment." Her razor-sharp gaze scraped the stunted length of his body. "Fortunately, you are *not* stupid. If you were, I would have nothing to work with." She produced a folded piece of parchment sealed with a wax stamp bearing the emblem of royalty. "It has taken me all morning to arrange this opportunity." She handed him the missive and tapped it with a claw-like nail. "Read it."

Maximus looked to Aeliana for a clue. His wife's quickly lowered eyes told him the letter did not contain good news. He slid a quivering finger along the seal.

Galerius Maximus is hereby appointed
Proconsul of Carthage.
Appointment effective immediately.
Terms of service shall include but not exceed one year.
Report to the first available ship sailing for Africa.
Restore the favor of the gods in the province of Tunisia.
Execute anyone who refuses to worship at the sacred temples.
Stop the plague by eliminating the Christians who spread it.

By order of Publius Licinius Valerianus Augustus,
Emperor of Rome.

MAXIMUS'S HEART hammered his chest. "What have you done, mother-in-law?"

"I have put an end to your ridiculous pursuit of the theater." Hortensia's nostrils flared. "Did you think I wouldn't find out about your bawdy theater actor and your secret training sessions in my stables? Servants talk." Her eyes were hard as paver stones. "A son-in-law with a reputation of prancing naked about the stage is *not* what I purchased with my daughter's very generous dowry."

"I will not do it, Hortensia." Maximus wadded the parchment and threw it across the room. "Africa resides in the bowels of Hades."

She leaned in close enough for him to catch the clayish scent of the henna she used to smother the gray sprouting from her head like the snakes of Medusa. "Listen to me, you wormy slug, you *will* go. Or I shall make certain you never return to see your child."

His eyes darted to Aeliana, but she knew better than to meet his gaze. "You can't keep us apart."

Hortensia laughed in the face of his belligerence. "There's no end to what I can and will do. Your future is already arranged. I'm counting on the southern sun of Africa to burn color into those pasty cheeks and add backbone to that soft body of yours. Because I expect you to return ready to do whatever it takes to assume the throne." She wheeled. "Come, Aeliana. The future proconsul of Carthage has to pack."

His wife put her hand to her large belly and mouthed *I'm sorry*, then hurriedly waddled after her mother.

12

W E'VE ASKED EVERYONE WHO left the church to reconsider." Barek followed Cyprian down another dark, lonely alley. So far both of them had refrained from stating the obvious. No one was coming to their aid.

"Not everyone." Cyprian paused beneath a wooden sign carved in the shape of a large tooth and reviewed his list once again, holding it at an angle to take advantage of the splinter of moonlight. A gust of wind whipped the jagged points of the tooth against the tenement building. "According to one of the tenants, we'll find your old landlord if we turn left here."

Barek scanned their surroundings. Unlike the stunning transformation in Maggie's appearance, a blossoming that had robbed him of sleep these past few nights, his old neighborhood had decayed since his family abandoned their flat above the dye shop and moved into Cyprian's villa in the posh part of town. Many of the shops and homes were empty. But if he closed his eyes, he could still smell the foul aroma of crushed snail shells clinging to his father's robe and hear his mother humming her sweet songs of the Lord's deliverance as her slender fingers worked the loom. How he missed them. And oh how his mother would enjoy seeing Maggie fill out a silk stola rather than trip over the hem as she had playing dress-up as a child.

Barek shoved his failure to protect all of them in with his guilt for betraying Cyprian. "Metras lived in one of the lower apartments because of his bad leg." Barek's empty belly had been howling since sunset. Sweat trickled down his back. Traipsing about in hooded cloaks and begging for help that would never come was perhaps God's way of giving him a taste of the punishment he deserved. "The old stonemason is the last name on our list, right?"

Cyprian glanced at their carefully reconstructed record. "He is."

Barek's father believed God kept the roll books, thus eliminating his need to record any believer's name. Had Caecilianus known his son's treachery would force Cyprian to reconstruct the roll, he might have left something more tangible. Thus, when Titus proposed dividing the tasks and decided to devote his time to finding out what he could about the new proconsul while Cyprian rallied the church, they all quickly realized there had been no reliable record of whom to rally. Cyprian had questioned Barek for hours, urging him to recall every person who'd ever attended the church gatherings in his home.

Sketchy list in hand, Barek and Cyprian had spent the past two days knocking on the doors of frightened people, all of whom had sided with Felicissimus in the church split. Barek barely had time to state his business before those who'd lapsed in faith would announce, "Your parents are gone and have taken my faith in the church to their graves. What's left for us now? As for me and my house, we'll put our faith in the slave trader's writs of libellus."

"Felicissimus had a pocketful of those worthless papers," Barek argued each time, all the while knowing the scowling faces glaring at him had procured their writs from Barek himself. "All the paper in the empire did not stop a Roman sword from piercing the traitor's heart."

Barek's arguments had gone unheeded. So far, not one person had changed his mind.

If he and Cyprian failed to muster some help, how would they manage the big job of converting the senator's home into a new hospital? Much as it pained Barek to admit it, Maggie was working hard, harder than he expected. She'd assembled a breathing tent similar to the ones her mother used to make, but so far Eggie had not regained his health. While Barek certainly didn't want the cocky stowaway to die, he worried that once Eggie recovered he would seek work at the docks. It wouldn't be long before Eggie told someone about his miraculous recovery. Word would get out and the house of Cicero would be swamped with more measles and typhoid cases than their inexperienced crew could handle.

After a couple of days of pounding the pavement, Cyprian and Barek had drawn a thick black mark through every name . . . but Metras. "What good is an old man?" Barek asked above the scrape of the wooden tooth sign on the stucco.

"That 'old man,' as you call him, can work both of us under the table." Cyprian raised his mask to block the stench of chamber pots emptied nightly upon the narrow streets and headed off down the first alley past the dentist shop.

Barek swallowed the reprimand without comment and hurried to catch up. Cyprian had lost everything because of him: Both of his wives. His daughter. His home. His influence. And for a while, even a bit of his faith. He needed the support, and Barek owed it to him to give him everything he had.

Barek stopped outside a door of warped planks lashed together with leather strips. "This is it."

"Are you certain?"

He nodded toward a small cross hanging on an oil lamp.

Cyprian's eyes met his with a weariness Barek could hardly stomach. "That's the best sign we've seen all day."

Barek held Cyprian back. "Let me knock, just in case."

"Metras is a loyal ally."

"Did you not think the very same thing of Felicissimus and myself?" Barek waited until Cyprian was safely concealed in the shadows, then rapped on the door of a slum apartment. The door opened a crack. Barek lowered his mask so he wouldn't look like a robber. "Metras?"

Gnarled fingers curled around the wood and two rheumy eyes cautiously peered into the alley. "What do *you* want?"

"It's Barek."

"I know who you are, boy. Used to help you and your father crush snails and harvest the purple tint from them." The door opened wide. A spare, stoop-shouldered man leaned on a cane. Metras hadn't worked in the quarries since a slab of rock slipped from the wench ropes and crushed his leg. His long beard had faded to the color of limestone dust, and years of working in the sun had chiseled deep crevices into his stoic face. "Can't believe you're the one who split the church over those worthless pieces of paper." Metras squared up his body and jabbed his cane into the center of Barek's chest. "Your mother would be ashamed."

"Listen, you may not want to help me, and I can't blame you, but"—Barek whistled Cyprian forward with their all-clear signal—"Magdalena is in trouble."

"I wouldn't trust a word you said if I hadn't heard it from several others."

"Then you know Magdalena did not kill the proconsul," Barek said.

The old man's shrunken frame made it easy to see into his single-room home. "I'm smarter than I look, boy." Women and children crowded in behind Metras, peering out at Barek with what he could see was disdain. "The healer couldn't any more kill someone than your sweet mother could turn away the sick. They both had too much heart."

"My friend." Cyprian stepped from the shadows, glancing around.

"Bishop." They shook hands. "Come in."

Cyprian surprised Barek and ducked beneath the low lintel. "You coming, Barek?"

"Am I welcome?" Barek asked.

"Long as you don't try to sell me anything, boy," Metras said.

"I'm done with that."

"Come on then."

Barek stepped inside the cramped little room. Women and children did their best to shuffle themselves into the farthest corner.

Cyprian didn't appear the least bit put off by the humble surroundings. "We're setting up a new hospital. Without Magdalena, we don't have enough help."

"Heard the soldiers destroyed your place. I'm sorry about that." Metras shifted his weight to his good leg. "Not easy to lose everything."

"A house is easily replaced, but without a place to treat the sick, I fear what will become of our city," Cyprian said apologetically, almost as if what had happened had been his fault, not Barek's. "I won't lie to you, Metras. What I'm asking is dangerous."

Metras's grip on his cane whitened his knuckles. "Not much safe this side of heaven, is there, Bishop?" Several children with concerned eyes backed tighter into the corner. "Who'll take care of these widows and orphans?"

"Bring them along," Cyprian said without hesitation. "We'll make room."

Metras studied the offer for a few moments. The cloudy fog in his eyes made it impossible to know what was going on in his bald head. Finally a slow smile pushed through his leathery wrinkles. He shuffled forward. "I think it best if we come at night."

Cyprian clasped the old man's shoulder. "Come whenever you think it safe, brother. Can you find the home of Titus Cicero?"

Metras gave a brief nod. "Give me a day or two to get things squared away."

They shook hands and Barek felt a strange surge of relief. Which made no sense. Metras was far from agile. How much assistance could a cripple offer? It was more likely someone would have to take care of him. Yet Barek couldn't help but admire an old man willing to put not only his comfort, but also his life in jeopardy for what he believed.

"Why did you call him 'brother'?" Barek asked once they were on their way. "His station is far beneath yours."

Cyprian stopped and gripped Barek's shoulders, his fingers digging in as if to root the point he intended to make. "You are not the only one who has made mistakes." Cyprian's eyes were intent. "Hear me well: we will not survive this struggle if we do not rely upon each other. Metras will stick closer than a brother."

Barek and Cyprian hadn't traveled a block, navigating the dark slums solely by the light of the full moon, when they spotted a small soldier patrol armed with torches and coming their way.

"Quick!" Cyprian whispered.

They drew their hoods and ducked out of sight. Praying the thrumming of his heart would not give them away, Barek dared not move. The rhythmic plink of metal studs on the cobblestone streets came closer, then suddenly stopped. The faces of the soldiers registered suspicion, and their bodies readied for action. Barek held his breath. Had the shadowed alcove of the apartment building obscured their presence, or could they be seen from this angle? He pressed his back tightly against the stucco.

"Halt!" a soldier shouted. The loud crunching sound of hobnail boots thundered past them and faded down the narrow alley.

They had not been seen. All they had to do now was wait. Once the patrols finished roughing up whomever they'd caught breaking curfew, he and Cyprian would slip out and go in the opposite direction. Relief quietly seeped from Barek's lips.

"Is something wrong, officer?" A woman's voice, faint and distant, carried through the corridor. Her Latin had a choppy familiarity that Barek and Cyprian recognized at the same instant. "My father and I are searching for—"

"Lisbeth?" Cyprian whispered, then started from his hiding place.

"Wait." Barek yanked him back, growling between clenched teeth, "You won't do her any good if you're dead." He pushed against Cyprian's chest and flailing arms, driving him deeper into the shadows. "Let me go in your stead. Please." He slammed Cyprian against the wall and shot out into the street. "Mother!"

Two of the soldiers spun on their heels, hands on the hilt of their swords.

"Barek?" Silvery light illuminated the joy on Lisbeth's face. She turned to the man who was with her. "I can't believe we found him, Papa."

He didn't dare look back to see if Cyprian was following. Instead he ran toward her with his arms open. "I'm sorry to make you worry, *Mother*."

The need to play along registered in Lisbeth's eyes. "It's well past curfew, naughty boy. You scared me half to death." She cuffed his ear, which he thought was taking the ruse a bit too far. "Your grandfather and I have been searching for hours."

"My supply wagon broke down near the market. I was left afoot."

"So you abandoned our goods?"

Barek wrapped his arm around her shoulders and squeezed tighter than necessary. "Don't worry, all is secure."

"Torch!" the taller soldier shouted. Light suddenly appeared, and Barek felt Lisbeth tense beneath his grasp. She too had recognized the redheaded soldier who'd led the raid of Cyprian's home. The soldier pressed in, and Barek caught a whiff of wine. Hopefully it had dulled the soldier's memory of thrusting his boot into Barek's ribs. "Remove your hoods." None of them complied with the soldier's orders. "Now!"

Barek could think of no convincing argument to protect his identity. His gaze slid sideways, hoping Lisbeth would send him some sort of cue. Her lips were pursed in an uncharacteristic silence for the women of her century. Someone had to do something or they wouldn't live long enough to debate who should have made the first move. With a sigh, Barek lifted his hands, slowly pulled back the heavy wool draped over his head, then quickly dropped his chin.

"You." The shorter soldier drew his sword and pressed the tip into Lisbeth's shoulder. "Remove your hood."

From the corner of his eye, Barek could see that Lisbeth did not flinch. He needed better light to be certain, but as best he could tell, the woman who'd dropped into and out of his life only days ago had aged, although not at Maggie's rapid pace. Had her face changed enough to make her unrecognizable to this armored killer? Barek stepped between Lisbeth and the soldier's blade. "Mother never shows her hair in public."

The tall soldier grabbed Lisbeth's arm, and a small moan of pain slipped through her lips. "She will tonight."

"How dare you try to disgrace my daughter!" The man who'd accompanied Lisbeth down this dark path, the man she'd referred to as her father, tried to pull Lisbeth free. "Let her go."

"Back off, old man," the tall soldier warned.

Barek's heart pounded his chest as he considered the different ways this confrontation could go. Lisbeth could lower her hood and risk recognition. They could run. He and Lisbeth might be fast enough to escape, but the old man with her would most assuredly be caught. Besides, fleeing the law would only make their punishment worse once they were apprehended. That left one option: Barek could start a fight. But he knew without a doubt the clank of swords would draw Cyprian immediately into the middle of the action. They would all be arrested and carted off to die on crosses next to Magdalena's.

The decision was his to make and he had to make it quickly. Hands shaking, Barek reached over and lowered Lisbeth's hood. Waves of ebony hair tumbled onto her shoulders and framed her fierce beauty.

The taller soldier brought the torch flame in so close to Barek's face that heat singed his nose hairs. "You, I don't know." He must have been too busy kicking the stuffing out of Barek's middle to remember his face. The soldier moved the flame near Lisbeth's head. "This one could be the older sister of the woman we seek."

"You've said that about every woman we've stopped." The shorter soldier holstered his sword. "You've had too much to drink."

"I never forget a face." Suspicion narrowed the soldier's eyes. "I've seen this plebeian plum somewhere."

"All plebs look alike, and right now they're all a little cocky," the shorter soldier warned. "Just because the commander patted your shoulder for catching Aspasius's killer doesn't mean you don't have to help the rest of us keep the peace. Hurt her, and you could cause a riot."

The taller soldier brushed off his fellow soldier's suggestion that they move on and held the flame close to Lisbeth's face. "Name, woman."

Again, Lisbeth did not flinch but stared him straight in the eye.

"I told you, she's my mother." The conviction in Barek's voice did not surprise him half as much as his sudden desire to protect this woman he'd hated for what she'd done to his mother.

The tall soldier ran the back of his hand along Lisbeth's cheek. "Lucky boy."

13

FIGHT OR FLIGHT SIGNALS surged from the soldier's grip upon Lisbeth's arm. This was the man who'd dragged her to the palace of the proconsul. A vile, bitter taste invaded her mouth. Lisbeth willed her rubbery legs to stand their ground and prayed he was too drunk and she'd aged too much in the past thirteen years for him to recognize her. She fastened her animosity upon the soldier who smelled of fish sauce and stale beer.

Keeping her wits would have been easier if Barek hadn't appeared out of nowhere. His betrayal had brought trouble crashing through Cyprian's door, and for that she wanted to slap him. But she also remembered this same angry young man planting his body between her and this soldier's blade. Why was he here and willing to save her again? She'd obviously misjudged Ruth's son, and she wanted to live long enough to apologize.

First she had to get rid of these goons. She blurted out the only name of status she knew. "Vivia, wife of Cicero." She prayed she'd delivered her lie with the conviction it would take to scare this overzealous soldier into letting her go.

"Well, Vivia, what do you say you and me find a quiet spot and—"

"How drunk are you, fool?" The stocky little soldier grabbed the redhead's arm. "Didn't you hear? She's a senator's wife. I'm leaving before you get us strapped." He wheeled and gathered up the other gawking patrols. "You're on your own." With their departure, the fine line between Lisbeth and trouble did not vanish.

The soldier with the death grip on her arm pulled her in so close torch flames coiled beneath her nose. "What's a senator's wife doing in the slums after curfew?"

She refused to let this excitable soldier think he was getting to her. "Many of my servants have died of the pox. There was no one to send to fetch my son."

"Why are you dressed like a pleb?"

"Advertising my wealth would be foolish in this neighborhood, don't you think?"

He wasn't buying her story. "Well, Vivia Cicero," he whispered coarsely in her ear, "ever bed a real man?"

A split-second glance at Barek pumped her pulse into overdrive. His nostrils flared in that hotheaded way of his, and both hands were clenched for a fight. The redhead had at least six inches on Barek. It would be a short-lived match sure to end with all of them arrested. If Lisbeth was stuck in prison, it would be impossible to locate Maggie. She summoned years of experience mastering panic in the OR and spoke with amazing calm. "Do you know a real man?" She fluttered her lashes.

The soldier's brows drew together, confirming her flirting skills had, in fact, become as rusty as her Latin. What did she expect? It had been years since she'd wanted the attention of a man. A teeny spark of fear licked at her righteous anger. This young man had lots to prove. Maybe she should rethink her approach.

Before Lisbeth could inject sappy sweetness into her tone, Barek had claimed her arm. "Mother!" His forceful jerk set off an immediate tug-of-war between him and the soldier for possession of her body. Barek was not about to let go. "We must fetch the wagon or the magistrate will be within his rights to fine us for having a wheeled vehicle on the streets after sunrise."

"Only a fool would dare fine the wife of Cicero." Lisbeth wrenched her arm from the soldier with a strong, freeing twist. "You do not want to tangle with the real man awaiting my arrival."

The soldier laughed, a disgusting guttural sound that made her want to rip his eyes out. "Feisty as a shepherd's cur." He reached for her again. "What's your hurry?"

"Stultissime!" Agitation raised Lisbeth's volume louder than she intended, but she had thirteen years of beef with this guy to get off her chest.

He came at her with both hands. "No woman calls me an idiot."

Lisbeth was starting to backpedal when a hooded man burst from the shadows and strode toward them, fury flashing in his eyes. Lisbeth instantly recognized the commanding gait and regal bearing of the former solicitor of Carthage. She stopped dead in her retreat. Incredulity erupted into elation she couldn't let show. The man charging to her rescue was the same man who'd barged into the slave trader's cell and bought her right out from under Aspasius. The man who'd thrown her over a horse like a caveman bringing home a fresh kill. The man who'd forever changed her life.

Her eyes locked with his and she shouted, "Go back!"

But Cyprian snatched the soldier by the collar. Before the soldier had a chance to draw his sword or jump back in surprise, Cyprian spun the redhead around to face him. "The lady said she had to go."

The soldier was probably fifteen years Cyprian's junior, six inches taller, and twenty pounds heavier—advantages he used to easily shake free. "You and whose army's gonna make me?"

"Me and the one God." Cyprian's clenched fist flew up hard and fast. A loud crack confirmed his angry jab had made a square connection with the soldier's jaw. The dazed man staggered backward. His helmet bounced off the wall opposite the sliver of space between the multistoried buildings. Startled for no more than a few seconds, the young man quickly regained his balance. Before Lisbeth could move, he shook off the punch and came at her with a flash of stained teeth.

"Fool!" He went for his blade, but the hilt had gotten hung up in the clasp of his scabbard.

"You don't want to do that!" Barek had his blade drawn and ready to thrust, as did Cyprian.

Panting, the redhead planted his feet and searched the alley for backup, but his friends had deserted him.

"Catch up to your cohorts, boy," Cyprian warned, pressing his advantage with a lunge that landed his daggertip at the soldier's throat. "No need to die for being an idiot."

The young soldier looked at the blade and then at Lisbeth. He held up his palms and took a step back. "I never forget a face, Vivia Cicero." He did a one-eighty and double-timed his way out of there.

All of them stood watching the flash of armor disappear into the night. But no one moved until the scrape of retreating cleats no longer echoed in the narrow passageway. With just their labored breathing rasping in their ears, Cyprian slid his dagger into his belt and turned to her.

"Lisbeth!" He pressed her to the wall, cupped her face in his hands, and kissed her solidly, reclaiming all that was his. Familiarity sparked vivid memories of midnight swims and making love beneath a blanket of stars. Old regrets and dreams stirred inside her like ashes goaded into flame. The past refused to change, yet here she was, allowing the sweet kiss of hope to consume the fears that hounded her future.

Alive! The man she thought she would never see again this side of heaven was alive!

Shock Lisbeth had managed to delay in the heat of battle crashed into her and buckled her knees. In a flash, Cyprian's roughened hands slid down the length of her neck like molten lava. His touch careened over the straps of the pack hanging from her back and drew her up in a supportive embrace. She'd lived the past thirteen years as the grieving widow. Some days the loss and sadness had been so crippling she'd wanted to stay in bed. And she would have if it weren't for the daughter she was determined to raise.

Heat spread from beneath his hungry touch and ignited a tiny moan of gratitude she'd meant for only God to hear. But defibrillating jolts radiated from Cyprian's heart, and her body couldn't help but arch toward the explosion of energy. Relief, warm and exhilarating, pumped darkness and despair from arteries she'd worried had hardened beyond repair.

There was no need for words in this private vortex, this place of completion she'd missed more than anything their vastly different worlds had to offer. Lisbeth wrapped her arms around her husband's neck and opened her lips to take in his hunger. His grip tightened upon her waist and numbed the ache she'd carried for so long. Within the span of a heartbeat, the weight of unbearable grief fell away. Her lungs inflated as if his breath had brought her back from the dead.

"Cyprian!" Barek's panic broke through the cocoon Cyprian's arms had spun around her. "We cannot stay here."

Cyprian released her lips but not his embrace. His forehead rested upon hers and he whispered, "I know why you've returned." He kissed her nose. "She's safe."

"Thank God." Lisbeth couldn't stop the tears. "Then you're not mad that I broke my promise?"

Cyprian stopped her apology with another quick kiss. "You had to come."

"Take me to her," Lisbeth said.

"I think there's someone you'll want to see on our way."

"Who?"

"Your mother."

"You know where to find Magdalena?" Papa asked anxiously.

Lisbeth peered over her husband's shoulder. Her father and Barek stood with their arms crossed and impatience drawing their faces into scowls. "Oh, I'm sorry, Papa." Lisbeth took her father's hand and placed it in Cyprian's. "Finally the two most important men in my life meet."

After brief hugs, expressions of mutual admiration, and Cyprian's assurances that he had a plan to free Magdalena, he sent Barek home to make sure the soldiers had not discovered the relocation of the hospital to the house of Cicero.

"But I don't want to leave you," Barek argued.

"You have proven yourself someone I can trust to take care of my daughter. I'd feel better knowing Maggie has every protection possible." Cyprian clasped Barek's shoulder. "Do this for me, please."

Lisbeth snagged Barek's arm. "Thank you. Your mother would be proud." She kissed his cheek and when she pulled back she was thrilled to see his lack of animosity. "Don't tell Maggie we're here. I think it would be best to surprise her the same way she surprised us. Don't you agree, Papa?"

After Barek had slipped away in the darkness, Lisbeth turned to Cyprian, not sure how she felt about his ability to carry on without her. "You've started a new hospital?"

"Without the help of the church or a healer, I'm afraid it offers little more than a place to die."

Guilt prickled Lisbeth's skin. "I can't stay. And you can't leave."

14

MAGGIE HAD SPENT THE past two days filling Eggie's vaporizer pot and sponging him down. She'd slept little and felt tired beyond her years. Stretching her aching muscles, she took a moment to evaluate her work. The crude tepee she'd constructed covered Eggie's head and chest. It was a little lopsided and if bumped in the wrong place, the shortest pole would slide out and drop the whole contraption on Eggie's face. But for her first attempt at being crafty, her vaporizer didn't look too bad. She couldn't help but wonder if her mother would have been impressed. Especially considering how many of Maggie's science projects usually went up in smoke.

But was it working? She lifted a corner of the tent and peeked inside. Eggie was finally sleeping.

Last night his skin was so hot she couldn't stand to touch him. He'd also had several bouts of delirium. Sometimes he shouted curses at imaginary demons or whimpered like a scolded child, begging his father to understand. More than once, he'd thrashed about in the bed while accusing Maggie of stealing his throne. Not knowing what else to do to calm him, Maggie had told him he could keep his old throne. Then, with a look of clarity that had almost had her convinced his fever had broken, he'd told her he didn't want it. Ever.

Strange. If she really thought about it, everything about this whole scenario was bizarre. Art, not health care, was her area of expertise. She had no business building vaporizers or trying to take her mother's place. If she hadn't been desperate to prove to her father that he couldn't live without her, she wouldn't be anywhere near a sickbed.

Maggie dipped a sea sponge into a mixture of cool water and warm beer. She never expected that finding her father would give her a whole new appreciation for her mother's dedication to her work. A few days ago she was anxious to get away from her. Now she was silently begging God to send her mom.

Maggie began to gently rub at the red spots on Eggie's face. The combination of stale alcohol and fevered skin stung her nostrils.

"Your mother always said to pat the sores." Naomi took the sponge from her hand. "Like this."

Maggie felt her back stiffen. She didn't mind her father's servant showing her what to do. After all, she and Naomi were friends. Maggie had helped Naomi in the kitchen after Ruth's death. Naomi knew Maggie had never nursed anyone before. So Naomi's tips weren't the problem. It was the way she said them. Like she knew what Mom would have done and Maggie didn't.

Naomi wrung the sponge and sat on the edge of Eggie's bed. "Let me show you again." She made a big deal out of gently dabbing Eggie's head.

"Okay, I've got it." Maggie tapped Naomi on the shoulder. The servant girl showed no signs of relinquishing her spot. Instead, she continued staring at Eggie, the sponge clutched tightly. Maggie tapped her again. "Naomi, don't you have pots on the fire?"

"Do you think he has family?"

Maggie said nothing for a moment, debating whether to mention Eggie's delirious renunciation of his father. "I don't know."

"Maybe your father will ask Titus if he can stay." Naomi handed Maggie the sponge, wiped her hands on her tunic, and rose. "Pat. Don't rub."

Maggie plunged the sponge into the brown liquid. "Got it."

"Look, Maggie." Across the room, Laurentius held up a piece of parchment. "Ith done."

She dropped the sponge in the basin and went to see Laurentius's latest work. "This little guy with the extra-long tail looks kind of sneaky, don't you think, Larry?"

Her uncle gave her a sideways glance followed by his adorable pie-faced grin. "That one ith you." He dipped his quill in the ink horn.

"Who's that?" She pointed at a mouse with a determined face and a bulging bag slung over its shoulder.

"Lithbutt." He smiled and lowered his head. "I mith her."

"Mom misses you too." Her mom wasn't the type to whine about things she missed, but the sad faraway look in her eyes had to come from somewhere and Maggie was pretty sure her mother's unhappiness stemmed from the loss of her brother and mother—and the man she loved. Maggie gave Laurentius a hug, then wiped a smudge of ink from his cheek. "If you come home with me, I promise not to torture you with fake shots and hair bows."

"You were little then. I forgive you."

"I was old enough to know better. I'm sorry, Larry." She patted his shoulder. "Are you sure you don't want to come?"

"No." With exacting precision, he added whiskers to the long snout of his mouse.

"Can you tell me why?"

He shrugged and jabbed his quill into the well again. "Me and Mama live here."

"Oh." His devotion to Jaddah was a punch in Maggie's gut. "If your mother came with us, would you want to come to Dallas then?"

Her uncle frowned. "No. I can't draw there." He dipped his pen and started crafting a larger mouse for his mouse family. Brilliant works of art, actually, considering his handicap.

"In Dallas, we have so many office supply stores you'd never run out of paper and ink."

Tears watered her uncle's almond-shaped eyes. "I can't leave Mama."

"Look at me, Larry." Maggie lifted his chin. "I'm not going anywhere without you or my Jaddah. We're family. Understand?"

Laurentius sniffed and shook his head. "Thyprian thays Mama is in prithon."

"You're right. She is. But my daddy is a very smart man. He'll think of a way to get her out. I promise."

Naomi came through the atrium lugging another pot of hot water for Eggie's vaporizer, the second one he'd needed since sunup and it wasn't even lunchtime yet.

"Excuse me, Larry." Maggie jumped to her feet. "I know I don't do things as well as my mother, but I can pull my weight, Naomi." She gathered the hem of her tunic and used it like a potholder and took one of the handles. "I said I'd take care of Eggie and I will."

"The water was boiling so I thought I'd go ahead and freshen his breathing tent."

Maggie swiped at a curl stuck to her forehead. "Everything in this century is ten times the work and takes ten times as long to accomplish." The first time she'd tried to lift the pot from the fire she'd grabbed hold of the handle and blistered her hands. Her back hurt from trying to keep sloshing hot water away from her legs.

Worst of all, she was afraid her hard work wasn't making any difference.

Eggie's sores were still oozing and he'd not been awake long enough to suck down more than a few sips of that awful drink Naomi whipped up. "No wonder my mother wasn't in a big hurry to come back to this century. She can't boil water without a microwave. How did she manage to treat critically ill patients with nothing but a campfire?"

"Microwave?"

"Best thing ever invented."

Naomi looked at her as if she had two heads or something. "Actually, all of us managed very well and with very little sleep most nights."

"I only meant things are tough here." Maggie lifted a corner of Eggie's tent.

"Then why did you come back?"

"I—"

"It doesn't matter. You always get your way."

The steam from the pot they were carrying together couldn't have stung any worse. Together she and Naomi emptied the boiling water into a pot at the base of the little tepee. Naomi stirred in crumbled eucalyptus leaves and in seconds fragrant steam fogged the room. "Do you think he's handsome?"

Handsome? Maggie cut a sideways glance at Naomi. Sure enough, she was staring at Eggie as if he were the best thing she'd ever seen. *So that's why she's picking on me.* "Hard to tell with all of those nasty boils."

Naomi started to reach for Eggie, then dropped her hand as though she'd reconsidered. "Think his fever has broken?"

What was with this girl? Maggie had seen her checking out Barek, which she had to admit made her a little jealous. Which was stupid, when she really thought about it. She wasn't staying here, so what did she care if Naomi had the hots for both Barek and Eggie? Maybe one of them would notice Naomi drooling and marry her.

Maggie laid her palm on Eggie's forehead the same way her mother did if she even hinted at not feeling well. "No."

Eggie's eyes fluttered open.

Maggie sponged his forehead and smiled. "You're awake."

"I hope not." His slate-gray eyes had a vaguely glazed quality. "I'm having the best dream ever." A silly smile slid across his cracked lips. He reached for her hand.

Maggie tingled with awareness. "You know you've been hallucinating, right?"

He shook his head. "A golden-haired goddess with a heart-shaped face is holding my hand and asking the gods to spare my life." He kissed her hand.

Heat flushed Maggie's cheeks. "God. I was asking *God* to help me help you."

"Please tell me you're not one of those Christians I've heard about." The guy knew how to flash a smile that could melt a girl's defenses.

But that didn't mean she should have given a total stranger information that could get them all killed. Both Dad and Barek had warned her not to tell this guy anything about what the people in this house believed, at least not before they knew more about him.

So much for keeping a low profile until she smuggled her father out of here.

Maggie removed her hand from his. "Okay, Romeo, I'm no doctor, but I know that when someone has a fever he needs to drink. A lot." She rinsed her hands in the nearby basin and dried them on the front of her tunic.

"Call me Eggie." A twinkle of mischief in his voice drew her in. "And I'll call you?"

"Maggie."

"Unusual name."

If his gaze hadn't been so bleary, she would have blushed at the way his eyes loitered on her figure. She could name only one other guy who'd ever made her blush, and in his eyes she would forever be the five-year-old irritant who'd interrupted his life.

"I was named after my grandmother, Magdalena."

"She must have been beautiful."

"The most beautiful woman I've ever met. And, if everything goes as planned, you'll get to meet her." Maggie could feel Naomi's eyes boring into her back so she decided to change the subject.

"So, *Eggie*, where are you from?" She slipped her hand behind his neck and elevated him enough to avoid drowning him in Naomi's magic tea.

"Far from here."

"Me too." *You have no idea how far, buddy.* "Mind handing me his drink, Naomi?" When the cup did not come, she glanced up to find Naomi's arms crossed and her lips pursed. "Please?"

"I have bread in the oven." Naomi rotated and ran smack into Barek. Flustered, she scuttled back, straightening her dress and hair. "The eel you pulled from the sea is awake," she told him, then stormed from the room.

"What was that about?" Barek picked up the cup and handed it to Maggie.

If he'd felt the same spark she did when their fingers brushed, the jolt hadn't knocked out his perturbed stare. How grown-up did she have to get before he considered her his equal?

"Maybe Naomi needs a nap." Eggie took a sip then promptly fell back on the pillow, sound asleep.

Maggie's gaze panned to Barek. "For a minute there I thought he was getting better."

Barek was squinting at her, a disapproving frown on his face. "Wonder where he heard about needing a nap?"

"I wouldn't know," she teased, hoping to lighten his sour mood.

"You're just like your mother."

Maggie cringed at the possibility. "Funny, you're nothing like yours."

They stood with eyes locked. Two cowboys in one of those standoffs in an old western G-Pa watched on Saturday afternoons. A muscle twitched in his clenched jaw, like any minute he'd explode from the strain of holding back. Why did Barek always take everything so seriously? Why did she care what he thought? She was here to get her father, not impress Barek. The urge to laugh at how ridiculous they both were acting bubbled inside her. She pursed her lips but the giggle would not be held back.

Then, a total surprise.

Barek burst into laughter at the exact same moment.

His laugh was rusty, as if it hadn't been used in so long it needed to be oiled. Maggie loved how the unexpected sound of it surprised him and caused him to sputter for a second. But instead of clamming up as he usually did whenever her antics shoved him off balance, his amusement gained speed. He threw his head back and really laughed. The more he laughed, the more limber and enticing the tone, and the softer the angles of his cheekbones.

Maggie was the first to catch her breath and she used the advantage to notice how handsome Barek's wide, white smile looked against his tanned complexion. "Maybe Eggie's right, we could all stand a good nap." She set the cup on a table. "Where's my dad?"

The smile slid from Barek's face, taking the magic with it. He quickly returned to his solemn, sour self, and Maggie felt a tremor of fear. "Tell me."

"Uh, Cyprian and uh . . . he decided to check on your Jaddah."

She didn't know how Barek had pulled off the writ of libellus thing because he wasn't a very good liar. He wasn't telling her something. Something important. "I wish he would have taken me."

Barek lifted her chin with his finger and Maggie caught a glimpse of her surprised reflection in his dark eyes. "He's going to do everything he can, but his hands are tied until Valerian sends someone to replace the proconsul."

Eggie mumbled something and turned over. His arm flopped off his chest and hung limp from the side of the bed.

"Oh, no." Barek snatched Eggie's wrist. "Somebody has marked him."

"It's just a tattoo." Maggie had noticed the Roman numeral III earlier and wondered what it meant, but so far the opportunity to ask Eggie about his choice of ink hadn't presented itself. "What's the big deal? Lots of people have them." She raised her sleeve and held out her wrist. "Even me."

Horror and disbelief widened Barek's eyes. "It's pagan to let someone cut your arm with a flint and stain the wound with gall and vitriol."

"You sound like my mom. She went ballistic when she found out. I told her I went to the same reputable place as my friend Kellie, but she was convinced I'd probably contracted hepatitis or something."

Barek leaned in for a better look at the delicate figure eight with the word DAD inked on the lower right loop. "That is a punishment mark reserved for slaves and criminals."

"No one punished me." Maggie knew she was quite capable of punishing herself, thank you very much. Her finger had traced the design so many times in the last two years she worried the ink would be worn away. "I did it to keep my father close."

Barek held Eggie's wrist high. "I can promise you this fugitive does not wear the mark of someone he wishes to remember." He dropped Eggie's limp wrist upon his chest. "This man is running from someone, and if whoever branded him finds him here, we are all subject to the wrath of his sword."

15

MAGDALENA'S CHAINS GAVE HER no room to stretch her legs. There was little she could do to pass the time but stare at the ceiling and wait for the moment the celestial lights reached their zeniths. She counted the small shafts of light that breached the mortar chinks as gifts from God. She took advantage of the illumination to write her thoughts upon the parchment Cyprian had left behind.

Across the narrow cell she could hear her three friends growing equally uncomfortable in their chains. "Kardide, how are you feeling?" In the silence, Magdalena noted that somewhere within their hearing, cicadas buzzed happily, free to go about their lives. She couldn't help but envy those winged creatures. She'd been someone's captive for so long she wondered if she could handle freedom. "Kardide?"

"Well enough," responded her friend feebly.

The dry rasp of Kardide's voice heightened Magdalena's fears of dehydration. Her friend had refused her ration of the water Cyprian brought. "Tabari, has Kardide's bleeding stopped?"

"I'm not sure." Tabari's slight frame scooted over stones, an abrasive scraping that caused Magdalena to worry the girl was grinding away skin along with the scant protection her thin tunic had to offer. "Do you want me to check when we have light next?"

"No. Best to keep the bandage tight for now." Magdalena wished her chains were a foot or two longer so she could access her friends, especially Iltani, who couldn't speak for herself. "Tabari, is Iltani well?" Magdalena could hear Tabari shuffling to the length of her tether.

"She is," Tabari said, then struggled back to her place, huffing from the added exertion.

Magdalena's friends had suffered so much on her behalf. Unless something miraculous happened, they would die alongside a healer whose own body was worn out from carrying her spirit through this dark world. She swallowed her regret for allowing their involvement in Aspasius's surgery and Lisbeth's escape and whispered, "Grace and peace to you all." Silvery streaks of light slowly sifted through the cracks. "I must write while the moon is high."

Magdalena spread the parchment across her lap and blindly searched the damp stones for the sharpened charcoal. Cyprian had asked her to record every detail of Aspasius's surgery, to construct an airtight defense for herself. But she'd witnessed enough of the criminal trials in the Forum to know guilt or innocence was decided long before the accused took the stand. Whether she had accidentally committed malpractice would be of little consequence.

Magdalena wiped away the perspiration dripping into her eyes and began.

If anyone finds this note, please see that it is delivered to the family of Dr. Lawrence Hastings, twenty-first century.

Magdalena read the line again. This scrap of parchment was far too small to write out all the names of those she loved. Besides, by the time it was discovered, her family could all be dead. She scratched out her greeting and started again.

To whoever finds this record . . .

It is the year AD 258 and I, Magdalena Hastings, along with three dear friends, have been accused of the murder of Aspasius Paternus, proconsul of Carthage. Cyprianus Thascius has offered to be our defense counsel. After Cyprian came to visit us in this dark prison, I allowed myself to feel hopeful. The man is a fine solicitor. If anyone can secure our release, it is he.

Yet the happy news of his willingness to plead our case brings great conflict to my soul. Defending us will put both Cyprian and the church at risk. Even if Cyprian is allowed to resume his legal practice, he has added the name of our dearly departed Bishop Caecilianus to his. The moment Cyprian states his new legal name in court, his convictions as a Christian will likely make the codicil to Aspasius's will null and void. By association, I too will be suspected of Christianity. The medical mercy I provided Aspasius will be declared an act of treason. And Cyprian will be accused of rendering aid to a traitor.

What shall I do? Demand that Cyprian withdraw from the case? While such action might save Cyprian and the church, it will most assuredly mean my death. And far more difficult to bear, the deaths of three innocent women whose only crime is loving me nearly as much as they love our Lord.

For those inclined to judge me, know that this decision torments me worse than any nightmare of wild beasts and angry gladiators. Every time I awake drenched in sweat and fear, I doubt my ability to remain brave. And then I remember the faithfulness of those who have gone before me, those trapped in this very same valley of decision. Men like our beloved Bishop Caecilianus, who died for his faith. I

*recount their courage and my spirit finds strength to trudge
from this interminable darkness toward eternal light.*

*I've spent much time in prayer and have reached this
conviction: if asked, I must confess Christ. There is no other
way for me. For I cannot imagine calling myself anything
other than what I am—a Christian.*

*Confident as I am in what I must do, know that I will go
to my death weeping for the time lost with my precious
family. Mingled with those tears are tears for Carthage.*

Who will be their healer once I am gone?

IMPATIENT VOICES penetrated the iron door. Keys rattled the
heavy lock.

Magdalena pressed the charcoal into a crack between the
stones and quickly rolled her parchment. She barely managed to
slip this tiny diary inside her tunic when then door banged open.
Her hand flew to her eyes to block the glare of their torches.

Two soldiers strode the cramped aisle. Swinging their lights
and rousing the prisoners by kicking their feet, they were obviously looking for a fight. They stopped in front of Magdalena.
"You. Stand."

Magdalena hadn't been on her feet since these same two ruffi-
ans had hauled her in. Had the new proconsul arrived? Where was
Cyprian? "What's wrong?"

"Up!"

Her joints were stiff and uncooperative, with every muscle
hurting after the beating she'd taken. "Give me a minute." Magdalena did her best to manipulate the ankle chains to keep her feet
from getting tangled. "How can I help you?"

"It's been reported that you know the whereabouts of Cyprianus Thascius."

Who could have alerted the authorities before the case came to trial? No one had been in or out of the prison since Cyprian was here and Magdalena was quite certain Cyprian had not given his name to Brutus, the guard who'd allowed him to access the new prisoners and now feared he'd be found out.

It had to be Pytros. The cunning little scribe of Aspasius had always hated her. Pytros had been present in their master's sickroom when Aspasius revealed he already knew of Cyprian's return. Pytros had also openly opposed the terms she'd imposed upon Aspasius before agreeing to provide him with medical care. She should have known Pytros would never allow her to get away with trumping him. Not only would he get even, he would do everything he could to have his master's addendum nullified. Of course, whether Cyprian was now a free man was a moot point if Cyprian could not locate the sealed parchment Lisbeth was supposed to have delivered into his hands. Without the actual paper it was Magdalena's word against that of Pytros. And Pytros wasn't the one with bloodstains on his tunic.

The only way she would know whether Cyprian had managed to retrieve that invaluable scrap of paper would be if he showed up to defend her on the day of her trial.

Magdalena fought the leg tingles protesting her lack of exercise and gingerly distributed her weight to restore her balance. "Curubis, last I heard. Exiled by my master."

"Liar!" A soldier's hand smacked her cheek. "Where is he?"

"Leave her alone!" Kardide had managed to stand and was swinging her fists across the aisle, managing only an occasional dull thunk against the soldier's armor. "She said she didn't know."

The soldier wrenched Kardide's arm behind her back and forced her to her knees. Then in a flash he raised the hilt of his blade and brought it down with a sickening crack upon Kardide's head. Tabari screamed as Kardide crumpled to the floor. A hush fell over the tunnel. Out of the corner of her eye, Magdalena could see Kardide pinned beneath the soldier's boot.

Magdalena pulled against the chains, the iron cuffs cutting into her ankles. "Kardide!"

The soldier lifted his boot and backhanded Magdalena again, sending her sailing. She hit the wall with a breath-robbing thud. Her legs buckled. Rough stones sanded her back as she slowly slid into a useless heap.

16

L ISBETH AND PAPA FOLLOWED Cyprian down the torch-lit path that led to the Hippodrome. Cyprian stopped and implored Lisbeth and her father to wait away from the prison's sinister entrance. He reached up and dragged a finger through the soot of the torch holder. He smeared a little on Lisbeth's face. "Can't risk one of the prisoners recognizing you."

"What about you?" she asked.

He added a bit of soot to his chin and lowered his hood to shade his eyes. "Let me do the talking."

Lisbeth hesitated for only a moment. "Mama is not taking the fall for this. I was there. She did everything medically possible to save that monster, especially considering the circumstances."

Cyprian drew her to him. The strength in his arms immediately reminded her of how difficult it would be to leave him again . . . and leaving him again was what she had to do because that's how her visits into his world always ended. "No one can know Magdalena is your mother."

"How can I allow Mama to die for a crime she did not commit?"

Papa came to Cyprian's aid and pulled her aside. "Perhaps it's best if you save your indignation for the judge."

"Lisbeth cannot testify." Cyprian had warned her and Papa of her mother's dire situation and the danger they might face in coming here. But neither she nor Papa had heeded his warning or discussed their next course of action. They'd headed toward the Hippodrome before Cyprian had time to reconsider his offer to take them. "Please, keep your voices low."

"What do you mean, I can't testify?" Her indignation was clear.

"You're taking our daughter and going home."

"Not without my mother."

"Shhhh," Papa warned. They all froze, listening intently.

The slam of a metal door was followed closely by a growing commotion at the base of the stairs. Without a word, Cyprian quickly pressed Lisbeth and her father into a nearby thicket and signaled they say nothing. Then he placed his body as a shield between them and the knot of soldiers marching up the stairs, laughing and discussing how they'd roughed up the old woman who'd hacked up the proconsul of Carthage. "Taught her a thing or two," bragged the redheaded soldier who'd left them in a dark alley not thirty minutes earlier.

Lisbeth struggled to stay put. The second the soldiers were out of earshot, Cyprian extracted another promise from her that she'd keep silent, then released her and hastily made his way to the pale-faced guard. Lisbeth and Papa hurried after him.

"Brutus, my good man."

"It's after curfew. You shouldn't be here."

"You seem upset. Are our prisoners well?" Cyprian approached cautiously.

The guard, a short, muscular fellow, reached for his weapon. "There wasn't much I could do. I think one of them is hurt pretty bad."

Cyprian didn't back away. "Let me help."

"Get us in there, boy," Papa said.

Brutus eyed them warily. "Who are they?"

"I'm a healer," Lisbeth said. "I can help."

Brutus's uncertain gaze shifted between Cyprian and Lisbeth. "You'll tell the proconsul I did what I could, right?"

"You have my word, Brutus." Cyprian turned and warned Lisbeth under his breath, "Remember what I told you."

"Fine." She hated tunnels. Not only did they rekindle the claustrophobia she'd fought so hard to overcome, she hated anything that reminded her of the proconsul's palace and the underground labyrinth she'd been forced to navigate several times: Once to care for her mother. Another time to save her brother. And the last time to save herself. Lisbeth steeled for whatever waited in the darkness: Rats. Plague. Death.

Brutus stood there weighing his options so long Lisbeth wanted to scream, but instead she stuck to her promise and kept her mouth shut.

"Brutus, please. Let us help," Cyprian said.

Finally, the guard fumbled with his keys. "Don't let her die on my watch." He heaved the door open. A putrid stench rushed at them.

"Smells like someone already did," Lisbeth said.

Cyprian shot Lisbeth a warning look and grabbed a torch. "Stay close."

Lisbeth reached to steady Papa, to protect him from whatever lay ahead. "It could be bad."

"I've got to see her." The color had drained from his face and his palms were sweaty, but he had a determined, hopeful look in his eyes.

In truth, it was she who needed bolstering. Whatever they found in this stink hole would only add to her guilt. She should never have left Mama in the third century. Nausea threatened to empty Lisbeth's stomach of the stale bread she'd found hidden in a jar in Cyprian's kitchen. She clamped her lips, held tightly to Papa's hand, and ducked beneath the lintel. Unprepared for the drop in temperature, she shivered. How long could anyone survive in here?

Cyprian waved the torch in front of him. "She's at the very end." Flashes of light swept human shapes chained along sixty feet of stone wall. The prisoners were filthy and too emaciated for her to determine whether they were men or women. She placed each footstep carefully to avoid the bony legs and arms reaching for her.

"Over here." Cyprian waved her forward.

Lisbeth stumbled across what felt like a knobby stick, but it was a leg so thin she could see the outline of the femur. "Sorry." Despite Cyprian's concerns that she might be recognized, she stopped and felt the prisoner's wrist for a pulse. Weak, but alive. "Watch your step, Papa. They don't have the strength to move." She spoke to the inmate. "I'll be back." She picked her way through the tangle of legs, forcing her mind to block out their cries for help.

"Lisbeth?"

The urgency of the woman's voice drew Lisbeth's attention to the cluster of bodies near where Cyprian waited. "Tabari?" Two of her mother's friends huddled over a woman sprawled on the floor. Panic radiated from their upturned faces. Much as Lisbeth wanted to stop and help, she couldn't because across the aisle Cyprian stared at a body rolled up like a carpet.

Bile seared Lisbeth's throat. "Is it my—?"

"Yes." Cyprian shoved the torch into a holder.

"Magdalena?" Papa raced around her and sank to his knees beside the body. "Magdalena?" His hands trembled over her hair-covered face.

"Let me have a look." Lisbeth gently moved her father aside, pulled her bag off her shoulder, then squatted beside her mother. Lisbeth pressed her fingers to Mama's carotid and prayed for a pulse. "She's alive." She stroked away ropes of matted hair. "I'm here now," she told her mother. "You're going to be fine." The sight of her mother's tunic stiff with blood nearly panicked her and forced the medical knowledge right out of her head. She nudged her mother's shoulder. "Ma . . . Magdalena, can you hear me?"

"Yes," she said in a feeble whisper.

"Thank you, Lord," Papa said.

Tears coursed down Lisbeth's face in hot release. "Can you name your injuries?"

"My pride." Mama rolled over. Her left eye was swollen shut and blood trickled from her split lip. "What are you doing here, Lisbeth?"

She hadn't meant to gasp, but now Mama knew she knew how badly she was hurt. "Long story."

Mama waved off Lisbeth's rush to help her sit up and started to push herself upright. "I just got the wind knocked out of me. Check on Kardide. She's taken a couple of hard blows to the head. The last one knocked her out for a minute or two."

Lisbeth remembered the tough old bird who'd once helped her escape the proconsul's palace. "Kardide," she whispered.

The older woman roused and slowly turned her head toward the sound of her name. Except for the bandage, she appeared to be in better shape than Mama. "I may have a little headache." Kardide made a fist and pumped it in the air. "But that soldier's shins will sting with my wrath for quite some time." Her fist fell to her chest as if someone had cut the string on a puppet. Then she rolled slightly in Lisbeth's direction and vomited.

"Kardide!" Mama called.

"I'm fine." Kardide wiped her lip. "Let Lisbeth help you first."

"No." Mama refused Lisbeth's attempt to check the damage to her eye. "Head injuries can't wait." She grabbed Lisbeth by the shoulders. "She may sound lucid, but she's lost strength in her right arm and now she's vomiting."

"But you're flush with fever and—"

"You can't let her die."

"Magdalena Hastings." Papa had been remarkably patient, but from his tone it was clear he was willing to wait no more for Mama to notice him. "You're still the most obstinate woman I've ever met."

"Lawrence?" Mama tilted her head. "I thought I was dreaming when I heard your voice, but it is you." Squinting sideways she tried to focus with her good eye. Her hand flew protectively to her face. "I didn't want you to see what I've become. Ever."

Papa's Adam's apple went up and down as if snagged upon decades of sorrow. "Seeing you again is all I've thought about for over forty years." Papa gently clasped Mama's hand and lowered it to her lap. His eyes navigated the changed landscape of Mama's face. A pained smile tugged at the regret and grief swimming in his eyes.

"I'm an old man now, my dear. But you, you are even more beautiful than I remember." His shaky hands cupped her puffy cheeks. He leaned forward and lightly brushed his lips across each bruise and scar as if he were removing years of sediment from a newly discovered artifact. Saving the broken place on her bottom lip for last, his kiss was light as a butterfly's wing. When he pulled away, he said with a satisfied air, "My treasure."

Mama tilted her good eye at him and said softly, "You came for me."

Tears glistened on Papa's cheeks. "I've been trying to get here since the moment I found out where you were."

Mama opened her arms and Papa fell into her embrace. They

clung together as if they never intended to let go again. Lisbeth's tears made it impossible to tell who was rescuing whom. Since she was five years old she'd wanted her family together. It was all she could do not to launch herself into the middle of the celebration. But this was her parents' private moment.

Lisbeth sensed Cyprian coming up behind her. His arm slipped around her waist. She couldn't help but lean into his strength. For a second she let her heart consider what it would be like to spend her life with the man she loved. Tempting as it was to fall back on the hope that they would be a family, she knew better. So far, history had refused to bend to her will. Either Cyprian would leave her through death or she would leave him through the portal.

"Please tell me Maggie is safe in Dallas," Mama whispered.

Papa's brows rose in the slow, easy way of a man who'd learned to conserve unnecessary efforts. "Well, Maggie's a long story."

"She's here, isn't she?"

He gave a reluctant nod.

"How did the child find her way back?"

Lisbeth waited for Papa to answer, but when it became obvious he didn't want to add to Mama's loss, she stepped in and answered for him. "Maggie's no longer a child."

"How many years have passed in your time?"

"Thirteen."

"Oh." Mama's lips trembled and Lisbeth wished she could take back this entire conversation.

"Maggie's a beautiful, artistic young woman and even more stubborn than her grandmother," Papa added, trying to cheer her up.

"How is that possible?"

His chuckle rumbled deep in his chest. "I do not know."

"Magdalena!" Tabari's voice interrupted. "Kardide will not wake up."

Lisbeth snatched her bag and rushed across the aisle. She felt for a pulse. Next she lifted Kardide's eyelids and flashed her penlight. "Unequal pupils."

"I'm telling you it's a classic epidural hematoma." Mama's teeth chattered.

Lisbeth wavered between getting to the root of her mother's chills and treating Kardide's possible brain bleed. "We don't know that for certain."

"Nausea is a sign of increased intracranial pressure and now she's unconscious. What else could it be?"

"Dehydration." Blood had seeped through the bandage wrapped around Kardide's head. "Maybe even typhoid."

"She took a pretty strong blow from a sword hilt. Her head hit the pavement in the fall." Mama's chills were making it difficult for her to speak. "And if we don't relieve the swelling her brain could herniate."

Of all the creative medical treatments her mother had asked her to give, this was well beyond the scope of reason. "Are you kidding?" Lisbeth said. "You want me to drill into her head?"

"I know it sounds frightening, but I'll talk you through it."

Maybe her mother was the one with the brain injury. "You've done craniotomies?"

"The gladiator docs do them all the time. I've assisted a very respectable Greek. Twice."

"Well, that's two more assists than I have, and I've been a surgeon for six years."

"You did a surgical residency?" Mama's pleasure slipped through her rattling teeth.

"She did," Papa said proudly, taking off his cloak and wrapping Mama tight. "Graduated top in her class." He leaned in close to Mama and whispered, "She's got your gifted hands."

"How many of the Greek's craniotomy patients lived?"

Mama lowered her good eye. "None. But the gladiators he operated on had suffered mortal injuries in the arena." Mama tried to get to her feet, winced at the pain the effort cost her, and sat back down. "We're wasting valuable time worrying about what might happen if we do surgery when we know for certain she'll die if we don't."

"I'm not a neurosurgeon."

"Then I guess you'll have to improvise."

"Not this time. A craniotomy would be risky in a perfectly sterile OR. Drilling into someone's head by torchlight in a filthy tunnel is insanely irresponsible."

"Standing by and watching a dear friend die is unforgivable." Mama hardly let the impact of that zinger sink in before she continued making her case. "The longer we wait, the more likely she will not recover." She spun her left index finger in a drilling motion over her clenched right fist. "You could save her just by making a small hole in the skull to relieve the pressure."

Having only one good eye had clearly hindered Mama's perspective. A top-flight surgical crew couldn't guarantee Kardide's recovery if she'd experienced a traumatic brain injury.

Judging stares came at Lisbeth from multiple pairs of eyes. No matter how many fellowships she completed or letters of distinction she added to the alphabet soup behind her name, she was not a savior. "I brought a few antibiotics, some oral typhoid vaccine, and the Kelly forceps you wanted. Unfortunately, I wasn't able to cram in a CT scanner or a high-speed air drill!"

"I've got the Greek's drill." Mama's announcement was followed by a little cough. "Bought it off him after he retired from his gladiator work."

"What?"

"It's in my bag. Those overzealous soldiers took my kit from me and gave it to the guard to hold as evidence when they brought us in." She cocked her head so that her good eye focused on Cyprian. "I'm sure you can sweet-talk Brutus into letting us have my tools for this small procedure."

"It's *not* a small procedure." Lisbeth let her exasperation show.

"The Greek could open and close in less than thirty minutes," Mama said confidently.

Screams of the wildcats held in adjoining cells echoed in the dark tunnel. Lisbeth knew exactly how these helpless creatures felt. Trapped against their will, yet forced to perform as if they had options.

"Lord, help me not to regret this." Lisbeth unclasped her cloak and spread it on the floor beside Kardide.

Papa and Cyprian helped her gently roll the patient into a supine position. After wadding Cyprian's cloak to elevate Kardide's head slightly, she sent him to fetch Mama's medical bag.

Through the metal door, Lisbeth could hear Brutus voicing his reluctance to relinquish care of the prisoners or the evidence bag until Cyprian agreed to let him watch the procedure. Brutus lit another torch and joined the ranks of the curious prisoners.

Feeling as if the stone walls were closing in, Lisbeth dug through her mother's tools: a couple of scalpels, a retractor, and a contraption that resembled a crude catheter. Just when she was about to call an end to Mama's game of chicken for lack of a drill, Lisbeth's hand came across a small wooden box buried beneath some fresh bandages. Inside, she found the infamous Greek drill wrapped in pristine white linen. The medieval-looking skull punch was no more than a polished metal shaft with a sharp, arrowhead-shaped tip and an attached horizontal crossbeam the size of a number two pencil.

Sheer panic shuddering through her, Lisbeth held it up. "Please tell me this isn't it."

"It's a brilliant design, don't you think?" Her mother motioned her closer, tilting her head so she could examine the tool with her good eye. She proceeded to tout the advantages of the lance's rounded edges and demonstrate via air gestures how to twist the attached crossbeam like a wine corkscrew. "Do beware of the danger of penetrating the dura."

"If by some miracle Kardide lives through this torture," Lisbeth said, nearly choking on the fact that she was actually discussing opening a woman's skull with a tent stake, "I'm sure she'll appreciate how we so thoughtfully lessened her risk of contracting meningitis by protecting her dura."

Mama waved off Lisbeth's sarcasm. "In my bag, you'll find the flask of the sterile wash we made for Aspasius. . . ." Sorrow trailed her unfinished statement. She turned to Papa. "I'm so sorry about everything, Lawrence."

He gently brushed her lip with his finger. "None of that matters now."

Lisbeth placed the drill back in the box and snapped it shut. "This is crazy."

"If you can't do it, perhaps Brutus would find it in his heart to free her long enough to set her up over here and I'll do it."

"You don't have the strength to turn the twist tie on a bread wrapper, let alone drill through bone." Lisbeth laid her palm on Magdalena's forehead. "Besides, I think you have fever."

Mama removed her hand. "Then we have reached a serious conundrum, haven't we?" She let her head rest upon Papa's shoulder. "Do nothing and let nature take its course. Or do what we can and let God steady our hands." They both knew Mama was referring to the long night of useless surgery they'd performed on the proconsul. "This time I'll concede. The final decision is yours, doctor."

"In that case, I want to go on record as saying this is a bad idea." Lisbeth looked around at all of the expectant eyes staring at her. Cyprian, Papa, Mama, even the other prisoners who'd stopped their crying out and put their own needs aside: all of them waited for her to pull some kind of a miracle out of a hat. Patients and their families did this to her all the time—expected her to fix broken bodies as easily as a mechanic repaired a car.

Which was more humane? Letting Kardide drift peacefully into the next life or doing a medieval procedure that would probably kill her? And if the surgery didn't do in the old woman, convalescing in a filthy dungeon would. "You know she'll never be able to drive after this, right?"

Mama laughed out loud. "It's a chance I'm sure Kardide would be willing to take."

The faces of Cyprian and Brutus scrunched in confusion.

She may not be the fearless surgeon her mother was, but neither could she stand by and do nothing. Lisbeth let out a long sigh. She stuffed her hand inside the bag in search of Mama's homemade disinfectant and nicked her finger. "Ouch."

"What is it?" Cyprian asked from his place at Kardide's head.

Lisbeth drew her finger to her mouth and closed the little gash with pressure from her teeth while she peered into the bag. A stainless steel bone saw.

Oh, no.

Her gaze darted to Mama, who was casting a one-eyed plea for silence. But then they didn't need to discuss how her mother came into possession of a twenty-first-century bone saw. They both knew exactly how this modern tool had gotten mixed in with her mother's primitive instruments. It was the saw Lisbeth had loaned her mother to amputate the gangrenous leg of Aspasius Paternus. Even more damning, the serrated blade was smeared with dried blood.

"Nothing." Lisbeth wheeled and spoke to the guard. "Brutus, we need every torch."

The moment Brutus left to get more light, Lisbeth turned her back to everyone and slipped the damning piece of evidence into her bag. By the time the guard returned, Lisbeth had used a little bit of Mama's sterile wash on her finger wound, applied a Band-Aid, and was rechecking Kardide's pupils as she and Mama discussed the hematoma's position. Without a CT scan she could never know with 100 percent certainty, but based on Kardide's arm weakness on the right and her blown pupil on the left, the most likely spot would be under the left temporal bone in the region of the middle meningeal artery.

Lisbeth marked the target area with her index finger. "Okay, now what?"

"Once you remove the bandage, measure two finger widths anterior to the tragus of the ear and then three finger widths above the tragus of the ear and you will have located the perfect spot," Mama instructed.

Lisbeth gloved up and offered Cyprian a pair. "Our patient's unconscious for now, but God forbid she wakes up during the procedure. I'll need you to hold her head very still."

Cyprian nodded and Lisbeth could almost see him turning green at the possibility of seeing so much blood.

"Papa, bring that extra torch in closer." Lisbeth unwrapped Kardide's head. To the naked eye, the injury appeared to be little more than a glancing blow that had scuffed the surface of the scalp. She shaved away a strip of Kardide's hair with a disposable razor she'd thrown in her bag at the last minute and took the makeshift measurements with her fingers.

Lisbeth retrieved a bottle of Betadine from her medical kit and a mask. "Cyprian, squirt this on the operative site and then douse the scalpel and drill." Her fingers brushed his and she hoped he could tell how grateful she was to have his help. She stretched her fingers. "Lord, I ask that you guide my hands."

"I've got a god right here." Brutus pulled a small stone statue from his pocket. Sweat poured out from beneath his helmet and his cheeks were flush. "Want to pray to it too?"

"No need. Perhaps you should step out for air, Brutus."

He shook his head. "Soldiers are used to blood."

"Stand back then." Lisbeth placed her right hand on Kardide's head. Memories all too fresh of the last surgery she and Mama had performed together washed over her. *Lord, help me.* She tightened her grip on the scalpel and glanced over her mask at Cyprian, whose face was dangerously pale. "Ready?"

He gulped and nodded. "God, don't let her wake up."

"Amen," Lisbeth muttered.

She sliced an incision along the curve of Kardide's head.

"Holy mother of Juno." Brutus's sword clattered across the pavers, his eyes rolled back in his head, and he crumpled in a heap.

"Lawrence, will you remove the helmet from our brave soldier and elevate his feet so Lisbeth can keep going?" Mama said, coughing.

Lisbeth didn't like the dry, raspy sound of her mother's cough, but there wasn't much she could do while in the middle of punching a hole in someone's skull. Hand shaking, she took up the drill.

"Whatever you do, once you start do not stop until you break through." Mama had stretched her chain to its limit and then strained against the iron links until she was nearly in Lisbeth's operating theater.

Sweat dripped from Lisbeth's forehead and she remembered the exertion it had taken for her mother to saw through the bone of Aspasius's leg with a first-class bone saw. How could she tap a skull with third-rate equipment?

Just when she thought her wrist would give out, Lisbeth felt the drill do its work, then disengage. An ominous gurgle was followed by the hiss of air bubbles as blood filled the hole, which was quickly followed by Lisbeth's sigh of relief. "I can't believe this worked."

Using one of Mama's blunt hooks she quickly removed a few bone fragments, then irrigated the burr hole with homemade disinfectant until the fluid ran clear. She inserted plastic tubing attached to a suction bulb drain she'd thrown in her backpack on a whim and stitched the scalp flap closed around the tube as quickly as possible.

"Drain needs to stay in place at least three days. I'll leave a clean scarf to cover it up and some antibiotics for when she wakes and can swallow, but you'll still have to watch for infection." Lisbeth leaned back on her heels and admired the neat baseball-seam stitches of Kardide's new scar. "Then we shall see if the results justify the treatment."

"Thanks to you, she'll only have a headache when she wakes up," Mama said proudly.

"*If* she regains consciousness. The next two hours are critical." Lisbeth rose, bent over, placed her hands on her knees, and let the rush of blood to her head sweep away the terror of the past thirty minutes.

Cyprian snapped off his gloves and came around and rubbed her back. "You did the best you could. The rest is up to God."

Tempting as it was to hang her head until she passed out, she had other patients. From the corner of her eye she caught a glance of Papa dragging Brutus upright. "How's your patient?"

"Still a little woozy, but not so green."

The guard's hair was plastered to his head, and his eyes were wild. "My keys." Brutus searched the dirty floor with his hands. "Where are my keys?"

"On your belt, man," Cyprian said.

Brutus's hand flew to his waist. When he discovered his keys had not been touched, Lisbeth's first thought was how Maggie would have enjoyed capturing the surprise on his face with her camera.

"You did not escape?"

"We are all still here," Papa assured him.

Brutus peered tentatively around Papa's shoulder. "And the woman?"

"She's going to live," Mama said, then promptly threw up on the soldier's boots.

17

"MAGDALENA?" PAPA LEFT BRUTUS swaying over his soiled shoes and rushed to Mama's side. "Lisbeth, do something. She's not well."

"I'm fine, Lawrence." Mama wiped her mouth. "It's just the flu."

Papa drew her tight. "You're shaking."

Lisbeth vaulted across the aisle. "Cyprian, take Brutus out of here." She tossed him a cylinder of foaming hand disinfectant she'd pulled from her bag. "Clean his shoes carefully, then rub this all over your hands." She helped Papa lean her mother against the wall. After conducting a thorough examination, Lisbeth sat back on her heels. Her mother's eyes begged her not to say what they both knew to be true. "You know it's typhoid, right?" She hated blowing Mama's valiant attempt to handle this herself, but there was no improvising on this one.

"You don't know that." A dry cough launched her mother's body into a convulsion that sounded as if her insides were being ripped out.

Lisbeth ticked off the symptoms: "Horrible cough. Temperature. Chills. A smattering of red spots on your chest. No booster since you arrived in Carthage, and more important, the surgery you performed a few days ago on Diona Cicero's perforated bowels exposed you to her bacteria. Even without the blood work, I can say 'typhoid' with more confidence than you said 'epidural hematoma' for Kardide." Lisbeth bent close to place a white tablet on her mother's tongue, the yeasty smell rising from her mother's skin eliminating any doubt. "I brought some Cipro."

Mama waved her away. "Save it for the others."

"Papa's right. Maggie inherited her stubborn streak from you."

"Leave me," Mama said, coughing. "Find your girl and go home."

Papa pressed his lips to Mama's forehead. "We're not going anywhere without you."

"He's right," Lisbeth said.

"You'll have no choice." Magdalena turned to Cyprian, who'd just returned from escorting Brutus out into the fresh air. "Tell them what happens to one accused of murdering the proconsul."

Cyprian knelt between them. "Her case will be brought before the local praetor. The prosecutor and I will be given the opportunity to frame the issues."

"You?" Lisbeth lowered her voice. "You can't go before the authorities. You're a wanted man."

"Not anymore," he whispered back. "Thanks to Maggie, I found the note your mother sent with you the night of your escape. This codicil to Aspasius's will grants me amnesty."

"I know what it says, but the wanted posters went up *after* the proconsul signed Mama's ultimatum. Aspasius's deathbed decree isn't worth the paper it was written on."

"A debatable technicality . . . a debate I intend to win, mind you," Cyprian said. "Don't look doubtful, you know I can be very persuasive when I want." He leaned over and kissed Lisbeth. "I cannot let this innocent woman go without representation."

The warmth of his lips upon hers cooled quickly. Winning as

he could be, Lisbeth knew where this decision would lead. "When are you doing this fool thing?"

He signaled to be careful they were not being overheard. "God willing, I plan to speak to the praetor tomorrow."

"And ask him what?"

"To reinstate my law privileges."

"Can he do that?"

"He has to go before the Senate with my request."

Cyprian's previous failure to change the minds of the authorities was a fact Lisbeth could not alter. Those same men who'd voted to exile her husband would not raise a finger to help him now. She'd come to terms with his destiny years ago. Arguing with him was pointless.

"I will not let Maggie watch you do something stupid. Those men will not embrace you."

"Lisbeth, please."

She held up her palms. "Since evacuating the prisoners is out of the question, the best I can do for now is distribute typhoid vaccine to the other inmates. Here, take one for yourself." She pushed the box of blister packs into Cyprian's hands. To her mother she said, "I'll leave enough Cipro to last a couple of days. The moment I find Maggie, I'm coming back for you."

"No, you won't." Mama held out her arms. "Look at my hands, Lisbeth. They've shriveled into chicken claws. I'm old and tired."

Lisbeth took her mother's hands in her own. They were clammy, hot, and fragile as an autumn leaf in her palms. Blue-ridged veins crisscrossed her mother's knuckles like lines on a faded road map. Each track was a tributary of connected memories: These hands deftly spreading peanut butter on crusty bread without letting a grain of sand get stuck in the mix. These hands massaging shampoo through her tangled curls. And most cherished of her memories . . . these hands gently examining a patient or wielding a scalpel.

"These are not chicken claws. These are the worn hands of Christ."

Mama pulled free and Lisbeth felt the same rumbling beneath her feet that accompanied the opening of the time portal. "And now it is time for me to go to him."

Lisbeth could almost taste the iron running through her mother's blood, that determined mettle to die by the same selfless standards by which she had lived. "No. Tell her, Papa."

Her father silently stroked his chin, dragging his finger across the stubble in an irritating back-and-forth rhythm.

"Papa, tell her!"

Her father lifted his chin. "If she can't go"—he reached inside the collar of his tunic and fished out the leather cord he wore around his neck—"then neither can I." He removed the ring from the cord and gently slid it onto Mama's finger. "Your mother and I are staying." He lifted Mama's hand to his lips and kissed each knuckle. "You go on, Lisbeth. Do what you have to do to keep our little girl safe."

"This isn't how it's supposed to end."

"Cyprian," Papa said. "I'm counting on you to keep my daughter from jeopardizing everyone's lives."

18

A T LONG LAST, STREAKS of light peeked through the slats in the bolted shutters. Maggie blew out the oil lamp and dragged the back of her hand across her forehead. On the opposite side of the room, Barek sat on the floor beside Eggie's bed. Maggie let out an exhausted sigh, picked up the breakfast tray Naomi had delivered without a word, and joined Barek on the floor.

She passed him the cup of warm wine. "Does he sound worse to you?"

Barek shrugged and took the cup. "Maybe a little." He'd refused to leave her, working as hard as she through the night to keep the vaporizer pot hot.

At first, Maggie hoped Barek's need to be near her was rooted in something deeper, something closer to the glimmer of interest he'd shown when they were laughing together. But as the hours wore on, and he acted more and more like the churlish guy she remembered, the real reason he refused to go to bed became evident. Her father had put him up to babysitting.

Her disappointment surprised her.

Maggie drew her knees to her chest and silently studied Eggie's body. With an odd-shaped tepee obscuring him from the waist up, the guy Barek had fished out of the harbor looked like some kind of mythical sea character with human legs. Her hands were itching for her camera. Even if she had it, nothing about a camera would be easy to explain—the flash would freak Barek out and spoil the shaky truce they'd forged.

Eggie's cough rattled his bed, if the short wooden frame with Eggie's size twelves hanging off the end could be called a bed. Her dorm bunk was bigger and probably a lot more comfortable. Especially after Titus had a servant remove the fancy down cushion and replace it with a thin mattress stuffed with something that crackled every time Eggie rolled over and hacked his lungs out. Maggie couldn't really fault Titus for his caution. There were enough dead bodies stacked between here and the time portal. She didn't blame him for not wanting his own family added to the heap.

In the rare lull between Eggie's coughing spells, Maggie dared a peek at Barek and confessed, "I don't know what else to do." She put her elbows on her knees and rested her chin in her hands. "He's hotter than a firecracker and coughing like a chain smoker."

"Firecracker? Chain smoker?"

"Never mind."

Barek cocked his head, looking at Eggie as if he too longed to get a better handle on the situation. "Have you ever seen anyone hold his ears like that?"

"Maybe it feels like his head is going to explode." Maggie stretched her legs and let her head fall back against the wall. "This is all my fault."

"You?" Barek turned to her. "I'm the one who found him."

"Yeah, but I said I could take care of him." Her arm drifted perilously close to Barek's. "What if he dies?"

"You've done everything you could." Barek threaded his fingers through hers and gave her hand a squeeze.

Nothing romantic. More of a big-brother, protective kind of grip.

So why was her arm on fire? "If Mom were here, she'd know

what to do." She hoped her voice wasn't laced with hormonal delirium.

"Maybe she'll come," he said, almost as if he expected Mom to walk in any minute.

"She's not coming."

"Why do you say that?"

Time to tell the truth. "She doesn't even know I'm gone."

Barek withdrew his hand and narrowed his eyes. "You ran away? Again?"

Maggie crossed her arms and tucked the hand Barek had held close to her chest in an attempt to capture the dissipating heat. "I'm eighteen."

"And no wiser than when you were five." Barek rubbed his temple, his mouth tightening with the pain of remembering the night his mother died. "Sorry. I didn't mean . . . you were just a child. I know you didn't mean for my mother to die." He was so tired he probably didn't realize that that rare glimpse of compassion she remembered fondly had leaked between the cracks of his crusty exterior and once again melted her heart.

Seizing upon this moment of contrition, Maggie asked, "Why did you create a diversion so my mother and I could get away that night I was sick?"

The question took him by surprise. He gave a humble half shrug. "It was the right thing to do."

"I saw what the soldiers did to those who couldn't get away. What you did was very brave, Barek."

"Don't think me a better man than I am." His gaze met hers briefly, then drifted past her and the walls of the villa. From the pinch of his brow she suspected Barek struggled with the memories of that horrible night the soldiers came in search of her father in the same way she was tortured with the slow-motion replay of his mother being flung about by an angry bull.

After a few seconds he said, "I told myself, 'Why not sell the writs? What would it hurt the one God for someone to say they'd burned a pinch of incense upon the altar of a pagan god when they didn't mean it?'" He took a sharp breath. "But I was wrong. Those writs of libellus destroyed everything. As all lies do."

Maggie grimaced at the prickle of her own guilt. "Everyone lies." The note she'd scribbled in the airport and intended to mail was still in her backpack. "Maybe not with words, but with the lack of them."

"But not everyone fails his own mother." Barek's eyes held neither judgment nor pity. "Cyprian had done so much for me, and I was such an ungrateful cur I couldn't see it. Saving you and your mother doesn't make up for half of what I have done. But it's a start."

Maggie envied how his confession rolled off his tongue—bravely. He'd screwed up and he knew it, but he was going forward, trying to make a difference no matter the consequences. The last time she'd done anything halfway noble, she was five and vowed never to play with dolls again. Who did that help? Her sacrifice did not give Ruth back to her son. No wonder she still felt guilty.

Eggie gasped and then coughed so hard he spit up blood.

"He's choking!" Maggie raced to the bed, flung back the tent flap, and tried to lift their patient into a sitting position. Eggie's body coiled out from under her grasp like limp spaghetti. "He can't catch his breath. I don't know what to do."

"I do."

The clear, intelligent, matter-of-fact voice that came from behind Maggie sent her heart plunging into the dark pit of her already upset stomach. The woman who belonged to this voice always knew what she was talking about and she loved to make sure Maggie knew it.

Maggie turned slowly. "Mom?"

"I've told you a hundred times not to leave your backpack lying around." Her mother tossed her the bag she'd left in her father's villa. "Don't just stand there." Her mother's skilled hands clasped Maggie's shoulders and moved her aside. "We've got a lot to do before we go home."

19

THE ELATION OF FINDING Maggie alive and scared half to death had dialed back Lisbeth's anger by several notches.

Hopefully her strong-willed girl had witnessed enough suffering that she'd never want to venture into this world again. Ever. Convincing Mama to leave was going to be tricky enough. She didn't need Maggie bucking their return as well.

Lisbeth pulled her stethoscope buds from her ears. "You nailed the measles diagnosis, and your vaporizer is well made."

Maggie dropped her backpack and inched in closer. "Then why isn't he getting better?"

"Complications are what every doctor fears. He could have just as easily developed pneumonia and a severe ear infection while under my care." She looped her stethoscope around her neck. "I'll give him a round of antibiotics, some Tylenol, and typhoid vaccine just in case. We'll have to keep the vaporizer going and pump him full of liquids until he's out of the woods."

"Is he going to live?" Maggie cowered beside Barek. Lisbeth couldn't help but notice Ruth's son's protective hand resting on her daughter's tense shoulder.

"He's strong." She pulled off the gloves she'd put on before conducting her exam. "Once his fever breaks I'll feel better about his prognosis. But know this: he's alive because of you."

Maggie let out a surprised breath. "But he'll recover because *you're* here."

As Lisbeth considered the best way to navigate the land mines between her and Maggie, Cyprian jumped in. "Young lady, I think your mother and I deserve to know why *you're* here."

Maggie's fists clenched in preparation for war. So much for any hope of a truce. Lisbeth braced, but to her surprise, Maggie turned and deployed her first missile at Barek. "Were you with my father when he found my mother?" Her frustration carried as far as the kitchen, drawing Naomi and Laurentius to the door. "Well?"

Barek grabbed hold of the finger she jabbed in his chest. "I didn't know you'd run away until just a few minutes ago."

"If you were any kind of friend, you would have told me *she* was here." Maggie's tears were being held in place by a wall of anger.

For all her travels across the centuries, Dr. Lisbeth Hastings knew one truth to be timeless: some people were like dangerous pathogens—unrelenting when it came to doing whatever they needed to survive. Her daughter was one of those people. She needed space. Whenever she felt trapped, she was willing to gnaw off her leg or worse, someone else's head, to get free.

Lisbeth stepped in to spare Barek the bloodletting that Maggie wanted to aim at her. "I asked him not to tell."

"Why is it always like that with you, Mom?"

"What are you talking about?"

"You can't keep me in that sterile box of yours forever."

"I did what I thought was best."

Maggie's hands flew in the air, her glare expanding the distance between them. "Were you ever going to tell me that my father would die a horrible martyr's death?" Hurt palpitated from her pursed lips.

"Cyprian's going to die?" Barek ripped his dagger from his scabbard. "When?"

"Everybody calm down," Cyprian said.

"My mother hates me for taking her from you!" Maggie's face blazed with accusation. "Admit it, Mom."

"How could I ever hate you? You're the best of both of us," Lisbeth answered.

"If I hadn't gotten sick, you could've stayed and stopped all of this."

There it was. The guilt Papa had alluded to, the sin from which Maggie sought absolution. What a fool she'd been to let the infection fester all these years. "Listen to me." Lisbeth gripped Maggie's shoulders. "If anyone is to blame for the way things turned out the last time we were here, it's me. When I brought you to the third century, I failed to take the proper precautions. I knew the dangers of a near drowning. I should have administered antibiotics the minute we climbed out of the well. But I didn't. By the time your typhoid vaccine failed, I'd given away my entire stock. You were dying. Aspasius was coming for us. Your father sent us back to save us both."

From the dagger stare Maggie was hurling her way, nothing she'd said had penetrated her daughter's hard head. Lisbeth sighed. "Hate me if you must, but I'd do it all again, exactly the same way."

Maggie's gaze shot between Lisbeth and Cyprian, evaluating this new information. "Even keep me from my father?" She snatched her backpack and stormed out.

Exasperated, Lisbeth turned to Cyprian and said with a sigh, "That went well, don't you think?"

20

AFTER A SLEEPLESS NIGHT sitting beside Eggie's bed, Lisbeth spent the next day hiding her parenting frustrations in the work of treating Eggie. Maggie spent the day avoiding everyone.

For the first time in her life, Lisbeth understood exactly how difficult it must have been for her mother when Lisbeth brought her anger and unmet expectations to their reunion. She was so angry at Mama for having to grow up without her that she wanted to hit something. She would have too if her mother hadn't been extremely patient.

Lisbeth wiped her hands. If only she had time to adopt the same tactic. But she didn't. Fall was coming, and with it, Cyprian's execution. While his hardheaded attitude angered her, she'd come to terms with his decision to face whatever lay ahead. Maggie obviously had not. There was only one way to prevent the emotional heartache her daughter would suffer if she had to witness her father's death and that was to extricate her from this place. Sooner rather than later.

Lisbeth forced her concentration on the task of lining up bundles of dried fennel, turmeric roots, and all-purpose margosa leaves on the kitchen table.

"Lisbeth?" Cyprian's voice was quiet, his arms careful as they slipped around her waist. His nose nuzzled the back of her neck. "This can wait until tomorrow."

Her body stiffened against a maelstrom of emotions she'd been fighting all day. Not because she didn't want to satisfy the longing she'd seen every time their eyes met, but to protect her own heart from being torn to pieces. Which was exactly what would happen when he had to go his way and she had to go hers. "I'm almost finished."

He came around and faced her. His eyes searched hers as he took the root bundle from her hand and laid it on the table. "You're finished for tonight." He picked up the oil lamp and offered his hand.

Lisbeth scooped up eucalyptus leaves. "You could have said something. Helped me with her."

Picking a fight with Cyprian was stupid. Her struggles with Maggie were not his fault. So why was she pulling the pin from the grenade? She knew why. Because, no matter what she told herself, coming here had disturbed the small seed of hope hibernating deep in her heart. The hope of becoming a family. Allowing this forbidden longing a chance to sprout was asking for her heart to be ripped out again. Their time together had limits. To pretend otherwise was setting herself up for a grief she would not survive a third time.

"It is herself she cannot forgive, Lisbeth."

"You sound like my father." Eucalyptus leaves crumbled to dust in her clenched palm. "I guess I'm tired of being her punching bag."

Cyprian considered her words for a moment, and she knew from the flicker of confusion he was trying to picture a punching bag. "I seem to remember someone having a wrestling match with her own mother in the middle of my garden."

Lisbeth hated how Cyprian could see the fear hidden in her

bluster. She made a feeble attempt at a smile. "That was different. Mama had stolen my stethoscope."

"Your mother had disappointed you and you couldn't let it go."

"How have I disappointed Maggie? I have given her everything."

"But me."

"I would have, but you made me promise never to bring her back." Even as the words left her mouth she regretted how they sounded. "You didn't deserve—"

His kiss silenced her apology. "Your sacrifices have been great." He offered his arm. "And that's what I told her. In the future, she's to direct her complaints to me."

"Future?" Lisbeth brushed the eucalyptus from her hands. "You know I can't stay."

"I know."

She abandoned her herbs and roots, and threaded her arm with his. His hand came over hers. Warm. Strong. And trembling. A small tremor, but one that shook her to the core. He was as frightened of losing her again as she was of losing him.

When Lisbeth had lost Cyprian the first time, she told herself she was coming back someday. So every moment of their brief life together played like a classic movie she'd watched so many times she knew every line. She remembered everything: The scent of his skin, salty with a hint of the expensive octopus ink he used for his ledgers. The quizzical look that quirked his lips whenever she used modern terms he didn't understand . . . and her favorite, the way the curls that fell across his forehead twisted around her finger when she plowed her hands through his hair and drew him so close they breathed the same air. Remembering these things, especially as she gave birth to his child, had kept him close and eased the fear of raising Maggie alone.

This last separation had been far more difficult. She'd told herself the agony was normal. After all, she was struggling to raise her daughter alone. Keeping up with Maggie drained both her mental and physical reserves. But she knew the truth: She wanted to be with him and she couldn't.

Cyprian pulled her to him. "We have tonight. Let's not waste it."

One night with this man she loved so much she ached inside was all she'd had on her last trip through the portal and it had not been enough. She would not put herself through that pain again.

His lips settled hers. He wasted no time pulling her close and she felt her heart melt. How could she live the rest of her life knowing she'd not taken advantage of the opportunity to make love to him again? She couldn't. When he finally released her, he smiled and offered his hand again.

Lisbeth laced her fingers with his and held tightly.

"You're limping," he said as he guided her from the kitchen.

"It's nothing."

"Let me take care of you for a change. I'll look at your foot when we get to our room." They made their way through the dark house via lamplight, dodging all the occupied sleeping mats in the halls.

Cyprian led her up the back stairs to a door tucked under the eaves. "Titus set this up for us." His eyes twinkled with anticipation and her heart quickened. There had been no one else for thirteen years.

"Wait until you see." Cyprian opened the door and drew her inside the tiny room. "Not our honeymoon suite, but more comfortable than the pergola on the beach."

Cyprian's lamp lit the details of the cozy space.

Titus had outdone himself. On the far side of the room, a plump double mattress covered in silky linens waited on the floor. Gauzy curtains billowed from the small window with a remarkable view of the sea. Shiny dots of lavender oil floated in a basin of fresh water. Beside the bed, someone had left a luxurious layout of wine, cheese, and an assortment of sweet cakes.

Cyprian set the lamp on the tray, then snatched one of the small biscuits. "Here, try this." He placed a piece of the little cake on her tongue, then gently kissed her lips. His touch melted the crumbs of wheat flour held together by rich goat's butter and sweetened with honey imported from Alemannia. How Titus had come by these delicacies when the rest of the city was starving affirmed once again how much power and wealth resided with the merchant who'd embraced them and their Lord. Tempting as it was to think the conversion of Titus could alter history's course, she couldn't allow her mind to go down that dead end road.

"Eat." Cyprian's mischievous gaze drifted to the bed, a grin tugging his lips. "You're going to need your strength." He pulled his tunic over his head and tossed the garment to the floor. "But first your foot." He stood before her, unashamed and still the beautiful specimen of cinematic dreams. "Sit."

A surprising wave of shyness lowered her eyes, and she sat upon the stool.

He knelt and removed her shoe and carefully began to remove the bandage wrapped around her foot. "Looks a little infected."

"I probably need to—"

"Shhhh." He poured water in a basin and gently lowered her foot into the warm water. "These legs have carried so many burdens." With one hand cupping her heel, he gently drizzled water over her shin. Next he slathered her leg with scented oil and began to massage her calf muscles. "Rest."

Lisbeth closed her eyes and let the tension drain from her body. A moan escaped her lips. "That feels fabulous."

Cyprian leaned forward and kissed her lightly. "Wait here. I'll get a towel." He went to the hook on the wall and retrieved the fresh linen. He lifted her foot and gently patted it dry. Pain shot from her heel to her knee.

She shifted so he wouldn't notice her flinch. "That's better. Thanks." Cyprian stood and tossed the towel across the room. He took her hand and drew her to her feet. He kissed her again, this time pulling her against him.

Her fingers worried the knot of her sash. Butterflies, bigger than the ones she'd battled on their wedding night, fluttered in her womb. Since the last time they were together, only a few days had passed for Cyprian. Her gaze toured his chiseled contours of shadow and light that danced in the lamp's flame. He hadn't aged at all. No new wrinkles. His waist was still trim. This man beckoning her to his bed looked exactly like the man of her memories, the one her dreams had called forth night after night for the past thirteen years. Examining him now was like looking at a picture of someone taken in the prime of his life and forever frozen in a state of perfection.

From the way Cyprian's eyes canvassed her body, drinking in the shape of her curves, Lisbeth wanted to believe she too had not aged. That her husband still thought he'd never seen anything so beautiful in his life. That her fears of disappointing him were unfounded.

But reality kept her belt knotted.

She didn't need a mirror to know time had taken its toll on her body. Lisbeth let her gaze drop to her hands. Thirteen years older. Veiny. Red and rough from years of scrubbing in for one surgery after another. Her biceps had softened from lack of time at the gym. Fine lines at the corners of her eyes crinkled into crow's-feet whenever she smiled.

"Blow out the lamp, please," she whispered.

"Not tonight," he said softly. In two steps he was so near that his breath warmed the top of her head. He lifted her chin and cupped her face with his hands. "I can't pretend to know how hard it has been in your world. How long our days apart have been for you. How frightening and difficult it must have been to raise our daughter alone." He kissed her nose, never taking his eyes from hers. "All I know is from the moment I sent you away until the moment you returned, it has been as if a thousand years have grieved my heart." He gently lowered his lips to hers, kissing her tenderly. "It was selfish, I know, but I wanted you back before I even let you go."

Tiny quivers, rhythmic as the distant waves rolling upon the shore, rippled from the heat of his lips. "I love you," she whispered. "Forever."

A hint of a smile curved his lips and he kissed her again. She drank in the salty taste of him as his kiss deepened. Her mind traveled to their last night together. The treasured memory was suddenly clear. She could feel the pergola tiles beneath her, see the bats leave their roost in the pergola's beams, and feel Cyprian's desire meld with hers. Having the memory securely in place settled her, steadied her breathing, and sent fear sailing. All too soon circumstances would rip them apart. But for tonight, they were together. And she refused to leave here with a single regret. She wrapped her arms around his neck, leaned into him, and loved him as if they had all the time in the world.

SQUAWKING GULLS outside the open window awakened Lisbeth from her first sound sleep in years. Still drowsy, she dragged her leg over Cyprian's. It was true. He was actually here. Not just a dream. She kissed his shoulder. He mumbled something unintelligible and drew her close. Though the room was warm, they'd clung to each other all night, soaking up the proof of the other's existence.

Outside their door, coughs and sickly moans rose from the

crowded halls. Lisbeth's patients would need her soon. She closed her eyes and prayed for one more minute of bliss. One more moment of not having to think about what would happen to these people when she had to leave. When she couldn't stand their cries for relief any longer, she started to rise.

Cyprian pulled her back. "Wait. Do you hear that?"

Maggie's lilting voice seeped through the cracks. Soothing. Graceful. Naive.

Pleasure spread across his face. "Our daughter is a good girl. Thanks to you."

"That's just it. If I let her see what is about to happen in this place, she won't be a little girl for long."

21

LISBETH KISSED THE SCOWL from her husband's forehead. "Maggie's going to need some help." She slid out of bed and went to the basin.

Cyprian rolled on his back, stretched lazily, then pillowed his clasped hands behind his head and watched as she emptied the sponge on her bare shoulders. "She's fully capable of changing Eggie's water pot."

"And if he's taken a turn for the worse?"

"Trust her to let you know."

"I do trust her." Lisbeth glanced over her shoulder, irritated at his implication.

"She says you hover."

"Really? Then how did she escape me long enough to come here?" She shimmied into her tunic. "It's not easy being two parents at once."

"I'm not saying you haven't done an excellent job raising our child. You have. It's because she is such a fine young woman that I think you can—"

"Don't let those big blue eyes of hers fool you." Lisbeth freed her hair from her collar. "Nothing is ever easy with our daughter."

"Or her mother."

"You should have married Diona Cicero if you wanted easy."

She chuckled at his surprise of her knowledge of his broken engagement to Titus's daughter and planted a kiss on Cyprian's forehead. "Come find me after you've prepared to face the praetor and we'll pray."

"I thought you weren't speaking to God."

"You're the one I'm not speaking to." Lisbeth smiled and slipped out the door just as Cyprian launched his tunic at her head.

She hurried down the stairs. Determined not to hover, she intentionally turned opposite the sound of Maggie's voice.

Titus's house was even larger and more spectacular than Cyprian's. Situated on prime real estate that overlooked the harbor, the structure had been strategically placed to maximize the breeze, which would be helpful for clearing the halls of the stench of sickness. Lisbeth dashed into the kitchen, stuffed her backpack with herbs, and wrapped her stethoscope around her neck. Her restocking complete, she could no longer put off her rounds or dealing with Maggie.

Lisbeth hoisted her bag and bustled toward the measles hall. She stopped at the door. Maggie was already dressed and filling Eggie's vaporizer pot with bubbling hot water.

"You're up early."

Maggie flashed a triumphant smile. "I think his fever has broken."

"Really?" Lisbeth set her bag beside Eggie's bed. "How are you feeling?"

"Tried to get this goddess to hold my hand, but she acts like I have the plague or something." Eggie pushed up on his elbows. "Her hair is the color of Scythian gold. Her eyes are jewels set in alabaster."

Lisbeth's gaze cut to Maggie. "How long has he been talking?"

Maggie rolled her eyes. "Too long."

Lisbeth couldn't help laughing. "Let's take his temperature."

"I don't think he can keep his mouth shut long enough to get an accurate read."

Lisbeth reached into her bag. "Don't worry, it's a rectal thermometer."

"Mom, that's gross."

"Just kidding." She kissed Maggie's cheek. "See, I can step out of the sterile box once in a while and have a little fun." Lisbeth removed the thermometer from her pack, watching Maggie cautiously consider the possibility. "Open wide, Eggie."

One of Titus's stable boys skidded into the room, waving his arms. "Come quick."

Lisbeth left Eggie with a thermometer hanging out of his mouth and scrambled after Maggie and the servant. "Well, what is it?" Lisbeth asked when she arrived at the front door.

The wild-haired servant licked his lips and became suddenly very interested in his shifting feet.

Lisbeth insisted. "Speak up."

The boy raised his dirty face. "When I helped the fishmonger water his horse at our troughs, he told me his daughter was ill."

"And?"

"I might have mentioned we had a healer." He undid the latch and slowly pulled back the carved wood. "I'm sorry."

Lisbeth gasped.

"Where did they come from?" Maggie blurted.

Fifteen new measles cases waited on the tiled portico and twenty more spilled out into the courtyard.

BY SUNDOWN Maggie and Naomi had helped Lisbeth add so many new sleeping mats they could barely pick their way through the atrium.

Titus was beside himself, shouting threats from the kitchen door. His rants alternated between warning Diona and Vivia he'd cut off their shopping funds if they set foot in the sick-ward and begging Lisbeth for medicine to keep his family safe. "I'll pay anything," he pleaded.

"I gave you what I have, Titus. But the typhoid vaccine will not protect you against measles. Stay out of here and wash your hands often." On her last visit Lisbeth planned for the measles epidemic and transported a few rounds of the vaccine in a small cooler. Unfortunately, most of it had spoiled. She'd been left with no choice but to throw out the unused vials. While packing her bag for this trip, she'd opted to use her limited space for the nonrefrigerated typhoid blister packs. Titus and Vivia had received the necessary doses. It would be several more days before Lisbeth knew whether it had been given early enough to preempt their exposure to the bacteria that had nearly killed their daughter and sickened Mama.

Long after dark, Cyprian brought a tray of cold lamb, warm cheese, and several rounds of crusty bread. "You need to eat."

"So far we're just seeing measles," Lisbeth said. She took a glass of wine from the tray. "If we start getting typhoid patients, I don't know what we're going to do. I've given Barek, Naomi, and Pontius the typhoid vaccine, but even if they manage to stay healthy that won't be enough help. I'll need Mama." She gulped the dark red wine. A tingling buzz traveled all the way to her aching feet. "Titus has graciously allowed his cook to assist Naomi with the oral hydration solutions and he's secretly opened a grain silo to keep us in bread, but even if we could handle the influx, I'm afraid as word spreads through the city that we have food and medical care they'll storm the villa."

"Sit with me for a moment."

Cyprian's grave face jerked her from her duties. "Has something happened to my mother? Tell me."

"Pontius delivered food and fresh water to the prison this morning. He reports she chided him for risking his life on such a fool's errand *and* that she and Kardide are making great improvements."

"Of course she would say that. I won't believe it until I see her again."

"Sit. You are exhausted."

"I don't have time."

His brows rose. "Now is all we have."

Her gut lurched. Lisbeth clung to her wineglass and let Cyprian lead her to a bench hidden in a small alcove.

Tempting as it was to beg him to keep on walking, Lisbeth settled in beside him. Another time and place this might have been the perfect spot for a romantic interlude, but the coughs and cries for mercy echoing in the corridor were more than mood killers. They were raw reminders of what she was up against . . . again. How had she allowed this to happen?

"Has it ever occurred to you that God may have sent you back for a reason?"

"God didn't do this. Maggie did."

"Just hear me out, please." Cyprian took the cup from her and then wrapped her hands in his. "What if *you* are the hope for the future—not me?"

"Me? That's ridiculous. According to everything I've read, *you're* the tragic hero."

His wan smile indicated his refusal to be sucked into her fears. "Tell me what you need to make a difference while you're here."

"While I'm here?" she whispered against the pressing inevitability of her departure. She'd made her position clear. She wouldn't stay and watch him die. So why did the acceptance in his voice constrict the air flow to her lungs? Lisbeth swallowed the acid mix burning her throat. "Same as before: the ports closed and the cemeteries opened. Lime to cover the bodies. Clean water for the tenements. More herbs for the oral hydration solutions and vaporizer tents. A hall cleared for possible typhoid patients. My staff is just a bunch of kids. Somebody has to relieve them before they drop from exhaustion. And somehow I've got to make time to check on my parents, while stealing every moment I can with you." She caught a shallow breath. "That's my short list."

His faint smile was lined with weariness. "Everything will be as God wills, my love." Cyprian folded her into his arms, drawing her against his chest. Scents of ink and parchment clung to his clothes. He'd been in Titus's library for hours poring over legal documents, searching for any loophole that would eliminate the necessity of his request for the reinstatement of his legal privileges before the Senate.

Though Lisbeth knew she shouldn't let herself be drawn into the problems of Cyprian's people again, she could more easily quit breathing than pull away from the steady beat of his heart. Each thump sank deeper into her soul, plowing through the crust she'd nurtured these past thirteen years. Softening her up. Preparing her for the moment they both knew could no longer be delayed. Tomorrow Cyprian would officially make his presence known in the city. He would stand before the praetor, beg the reinstatement of his rightful place, and officially set into motion events neither of them could stop.

"You have the note?" she whispered.

"I have the note."

"And you'll tell Xystus to explain to the Senate that Aspasius set you free—"

"I'll tell him." Cyprian's finger skimmed her cheek. "I'll seek an expedited decision and press to go to trial immediately."

"And if Xystus refuses your requests?"

"I'll remind him of my father's generosity to his family over the years."

"But a trial may not go—"

Across the atrium, someone rapped on the door. Lisbeth couldn't help the frustrated sigh that stirred the hair escaping her loose braid. "More sick have found us."

Cyprian planted a soft kiss on her forehead. "I'll get it. You rest a little longer."

"If it's an emergency—"

"I'll call you."

She heard Cyprian open and close the peephole, then throw open the door. "Metras!"

Metras? Lisbeth peeked around the pillar. The old man who'd stuck by them while the rest of the church followed the traitor Felicissimus out the door was shaking Cyprian's hand.

"Tappo!" Cyprian turned and offered his hand, but the Egyptian stonemason tromped in without a word. After him came twenty more adults and at least that many children, Cyprian's pleasure growing with each guest. "Thank you all for coming."

Lisbeth left her plate and went to investigate. "What's going on?"

These were not new patients. In fact, it was easy to see none of the new arrivals crowding into the atrium were even sick. Some she recognized as former patients she and her mother had already nursed to health. All of them were members of the church who had at one time or another served alongside Ruth and herself.

Metras made his way to the front of the group. "Lisbeth, you look worn out," he said with a gummy smile. "Good thing I brought some help." The hairs on the back of her neck bristled. Except for Metras, these people had abandoned her husband and left him to face the Roman soldiers alone. She never wanted to see these traitors again. She opened her mouth to express those very sentiments when an exhausted sigh drew her attention. An emaciated woman suddenly slumped into Metras. Her sunken cheeks were flush with fever. In her arms, she clutched a bundle in the shape of an infant. Lisbeth would have thought her another pleb from the slums except for the expensive clothes on her back and the gold jewelry draped around her neck. "And who is this?"

"Don't know." Metras shifted his cane to better support the weight of the woman swaying from his arm. "Found her wandering the street not a block from here. If the rich coward who left his family isn't dead, someone ought to kill him."

"You were right to bring her to us." Cyprian led the woman to a bench. "Lisbeth, this woman could use your help." The room went silent. "Lisbeth?"

All eyes turned on her. This woman was a patrician. She could bring trouble. Lisbeth willed her feet to move toward the bench. "What's your name?" she asked the woman.

"Arria." The bundle in the woman's clenched arms didn't move.

"Can I see your baby?"

Arria gave a cautious nod and eased her grasp on the child. Lisbeth pulled back the blanket and peered at a tiny blue face not more than a month old. The woman had come too late. Lisbeth lifted her eyes to deliver the bad news, but Arria's anxious eyes compelled her to run the stethoscope bell under the bindings and listen for a heartbeat anyway.

Lisbeth swallowed the sting that always swamped her when someone died, and she tucked the bindings back in place. She gently touched Arria's arm. "Wait here." She caught Cyprian's eye and cocked her head toward the alcove. He excused himself and followed after her.

"I hate to throw cold water on your excitement," Lisbeth whispered. "But that woman with Metras is obviously somebody important. Perhaps even the wife of one of the senators who voted in favor of your exile."

He brushed her lips with his. "I seem to remember someone I know rather well proposing we care for *anyone* who was sick."

"A lot has happened since then and you know it." Lisbeth's rising volume caused everyone to turn and stare. She leaned in and lowered her voice. "Her baby is dead. If the praetor sends you to face the senate, you don't need to give them reason to blame you for the death of one of their children. And I'd hate to think what would happen if she dies and—"

"Shhhh. Tomorrow has enough worries of its own."

"But she could—"

"Lisbeth, her husband has clearly abandoned her. Many of the senators have left town. I know you can see it's a difficult time for her, but what you may not see is that this could be good news for us. If there aren't many senators left to rally, Xystus will be free to reinstate my solicitorship on his own."

"Wait." Lisbeth pulled Cyprian back into the alcove. "Contrary to what you and Maggie may think of me, I'm not made of stone. I'll help her." She jerked her head in the direction of the crowd staring at them. "But these people whom you seem so happy to welcome back into the fold are the same backstabbing cowards who walked out on us."

"They are."

"And all is forgiven? No questions asked? Is that wise?"

"Is it not enough that followers of Christ have to fight against the court of public opinion? How will it help the dying in Carthage if Christians bicker among themselves?" Cyprian clasped her shoulders, a stern look in his eyes. "Neither you nor I can claim to be free of mistakes." He didn't have to list the reasons for the tangled emotions in his voice. His decision to marry Ruth had changed everything for both of them. "These good men and women had to swallow a great deal of pride to come to our aid. Being here is the same as admitting they were wrong. I must forgive them."

"I'm all for grace, but what if the new proconsul makes them a better offer? Food for their bellies? Their properties restored? Assurances of safety for their families? Who's to say they won't desert you again?"

The meaning of his heavy sigh was not lost on her. Cyprian was disappointed in her inability to back him up, and frankly, so was she.

His fingers dug into her shoulders as if he was attempting to pull her back from a dangerous ledge. "When the soldiers came for Christ, he looked about the garden and found he stood alone." Cyprian released her. "Do I deserve better than our Lord?"

"You're right. You can choose to trust whomever you like just as you can foolishly choose to go before the praetor." She peeled from his grasp. "But forgive me if I sleep with one eye open."

"If I fail before the praetor, I want to know I've left you surrounded by friends, people who can help you do whatever you must to take our family home." Cyprian brought her hand to his lips. "A few days. It's all I'm asking."

Lisbeth let her gaze sand the ragged group staring at her. They distrusted her as much as she distrusted them. These were not her friends. She fastened her apprehension on Cyprian. "Three days."

22

MAGGIE COULDN'T HELP THE little flutter of pride when her mother congratulated her on Eggie's recovery and told her to transfer his vaporizer to someone in greater need. Maybe Mom was beginning to see that she wasn't a total screwup.

"Cool your jets, Eggie. This will only take a second." Maggie freed the silky fabric draped over the tent. The stowaway's seal-gray eyes peered at her through the tepee stakes. "What are you looking at?" She shook out the cloth.

"You." Eggie grinned. "You don't talk or look like anyone I've ever met before."

"Well, stare at something else."

Although her patient had definitely gained strength since Mom arrived and shot him full of antibiotics, he was still a frightful mess. Brown crusty scabs dotted his face. Cracks deep as a Texas blacktop in August split his lips. His hair was a tangled bird's nest her own mother couldn't tame, and her mother thought she could conquer everything.

"You're beautiful." Eggie's voice was still raspy from healing pustules in his throat.

"My mom says measles can ruin your eyesight." Maggie lifted the tripod she'd cobbled together, taking care to keep the frame intact so she wouldn't have to reassemble it for the next patient.

Eggie pushed up on his elbows. "I see things others do not."

"Those are hallucinations from the high fever."

He glanced around the room. "See the cloisonné vase on the pedestal?"

Maggie looked over her shoulder "What do you know about cloisonné?"

"It's Greek. A copy, but a fairly expensive one." Eggie pointed at the wall mural. "Rural and common in flavor. Most likely a Peiraikos." He directed her gaze to the floor. "The mosaic is Roman in design, but judging from the color combinations, the artist was Etruscan." He smirked at her surprise. "As you can tell, I have a very refined appreciation of beauty. So when I say your beauty is of more value than any of these things"—he scooped her hand and brought it to his lips—"you may take my observations on the highest authority."

"Okay, anyone who knows the difference between cloisonné and a mosaic has my attention."

"Finally." Eggie's grin tilted mischievously toward his dimple. "I didn't think I stood a chance of redirecting those magnificent eyes from our heroic fisherman."

"Don't know what you're talking about."

"I've seen you sketching him when you think no one is looking."

Heat swept up her neck and flamed scarlet on her cheeks. Her free hand slid to her pocket where she'd hidden the small pen-and-ink sketch she'd finished late last night. Maggie wasn't going to talk about Barek, not to anyone. "And you came by this appreciation of art while swabbing the decks of fishing vessels?"

"Give me a kiss and I'll tell you how I came to possess my appreciation."

Maggie removed her hand. "I don't need you to teach me about art, or kissing." She folded the tripod and started to leave but something inside her screamed *Stay!*

What was it about this guy? Maggie tucked the tripod under her arm. "So why would you tell me your secrets?"

Eggie crammed a pillow behind his back. "Because I trust you?"

Trust? Nobody trusted her. Not her mother. Not her father. And especially not Barek. She gave Eggie a doubtful look. "Whatever."

"Really, I do." Okay, he was a smooth talker and possibly an escaped convict, but she liked him.

Eggie had a creative side he wasn't afraid to express. Maggie liked the hint of trouble brewing in the depths of his eyes. She liked how the richness of his voice beat inside her chest and made her feel alive.

"Girl! Come here!" an impatient male voice shouted at her from the doorway. "Quick!"

Maggie turned to find Titus waving her toward him. Never thought she would have considered Friar Tuck a lifesaver, but his interruption had saved her from doing something stupid like divulging her silly thoughts and giving Eggie the wrong idea.

Titus smoothed his bangs impatiently as Maggie made her way to him. "Tell your mother word has come of the new proconsul's arrival. I'm heading to the harbor to meet him."

"Now?" Maggie stared after his hurried exit, then turned to Eggie. "We are in so much trouble."

Her fright must have shown on her face because Eggie took her hand and asked, "Why does the new proconsul's arrival matter to you?"

"He doesn't. It's the emperor who sent him. I've read all about Valerian and everybody's thinking he's wonderful, but history records him as a jerk who thinks Christians should be eliminated."

"Whoa! You talk faster than a runaway horse. History? What records are you talking about?"

Her mouth fell silent. Maggie had once again said too much. "Never mind."

"Do these history records also say the great Valerian is a pompous, self-righteous pig who's more concerned about keeping Rome together than his family?" Eggie let his shoulders fall back upon his pillow. "I hope the Sassanids remove the old man's head."

Maggie stepped back, unsure if he was teasing or if he was an emperor-lover setting her up. "You talk like you know him."

Eggie lifted his head and eyed her coolly. "Valerian is my grandfather." He ripped his sleeve from his wrist. "I will bear his mark to my grave."

"Holy cow." She shuttled back even farther, knocking over a chamber pot as her eyes skimmed the premises for Barek. "Who are you?"

"Publius Licinius Egnatius Marinianus. Youngest son of Gallienus Augustus and Cornelia Salonina." He nodded his head in a half bow. "At your service, my lady." For once he wasn't smiling, and neither was she. "Are you going to tell your fisherman friend he saved the successor to the throne?"

All of Barek's warnings beat in her ears. "What do you think?"

"Please"—he reached for her hand, his eyes pleading—"if your father sends me home, my fate will mirror that of my brothers."

"What happened to them?"

"They pursued the purple and now they are dead."

"What does that even mean?"

"To see who was worthy of the throne, my grandfather sent my oldest brother, Valerianus, to deal with the troubled Illyrian provinces and my middle brother, Saloninus, was sent to help my father deal with the Gauls. After both brothers were killed, my grandfather expected me to take their place, to prepare for the day I would succeed my father. When I confessed my love of sculpture and my distaste for his bloody wars, he called me the son of a Bithynian Greek witch and had this little reminder of my forfeited place in this world branded upon my wrist. That's when I decided to take my leave."

Maggie remembered how upset Barek had become when he saw Eggie's tattoo. "How do I know you're not really some criminal or an escaped slave or something?"

"Because like me, my beautiful little goddess, you see what no one else can see . . . the beauty of truth."

23

THE PORT OF OSTIA stank like fish, brackish water, and moldy wheat. Maximus lifted a piece of linen to his nose and continued his inspection of the towering ship. "I'm to be ferried to my new position aboard a grain freighter?"

"Your orders said 'first available ship.'" Kaeso hoisted a trunk to his bare shoulder. "At least it is not an exotic animal transport vessel."

Stevedores rolled large, empty wooden casks up the gangplank. Maximus had not slept a wink since Hortensia's carriage dumped him and Kaeso at the port three days earlier. "I have died and gone to Hades." He let out a long, dramatic sigh, certain nothing would wash this salty bitterness from his mouth, and trudged the briny two-board bridge with the zeal of a man going to his execution.

Before he was settled in his hammock belowdeck, favorable winds snapped a billow into the sails and hauled them from the port. They'd not been in deep water more than a day when the weather turned foul. The boat pitched and tossed Maximus as if he were a worm in a cocoon.

He pried the hemp with his fingers and shouted at Kaeso, "What in the name of the gods is happening?!"

"Shall I go see?"

"No. Another minute in this rank hole and I shall lose my mind." He flipped to the floor. The hard landing upon his belly emptied the last of the sustenance he'd managed to choke down. Maximus pushed himself to his hands and knees, then clawed his way to the ladder. He climbed to the deck and poked his head through the opening. The horizon toward which they plowed was black with storm and menace. He suggested to the captain that they turn around, but his pleas could not be heard over the crew's prayers begging the gods to allow the rain to follow them to Carthage.

"One season of moisture," the captain had explained, "is all it would take to break Africa's drought and transform the breadbasket of Rome from brown to green. And if the good proconsul prayed hard enough, the rain might wash away the sickness marching toward Rome faster than the angry Persians."

The massive ship rose, then dipped sharply. Masts creaked and swayed in the pounding rain. Maximus did not care what became of those pompous dignitaries who'd bowed to his mother-in-law. He slunk back to his sling and cursed the woman who'd arranged his exile to Africa.

It would serve Hortensia right if he threw himself overboard and impaled her dreams of his rise to power upon the trident of Neptune. Instead, he sipped a camphorous mixture of crushed horse heal root and warm wine, but Kaeso's sure cure for seasickness failed to hold his nausea at bay. Hand clasped over his mouth, Maximus was once again forced to make a hasty dash for the ladder. He staggered to the ship's railing and hurled a sour offering into the saltwater sanding his face.

It was time he faced the horrible truth: he was neither a politician nor a man equipped to tame savages raised from a primordial sea. And since he'd not convinced his mother-in-law otherwise, he was not even a very good actor. Maximus swiped at the bile trailing his lip. Oh, that the gods would put him out of his misery.

"Master!" Kaeso pulled him back from the edge and shouted into the howling winds, "Come below! Land has been sighted. You cannot arrive at your new post looking like a drowned tiger cub."

"I prefer to wear my traveling clothes. Men who wear snowy white togas end up with daggers in their backs or their legs sawed off in their sleep."

"Come, master."

Huddled between their hammocks, Maximus clung to a low beam as Kaeso peeled away his wet tunic. It no longer mattered that the sailors snickered and pointed at his pale frame. "The gods have left me to die without ever having applause echo in my ears, Kaeso."

His servant dipped a sponge in a basin of fresh water and squeezed it over Maximus's head. "Have you considered using your time in Carthage to learn the theater techniques of Terence?"

"Terence?" Maximus felt his briny face crack with a faint smile, his first since Hortensia had rearranged his fate. "His name is known on every Roman stage." Water trickled over the contours of Maximus's body and puddled at his feet. "I adore his work. *Hecyra* is my favorite comedy of all time. Sostra, the pushy mother-in-law, is written so true to form." Maximus extended his arm and Kaeso ran the sponge to his fingertips. "Is it too much to hope that a backwater hole has a theater and a company that practices the philosophies of the greatest actor the world has ever seen?"

"Terence hails from Carthage and I've heard a marvelous structure, with perfect acoustics and overlooking the harbor, has been resurrected in his name." Kaeso held out a fresh garment.

"But would they want me?"

"Think of the prestige the theater would gain if a man of your political stature joined their company."

Maximus lifted his arms and the silky tunic slid easily over the intriguing possibilities whirling in his head. "They *would* be lucky to have me, wouldn't they?"

"Do your duty to Rome"—Kaeso draped the heavy woolen toga over Maximus's shoulder—"and when you go home, Valerian will be obligated to grant you anything you desire . . . perhaps your own stage, or better yet, your mother-in-law's head upon a spike."

By the time their ship had moored, the rain had stopped and Maximus's spirits had lifted. Gulls swooped overhead and steam rose from the miles of wet concrete that circled the harbor.

"Galerius Maximus?" On the dock, a monkey-faced man with a bowl haircut and apelike arms summoned him from a golden two-wheeled cart. "Proconsul, your chariot awaits."

Maximus wrinkled his nose and whispered under his breath, "Kaeso, are you sure this dump has a theater?"

His servant shrugged. "You will do well to remember that you are already onstage."

Maximus gathered the hem of his toga, plastered on the aloof expression his mother-in-law always used on him, and followed Kaeso's glistening back down the gangplank.

The gangly man leaped from the chariot and rushed forward. "I am Titus Cicero." His fine robes and polished red shoes were those of a patrician. "I'm sorry to burden your arrival with such troubling news, but there is sickness in Carthage." He offered two white cloths. "You and your man might want to cover your noses."

Maximus couldn't deny the wind carried an unpleasant odor. "I thought the stench merely the scent of barbarism." The hint of disdain he'd injected into his response, so reminiscent of Hortensia's voice, had done its trick, for Titus immediately took an appropriate step back. Maximus tied the cloth around his growing smile. "I suspect this sickness has been greatly exaggerated."

"I wish that were so, my lord."

My lord. No one had addressed him with such respect in quite some time. Perhaps Kaeso was right. No one here need know about the black eye his father had given his family. This was his chance to make a new name for himself. A respected name. A powerful name. This was his chance to finally have what *he* wanted.

Maximus straightened his shoulders and asked boldly, "Have you a theater in this rat's hole?"

Titus's face looked puzzled. "Yes."

"How does it compare to the one in Rome?" Maximus could tell his driver thought his questions odd but he didn't care. He was lord here.

"I've been to both. This one is far superior, my lord."

"Take me."

"But wouldn't you rather see—"

"The theater. Now!"

"Very well."

The closer they came to the city, the more fetid the smell. Crusty brown treetops crackled in the hot breeze sweeping in from the desert. Carthage burned hotter than his worst imaginings. Maximus dabbed at his neck with his personal linen. Perhaps he'd been a bit shortsighted not to beg the rain gods to wash the air clean and cool. He'd maintained his breathing exercises as best he could on that horrible sea crossing, but even he could not hold his breath for a year.

Titus drove far too slow, dropping useless tidbits of information like bread crumbs Maximus could follow back to his ship should he desire to get out of this pigsty while he still could. "From our spectacular man-made harbor, the city is accessed via one of its twelve guarded gates." Titus motioned to the stone lintel marked *Qrt Hdcht* . . . Carthage New City.

"Move along, man," Maximus ordered.

Titus flicked the reins and the white horses trotted past refuse clogging the gutters and bodies covered in powdery ash.

Maximus pressed his mask to his nose. "So this is why there is no one to welcome me?"

"I told you, there is sickness. We are battling *two* plagues. The death toll continues to rise. The lime kilns of Egypt are burning night and day, but they cannot keep up with the demand of our burial needs. I suggest you reopen the cemeteries as quickly as possible."

"Why are the burial grounds closed?"

"Aspasius thought it . . . best."

"That is absolute folly. The emperor has directed me to clean up this mess. Open the cemeteries immediately."

A very pleased smile drew Titus's lips apart and exposed large gums and small teeth. "Good to hear that our great emperor believes Carthage a worthy investment."

"Rome fought three wars to own this port. I wouldn't be here if they were going to let it rot."

Titus smiled. "Then Rome will want you to do what's best for the province, I'm sure." He clicked the reins. "You'll have a full court, a military and civil staff, a privy council, a full consortium of well-connected dignitaries, and several subaltern clerks at your disposal."

"And which one are you?"

"I, sir, am one of your more tenured senators."

"I won't be relying on senatorial rule." Maximus nearly laughed out loud at the shock on Titus's face.

"In the past, the emperor endeavored to keep the senators in good humor," Titus pouted.

Maximus could do an intoxicating monologue using the senator's dramatic facial expressions alone. "And why would he do that?"

"The details of the city's government come under our supervision, and so far it is the senators of Carthage who have managed to maintain law and order. We should be rewarded for our efforts."

Maximus flicked a fly from his toga. "Rome is fighting wars on nearly every border. Whether the details of this little frontier outpost are handled with good humor is of little concern to the emperor."

"The emperor knows the only extra stores of grain and oil lay in the silos of the African provinces." Titus lifted his snub nose. "I know because I own the majority of the surplus."

Apparently there was a learning curve to ruling without question. The first rule was: find out who believed themselves to be in power. The second: let them continue in their error.

Maximus fanned his face with the linen Titus had given him. "And what would make you happy, my most esteemed senator?"

"Aspasius left many pressing matters . . . unattended." A hint of a threat lowered the senator's enunciation of *pressing matters.*

"Such as?"

"Persecution of the Christians. Some say it is a necessity. Others claim it barbaric." Titus's gaze slid toward his. "What say you?"

"Unlike the last proconsul, I do not view Christians as unprofitable members of society or a miserable bunch of weaklings. They are simply ill-informed and misguided plebeians." Maximus pondered Titus's huge sigh. Expressing relief for the welfare of plebs must be a southern thing. "Once these Christians understand how their refusal to acknowledge the gods of Rome has brought about plague on this province, their thinking should be easily corrected, don't you agree?"

"An undertaking that would consume a considerable amount of your time; therefore I'm offering my services."

"What do you know of these Christians?"

Titus shrugged. "Only that they are peaceful people."

"Peaceful people who spread sickness and death."

Titus pulled hard on the reins. "Quite the opposite, my lord. They are doing everything within their powers to help curb the tragedy that has befallen Carthage."

"So you are a sympathizer with these Christians?"

"I'm simply saying that I'm actually quite versed in the law. If you were to appoint me as judge, you would be relieved of the nasty duty of sorting these types of matters."

"Are you asking for special favor?"

"Simply offering my services."

Maximus tugged at the neck of his tunic, once again mindful of the danger of wearing the white toga. "Tell me the details of this role of judge."

Titus eyed him as if he had two heads and no common sense. "Court is held in the Forum. A prosecutor presents the evidence and a defender presents his defense. And the judge, a man of means and high standing in the city, decides the fate of the accused."

"I know how trials work. My question is: will everyone in the city come to see the proconsul's murderer tried?"

"My lord, you will be pleased to know that even the frontier provinces have a keen appreciation of justice. You can rest assured this trial will be well attended and fairly judged if you allow me to—"

"I shall act as judge."

24

LISBETH TREATED THE SICK and more kept coming. Even if she could climb the stairs and sink into the little mattress beneath the eaves, she wouldn't be able to sleep, not when there was so much at stake.

For Maggie's sake, Lisbeth had kept to herself her reservations concerning the plan Titus and Cyprian had devised to free her mother. Titus was to greet the new proconsul and work to get himself appointed judge while Cyprian presented his case for reinstatement of his proper place in society before the praetor.

This afternoon, Lisbeth had washed her hands and helped her husband dress in one of Titus's best togas. She'd even followed him to the door and kissed him soundly. But when he set off with his neatly written petition tucked beneath his cloak, she couldn't watch.

Worst-case scenarios played in her head as the hours dragged by and no word came from Cyprian or Titus. At about sunset, her jubilant husband had returned. The current praetor, a longtime family friend indebted to Cyprian's father, had readily restored Cyprian's citizenship along with his right to practice law. She'd worried about Cyprian being a wanted man for nothing. Xystus had not asked to see the note. Even more surprising, the praetor agreed with Cyprian: to delay Magdalena's trial by waiting upon Senate approval of Cyprian's petition would not be in the best interest of the city. Already, maintaining law and order was becoming more difficult. No one wanted Rome to send in more troops.

Cyprian was so encouraged by the meeting, he felt certain he could present her mother's case before Xystus and have the trumped-up charges dismissed before the new proconsul had a chance to unpack his bags.

"And if Xystus does not rule in Mama's favor, what then?"

"There is that slight possibility. In that case, your mother would be forced to stand trial, thus the precaution of having Titus appointed as judge."

Neither of them commented on the fact that Titus had yet to return from his treacherous errand. His delay was nearly as disconcerting as the idea of Mama's fate resting in the hands of Valerian's new man. Neither Valerian nor his appointees could be trusted. Cyprian, on the other hand, believed an emperor who'd arranged for all exiled bishops to be brought home was exhibiting a change of heart.

"Don't worry," Cyprian had said, "I'll make certain I present a pretrial case that leaves the praetor no choice but to dismiss the charges." The odds were in their favor, he had assured her, and her mother would never stand trial. "God has not forgotten us after all."

Cyprian seemed so grateful for the opportunity to witness the workings of God, how could she argue with that? When Lisbeth stopped to count all that God had done for her in the past eighteen years—bringing her to this place, helping her find her mother, letting her fall in love with an incredible man, and most important, giving her a beautiful daughter—she would be a fool not to count on God to work things out for her mother. But she wasn't willing to go so far as to claim the ease with which Cyprian had reentered public life was a sign that God intended to spare him ... or that Valerian would prove a leopard could change its spots.

Lisbeth could not argue that the restoration of her husband's place in his world was a giant victory, one history had not recorded.

Lisbeth checked with the servants one more time. Titus had not returned. Had he stopped by the prison to inform her mother? Willing her exhausted legs to move, she climbed the shallow steps to the bedroom tucked beneath the eaves of the villa. She lit the oil lamp and opened the window. The desert breeze did little to cool the small space. She stripped from her tunic and poured water into the basin. Though she was in a hurry to run her errand, she indulged in a quick sponge bath. She checked the gash on her foot from the pottery shard. It appeared to be healing slower than she would have liked. Every step was a painful reminder of the damage an incensed Rome could bring down on this house.

Lisbeth redressed the wound and exchanged her old tunic, covered with phlegm, for a fresh one. She grabbed her bag. Her supplies were low. She hurried down the back steps to the kitchen. Chickens roosting near the door squawked at the intrusion. She stepped inside and was surprised to find Eggie watching Naomi and Junia trying to teach Maggie the art of kneading wheat meal and water into a usable dough. If Aisa were here, he would beam at Maggie's progress.

Lisbeth remembered watching these same girls make popcorn over an open flame and now here they were, acting like responsible adults, even though Junia and Naomi hadn't matured past the point she'd left them. It was good to see that although Maggie was a foot taller and far more filled out than Junia, Maggie's changes hadn't lessened the bond the two had formed the night an ox trampled Ruth to death in a tenement alley. On the other hand,

Naomi's glare communicated sheer disdain for Maggie's transformation.

Maggie looked up from her dough, flour dusting the end of her nose. "Mom? Where are you going?"

"To check on your grandparents." Lisbeth loaded fresh bread into her pack.

Maggie wiped her hands on her dress and went to check the pot of water sitting on the grate above the fire. "But there's a curfew."

"I'll be careful."

"Does Dad know you're going?"

"He's busy preparing your grandmother's case."

"So you didn't tell him?"

Lisbeth stuffed a jug of wine into her bag. "No. I didn't tell him."

"Take me with you. I'm dying to see G-Pa and Jaddah." Her daughter passed the pot of boiling water to Eggie. Since the handsome young man's recovery, he'd become Maggie's shadow. Lisbeth could tell from the way his eyes never left Maggie's, Eggie was smitten. Too bad she and Maggie were leaving for home as soon as her mama was a free woman. Maggie deserved the attention of a nice young man, but someone from her own century. Lisbeth shoved her longings to the back of her mind. She didn't want her daughter to spend her life torn between two very different worlds.

"That's not a good idea." Lisbeth hefted the heavy bag to her shoulder.

"What if you run into trouble or need help?"

"I'll be fine."

"With that limp? You couldn't outrun Metras." Maggie wiped wheat dust from her nose. "Please, Mom. I haven't been out of this house since Dad brought me here."

"Navigating this city is not like going to the mall, Mags." She saw her daughter recoil, face flaming as if she'd been slapped. "I'm sorry, I—"

Her daughter's eyes burned into hers with a look of total disbelief. "I got myself here, didn't I?"

Her words were a scalpel meant to carve a serious dent in the notion that Lisbeth could protect her forever. "Okay, get your cloak. But once we leave these doors, you don't take a step out of my sight. Understand?"

"Is that even possible?" Maggie whispered. "You tracked me down in another century."

"Do you want to go or not?"

METRAS WAS waiting at the door, his extended cane barring their exit. His lips hugged his bare gums in a pained expression, raising the possibility he'd overheard their conversation about going out without telling Cyprian and didn't approve. "You remember Quinta?" he asked Lisbeth.

She was in no mood for a lecture. "The feisty grandmother who followed Felicissimus and half the church out the door with her grandchild on one hip and a giant grudge against Cyprian on the other?"

"That's the one."

From the set of Metras's jaw, Lisbeth knew she was in for a good head rapping if she tried to get past without hearing him out. "Why are we discussing Quinta?"

"I asked her to come help us."

"Well, she didn't. I guess she's content with her writ of libellus."

"She's torn that worthless piece of paper to shreds." Metras dragged his hand over his thinning hair. "She would have been here if she could."

"Why didn't she come with the rest of you?"

"Too sick."

"Why didn't you say so earlier? Send one of our carts for her immediately."

He leaned his entire weight against the cane. "She won't come. Doesn't think you'd want her . . ." He lowered his eyes, leaving his explanation for her to finish on her own.

"Let me see if I've got this straight: she trusted that lying weasel Felicissimus and his counterfeit protections against Rome, but she won't trust me? She's seen me treat people I didn't like."

"I didn't say Quinta's thinking made sense," Metras said. "I said she's sick and needs help."

Lisbeth could feel Maggie's eyes boring into her back. "All right, I'll make a house call. But I'm not making any promises."

Metras's satisfied smile revealed an enviable full heart. "Forgiveness is the sweetest honey you'll ever eat." His eyes skated between her and Maggie. "But sometimes you've got to be a persistent bear to get a pawful." He lowered his cane. "Thank you."

Persistent? Lisbeth wasn't one to give up easily, but even a bear will abandon a honeycomb if he gets stung enough times. At least that was the reason she gave whenever she backed away from this growing rift with her daughter. Had she really become so hardened and thick-skinned from all the years of work and death?

Lisbeth opted to visit Quinta first, praying that along the way she and Maggie would find more than the supplies she needed. Maybe, if they were lucky, she and her daughter would stumble upon a pinch of grace. Something that would allow them to forgive one another the way Cyprian had forgiven the church members who'd hurt him so badly.

"Remember, stay close," she whispered to Maggie. "Draw your cloth across your face."

Huge grain freighters sent from the capital waited in the harbor. Valerian had ordered the storage silos of Africa emptied. Full-time guards patrolled the mountains of corn piled high upon the quays, awaiting shipment to Rome. Not a single kernel was to be distributed to the starving in Carthage. Whatever Rome won by the sword it secured with the plow and made certain the citizens of the capital were the ones who enjoyed the bounty. It was a wonder, Lisbeth mused, that the desperate and oppressed had not rioted. The closer the two women came to the heart of the tenements, the more intense the damage. Once-robust neighborhoods had taken on the skeletal appearance of the terminally ill. Buildings with peeling paint and dying shrubbery sat empty, the doors kicked in by looters. Drought, famine, and plague had ravaged the city much the way Lisbeth's refusal to get behind Maggie's campaign to bring Cyprian to the twenty-first century had nearly destroyed her relationship with her daughter.

Desperate to locate some common ground she and her daughter could use as a foundation for rebuilding, Lisbeth asked, "So what do you know about Eggie?"

"Nothing." Obviously Maggie was still stinging from Lisbeth's insistence that she stay close.

"I saw you sketching him the other day. He seems pretty chatty to me."

"His mother is a Bithynian Greek."

"That's it?"

"His older brothers are dead."

"That's sad." Lisbeth steered Maggie around some bloated bodies. "What about his father?"

She shrugged. "They don't get along."

Bull's-eye! The barb lodged and deflated Lisbeth's hopes of coming to a point of shared grace. "Is that why Eggie ran away?"

"Are we almost there?" Maggie's change of subject meant this discussion was finished.

Kicking herself for once again pushing too hard, Lisbeth turned down an alley with vulgar graffiti scribbled on walls. Several doors down, a wooden tooth swayed overhead. "We might find some supplies in the dentist shop." Lisbeth lifted the latch and cautiously peeked inside. Dusty abandonment wafted from the quiet sanctuary. "All clear." She waved Maggie in, instructing her to leave the door open to allow the moon to light the dark space. From the corner of her eye, she saw Maggie draw something shiny from her sash. "What is that?"

"A knife."

"Where in the world did you get a knife?"

"I bought it from a local vendor outside the airport."

"Oh." She couldn't believe Maggie had thought ahead, which was more than she'd done. "Well, hopefully you won't need it." Once Lisbeth's eyes adjusted to the dimness, she could see they'd come too late. "Looters have already taken the tools and herbs."

Outside, the stamp of hooves on the cobblestones was quickly followed by the rattle of chains and buckles. Lisbeth grabbed Maggie and pressed both of them behind the door. A slit between the leather hinges afforded Lisbeth a view of what was happening in the alley. The centurion sitting atop a pawing horse was flanked by foot soldiers with torches.

"Secure the perimeter," the commander ordered.

One of the soldiers strode to the threshold of the dentist shop. Lisbeth could feel Maggie's fingers digging deeper into her arm. Any moment she expected her claustrophobic daughter to bolt, to scream that she couldn't breathe, but she was still as a statue, the knife raised and poised near Lisbeth's ear. The soldier extended his torch through the shop's doorway and waved the flames. "This place has already been stripped." He backed out and moved on.

Neither Lisbeth nor Maggie dared speak, let alone move until the sound of iron cleats retreated beyond their hearing. This scare was too close for comfort. "You're going back to the villa," Lisbeth whispered.

"Only if you do." Maggie's voice had a steel edge.

"Sometimes you're as stubborn as your father."

"That's what you get when you cross a mule with a wildcat."

"Where did you hear that?"

"G-Pa."

Lisbeth couldn't help but smile at the effort it was taking for Maggie to push her away. "Not sure which one you think I am and I don't think I want to know." She kissed Maggie's cheek. "Come on. Stay alert. And keep that knife handy."

Lisbeth did not know what to expect once they finally found Quinta's apartment, but instinct told her it could be bad. Lisbeth assigned Maggie lookout duty, then knocked lightly so as not to alert the neighbors. No moans, no cries, even worse—no sound at all. She knocked again and noticed a lamp's flicker in the apartment across the street.

"Quick." She pushed against the unlocked door. Scents of rotting hay and wet feathers mingled with the stench of soiled sheets, sweat, and vomit. "Don't touch anything," she warned Maggie, who was pinching her mask against her nose.

It took a moment for Lisbeth's eyes to adjust to the dim light filtering through the cracks in the closed shutters. Bodies. Two of them were huddled together in the middle of the sleeping mat. Hard to tell if they were dead or alive. She could hear the sounds of a crowd gathering outside. The moment she declared those inside dead, looters would storm the house and take anything they could get their hands on.

Lisbeth opened the door and hissed, "Plague!" The curious scattered. For now. From their hungry faces, she could tell they wouldn't be held off for long. "We'll have to work fast. Find the lamp."

With surprising efficiency, Maggie located oil and flint. A few quick strikes and she had the wick flaming. "Now what?"

Lisbeth squatted beside Quinta. A faint pulse beat against the fingers she pressed to the carotid. "Now the real work begins."

25

CYPRIAN DRAGGED HIS HAND across the ache in his neck. "So Galerius Maximus comes to town and all of a sudden the praetor promptly packs his litter, loads his slaves with anything they can carry, and leaves?"

"So it would appear," Titus said. "And Maximus has also skirted the senate and appointed himself as judge."

"I'm not surprised Maximus wants to be judge, but I am surprised the new proconsul would choose such a blatant affront to precedent as his first official action. Did Xystus offer no contest?"

"None."

"What does Xystus know about this emissary of Valerian that we don't?"

"Perhaps it's not as bad as you think. Maximus is a vain little banty rooster, intent on standing before crowds, but he seemed amenable enough toward Christians."

"Did he seem as benevolent toward murderers?"

Titus gave a one-shouldered shrug. "He might draw the line at having someone come after his leg with a saw, but who wouldn't?"

"If Maximus finds Magdalena to be the property of the state, her ownership reverts to him and he can do with her as he wishes." Cyprian's eyes burned from the strain of researching the legal parchments spread upon the desk of Titus. Now that Maximus had run Xystus out of town and appointed himself judge, Cyprian's hopes of having the trial dismissed in the pretrial stage had been destroyed. Cyprian didn't dare go to trial before a possibly hostile judge without every angle carefully researched and supported.

"I would feel much better if you were sitting in the judge's seat, Titus. Is there nothing we can do to overturn the proconsul's self-appointment?"

"Unfortunately our shiny new proconsul glows with the emperor's blessing, and the glare has blinded those left in the Senate. Our best bet is to stay within Maximus's good graces and pray Valerian's recall of exiled bishops is a sign of the throne's changed heart."

Cyprian sighed. "In that case, my goal will be to discredit the state's witness and convince the proconsul he needs the healer to help him restore this portion of the empire."

"I know you are a student of Tertullian." Titus's brow cocked over his steepled fingers. "But I have the original works of Antoninus Pius squirreled away, and there may be a loophole we have overlooked."

"We cannot leave any stone unturned. Fetch them, quickly."

Titus mounted a small stool. His long fingers searched the top shelf and retrieved a scroll tucked behind some urns. He brushed a puff of dust from the century-old text. "Care to do the honors?"

Cyprian fingered the treasured work, unable to dismiss the pang of longing for the shelves of simple parchments he'd left behind in his library, the ones scratched out some two hundred years earlier by men who sought to know only one thing about their future: where they would spend eternity.

"Your collection rivals the scriptures Caecilianus and I had collected."

"Justice and mercy suffered an irreplaceable loss with the destruction of your property." Titus's face was truly sad.

Gratitude overwhelmed Cyprian. Were it not for the surprising generosity of a man whose newfound faith had transformed him from enemy to friend, Cyprian would have faced tomorrow unprepared. "I'm finding faith and friends are the possessions that matter, brother."

Pontius burst through the door waving a small scrap of paper. "An urgent message has come from the bishops of Numidia."

His deacon's unusual distress led Cyprian and Titus to abandon the law.

Dearest brothers in Carthage,

We write as captives of the faith. Valerian has issued a new edict, one that says bishops should be imprisoned or put to death. His orders have sent us to the mines to work with half our hair shorn and insufficient food and clothing. On the sixth of this month, Bishop Sixtus and four of his faithful deacons refused to recant their love of our Lord. They were put to death. We have been told that senators and knights, and anyone else of rank who does not bow to the gods of Rome, will likewise lose all his goods and properties. If these men persist in their "heresies," they shall also forfeit their lives and their women shall be exiled. Only God's divine intervention will save us. Praying he will also intervene on your behalf.

Do not believe, dear brothers, that Cyprian has been summoned from exile for your good. He has been brought home to die.

"WHAT DOES it say?" Titus asked anxiously.

"Lisbeth was right." There was no point in hiding what would soon become public knowledge. Cyprian handed him the parchment. "The end is coming."

Titus's face acquired a ghostly pallor. "Senators executed?" His shaking hands rattled the parchment. "My wife and daughter exiled? What have I done?"

"Settle down, man. Our one God has not forsaken us." Cyprian slid a chair beneath Titus's buckling legs. "Pontius, take a letter thanking our brothers in Numidia for their warning. Enclose seven hundred denarii for the relief of the saints in the mines."

Titus rolled the parchment and tapped it on his knee. "You can't risk going before Maximus."

"If our end is coming, what good will it do to hide?"

26

MAGGIE RAN ALL THE way from Quinta's apartment to Titus's villa to fetch the cart. If she didn't hurry, the sun would break over the horizon before they had Quinta safely delivered. She had to get this right if she wanted to see her grandparents. That run-in with the soldiers had made Mom really jumpy. She never would have agreed to Maggie's suggestion that she go for help if there had been any other choice.

While her mother instructed Barek and Eggie on how to move Quinta from the apartment to the wagon without spilling her from the soiled sheet, Maggie scooped up the limp baby and carried him from the squalid room. His diaper was wet and sour and his tiny body was speckled with the same red rash that had left brown scabs on Eggie's face.

Once the guys had Quinta settled in the cart, Maggie placed the baby in her arms. If her mother's stomach buzzed with this same sense of satisfaction every time she helped someone, no wonder she didn't mind the hours at the hospital. Helping people get well did feel rewarding. Maggie's gaze cut to her mother. Earlier, her mother had been telling Metras how much she didn't appreciate what Quinta had done. Now here she was, holding Quinta's hand and talking as if all were forgiven.

Throughout Maggie's life she'd tried to be brave, to be like her mother—an uphill battle for someone with no interest in the peri-odic table. But it wasn't until she saw gratitude seeping from Quin-ta's eyes that she realized the characteristic she most wanted to imitate was her mom's compassion.

Back at the villa, Barek and Eggie resumed the endless job of filling vaporizer pots while Maggie paid extra close attention to the construction of the breathing tents for Quinta and her grandbaby.

"They should rest now." Mom closed her backpack and in-spected Maggie's work. "These tents are a work of art."

That buzzy feeling hit Maggie's stomach again and sparked a smile. "Maybe I'll make one for my senior art show."

"Good to know you're going back to college. That I haven't wasted the price of a nice luxury car on your first semester." Mom stopped and looked at her. "You are planning on coming home with me, right?"

"I'm sorry I didn't tell you when I left school, but I had to try to save him."

Mom wiped her hands on the front of her dress. "Of course you did. You're *my* daughter too, you know?" She slung her back-pack strap over her shoulder and offered Maggie her hand. "Come on. Let's go tell your father we've rounded up another one of his lost sheep."

They found Cyprian in the dimly lit library, the shutters sealed tightly. Dad and Titus were hunched over a bunch of dusty-looking papers. It was clear from Titus's mussed hair and wild eyes that something was terribly wrong.

"Cyprian? What's happened?" From the crack in Mom's voice, she sensed bad news. "Tell me."

Dad handed Mom a piece of paper. "Valerian."

The color drained from her mother's face and Maggie knew she wasn't the only one who'd flipped to the end of the history books to see how her father's story ended.

Mom managed to speak despite her trembling lip. "You can't defend my mother."

"I've tried to tell him!" Titus blurted out. "Maximus has removed Xystus, appointed himself as judge, and set Magdalena's trial for tomorrow."

Maggie put voice to the question frozen on her mother's lips. "So does this mean Maximus will come after you, Dad?"

"We're searching the law." Cyprian was trying his best to appear confident. In all of her research, Maggie had never found a record of her grandmother's trial, but she and Mom both knew there was ample record of her father's death. And they both knew who was behind it.

"Maybe Titus could argue for a continuance or something," Mom muttered.

Her father shook his head.

"Why not?" Mom insisted. "It would at least give us time to think."

Dad put his hands on Mom's shoulders and led her to a nearby bench as if trying to steer a careening car back from the ledge. "The Goths are invading Rome from the east, the Germans are attacking the empire on the Rhine, and in Asia the great King Sapor is rallying the Persians. Valerian has sent Maximus here with one purpose: to secure his southern provinces. The new proconsul has a point to make. If I were ruler, I would make it at the murder trial of my predecessor, and I would start by discrediting me."

"But you have Aspasius's note," Mom argued. "The one that says you are a free man."

"We don't even know if the note will hold up," Titus said.

"But you seemed so certain."

"That was before my father's friend left town."

"Then Titus has to defend her and he can put me on the

stand," Mom said, the color rushing back to her cheeks with a vengeance.

"Absolutely not."

"I was there. I can tell them exactly what happened."

"You have only the word of servants to prove you were there." Dad's eyes were fierce, a look Maggie hadn't seen since Ruth's funeral when he declared he would not rest until Carthage was free of persecution.

Mom pulled a shiny, stainless steel saw from her backpack. "Here's your proof."

Dad's eyes widened. "Where did you get that?"

"From Mama's bag. But I'll say it's mine."

Maggie felt her whole world shift. Mom was basically offering herself up for Jaddah, and Dad wasn't having it.

He took the saw and crammed it into Mom's backpack and zipped it shut. "I don't want either of you at this trial, understood?"

"If you're going, I'm going," Mom said, not the least bit ruffled. "Don't even try to stop me."

Maggie jumped between them. "I'm going too."

"No you're not," both parents said simultaneously.

"Wait a minute," Maggie declared. "I'm eighteen. I can go anywhere I want to."

"Maybe in your world," Dad said. "But in my world, I'm your father and I say you are not going."

Maggie turned to her mother for support. "Can he do that?"

Lisbeth's slow sigh was a hard one to read. Either she didn't want to be in the middle or she was glad to have someone share the burden of being the bad guy. "He just did."

They may think her a baby, one they could tell where she could and could not go, but they wouldn't see her cry like one. "This isn't right." Maggie stormed from the library. Head down and eyes bleary, she crashed into something solid, something with warm arms that immediately wrapped around her in comfort.

"Whoa!" Eggie, his scars now faded, had her by the waist. "What's wrong, my little goddess?"

The tears she'd been fighting sprang free. "My parents have forbidden me to attend my grandmother's trial and it's going to be a bloodbath." She swiped her cheeks.

Eggie scanned the hall, including a brief glance over his shoulder, and grabbed her hand. "Come on." He led her through the maze of mats and out to a shady corner of the courtyard. "When is this trial?"

"Tomorrow."

"Then we've no time to waste."

"We?"

"Your father forbade you to go to the trial, right?"

"Didn't I just say that?" she said with a sniff.

"Think." Eggie was asking a lot considering he was still holding her hand. "Did he say you couldn't go into the market for more herbs?" His insistent squeeze flipped a mental breaker, and what he was asking registered.

Maggie's smile was not from her surprise at Eggie's suggestion, but rather her astonishment of how much they thought alike. "Now that you mention it, he didn't."

"While I was filling the pots for those two we just picked up, I noticed we were running dangerously low on eucalyptus."

Maggie nodded conspiratorially. "My father wouldn't want Quinta or her grandbaby to suffer because we lacked supplies."

Eggie's gleaming eyes were intoxicating. "In Rome, vendors line the path to the Forum. I'm sure it is the same here. If the herb vendor's booth happens to be within earshot of the witness stand, can you help what you overhear?"

Maggie smiled. "It would be a dereliction of my duty to let our supplies run low because of what I *might* overhear." She rose on her tiptoes, kissed Eggie's cheek, and whispered, "Too bad you will never be emperor."

"Ah, but then I would never have gotten that kiss or this one." He cupped her face with his hands and kissed her on the lips.

Maggie took a step back. She knew his lips, had watched the various changes in coloring during his illness, and saw now that they were healed. Yet somehow she didn't feel much from his kiss, not the way she would have hoped.

She stepped away from him in surprise, but Eggie just smiled and offered his crooked arm. "The moment the coast is clear, we shall head to the market. Shall we peruse the supplies and make our shopping list?"

She threaded her arm through his. "You're a good friend."

27

Barek searched the hall, the steaming pot of hot water he was lugging burning against his hands. "Eggie, can you . . . Eggie?" The man had been right behind him a moment ago. "Eggie!" Barek headed down the hall, past the open door to the courtyard. Laughter wafted to his ears. He stopped and surveyed the shadows. Movement caught his eye.

Eggie. And he was with someone. A woman. No. Maggie. And she was planting a kiss on his cheek.

"Maggie!" Barek dropped his jug of boiling water, unconcerned by the sizzle of his flesh, and stormed to the secluded corner of the garden. "What are you doing?" He unwrapped Maggie from Eggie's arms and dragged her clear of his reach.

"Barek." Maggie pounded on his arm. "Let me go."

"If he tried anything, I'll—"

"Stop acting like an older brother."

He didn't know why he should be surprised by her flippant attitude, but he was. "Somebody's got to watch out for you."

"I can take care of myself." Maggie jerked her arm free. "Not that it's any of your business, but I was thanking a friend."

"Thanking him for what?"

"Helping her empty chamber pots," Eggie said, grinning.

Barek wheeled and poked Eggie in the chest. "I've had enough of you and your starry-eyed advances toward this girl."

"Advances?" Maggie shouted. "Are you trying to be my dad too?"

Barek's forehead creased and he studied her more carefully. "Have you been crying?"

"What's it to you?" Maggie defended.

"Did *he* make you cry?"

"No."

"Someone made you cry!"

Maggie held up her palms in surrender. "Okay. Mom and Dad said I can't go to my Jaddah's trial tomorrow and I was crying about it." Her lifted chin dared him to keep on with this line of questioning.

"Tomorrow?"

"Yes. Go ahead. Call me a baby."

"I didn't say you were a baby."

"You're treating me like one."

"A mature person would probably understand your parents' concern and agree there's no point of putting you in danger."

"I can keep her safe." Eggie dropped his playfulness, and Barek could see he wasn't going to be easily bullied.

"You know nothing of keeping her safe and even less about politics." This fellow hadn't been in Carthage a week and he was acting as if he was an expert on everything, including Maggie. "No one knows what to expect from the new proconsul."

Eggie squared off nose to nose with Barek. "The man Valerian sends will be obligated to follow his orders and—"

Maggie stepped between him and Eggie. "I didn't come all this way to nurse a bunch of sick people. I came here for my Jaddah and father. I'm going to that trial." She wheeled and snatched Eggie's hand. "And lucky for me, I have a *real* friend who's not afraid to help me."

Barek snagged her arm. "You're not going anywhere with him."

"What are you going to do, chain me in some dungeon and tell my mom?"

What was it about this girl that made his blood boil? "No. *I'm* taking you."

28

"I THOUGHT LISBETH WOULD BE here by now." Lawrence smoked his pipe, pacing like the caged cats next door. "That Pontius fellow made it sound as if she'd come as soon as they had a plan."

Magdalena drew in a deep breath of the fruity, soothing aroma of her husband's Erinmore. "You made it clear that she was to go home."

"She never listens to me." He stopped and raised his brow. "Does she listen to you?"

"She'll come when she can." Magdalena coughed and pulled the blanket around her shoulders, knowing her inability to get warm meant she needed more Cipro to break her fever. She patted the stones upon which she sat. "You know how unpredictable medicine can be." Their gaze met and for a moment she knew they were wishing the same thing . . . for a way to rewind the clock and reclaim all of those nights lost to her operating schedule and his excavation adventures in faraway places.

"You're still coughing." Lawrence quit his pacing and came to her side, concern knitting his white brows. Time had taken a toll on him as well. "Pontius said Lisbeth was bringing more meds."

"And Maggie." She coughed into the crook of her arm.

"I wish she wouldn't risk my granddaughter."

"She's my granddaughter too, Lawrence."

He dropped to his knees beside her. "I only meant—"

She put a finger to his lips. "I know what you meant. It's all right. I knew you wouldn't let Lisbeth raise our granddaughter alone. It's why I sent her home to you." She felt a cough coming and drew the crook of her arm to her mouth again. "I'm sorry you—"

"No regrets." Lawrence kissed her forehead. The keys rattled in the lock. "I told you she'd come."

Both of them turned hopefully toward the door. The sound of a shoulder pushing against the heavy metal was followed by a grunt, which was followed by the creak of the door and torchlight. Brutus tromped toward them with a large jug tucked under one arm and a flaming bundle of sticks in the other.

"Are you alone?" Lawrence asked.

Brutus waved the torch behind him. "You see anyone else?"

"We were expecting—" Magdalena coughed again. "Never mind. It doesn't matter."

"Your fool coughing is wearing me out, woman." Brutus set the jug at her feet, lifted the gourd hanging from a string around his neck, and plunged it into the water. "Had this brought up from the well."

"You didn't drink any, did you, Brutus?"

"'Course. A man can develop a powerful thirst standing about in the heat."

"Oh, no." Magdalena struggled to stand. "Lawrence, give him those tablets."

"I took the pill your friend gave me," Brutus said.

"Your vaccine hasn't had enough time to become effective. The Cipro's an added precaution." Magdalena waved her hand. "The decision is made."

"No. You need them," Lawrence protested.

She laid a hand gently on his. "I'm not going to need them."

Lawrence's eyes darkened with worry and she knew he'd caught her meaning. If her trial went well, she would be free. Any Cipro Lisbeth had left she'd pump into her, no matter how many times she'd beg her to give it to someone in greater need. If her trial went badly, she would die in the arena that same day. In either case, whether she was cured of typhoid right this minute was a moot point.

Lawrence reluctantly pulled the brown plastic bottle from his pocket and handed it to Brutus. "Take one now and one with your lunch."

Brutus's eyes grew wide as he looked to Lawrence and then to her. She could see the color slipping from his cheeks. "Do I have what she has?"

If this stocky guard passed out again, she didn't think she and Lawrence could handle his limp body on their own. "Some of the wells are contaminated." Magdalena pointed at the jug. "No point in taking any chances."

"How long before my insides turn wrong side out?" A loud gulp accompanied his attempt to swallow his fear.

"They won't if you take these tablets."

Brutus's face bunched into a confused puzzle. "You're giving me your medicine?"

"I think it will help you."

"Why would you help me?"

"It's what Christ would do." Magdalena held out her empty hands, palms up. "Help is all I have to give."

"I can't pay."

"You don't have to. It's free."

"You're some of the strangest people I've ever met." Brutus fumbled with the childproof cap. "How do you get into this thing?"

Lawrence showed him how to press and turn at the same time.

Brutus's thick fingers didn't cooperate, so Lawrence opened the bottle and emptied a tablet into the guard's dirty palm. "One now. One later."

"You wouldn't be trying to trick ole Brutus, now would you?"

"Been giving the same thing to my wife."

"Like I said." Brutus tossed the pill back and swallowed it without water. "Strangest people I ever met."

29

MAXIMUS STORMED INTO THE torch-lit palace aviary still huffing from the stiff, uphill walk from the theater. "Kaeso!"

His roar sent the caged field fares, ortolans, nightingales, and thrushes into a screeching flurry. Like ambitious senators determined to be heard over the other, the brightly colored birds he'd inherited from his predecessor fluttered to higher and higher perches.

Filthy birds and their messes were not all he'd inherited. Since his arrival, a small parade of senators had burdened him with multiple complaints. He was tempted to herd all those white togas into gilded cages and have them carted off to the tunnels beneath these marbled floors.

Maximus stuck his index finger through the gold bars and smiled at the parakeet pecking at his large ring. "Kaeso!"

His servant slipped from the shadows of the garden wearing a perturbed expression. "Bellowing does not become your station."

Maximus shook the bird from his finger, slammed the cage door, and plopped down upon an upholstered sofa inlaid with tortoiseshell and gold. "How can I be expected to prepare for my role as judge when these unnecessary interruptions continue to cut my acting lessons short? Epolon says I have some work to do."

"The freedman will have to wait. Titus has requested an audience."

"Again? What could that infuriating baboon possibly want now?"

"Baboon?" Titus strode into the atrium from the open door of the center courtyard where he'd obviously been waiting. The depth of his scowl indicated he'd been waiting long enough to hear himself referred to as a hairy primate.

Maximus offered Titus a seat next to him, but he remained standing. "A term of endearment where I come from." His delivery of the quip failed to soften the frown drawing Titus's brows. "A sense of humor would broaden your appeal greatly, Senator."

"What I have to say does not require humor." Titus's chin jutted like a pointing finger at Maximus. "My lord, I'm asking you to seriously consider recusing yourself from presiding over the murder trial."

"Absolutely not."

"At the very least, you should reinstate a new praetor and follow the rule of law."

"And why would I do that?"

"The trial of the healer of Carthage is a very delicate matter, my lord. One that perhaps is best understood by someone local."

"A healer who is a murderer. Strange combination."

"You're presuming her guilty before you've even heard the case." Titus paced with such an interesting gait. Maximus could not wait to apply this hip-forward lope to a characterization he'd been working on with the protégé of Terence. "If I didn't know better, I'd think you were implying me inept, Senator."

"I have only *your* best interest at heart." Titus's beady eyes glared at Maximus. "The people adore the healer. No sense starting your tenure on the wrong foot."

"Your concern is gratifying, but I intend to have a very public presence during my stay in Carthage, and I think the trial of this murderer is a matter better understood by a ruler who would prefer not to have his leg sawed off in his royal bed." Maximus held up his palm and silenced Titus's argument, proving he was indeed a quick study of the art of ruling well. He couldn't wait to get back to Rome and try his hand at shutting his mother-in-law's mouth with a simple gesture. "I shall have my chariot deliver me to the trial of this impudent slave in the grandest of fashion. I assure you, Titus Cicero, my debut entrance as ruler of Carthage will be one this city will never forget."

Titus turned his long face toward the door, but not before Maximus could see that his decision had not made the senator happy. He didn't care. Far wealthier people than Titus Cicero had tried to tell him what to do. It felt good to get his own way for once, even if the idea of judging terrified him.

But, by the gods, he was an actor. He'd successfully pulled off the role of proconsul when he first landed, hadn't he? Although Maximus had not finished his private lessons, he'd acquired enough skills to pretend he knew how to preside over a murder trial. He'd set to work immediately after his arrival. The theater was within walking distance of his palace. Kaeso worried the exercise was beneath the station of a proconsul, but Maximus found taking the stairs a perfect way to warm up his lungs for the breathing drills dear Epolon put him through.

The accomplished actor had sorted his skills in one session. Since then, they'd worked to capitalize on Maximus's few strengths and eliminate his many weaknesses.

"Not to worry," Epolon had said as he flittered around Maximus as he left the theater. "When you make your grand appearance upon the judge's seat, no one will suspect you have just given the first public performance of your illustrious career."

Maximus longed for the day when he possessed Epolon's confidence. This year would fly by far too quickly.

30

MAXIMUS PULLED THE COVER over his head. "Please, Kaeso, let me sleep a few more minutes."

"If you insist on missing your cue, I shall have no choice but to contact the senator and tell him you have changed your mind."

Maximus growled and tugged the blanket tighter around his ears.

Kaeso threw open the shutters. "The sun is fast approaching its noonday height. You have less than an hour to make your first appearance as the new proconsul of Carthage. What shall it be?"

Maximus lowered the cover and studied the ceiling. What a pleasure it was not to have that shrewish goddess staring down at him. Kaeso was right, this was a new day and he was the author of this next act.

"I shall go." He rolled out of bed, relieved himself of the jug of wine he'd downed after his all-night rehearsal with Epolon. He splashed his face with the warm water Kaeso had just emptied into a basin. Maximus leaned in close to the polished brass and poked at the dark circles beneath his eyes. "If you line my eyes with kohl, perhaps they will give me the fierce look Epolon said I would need in the Forum."

"You don't have to do this. That long-armed senator seemed more than happy to take your place as judge." Kaeso layered heavy folds of purple-trimmed wool upon Maximus's shoulder. "However, plum roles do not come along every day. And judging the murderer of your predecessor is plum."

"You're right. I shall not let some frontier senator upstage me."

"Still, anyone as new as you could easily step into dung and not know of his misfortune until others smelled it upon his shoes."

"You worry too much, my friend." Maximus turned in front of the mirror and caught a glimpse of Kaeso's concerned expression. "After you double-check my pleats, add a touch of color to my cheeks." He patted his churning belly. "Do you have any more of that awful brew for stomach upsets?"

"The gods could be trying to tell you something."

"It's nothing but a small case of stage fright. Epolon said a nervous stomach can actually propel one's performance if the force of the discomfort is harnessed."

To regain control of errant thoughts, Epolon had also suggested mind games. One of Epolon's favorites required Maximus to visualize his idea of a perfect day. So as Kaeso finished dressing him, Maximus launched into deep breathing exercises and forced his mind on an imaginary journey. He pictured himself going to the theater instead of the Forum, then taking the stage and delivering his lines flawlessly. He'd even conjured scenes of the entire audience leaping to its feet and applauding him as one greater than Terence.

But when Kaeso tapped him on the shoulder and said, "Master, your chariot is here," Maximus knew neither his breathing nor imagining had worked. His stomach rolled the way it had aboard the moldy grain freighter, and his confidence was sinking beneath a wave of doubt.

Maximus reluctantly tossed his toga's excess fabric over his arm and filled his lungs. "Let the show begin."

In a swirl of white and purple, Maximus descended the palace stairs and waited as Kaeso raised the sunshade on the four-wheeled chariot Maximus had discovered hidden beneath a tattered sail-cloth in the corner of his newly acquired stable. According to the head groom, Aspasius had been murdered just hours after the special-order chariot arrived from Bulgaria. Not knowing what else to do with the expensive vehicle, the servants disguised the lavish cart as best they could to keep looters from stripping parts.

Maximus gripped the fine leather dash and climbed aboard. Showing off the exquisite bronze carvings made by illiterate horse-breeders captured nearly two hundred years earlier would remind his subjects not only of their place in perpetuating the success of the empire, but also of his place as the new voice of justice in Carthage. Nothing screamed "cunning" and "just" like mytho-logical panthers with the bodies of wildcats and tails of dolphins. According to Maximus's new acting coach, proper props were as important as a grand entrance when it came to creating a believ-able character.

Maximus gathered his courage, summoned the lower register of his voice, and instructed his driver, "Proceed to the Forum via the main street."

The slave looked to Kaeso, then back to Maximus. "Carthagin-ian tradition demands you ride past the prison so they know when to bring the accused forward."

"What do I care of your barbaric traditions?"

Kaeso gently placed his hand on Maximus's arm. "Today, you care."

"But I'll be late."

"You're late because you would not get out of bed."

"But a fashionably late entrance can also make for a very grand entrance. A little trick Hortensia taught me." Maximus issued his next order as firmly as possible. "Drive me past this horrid prison, but then circle back and proceed as I instructed."

Bodies were stacked along the paved corridor like rotting cordwood. "Will there even be anyone to watch my performance?" Maximus asked Kaeso as they bounced along.

Kaeso shrugged. "We shall see."

The driver pulled to a stop near the stairs leading down to the prison's metal door. "Do you wish to speak to the prisoner?"

"My words for that wench"—he smiled—"shall be delivered when a well-delivered line counts."

31

Brutus held a torch over the place where Magdalena and Lawrence clung together like survivors on a leaky raft. "It's time," the guard said quietly.

Lawrence cinched Magdalena with his ropy arms. "Can we have a few more moments?" he begged the guard. "Our daughter will be here any minute—"

"The judge has already ridden past," Brutus said glumly. "Your escorts will be here any second. No time for long farewells." He reached beneath his breastplate and retrieved a freshly pressed tunic. "It's not much, but at least it's clean. Woke a washerwoman and paid her a silver piece to launder it proper." He held out a brown woolen garment, scuffing his boots like a nervous child. "Told her the wearer would be as fine a lady as my momma. And my mother, may the gods . . . uh, the one God rest her soul, always insisted her dress hold a good crease."

Magdalena peeled herself from Lawrence's embrace and pressed the stiff wool of Brutus's offered garment to her nose. Sunshine and sea breeze, a gentle reminder of God's continual presence. "Thank you, Brutus."

"I've heard your prayers and seen how those who profess the faith in your one God have risked their lives to care for you." Brutus offered his hand and helped her to her feet. "It would have been an honor to be healed by your hands."

Magdalena blinked back tears. "To see your heart healed has been my honor."

Brutus nodded, then turned to Lawrence and whispered, "Now would be the time to say your good-byes and disappear into the crowd."

Lawrence planted his feet, his jaw set for a fight. "She's innocent!"

"If they find her guilty, you won't get another chance," Brutus continued whispering. "If they find her innocent and set her free, you can determine a meeting place and she can find you easy enough."

Magdalena laced her fingers with her husband's. "I love you, Lawrence, but one of us has to take care of the kids."

"It took me years to find you"—he tightened his arm around her waist—"don't ask me to leave you now."

"Tell our girls how much I love them." The tears stinging her eyes would not be held back forever. "I'm counting on you to love Laurentius like your own son."

Lawrence cast aside the precautions they'd taken with her typhoid and cupped her face with his hands. "I won't go without you." In his eyes, she could see her distorted face. Ridged slashes that extended her lips almost to her ears. Old before her time. She laid a hand on his chest in an effort to turn him away, to keep him from kissing her out of pity. He drew a deep, shuddering breath, as if her fevered hand had burned straight to his heart.

Magdalena could feel the pain beating inside him, and her own emotions threatened to boil over. "What we see is not all there is. God will not fail us."

"I love you." Lawrence lowered his lips to hers. His beard,

which had passed the bristly stage a couple of days earlier, was a soft, private curtain drawn around her mouth. He kissed her deeply, as if he wanted the ridges of her scars permanently etched into his lips. He pulled back only when Brutus gave him a little nudge.

"You can't stay, my love. Go."

His eyes brimming with tears, Lawrence told her, "Look for me." His eyes lingered. This time, when her gaze wavered over the watery depths of his love, she saw a woman she'd not seen in years: One who was perfect. Beautiful. Young. "I'm coming for you," he whispered, and then he was gone.

Magdalena teetered on the edge of running after him, clutching the clean tunic to her chest as if it were a promise Lawrence could actually keep. Short of trying to jump down the time portal with everyone they loved, they could do nothing and they both knew it. She wanted to be brave, to go to her death as those before her had. With her head held high. But her mouth was paper dry, her eyes flooded with tears, and her courage a puddle of candle wax.

Brutus freed Kardide from the wall. The old woman, her drainage tube flopping from her headscarf like a snake trying to escape Medusa's turban, rushed to Magdalena and wrapped her in a steadying hug. Magdalena melted into her embrace, counting her friend's remarkable recovery more than a testament to Lisbeth's excellent surgical skills; her presence was a gift from God. Though they were both unwashed and sour-smelling, each was unwilling to relinquish the support of the other.

"I wish I had time to give your head wound proper attention, Kardide."

"It can wait," Kardide assured her.

Brutus unlocked Magdalena's chain from the wall hook, then turned his back to allow Kardide's assistance with Magdalena's garment change. Next he freed Tabari, and she hurried across the aisle and insisted on finger combing Magdalena's hair. Within minutes Magdalena's hopeless tangles had been subdued into one neat plait that hung down her back. Once Iltani was freed, she silently raised the hem of her dress and wiped the grime from Magdalena's face.

"Thank you, my friends"—Magdalena swallowed the lump in her throat—"for everything."

"Today's hearing is just a formality, right?" Kardide asked. "Our chance to tell them you did not kill that monster."

Magdalena didn't have a definitive answer. She'd been counting on Lisbeth to give her the latest information. When her daughter failed to show up, Magdalena knew in her gut that something wasn't right. Doing her best to remove any trace of fear from her voice, she said, "You heard Pontius. Cyprian and Lisbeth are making a plan."

"Brutus!" a soldier bellowed from the open door. "I swear upon Juno's stone, if you don't get those prisoners out here, I'll beat you along with them."

"Coming!" Brutus shouted.

If the soldier had captured Lawrence he would have sounded much happier. Magdalena breathed a sigh of relief. "Fear not, my friends." She gave Brutus's hand a covert squeeze. "I'm ready." On shaky legs, Magdalena traversed the narrow tunnel, wishing for time to stop and assess each prisoner.

"We're praying for you, lady," they said as she passed.

Magdalena thanked each one, then bent beneath the stone lintel and came forth from the tunnel like one raised from the grave. Her hands flew to shield her eyes from the white-hot glare. She'd lost count of how many days it had been since she'd seen the sun. She lifted her face and boldly said aloud a prayer of thanks as the blinding rays warmed the chilly dread pumping through her veins.

"Move it," a soldier ordered.

Magdalena lowered her hands. The redhead who'd taken such great pleasure in dragging her into custody now had a whip. The law was clear. In cases that involved a slave murdering her owner, she could be flogged in the Forum so that no other slaves would consider the possibility of hurting those who enslaved them. Should she be found guilty, the state would exercise its right to inflict the death penalty and she could be flogged yet again. Since she was not considered a Roman citizen, she would die on a cross erected in the center of the arena.

Before her weak knees could betray her, Magdalena checked over her shoulder. One by one her friends emerged into the light, ducking their heads as she had in response to the brightness. In the sunlight, she could see how they were in worse shape than she'd thought: filthy, bruised, broken as she, and unsure of what lay ahead.

The redheaded soldier yanked the chain connecting their shackles. Magdalena and her friends stumbled after their armed escorts.

More people than Magdalena had seen on the streets since the beginning of the measles outbreak lined the steep path to the Forum. Quiet and somber, they stared at the degradation of her body.

"Healer!" A bent old woman stepped in front of the soldiers who flanked Magdalena and handed her a beautiful head covering. "For saving my son."

Another woman, younger and toting a toddler, pressed an ivory comb into her hand. "For saving my mother."

Before they could move on, another woman ran up and swiped a cool cloth across her face. "For healing my baby."

"Stand back." The redhead withdrew his sword and the murmuring crowd backed down, but just for a moment.

Magdalena slid the comb into her pocket, draped her head with the shawl, and then marched toward the Forum with her spirits buoyed and her shoulders raised a little higher.

By the time they made the turn toward Byrsa Hill the follow-ing had doubled in size. A woman with a face scabbed by a recent case of the measles burst through the guard line. "You may not remember me, dear lady, but I shall never forget my family ate because of your kindnesses." She pressed into Magdalena's palm a pouch of dried dates.

People she recognized as those she'd helped, and even some she had not, wormed their way through the throng and gifted her with scraps of bread or pieces of cheese.

The redhead squeezed her arm. "Keep moving," he growled into her ear. Even he knew an order to stop the gifting could ignite into a riot.

Magdalena received so many tokens of appreciation her pock-ets bulged. She cradled a flask of wine against her chest, a treasure she did not take for granted. The generosity these people had shown her was not without cost. Many of them and their families would go hungry tonight.

Had Christ felt the same mix of gratitude and responsibility as he rode into Jerusalem to face his end? Magdalena's chains dragged behind her, stirring the dust and unstoppable tears.

Long before Magdalena was ready, the covered walkways of the Forum came into view. The redheaded soldier led them up steep steps and hurried them past the bored luxury stall vendors. Hungry patrons weren't interested in silk, incense, glass, alabaster, ivory, or hammered copper. The only vendors doing any business were the seafood salesmen. And they'd had to reduce their prices so drastically that they were practically giving away the last of their salted Atlantic fish to the few families who still had a bit of gold in their purse.

At the Forum, an even larger crowd had gathered. Rumor of her trial must have spread through the city faster than the plague. Though Magdalena was preoccupied with praying her stomach would calm, she was quietly pleased to see how God had answered her prayers and allowed more than she expected to survive the drought and sickness.

The redheaded soldier towed them through the Forum's arched entry and into the pillared circle. The temple of Jupiter dominated the northern quadrant. Sunlight bounced off the bronze roof tiles and lit up three statues perched high atop stone pediments. The god of thunder commanded center attention. Beside him stood his regal queen, Juno, the goddess of love. On Jupiter's left, his virgin daughter, Minerva, the goddess of medicine, looked down her sculpted nose at the sickly healer being hauled before her court.

Magdalena's gaze skipped over the public weights and measures tables scattered about. In the center of the Forum, four serious-faced trumpeters with shiny brass horns guarded the podium where the town crier shouted the daily news. The small stage, swept clean of trash and pigeons, had been decorated with one massive ivory seat.

In all her years, Magdalena had never seen so much ceremony dedicated to a simple pretrial hearing. Usually the hearings were so insignificant they drew scarcely any notice from those conducting business at the vendors' stalls.

Stifling heat, along with the growing throng, sucked up the fresh air Magdalena craved. Her gaze ricocheted over the people, searching for one tall gangly man with gray hair and lips she longed to kiss one more time. But Lawrence was nowhere to be found.

Suddenly, Pontius was at her side and Cyprian on the other. Their protective grasp on her elbows felt as if God had come to carry her across the finish line.

"Once the judge arrives, this should be over quickly." The folds in Cyprian's white toga were crisp.

"Judge? What happened?"

"Try not to borrow trouble." Though his voice was steady, Cyprian couldn't conceal the worry in his eyes.

"No matter what happens to me, please see what you can do for those still in chains in Perpetua's prison," Magdalena said.

"Let's get you acquitted first," Cyprian said to the redheaded soldier. "I'm allowed a moment of privacy with my clients."

The brazen young cadet eyed Pontius. "Is this your man?"

"He is."

The soldier reluctantly relinquished custody of the chain into Pontius's outstretched hand. Magdalena and her friends followed Cyprian to the bench reserved for the accused. Pontius stood guard as the women formed a little huddle around Cyprian. She shared the spoils in her pockets with them as Cyprian caught them up. "Titus could not persuade the new proconsul to recuse himself from your trial, so we went with a different plan."

"And what is this plan?" Kardide gnawed on a crust of bread.

Magdalena patted her hand. "He'll do his best, my friend." From the corner of her eye, she spotted Lisbeth wearing a hooded cloak and working her way to the front of the crowd, her face determined and stronger than anyone should ever have to be. It was all Magdalena could do not to run to her daughter and beg her to take everyone they loved as far from this time as possible. "What is Lisbeth doing here?"

Cyprian leaned in close. "You know chains would not have kept her away."

Magdalena searched the crowd for a striking blonde matching Lawrence's description of their granddaughter. "Please tell me Maggie is not here as well."

"I've tasked Barek with Maggie's safety," Cyprian assured her. "She's not to set foot outside of Titus's villa."

Grateful relief quivered in her nervous belly. "Then let's get this over with."

32

"I HEAR TRUMPETS!" MAGGIE TRAILED only a few steps behind Barek, determined to keep up. "Does that mean we are missing the trial?"

"We will if you don't stop talking and start walking." Barek, it seemed to her, purposely increased the length of his stride just to irritate her. Not only had he insisted on escorting her to the trial, he'd taken over the plan. Already this morning, he'd found one chore after another to delay their departure.

Maggie understood why he'd insisted they wait until her parents left for the Forum before they set out. She even understood that Barek had agreed to take her only because he knew that with or without him, she was going. Tempting as it was to let herself imagine Barek's overprotectiveness was about more than his irritating big-brother tendencies, his sullen face and narrowed eyes told the real story. Taking Maggie to her grandmother's trial after he'd given his word to Cyprian that he'd keep her home was, in Barek's mind, as deceptive as selling writs of libellus. The one time she'd forced him to look at her, she'd felt the same twinge of guilt she'd experienced the night he'd risked his life to keep a bratty five-year-old safe from pursuing soldiers. She hadn't meant to put him in a compromising position then and she hadn't meant to do it now.

Eggie sidled up and let his fingers brush hers. "I told you we should have left earlier."

"And what excuse would you have given if her parents had caught us?" Barek tossed over his shoulder.

Guilt or not, Maggie didn't think it fair to allow Barek to take out his frustration with her on Eggie. "Same one I gave the night we had to outrun the soldiers at the Tophet."

Barek stopped so abruptly that she face-planted in the middle of his back. He wheeled, his eyes simmering coals and his temper flared. "And what exactly did you tell them?"

"I told them you made me go against my will."

He crammed his hands upon his hips. "Me?" He shouted so loudly a couple of peasants hurrying along beside them stopped to look. "*You* were the one who nearly got us killed and you know it."

Okay, he had her there. She was the one who'd insisted on tagging along to help him bury his mother's ashes. It was her scream, when she tripped and twisted her ankle, that had alerted the soldiers to possible curfew breakers in the area. And her claustrophobia inside the Tophet morphed into a hyperventilating tantrum that gave away their location and sent the soldiers thundering their way. If Barek hadn't abandoned his mother's ashes and scooped her up, both of them would have been caught.

Maggie waited until the peasants moved along. "Lighten up, Barek. I was just kidding. I didn't really tell them that. I'm sorry for everything about that night." He flinched at her touch, but he didn't pull away. "Why are you always so serious?"

"Because somebody has to think ahead."

"Look out!" Eggie flew at them like a superhero, plowing into Maggie and Barek with a force that sent all three of them sprawling onto the sidewalk. A split second later five black horses pulling a golden chariot whizzed past, the driver's whip snapping in the air.

Maggie's skull throbbed where the back of her head had hit the pavement. She tried to move but Eggie had her pinned down. His gray eyes were less than two inches from hers. "I can't breathe," she said, gasping.

"Are you hurt?" Eggie's chest pressed so tightly against hers she could feel his heart beating. His lips hovered above her, close enough she could kiss them without moving.

From the corner of her eye, Maggie saw Barek hustle to get his legs under him. He came up huffing. "She said she can't breathe."

Eggie grinned, not making any effort to shift his weight or remedy their compromising position. "Trust me, she's breathing."

Barek grabbed Eggie's tunic and roughly hauled him upright. "When she says she can't breathe, she can't breathe."

Maggie struggled to her feet. "Stop it, Barek." She brushed herself off, dug her phone out of her backpack, and examined the pink case. "You both would have been so dead if this were broken."

"What is that?" Eggie asked.

"It's my camera." She held it up, extended her arm, and snapped a picture of their stunned faces. "Well, not my good camera. My phone's easier to conceal."

A few clicks in the edit program and she'd cropped out a couple of curious rubberneckers and corrected Barek and Eggie's red wide-eyed stare. "Pictures." She turned the screen and showed them the image. "Of my friends."

Eggie lurched backward, his eyes growing bigger still. "Are you a witch?"

"No." Barek took Maggie by the elbow. "She's just sneaky." He poked Eggie in the chest. "That's why you're going to help me keep an eye on her."

33

LISBETH RAN ALL THE way from Titus's villa to the Forum, her bag tucked inside her cloak. She hit the steps without taking the time to catch her breath and pushed through the restless crowd with equal parts gratitude and anger: Gratitude for Cyprian's willingness to step in and sternly forbid Maggie to attend the trial. Anger at his unwillingness to allow Titus to take his place.

When it came to Maggie, it was nice not to be the disciplinarian for once. Or to be the sole brunt of her wrath when they tried to explain why she had no business being in the middle of a political hotbed. But when it came to Cyprian's refusal to heed her fears for his life or to allow her to take the stand on behalf of her mama, Lisbeth wasn't as enamored.

Her mother's friends were there that night, but she was the only one who could give accurate medical testimony as to Aspasius's deteriorated state. And Lisbeth would say the evil man would have died much sooner and in far more pain if Magdalena hadn't tried to help him.

The second Lisbeth had Quinta and her grandson stabilized, she'd left a rather subdued Maggie a list of chores and sprinted toward Byrsa Hill. Lisbeth elbowed her way through the crowd. The stink of unwashed bodies and the distinctive scent of wet chicken feathers triggered her gag reflex. Measles, and possibly their nasty accomplice typhoid, were in this mob. Holding her breath, she burst into the circle, her eyes frantically trying to take in the proceedings. Shimmers of heat rose from the uneven cobblestones in the center of the Forum.

She spotted Pontius first. Ever vigilant, Cyprian's most trusted friend was only a few feet from her husband. "Cyprian!" she shouted, but he was preoccupied speaking to Mama and her friends. Mama looked haggard, thin, and fever-flushed. A woman who should have been in a hospital, receiving the selfless medical care she deserved instead of being forced to risk her health for this ridiculous murder charge.

Not wanting to add to her mother's worries, Lisbeth slipped back into the crowd. On the other side of the wooden stage, a barrel-shaped man with hands thick as cement blocks worked the crowd with the flourish of a TV prosecutor. If he was Cyprian's opponent, where was the judge?

Thundering hoofbeats prompted trumpet blasts. Heads turned toward the Forum entrance. Five black horses hitched to a golden chariot roared into the center of the circle. A cloud of choking dust swirled in their wake. People scattered from their path. The man executing a perfect pageant wave from beneath the sunshade was pale, slight, and puffed up proud as an adder.

Lisbeth's hands turned clammy. "The ghost of Aspasius," she muttered, but she could have shouted, for it would not have been heard over the rhythmic clop of the magnificent team prancing round and round the witness stand. *God, please don't let anyone question Cyprian's right to be here.*

She rose on tiptoes for a better look at the man who now held the power of life and death over her mother and her husband. Maximus was a pasty, high-browed man who wore a lopsided crown of greenery. He had narrow eyes, narrow shoulders, and from the sneer on his face, Lisbeth guessed, the emperor's narrow thinking when it came to Christians. There would be no justice here today. This trial was a sham.

Heart pounding, Lisbeth raised her arms to capture Cyprian's attention. Before she could work her way to a place where Cyprian would see her, she was snagged by her mother's gaze. Terror registered in Mama's eyes. With a slight shake of her head her mother warned Lisbeth to do nothing.

How could she do nothing?

Lisbeth tried to move toward her mother but a solid body pressed her from either side. From the sour-milk smell of them they were cheese merchants. Since she couldn't go forward, she attempted to maneuver backward. But people determined to see the day's events had filled in behind and effectively cut off her ability to do anything for now.

The servant of Maximus exited the chariot first. He dropped on all fours and made himself into a human footstool. The proconsul placed a red boot upon his servant's back and descended with great pomp, careful not to allow the folds of the toga draped over his arm to touch the dirty pavers. His nose lifted as if trying to rise above the displeasing scents of Carthage. One step at a time, he made his way center stage, slowly assessed the crowd, then seated himself in the empty judge's seat.

"I am Galerius Maximus, the new proconsul and judge of Carthage." Maximus's voice carried well beyond what she would have thought possible from such a scrawny guy. He waved his hand at the prosecutor, who was strutting before a group of senators clustered together in the shade, one of whom was Titus Cicero. Cyprian had stationed the land merchant among the patricians with the express purpose of silencing any adversaries.

"Call your first witness," Maximus ordered the prosecutor.

Lisbeth held her breath. If the prosecutor was going to protest Cyprian's presence, this was his opportunity.

"Honorable proconsul." The prosecutor bowed respectfully to Maximus, then wheeled and pointed at a smug little man standing within arm's reach of the platform. "I summon Pytros, former scribe of Aspasius Paternus."

For now, Cyprian was safe. Titus caught her eye. With a nod, Lisbeth knew he had held up his end of their plan and convinced the prosecutor Cyprian's reinstatement by Xystus was all on the up and up. Lisbeth gave him a grateful nod, but her relief was short-lived. The man the prosecutor had summoned was the devious and conniving weasel who'd worked behind the scenes and arranged Felicissimus's betrayal of Cyprian. Pytros had always been jealous of Mama's influence over his master and from his pleased prance to the podium he intended to get even for the slight. Cold slithered over her skin and seeped into her pores.

The prosecutor clasped his hands over his belly. "Pytros, were you a slave of Aspasius Paternus, the beloved proconsul of Carthage?"

Beloved? Lisbeth wanted to throw up. The only person who loved Aspasius Paternus was he himself.

Pytros withdrew a hanky from his sleeve and dabbed his eyes. "I was."

"And how were you treated while in his service?"

"I received a new tunic every year, a cloak, and a new pair of wooden shoes. Now that I am free and forced to provide for my own needs, I realize the generous care my master afforded all his servants."

"Objection!" Cyprian's powerful voice rang out. "Death of a master does not free a slave. Yet Pytros is free? How can this be?" He waited, but when his objection went unanswered by the judge, he gave an impatient shrug of the shoulders and continued, "Should I be afforded the opportunity to review the will of Aspasius, will I find evidence of this man's *manumission liberta*?"

Pytros eagerly jumped in with his own explanation: "I am a freedman."

"How is it possible you are able to testify as one granted the freedoms of a citizen of Rome without a reading of the deceased's will?"

"Objection!" the prosecutor yelled. "My witness is not on trial."

"Pytros's ability to testify should certainly be of interest to this court," Cyprian protested.

All eyes turned to Maximus.

The proconsul shifted in his seat. "I want to know what this man saw, whether or not he has the right to tell me."

"Then Pytros is a very fortunate man indeed." Cyprian pivoted and charged back to his bench, speaking loudly enough for his sentiments to be heard throughout the Forum. "It appears a political sleight-of-hand has magically brewed royal purple from a cheap vegetable."

"Maximus, please, remind our eager solicitor of his place."

The prosecutor's pointed threat was not lost on Cyprian. He raised his hands. "I withdraw my comment, my lord."

"There's no need." Pytros fanned his white hanky. "I would gladly forfeit my freedoms would it bring my beloved master back from the dead." He jabbed his finger in Mama's direction. "She killed him. I saw her bloody hands pounding his chest."

The crowd clamored behind Lisbeth. It was all she could do not to scream, "She was doing CPR, you fool!"

"Magdalena's an angel!" shouted someone to the right. Agreement, a tiny murmur at first, began to ripple around the Forum, picking up steam as it moved from person to person. Soon people started shouting things like "She's the only one who can save us!"

"As she saved the proconsul?" Pytros shouted indignantly and the crowd quieted.

A satisfied smirk spread across the prosecutor's face. He brushed his hands together and waddled back to his side of the podium. "The state has no more questions for this witness."

Cyprian cleared his throat. In one well-seasoned move, he approached Pytros congenially, smiling as if they were friends. "I hope you did not take offense at my comments."

"Well, I suppose it would be asking a lot for a patrician to immediately accept a slave's good fortune."

"My congratulations on your *luck*."

Pytros's posture straightened and he seemed pleased by Cyprian's concessions. "Thank you, my lord."

"You served the proconsul as scribe, did you not?"

"I did."

"Can you tell us your duties?"

"Correspondence, errands, managing his schedule."

"Exacting and taxing work, I'm sure."

"Indeed."

"And your training, it must have been extensive?"

"Indeed. I sat at the feet of the best scribe in all of Rome to learn my craft."

"Impressive." Cyprian gave a slight nod. "No wonder Aspasius was quick to grant one so accomplished his liberty. Well earned, I'm sure." Cyprian smiled. "Would you say Magdalena was treated with the same generosity you claim Aspasius afforded you?"

"Far better," Pytros said, his former wariness all but vanished.

"How unjust."

"My thoughts exactly."

Concern furrowed Cyprian's brow. "Was this because of Aspasius's appreciation for her expert training?"

"Oh, no." Pytros had become putty in Cyprian's expert hands. He leaned forward eagerly. "She escaped numerous times. My master could have branded her forehead or had an iron collar permanently riveted around her neck. Her medical services were not the reasons for my master's generosity toward this woman."

"Her face is seamed with the marks of your master's generosity." Cyprian's mention of her mother's scars brought Mama's hand to her mouth and Lisbeth's ire to the boiling point. She attempted to wriggle free of the cheese merchants but failed.

Cyprian moved closer, forcing Pytros to take a startled step back on the witness stand. "Is it true that Aspasius paid six thousand denarii for this woman and only five hundred drachmas for you, Pytros?"

The scribe's nose twitched like an animal sensing a waiting predator. He shifted uncomfortably. "I wouldn't know what he paid to have her in his bed."

Lisbeth clawed at the cheese merchants' arms, but they were too engrossed in the unfolding drama to give way.

Cyprian planted his feet and poised his body to wield the final blow, any pretense of nurturing their friendship gone. "Did it ever occur to you that Aspasius considered you nothing more than a cheap commodity?"

"My value was not only in my skill, but in my undying loyalty." Pytros dabbed his eyes with a cloth. "*I* did not mutilate and murder my master."

"Were you not in charge of his medical care once Magdalena left?"

"I was."

"Did you seek potions to treat your master's wounds and administer those salves and tonics yourself?"

"I did what any attentive slave would do to ease my master's pain."

"And yet he worsened," Cyprian said. "Are you trained in the healing arts?"

"No."

"Isn't it possible it was *your* mistakes and pitiful ministrations that ultimately hastened your master's death?"

"Don't try to blame me." Pytros jabbed his finger in Magdalena's direction. "No one wanted the proconsul dead more than me . . . I mean her."

"*You* wanted him dead?" Cyprian's grin could not be contained. "Were you jealous of the respect and love Aspasius had for the healer?"

"Free the healer!" Townspeople pressed toward the platform. "Free her!"

Cyprian's brilliant checkmate of Pytros had the prosecutor running toward Maximus. "He's putting words into the mouth of the witness. Make him stop!"

"No more questions!" Cyprian shouted over the cries for Mama's release. He strode to stand beside his client.

Maximus raised his hands and the crowd quieted. "I've heard enough." He stood. "I find on behalf of—"

"My lord," the prosecutor said, "the state has yet to call the accused."

Maximus sat back down abruptly. "Call her."

The flustered prosecutor boldly summoned Mama to the stand.

Mama didn't move. Had she not heard the prosecutor call her name above the ruckus? Lisbeth shimmied her shoulders against the burly arms of the cheese merchants. Cyprian leaned over and whispered into Mama's ear. She nodded and rose slowly. Her weight was down ten pounds and her complexion had sallowed. She stood planted in that spot but there was no hiding the tremble that said she was acutely aware of the danger.

Lisbeth saw that the bruise around her eye had faded from deep purple to more of a mustard green and the reduction in swelling allowed both eyes to complete a panoramic assessment of the crowd. Lisbeth lunged against the cheese merchants. Mama's countenance suddenly seemed to soften, as if she'd seen something that gave her a shot of courage. She lifted her chin and dragged her chains across the pavers. Once she mounted the platform, she clasped her hands in front of her. In a show of defiance, Mama fastened her gaze on Pytros, who'd sandwiched himself among the senators.

The prosecutor had regained his composure. He licked his lips and began his interrogation. "Are you the one the plebs call 'the healer'?"

"I have done what I could for their sick."

Cheers rose up across the gallery. Was the crowd's support a good thing? Lisbeth craned her neck for a better view of Maximus, but the prosecutor silenced the mob and quickly moved on with his questioning before she could correctly frame the proconsul's scowl.

"Did you or did you not conceal a child of deformity?" A gasp echoed in the pillared circle. This charge alone, should it stick, could seal her mother's doom.

Lisbeth's gaze followed the trajectory of Mama's fixation to the opposite side of the Forum. *Papa?* No wonder her mother had settled after her gaze swept the venue. Of course her father would be here. Lisbeth tried waving at him, but she knew her father's attention was so intently fastened on his wife he wouldn't have noticed Lisbeth if she'd been close enough to slap him.

The days he'd spent tending Mama in the prison had taken a toll on him as well. His beard had grown in gray and shaggy, and the dark circles under his eyes suggested he hadn't dared fall asleep for fear his beloved wife would disappear again. But it was the intense helplessness on his face Lisbeth couldn't take. She shouldn't have left him alone with Mama for so long.

Sunlight bounced off a small hot pink box held high in the

general vicinity of Mama's gaze. Neon colors of the twenty-first century were as out of place in this drab crowd as the snowy white togas of those conducting the trial.

Maggie?

Lisbeth strained her neck for confirmation. Not more than two steps behind Papa, Maggie was doing her best to get the perfect shot with her phone camera, and beside her was the boy who'd promised Cyprian he'd make sure Maggie didn't leave the house. Eggie was also there. Every cell in Lisbeth's body prepared for battle.

"I'll kill her," Lisbeth muttered under her breath, her mind planning the fastest route to her child. "No, I'll kill all three of them." Her frantic attempt to move yielded no gain.

"Deformity?" Mama's shoulders visibly stiffened. "Did your father rail when he saw your unusually large ears and order you exposed?"

"My lord," the blushing prosecutor demanded over the tittering crowd, "instruct the witness to answer."

Maximus flicked his wrist. "Slave, you heard the man. Did you or did you not conceal a deformed and cursed child?"

Papa gave Mama a slight nod of encouragement.

"It is true that Aspasius Paternus fathered my son." Mama returned her focus to the antagonistic man standing before her. "But my beautiful boy is neither deformed nor cursed. He is a light in the darkness."

"It has been reported that his eyes are unnaturally slanted and that his mind remains forever childlike."

"Thankfully, he does not resemble his father in appearance or temperament."

A sly smile dimpled the prosecutor's face. "The child of a free man and a slave woman is still . . . a slave. Was it or was it not the legal obligation of the father to order the child's exposure?"

Mama swallowed. "Your laws granted Aspasius that preroga-
tive, yes."

"And did the proconsul order it so?"

Silence echoed in the Forum. Lisbeth could feel the people
leaning forward as they awaited her response.

"He did."

"And yet you, a lowly slave in the house of the proconsul of
Carthage, took it upon yourself to circumvent a direct order of
your master?"

"I live by a higher law."

The prosecutor's brows rose. "And what is this law that is
higher than that of Rome?"

A slow, deliberate smile spread across Mama's face. "The law of
Christ."

Murmurings that had been but a pebble thrown into a pond
blossomed into nervous ripples through the crowd.

"So." The prosecutor's delight curled his lips. "This *Christ* had
you circumvent Roman law and hide your deformed son from his
father. Did he also instruct you to take a jagged instrument to your
master's leg and saw it off with malice and forethought?"

"When a doctor loses a patient"—Mama's voice was remarkably steady—"it is something we never forget. I have had ample
time to think about my decision. I have gone over and over that
day in my mind. What could I have done differently? Whether it
was a blood clot or septic shock that brought about Aspasius's ulti-
mate death, I'm still convinced amputation was the best choice of
treatment and the proconsul's only hope."

"May I never be at your mercy," the prosecutor said with a hu-
morless chuckle. "Is it true you oppose the bloodletting of the
Roman physicians?"

"What does this have to do with the proconsul?" Cyprian
objected.

"True or not?" the proconsul demanded.

Mama held up her palm to stop the arguing. "Yes," she said. "Bloodletting is a barbaric, ineffective, and dangerous form of treatment in my opinion."

"Then why did you step in and perform your own manner of bloodletting upon the daughter of Titus Cicero?"

The senators, all clustered together near the stage, turned shocked faces in Titus's direction.

To Lisbeth's surprise, the rich land merchant kept his eyes on Mama. Ever so slightly, his shoulders rose and he stepped away from his colleagues. The worry pinching his face dissipated and he acquired a rather proud and pleased expression as he said, "The skills of this accomplished surgeon saved my daughter from the sickness ravaging her bowels."

Mama rewarded Titus's confession with a smile of her own, then answered the prosecutor, "Titus is correct. Bloodletting and repairing a perforated colon are two very different things."

"And amputation?"

"A proven treatment for gangrene used from the days of ancient Egypt."

"Isn't it true that you administered a large dose of madder root to the proconsul?"

"Everyone knows madder root relieves pain."

"So you confess you drugged the proconsul and then coerced him into granting you permission to mutilate his body?" Before Mama could refute his implications, the prosecutor held up his palm. "That with the proconsul's death, you hoped to escape once again and achieve your freedom?"

"Objection!" Cyprian shouted. "The prosecutor has presented no evidence to support these allegations."

"It all sounds very convincing to me," Maximus said. "Unless you can produce evidence to the contrary, I will have to rule in the state's favor."

Cyprian reached inside his toga and retrieved a wrinkled parchment.

"Yes!" Lisbeth shouted.

Cyprian continued, "I have the signed addendum to the proconsul's will, the codicil that changes everything." The crowd gasped. Cyprian brought the paper to Maximus. "As you can see, his signature is clearly legible, proof Aspasius was of sound mind when he consented to these changes."

"He was in so much pain he would have agreed to anything!" Pytros shouted, waving his hanky at Mama. "She said she wouldn't help him if he didn't agree to her terms!"

No one moved. No one breathed.

Cyprian turned slowly and faced the wide-eyed scribe. "So you are changing your testimony, Pytros?" Cyprian ignored the rapid shaking of the scribe's head and moved in. "Are you saying the healer *helped* rather than harmed the proconsul?" Cyprian had trapped the scribe with such finesse Lisbeth would have applauded his strategy were her arms free. "Which is it?"

"How does the court know this piece of paper is not a forgery?" the prosecutor argued to Maximus. "The accused could have mastered his signature . . . and . . . and this scrap of paper lacks the proconsul's official seal." He stormed to his bench and produced a thick scroll from a bag. "This is the proconsul's sealed will."

Maximus's gaze ping-ponged between the scroll in the prosecutor's hand and the crumpled piece of paper Cyprian had given him. From the confusion knitting his brows, Lisbeth could see the new proconsul of Carthage wasn't sure what to do next.

Titus stepped out from the senators' huddle. "You must compare the will against the document in question, my lord."

"I was just about to suggest the same, Senator." Maximus ran his finger along the edge of the scroll and broke through the blood-red wax. He unrolled the scroll and scanned to the signature, then back to the note. "The signatures appear to match."

"Then let us hear the terms of this will," Cyprian demanded.

Maximus handed the note back to Cyprian, then stood with the parchment held to his chest until complete silence descended upon the Forum. Satisfied he had everyone's attention, Maximus cleared his throat and began to read in a loud voice, "I, Aspasius Paternus, bequeath my personal effects, et cetera, et cetera, et cetera . . ." as he scanned the document. "Oh, here we are. My slaves are to become the property of the succeeding proconsul."

Maximus lifted his eyes and smiled in a way that suggested he expected these starving people to salute his good fortune. When they did not, he dropped his eyes and continued reading, "Including footmen, litter-bearers, overseers of the furniture, overseers of the lighting of the palace, valets, tailors, wine stewards, chamberlains, cooks, bakers, fullers, bath-keepers. . . ." He skipped down the list. "Ah, yes, here it is, and my personal physician, Magdalena." Maximus made a great show of rolling the scroll as if it were sacred. "According to this, I am a very rich man and the healer is my property to use as I see fit."

"She is forever bound to you," the prosecutor confirmed, "in death or in life."

"Unless this codicil states otherwise, correct?" Cyprian said. "The codicil Pytros has already confirmed that the proconsul signed."

The prosecutor gave a reluctant half nod.

"Cyprian, the addendum." Maximus held out his hand and Cyprian relinquished the flimsy piece of paper upon which his whole case rested. "I see that it is dated the day of the proconsul's unfortunate death," Maximus said. "It reads, 'I, Aspasius Paternus, do hereby agree to restore running water to the tenements, clear the streets of dead bodies, close the harbors and highways until the sickness passes, forgive the complicity of the worthless slaves Kardide, Tabari, and Iltani, and grant the immediate pardon of Cyprianus Thascius. The solicitor is hereby empowered to facilitate the restoration of Carthage.'" Maximus raised his eyes. "A pardon? Why would a solicitor of Carthage need a pardon, Cyprian?"

"Now that I am a free man, the injustice of my exile no longer matters."

The crowd broke into cheers. One of the beefy cheese merchants scooped Lisbeth off her feet and tried to kiss her on the mouth. She pounded on his chest until he released her. He licked his lips and wedged her back into the space that had grown even smaller between the two freedmen.

Cyprian raised his palms to silence the celebration. "My lord, you will note the codicil contains no mention of my client's desire for or attempt to seek her own manumission. May I ask her why?"

"That is a curiosity to me as well," Maximus agreed. "Ask her."

"Magdalena, why didn't you ask for your own freedom?"

"I asked for what was important."

Cyprian flashed a grin at the red-faced prosecutor. "Magdalena thought nothing of her own welfare, as has been her practice throughout her years in Carthage. Instead, she sought only the good of the empire." Again everyone shouted approval. "I ask you, my lord, would someone who possessed such a selfless nature kill the man who'd just granted her everything she wanted?"

"If she had no further need of him, yes, I believe she would," the prosecutor said.

"Then produce her weapon and prove it," Cyprian replied.

Lisbeth blew Cyprian a kiss and kicked the shin of the cheese merchant who'd tried to kiss her. When he grabbed at his injury, a hole opened up and she dashed toward the defendant's bench.

34

SWEAT TRICKLED DOWN MAXIMUS'S back in great rivulets. The eyes of Carthage were upon him. Not in the condemning manner of his mother-in-law, but with the same high expectations. From the way the plebs rallied at the news of Cyprian's pardon, Maximus could only guess how thrilled the poor would be if he released their healer. The happiness of the patricians would be an altogether different matter. These men of rank obviously were the ones who'd voted Cyprian into exile. Would it be too much to expect them to tolerate the solicitor's pardon? The very real possibility existed that freeing a slave who'd killed her master would, in fact, incite other slaves to attempt the same thing. If so, no one of rank and means was safe.

Maximus surveyed those gathered. Low-voiced opinions buzzed around him like a swarm of bees. How he wished someone had written his final line so that all he had to do now was take a deep breath, deliver it, and take his bow. But alas, that was not the case. The time had come for him to pronounce the verdict of his choosing. *Courage*, he told himself, and set to work weighing his options.

Maximus studied the pitiful woman who stood before him. Though obviously frail and possibly ill, power radiated from the knife lines drawn across her face like rays of sunshine. Not the power of flesh and blood, but the confidence of one who knew the outcome and was not afraid. If the healer were a patrician, Carthage would probably celebrate her as one who'd accomplished what no one had managed to do: ousted Aspasius Paternus from office. The hairs on Maximus's arms rose.

Whether her deed was accidental or intentional mattered little. What mattered was that if a woman could so easily accomplish the death of a man greater than he, where did that leave him? With his very life in jeopardy.

Fear began to coil inside him. Maximus, like all the other patricians staring at him, did not want to spend the rest of his tenure sleeping with a dagger beneath his pillow. And that's exactly what he would have to do if he claimed his inheritance from Aspasius and took his predecessor's healer into his house. If she didn't kill him, her supporters would. This slave possessed powers far too great for her to be allowed to live.

Maximus stood, held up his hands. When the silence he desired had been achieved, he spoke with feigned confidence: "Guilty!"

Silence hung in the Forum for but a brief instant.

"No!" The protest came from a single female voice on the opposite side of the Forum. Before Maximus could locate the dissenter, a woman leaped over the defendant's bench and was making her way straight toward him. "This isn't right!" she squawked like a mad banshee hen. "Magdalena did everything she could for that monster, but his insides were rotted beyond repair." The angry woman waved a shiny blade of some sort. "I was there!"

"Lisbeth, go back!" the accused screamed.

"She didn't kill him!" The woman came at his neck with the jagged saw blade. "She tried to save him!"

"Lisbeth, no!" Cyprian lunged for her, knocking her to the ground seconds before her saw would have found Maximus's throat.

The crazy woman would not be kept down. She squirmed from the defender's hold and leaped to her feet. "She's innocent!" she shouted, saw still in hand. "You're killing the only hope of Carthage!"

Somewhere in the Forum the sound of breaking glass ignited the murmurs into heated shouts. Broken broom handles and clubs made from sticks and steel rods were pulled from beneath cloaks. Anger exploded in the Forum as the crowd members rolled forward, waving their weapons like a great tide intent on sweeping the footprints of oppression and desperation from the sand. Sounds of steel blades being withdrawn from military scabbards accompanied the quick movement of soldiers double-timing into place around the judge's platform.

Safe behind the perimeter of crossed swords, Maximus issued his final line of the show: "Crucify this murderer and her accomplices immediately! Cast their bodies outside my city!"

35

MAGGIE STOOD FROZEN, WATCHING the chaotic scene record on her phone screen. People were shouting, pressing toward the stage, and throwing stones. Soldiers charged in and formed a perimeter of shields and spears. Jaddah had dropped out of the screen. Fear skittered over Maggie's skin. She panned her phone camera, zooming in on individuals and the anger on their faces.

Suddenly her mother's face filled the screen with a mixture of fury and terror. "She's innocent! If anyone is to blame, blame me!"

Maggie pulled down the phone. "Mom!"

Her mother snapped into action, jerked free of Maggie's father, then charged in to fight against the soldiers surrounding Jaddah.

"Mom!" Maggie shrieked, but her voice was lost in the surge of the inflamed mob.

"We've got to get out of here!" Eggie grabbed her elbow.

"No!" Maggie lunged toward the podium, but Barek held her back. "Let me go!"

His hand cuffed her wrist. "What do you think you're doing?"

"I'm going to help my mom!"

"No you're not!"

"You can't expect me to stand here and do nothing!" Maggie yelled above the noise. "Please, Barek."

A big man brandishing a broken broom handle knocked them aside. Barek pulled her to him. "I know you want to help her. But look around!" he shouted. "Have you counted the troops Maximus had brought in? We've got to think of another way."

Maggie watched helplessly as across the teeming mass of people a soldier lifted his sword over her mother's head. "Mom! Run!"

Her mother turned toward Maggie's voice just as the soldier brought the hilt down hard upon her head. Maggie watched helplessly as her mother, a tower of strength and determination, crumbled. "Mom!" Maggie felt Barek's arm hook her waist. She kicked at his shins but couldn't break free.

"Let's get her out of this crowd." Eggie nodded in the direction opposite the mob storming the podium.

Maggie's feet left the pavement. Before she could protest, she was hanging upside down over Barek's shoulder. "Put me down!" Blood rushing to her head, she pounded Barek's back. "Now!"

His grip tightened. His speed increased, jostling her like a rag doll. She felt him veer out of the crowd and duck down an alley. He stopped in a quiet, shaded nook of a large building.

"Where will they take Maggie's grandmother?" Eggie asked Barek, his breath coming in short huffs.

"To the arena," Barek spat out between his own labored breaths.

"They can't crucify someone they don't have," Eggie said.

Maggie raised her head. "Let me go!"

Barek squeezed Maggie's legs even tighter. "What are you saying, man?"

Eggie looked around as if worried they'd been followed. "You know the route they'll take to the arena, right?"

"The longest. To give the news time to spread and draw the biggest crowd," Barek said.

"Which way?"

"Past the theater, probably."

"Perfect. Find a place between here and there where you can hide."

"Then what?"

"Then jump out and grab the old lady when they come by."

"And what shall we use as weapons to fight off the soldier escort? Your charm?"

"Put me down!" Maggie demanded. "I've got to get to my mother."

Finally Barek acknowledged her. "I'll put you down, but if you try to run I'll beat your backside." He hauled her off his shoulder and dropped her with a thump.

She scrambled to her feet. "I have a knife." Maggie pulled the blade she'd bought from the airport vendor from her sash.

"Whoa!" Barek ripped it out of her hand. "Give me that before you hurt yourself."

"There, now you're armed, Barek. Feel better?" Eggie smirked. "The awkward way you're handling the weapon, hopefully you won't need it."

Barek slammed his forearm into Eggie's throat and pinned him against the wall. He brought the knife against Eggie's cheek with his other hand. "So you think the soldiers are just going to hand Magdalena over if I show them a weapon?"

"Barek! Stop it!" Maggie tugged on his sleeve but he wouldn't budge from his stance.

"I'll create a diversion," Eggie croaked.

"What kind of diversion?" Maggie asked.

"I'll think of something that will get everyone's attention."

"Then what?" she demanded.

"Then you and Barek grab your grandmother and run like ga-zelles. I'll circle back for your mother."

"We can't do this." Barek had dug in the way he did the night she'd wanted to go with him to bury his mother. She'd won then and she'd win now.

"Why not?" Maggie hoped neither guy could see the terror clawing her insides.

"I promised your father I'd keep you safe."

"And he promised my mother he'd save my grandmother," she argued. "Some promises get broken."

Barek looked between her and Eggie. He slowly lowered the knife, released Eggie's throat, and stepped back. "We can't take her back to Titus. They'll kill him for harboring a criminal."

Eggie rubbed his throat. "Got any better ideas?"

Maggie didn't know whether to be relieved or terrified that she'd gotten her way so easily. "You'll do it, Barek?"

"If I don't, you'll go anyway."

"Barek—"

His scowl silenced her explanation. "I know how you are! Once your mind is set, there's no changing your course. Don't try to deny it. I know you better than you think."

"Hate to interrupt your admiration for each other"—Eggie grabbed an unlit torch from a nearby streetlamp—"but if we do this, we'll need someplace to hole up until everything settles down."

Barek didn't hesitate a moment. "My parents' dye shop is vacant."

"Wait for the diversion, then grab her grandmother and go there." Eggie waved the bundle of sticks in a little farewell salute. "I'll catch up with you later."

Maggie ran after him. "Wait! How will you find us?"

"Smart as you are beautiful." Eggie clasped her face, pulled her to him, and planted a kiss on her forehead. "Tastes even sweeter." His release left her speechless. He shot a pleased smile to Barek. "Now, where is this dye shop?"

Barek threaded his fingers through Maggie's as if reclaiming what Eggie had so brazenly taken. "Southernmost fringe of the city." His eyes narrowed. "Follow the foul smell to a wooden tooth, then turn left."

36

AT THE SOUND OF Maggie's cries for help, a switch snapped in Lisbeth's head. She staggered to her feet. Righteous indignation at the proconsul's verdict had quickly morphed into something far more deadly than the headache she had from the blow to the head. She was a desperate mother determined to protect her child. Lisbeth fought wildly to free herself from the soldier dragging her away from the podium. He pinned her arms by wrapping them across her chest. She sank her teeth into his exposed flesh and didn't let up until she tasted blood.

"Ahhh! You little witch!"

While he writhed in pain, Lisbeth seized her chance. She broke loose and ran toward where she'd heard someone screaming for her in English.

"Maggie!" Her eyes frantically scanned the sea of angry protestors. Far beyond her reach, she caught a glimpse of blond curls. "Maggie!" She shifted her eyes over the crowd but her daughter was gone—swallowed by the surge of people like a footprint in sand. She began to spin, calling and searching with each rotation.

Someone grabbed her from behind and drew her to an instant halt. "Get out of here."

It took a second for recognition to pierce her blinding rage. "Cyprian! Maggie's here!"

He shook his head. "She's home with Barek."

Lisbeth waved the bone saw she'd somehow managed to hang on to in the direction she'd last seen their daughter. "I spotted her a minute ago but I couldn't get to her."

"Put that thing away." He pulled her tighter still and kissed her forehead. "I'll find her. Go home."

"Not without Maggie!" Lisbeth called after him, but he was gone. She turned back to the podium. Broad-shouldered military handlers had surrounded Maximus. Her mother's hands were being bound behind her back. Papa had made his way to the stage and was desperately ramming his body into the barrier of shields.

"Papa!" Lisbeth fought past brawling fishmongers and belligerent cheese merchants. "Papa!"

"I know you!" The redheaded soldier grabbed her arm and yanked her onto the podium. "You're the one from the dark alley. The one who claimed to be the wife of Cicero." He ripped the saw from her hands. From the recognition on his face, she could see that the combination of better light and the saw had made it easy for him to connect the dots. "You're not the senator's wife, you're the servant I brought to the proconsul's house the night of his surgery. She was there!" He flung her before Maximus. "She was the one who disappeared after the murderous deed was done."

"Arrest her!" Maximus ordered.

Lisbeth lunged for the soldier's throat. Her doubled fists hit his breastplate so hard she could feel her knuckles instantly swelling. The redhead laughed and grabbed hold of her elbow and jerked her close. He held her in a tight bear hug she couldn't break. Panic rushed in like a whirlwind.

"Let her go!" said an authoritative voice, then from out of nowhere, Cyprian launched his body at the redheaded soldier.

Lisbeth sailed backward. She rolled to a stop just as the redhead raised his whip. It came down with an electrifying crack across Cyprian's face.

Cyprian staggered backward but managed to stay upright. "Get Maggie and go home!" he shouted at Lisbeth as he quickly regained his balance and charged toward the redhead. "I'm the one you want!" He drew back his fist, anger flaring his nostrils. "Let's see how tough you are when you have to fight a man." He stood poised to release the full fury of the years of injustice he'd suffered at the hands of Rome.

Lisbeth crawled forward, her eyes on Cyprian. Halfway there, it was as if the wind changed, bringing with it a great, cooling sort of power. There could be no other explanation. For in the blink of an eye, Cyprian's will to fight was snuffed out. Vanished.

Cyprian slowly lowered his fist, stepped forward, and held out his hands for the cuffs. "I surrender."

"Cyprian! Don't!" Lisbeth felt a strong hand clasp her arm and yank her into the crowd.

WITH THE tip of a soldier's blade in his back, Cyprian kept his face straight ahead. He didn't dare look back, for one more glimpse of the terror on Lisbeth's face as Pontius dragged her away would compel him to fight to stay alive. She'd given up everything to save him: Her world. Her career. Her family. And yet, despite her sacrifices, Lisbeth could not change his destiny. He would not let her give up her ability to return home.

God, be with her because I can't.

Cyprian threaded his way through the mob, hoping to keep the redheaded guard escorting him from the Forum so busy Lisbeth would have an opportunity to escape. He set a course toward his client. He was intent on reaching Magdalena before they took her to be crucified. He wanted to tell her . . . to tell her his mistake was not in his arguments, for the law was on his side. His mistake was that he'd underestimated the reach of a dead man. Aspasius had tried to ruin his reputation with nasty rumors. Stripped him of his wife and friends. Charged him with treason against the throne. Rallied the support to exile him like a common criminal. And now, he'd taken his ability to make a difference.

A fresh pang of grief ripped through Cyprian. Those were not the things he really wanted to tell Magdalena Hastings. He wanted to say he didn't understand why God had allowed the most selfless woman Carthage had ever known to be sentenced to death. This city was sick. They needed a healer. They needed someone to show them Christ. They needed her, especially since Lisbeth was going home. He wanted to say he was sorry he was not the bishop his predecessor had been.

Dodging flying fists, elbows, and stones, he shouted, "Magdalena!" He pushed against the soldiers trying to hurry him to wherever they would hold him captive. He was a Roman citizen and a patrician through birth. By law he had the right to house arrest. He pressed against the swords holding him back. "She's my client. I have a right to speak to my client!"

"She's my prisoner." The redheaded soldier shoved him into the arms of another soldier. "Get him out of here!"

Two guards led him through the crowd and dragged him from any hope of saving the ones he loved.

A coldness seeped into his gut. Whatever was coming next, he would have to face the trial alone.

LISBETH PULLED against Pontius's iron grip, watching Cyprian calmly agreeing to be led from the Forum like a common criminal. His wrists were bound in metal cuffs. Her heart sped in several directions at once: *Cyprian. Maggie. Her parents.* She didn't know which way to run. Her family had been torn into pieces she might never stitch together again.

Lisbeth had never experienced this level of fear. From her very first visit to the third century, she'd faced one difficult situation after another. There'd been losses—huge ones. Yet somehow through it all, she'd always managed to hang on to a fragment of her family. Even all those years ago when her mother disappeared from the Cave of the Swimmers she'd had Papa. And when she'd had to leave Cyprian and Mama behind, she'd had Maggie. But this time things were different. At this moment, everyone she loved was beyond her reach.

Rioters rushed the tables of weights and measures and flipped them with ease. People dove for the scattered coins. Nearby someone picked up a stone and hurled it at the judge's podium. In an instant, stones whizzed through the Forum.

"We've got to go."

Lisbeth turned toward the hand pulling her in yet another direction. "Pontius, what are you doing?"

"What Cyprian would want!" he yelled over the bedlam. "Protecting you."

She shook her head. "I've got to find Maggie and my parents."

"I know a shortcut." Pontius waved his hand and suddenly Tappo, the brawny stonemason whose original desertion had left her and Cyprian to fend for themselves, flanked her. "If we hurry maybe we can cut them off on the way to the arena."

37

MAGGIE STUMBLED ALONG AFTER Barek, his grip on her
wrist so tight it was cutting off the circulation to her hand.
She'd crossed a line by convincing him to do this with her. These
people were not his family. Yet here he was, risking his life. If this
didn't work, there would be no going back to the time when they
were just two kids accidentally thrown together.

They rounded a corner and ducked into an alley. Barek held
her against the wall and pinned her with his arms. Breathing hard,
he said, "Not a word." He slid her knife from his sash. "I'll draw the
soldiers' attention. You grab your grandmother."

Maggie was determined to prove to him that she could carry
her weight in this plan. "Which way to your father's dye shop?"

His arms were a protective cage around her, holding her captive. Every nerve in her body tingled. He pressed his cheek against
hers, his stubble scratchy against her face as he whispered directions. She repeated them back in a muted breathlessness that drew
him even closer. "Mom and I searched the shop with the tooth
sign for herbs. I'll recognize it when I see it."

"You must make certain you are not followed." Barek's breath
warmed her neck and heated her blood. She prayed his buried face
meant he couldn't see the rush of heat to her cheeks.

The distant clamor of the approaching crowd scratched at Maggie's subconscious and lifted Barek's head in alert. Her eyes sought his for confirmation. He was staring at her lips. When she parted them to speak he laid his finger upon them. He must have felt the jolt of the connection because his eyes jerked to hers. Barek was no longer a terrified teen who didn't know what to do with a violently ill child. In the space of the past few days, he'd become a man willing to shield her with his own body.

"I can't breathe," she squeaked past the force of his finger.

Barek removed his hand and leaned in. Then in a totally unexpected move, his lips brushed hers. "You're breathing."

His voice, low and sure, pushed through the tangle of fear closing in on her. Maggie's throat opened and her lungs flooded not with air, but with a freeing realization. She didn't want to be the annoying reminder of Barek's tragic past. She wanted to be someone he could trust with his future. Her limbs grew loose and she threw her arms around his neck. For a second it was like one of those crazy slow-motion moments in a romance movie, that moment when both people want the world to stop so they can kiss at their leisure. She leaned toward Barek.

Shouts of "Free the healer!" came closer.

"They're coming." Her voice was barely a whisper he seemed to inhale.

Barek's body tensed. "Stay quiet." He leaned in and kissed her hard.

The threats of danger melted into Maggie's puddled heart. All too soon the moment was over. He released her and she pitched toward him like a moth to a flame, but he reached behind his neck and undid her hands. In one decisive movement, he pushed away.

She covered her mouth with her hand, hoping he'd read the clumsy move as her willingness to follow his instructions and not her attempt to keep the warmth of his touch from evaporating. She pressed her trembling core hard against the wall and listened. The distant roar of several hundred outraged plebeians was louder now.

"Wait for my signal." Barek eased his head slowly around the wall for a brief peek. He turned back to her. "Whatever happens, after you grab your grandmother I want you to run and don't look back."

"I'm not going to leave you to fight them alone." Maggie wiggled around for a peek of her own.

"Yes you are." Barek's strong arm lassoed her waist but he couldn't reel her in.

"They're beating her." Maggie strained against his hold, a magnet drawn to the iron of her grandmother's backbone. Jaddah's neck was unbowed, her head raised high. She seemed totally oblivious to the riots and the whip coming down upon her back. Instead, she kept trying to reach for G-Pa, who was running alongside her.

"Recant, Magdalena," Maggie could hear her grandfather begging. "Crucifixion will be your punishment. Please recant, my love."

The tall redheaded soldier cracked his whip, nicking Jaddah's shoulder. Maggie lunged against Barek's hold as the crowd surged forward in raucous disapproval. The armed escort that flanked the prisoner held the mob at bay with heavy bronze shields, the muscles in their legs bulging against their bootlaces. The redheaded soldier raised his whip again and brought the lash down with a sizzling slash upon G-Pa's back.

"Lawrence!" Jaddah screamed.

"No!" Maggie shot out from under Barek's arm and charged toward her grandparents.

She could hear Barek's frantic steps as he shouted curses at her refusal to heed his command, but she couldn't stop herself. "Let her go!" Maggie flew at the first soldier she came to, a short, stocky fellow not the least bit fazed by her attack. He wrapped his arms around her waist and lifted her kicking and screaming above the pavers. "Let my Jaddah go!" Maggie screamed.

Before she could think of what to do next, Barek plowed into the soldier from behind and sent the three of them somersaulting into the crowd. Maggie's back took the brunt of the landing. As they rolled around she struggled to catch her breath. Barek pulled the soldier off her and threw him into the crowd.

Clubs and knives appeared in hands that had been empty. Soldiers readied their spears and issued "Stand down" warnings. The mob disregarded the orders and jumped into the fray.

On her hands and knees Maggie scrambled to dodge boots and sandals. She crawled out from under several legs just as a soldier's whip came across her Jaddah's back and knocked her to the ground.

"No!" Maggie bolted to her feet and fought her way to her grandparents.

"Maggie?" G-Pa yelled over people pushing and shoving. "What are you doing here?"

She threw herself between her grandmother and the soldier rearing back to swing his whip again. "I could ask you the same thing!" Maggie cried out.

"Go home!" G-Pa ordered, hanging on to Jaddah's chain.

"No! Not without you."

"Step away from the prisoners." The redheaded soldier came at Maggie with the whip. He drew back his arm, set his legs, and prepared to unleash the full fury of his lash.

"Don't touch her." The short, stocky soldier who'd been wrestling with Barek when last she saw him grabbed the leather cord of the redhead's whip and held it steady. "That's enough."

"You stupid scut, I'll see you stripped of your rank and hanged." The redhead ripped the lash from the hands of the stocky soldier and released the leather strap with a blinding force across his fellow soldier's face. The short soldier reeled backward, found his footing, then lowered his head and charged. His helmet rammed into the redhead with velocity comparable to that of the ox who'd attacked Ruth not far from this very spot.

Maggie scanned the street fight for Barek. He was picking himself up and coming toward her with his knife raised.

"Smoke!"

Everything came to a halt. Sweaty faces lifted to the sky. A dark, angry cloud churned above them.

"Fire!" Maggie shouted. "Fire!"

Weapons clattered upon the pavement. The mob scattered into the gray wisps, calling to each other to grab jugs and head for the wells. Smoke stung Maggie's nostrils and burned her throat. The soldier brigade broke its line of defense and fled in the direction of the black cloud. All but two: the tall redheaded soldier with the dented chest armor and the short stocky one with a lopsided helmet. They were locked in a standoff.

"You dare to attack your superior?" the redhead said with a growl. He cast his whip aside and drew his sword. "I'll cut you down right here and earn a gold piece for it." The sword flashed in his hand.

The short one, breathing hard from his defensive tackle, ripped keys from his belt and tossed them to Barek. "Take them and go!"

"No, Brutus!" Jaddah reached a bloody hand toward the soldier. "They'll kill you."

"Go!" Brutus shouted as he freed his sword. He raised his blade and faced the redhead. "There is but *one* God!" Brutus fastened his gaze on the redhead and charged straight at the glistening steel pointed at his throat.

38

"MAGGIE!" BAREK TUGGED HER wrist but she was too dumbfounded by what the soldier had done to move. Watching someone die on a movie screen was nothing like being only a few feet away from the gruesome reality playing out before her.

"Come on!" The urgency of Barek's command wrestled her free of her stupor, giving her no time to process the sights and sounds of someone losing his life on her behalf. "Help them!" he shouted. From the corner of her eye she saw a chain being hurled her way. "Now!"

Barek had taken advantage of the redhead's focus on the sword fight and launched into action. He'd used Brutus's key and managed to free her grandmother of her chains, but before Barek could free Jaddah's friends, the redheaded soldier withdrew the sword he'd plunged through Brutus.

The soldier's eyes lifted, full of hate and revenge. Blood dripped from his blade. "I'll kill all of you."

"Run, Maggie!" Barek linked arms with G-Pa and practically lifted Jaddah's feet from the ground. The three sprinted away. The chain connecting Jaddah's friends snapped taut in Maggie's hand, leaving her no choice but to drop it or run along after them.

Hobnail cleats fast approached. The quick clip had an eerily similar ring to what she'd heard the night she and Barek sneaked out to bury his mother and ended up ducking into the Tophet to ditch the soldiers. Remembering the underground burial chamber as a place of safety surprised her. No matter its attachment to death, it was the perfect place to give this mad dog the slip. "Barek, we must find your mother's urn."

She could tell from his quick nod that he'd caught her meaning. Barek was now nearly carrying her grandmother as he tried to run faster. Determined to keep up, Maggie pulled Jaddah's weary friends along as she fought the smoke constricting her throat. Where was Eggie? Had he been caught creating a diversion, whatever it was?

As their entourage skidded around a corner, Maggie glanced behind her. A couple of old people, three chained women, and one terrified college dropout were easy catches for the highly trained foot soldier in hot pursuit. The redheaded soldier quickly overtook them. He bypassed the servants and went straight for Maggie. He grabbed a handful of her hair, snapping her head backward. The pain was so sharp and sudden, she dropped the chain.

"Barek!" She slammed into the ground. Before another word could leave her mouth, Barek was between her and the soldier, his knife extended and his nostrils flaring.

"Run!" he yelled.

Maggie struggled to her feet, but she was too late. Barek and the redhead were locked in hand-to-hand combat.

G-Pa grabbed her from behind. "Which way?"

"I can't—"

G-Pa shook her. "Which way?"

Hot tears stinging her cheeks, Maggie picked up the chain. She didn't dare look back or she wouldn't be able to choose between saving Barek and saving her family.

A few breathless minutes later, she, Jaddah, G-Pa, and her grandmother's three friends were well out of earshot of Barek's scuffle. As they stood huffing among the burial urns stored in the cavernous tomb of the Tophet, she had no way of knowing what happened after she fled. The guilt was nauseating. Had Barek escaped? Or had . . .

She didn't dare think about what she would do if Barek didn't come for them.

Outside the Tophet, the frantic calls of citizens and soldiers scurrying to put out the fire continued. Maggie and her little band of escapees plastered themselves against the nearest wall and listened. Fingers of smoke crept through the arched doorway. Maggie surveyed the burial chamber in the dim light. Somewhere among the stacks and stacks of urns were the remains of Barek's beloved mother and the premature baby who'd died with her.

Maggie swallowed the sour taste this memory always brought to her mouth. If she didn't come up with some kind of plan, very likely her own remains would be excavated from this place someday. She listened carefully to the noise filtering through the doorway.

"This is the place that changed our lives," her g-pa whispered as he helped Jaddah lower herself to the dusty cave floor.

Maggie kept one eye on the door, the other on the pain creasing her grandmother's face. "What do you mean?"

"I was poking around the ancient ruins and fell through about right there." He pointed to a place in the domed ceiling, a place still intact. "Landed on an urn." He squatted beside Jaddah and wrapped his arm around her shoulders. "Met your grandmother when she had to dig the potsherd out of my backside. She was the one who noticed the little swimmer."

Maggie's heart stopped. "Swimmer?"

G-Pa nodded. "When I pieced it all together, I discovered the little swimmer was a replica of Neolithic art I'd seen in a book about the Cave of the Swimmers. Got me to thinking, how did this exact same picture end up in Carthage? A thousand miles from the point of origin. So I went to the desert looking for answers."

Lightning-hot guilt rattled Maggie's limbs. Memories swirled like the ashes in Ruth's burial fire. Maggie was the one who'd drawn the swimmers on the urn. She was the one who'd changed their lives. This whole big mess was her fault. None of her family would have even known about the time portal if she'd only let Barek bury his mother in peace. Jaddah wouldn't have suffered for years at the hands of a madman. Mom wouldn't have had to grow up without her mother and she never would have come here. But if Mom hadn't come here, would Barek's mom be dead? And even more sobering, would Maggie exist at all?

"Lawrence, grab her," Jaddah said.

Maggie's legs went out from under her and she slumped into her grandfather's arms.

WHEN MAGGIE came to a few minutes later, her head rested in her Jaddah's lap. "Maggie." Her grandmother's velvet touch stroked her hair away from her face. "You've grown up to be every bit as beautiful as I had imagined."

Maggie shifted uncomfortably beneath the praise. Urns stacked fifty to a hundred high surrounded them. "We can't stay here." She tried to push up, but the sudden motion gave her the feeling jugs of ashes were flying around her head.

G-Pa eased her back into her grandmother's lap. "You aren't going anywhere just yet, young lady."

"Did I say anything while I was out?"

"You said 'Forgive me' over and over," Jaddah whispered.

Maggie moaned.

"Forgive you for what?" G-Pa wanted to know.

The knot began to uncoil inside her. Maggie emptied herself of the shameful story of Ruth's urn: How she'd been so desperate to make it up to Barek for her part in Ruth's death that she'd thrown a fit until he finally agreed to take her with him to bury his mother outside the city. How she'd twisted her ankle and cried like a baby and that's how and why she and Barek had come to hide in this place. And when the soldiers discovered them, Barek had to choose between saving her or his mother's ashes.

"I'm sorry. I never thought"—she dared to raise her eyes and saw her grandparents sitting with their mouths open, too stunned to speak—"a little picture could cause so much hurt. But that's always been my problem . . . I don't think."

G-Pa reached for her. "I'm glad the mystery is solved." Tears glittered in his eyes. "Aren't you, Magdalena?" Where was his rage? His anger at being separated from his wife for nearly thirty years.

"I can't imagine our lives without our precious Maggie." Her grandmother leaned over and kissed her forehead. "You and your mother are proof of how splendidly God uses broken potsherds."

She wondered how her mother would feel once she learned Maggie was the artist responsible for bringing her parents together and for tearing them apart. Her mom was still trying to compensate for feeling abandoned by Magdalena. Deep down, Maggie knew her mother didn't want her ever to feel abandoned. That's why she never let her out of her sight. The truth that she had been too self-absorbed to see it hit her hard now.

Maggie accepted hugs and reassurances she did not deserve. She would make it up to her mom by taking very good care of her mother's parents until they could all be together again. She'd need a plan. Possibly it was a little late to perfect this skill, but from here on out, she was determined to use more than the artistic half of her brain. Who knew? She might even surprise both Barek and her mother by actually coming up with a viable way to get them all out of this mess. At the very least, she owed it to these people she loved to try.

39

STONES AND VEGETABLES WHIZZED across the melee in the Forum. A rotten tomato smacked Maximus in the chest. The bloody stain spreading across the front of his snowy white toga matched the fear sweeping through his body. He dove behind the judge's seat and pressed his upset stomach to the stage floor.

His bodyguard snatched a shield from the hands of the nearest soldier and flew to his aid. "Why did you order Cyprianus Thascius to be taken under house arrest?" Kaeso shouted, deflecting a pomegranate. "Could you not see that the people hated your verdict?"

"Save your lecture." Maximus poked his head up long enough to shout, "Get me out of here!" A rock hit him square between the eyes. "Ahhhh!" He pressed his hand to the stinging insult. "See what you've done!"

"Me?" His servant deflected flying debris with the fleet-footed skill of a trained soldier. "I did not condemn their healer to death."

Maximus used his elbows to slither closer to the protection of his servant's shield. "Think of the chaos that would ensue if servants got away with killing their masters."

"And what do you call this?" Kaeso veered right to fend off a rotten fish, leaving Maximus in the open.

"Don't look at me like that. I had no choice." A fist-size stone grazed Maximus's shoulder. He rolled behind Kaeso's shield.

"There's always a choice." Kaeso hooked him under the arm. "I hear your chariot approaching." He hauled him to his feet. "Stay close, and keep your head down."

Maximus clung to Kaeso's shoulders. His nails dug into his servant's sinewy flesh in hopes of salvaging more than this day. His self-respect was at stake.

Five black horses galloped into the Forum, clearing a wide path on their way to the podium. The driver reined them hard, and the lead horse reared and pawed at the startled protestors.

"Run!" Kaeso moved forward, shield in front, head down. Maximus raised his hands to protect his face and made a flying dive into the chariot. "To the arena," Kaeso ordered.

"No!" Maximus rose to his knees and grabbed his servant's tunic. "I can't go there! They'll kill me!"

"You can issue pardons and undo all of this." He pried Maximus loose. "Now, get down." Kaeso shoved him to the floorboard and snapped the shield over the tiny space as if trapping a lizard in a jar.

The driver cracked the whip and they spun out of the Forum. From his crouched position, Maximus could hear women and children screaming, dropping their stones, and diving out of the path of the speeding vehicle.

What had he done?

He'd expected a smattering of disappointment when he announced his judgment, for every person of note had his followers, but how had a slave woman and an above-average solicitor garnered such support? If only he'd listened to Titus and allowed someone local to preside over the trial, he would not be fleeing the Forum like some cheap herbalist whose tonics were nothing more than colored water.

As his chariot raced through the city, Maximus dropped his head to his knees and wrapped his arms around the terror twisting in his gut. The farther they traveled from the Forum, the louder the roar of the crowd and the faster his heartbeat. He would be lucky if these barbarians didn't crucify him. Shudders of sheer terror shook his body.

Who was he kidding? He wasn't brave, and after he learned the acting trade he wouldn't have to act brave anymore. What would it hurt if he released his prisoners? Crucifying the healer would not bring back Aspasius from the dead. Why should Maximus be the one to suffer for the evil deeds of the former proconsul? Besides, a little goodwill could go a long way toward making his tenure here tolerable. If he granted Cyprian a pardon, he could dump the restoration of Carthage into the solicitor's lap and free his time to do what he really wanted to do: study under Epolon and become the greatest actor the world had ever seen.

Kaeso was right. It wasn't too late to fix this. He would grant the pardons. Set both Magdalena and Cyprian free. His frowning face relaxed as he imagined an appreciative and adoring audience.

Maximus tapped on the shield to signal his servant and announce his plan. But the shield was not removed. He pounded. Still the barrier was not removed. His cramped space seemed to be growing warmer and warmer. He ripped the greenery from his head and used the edge of his toga to sop the sweat and blood trickling down his neck. The more he mopped, the thicker the air became inside the chariot. An acrid burn sizzled in his throat. His knuckles rubbed the sting in his eyes.

Smoke!

Was his vehicle on fire? Gasping for air, he pounded frantically on the bottom of the shield. "Kaeso, I smell smoke. Stop! Let me out!"

The chariot ground to a sudden halt. Jumpy horses skittered over the curb. The chariot rolled right, sending Maximus crashing into the side. Then the vehicle box teetered as if it were going to go over and fell back on its wheels.

"Kaeso! Let me out!"

His servant lifted the shield. Thick smoke flooded the cramped compartment. "You don't want to see this."

Maximus burst out coughing. Intense heat warmed his back. He pivoted toward the strange roar.

"My theater!" White-hot flames danced across the stage, pillaging the set pieces and his aspirations of freedom. "Noooo!" His horrified shout sliced through every flight of fancy he'd dared consider since his banishment to Carthage. "Not my theater!"

He flew from the chariot. Giving no heed to Kaeso's pleas for his return, he pulled his toga over his head and raced to save his dreams.

Blasts of heat hit him in the face, sucking the air from his lungs. But he would not be deterred. As if chopping wood, Maximus slapped his heavy wool toga at the hungry fingers of fire tearing into the newly painted props—a forest of gnarled trunks and leafless branches. He inhaled noxious fumes and soldiered on, beating his way to the misanthropic farmer's cottage that had been designed for the upcoming show. Epolon had promised to reward his hard work with a part in this tale of a young noble who falls in love with a peasant girl. Of course, the director had made it clear Maximus wasn't ready to have a speaking role, but portraying a mute woodland nymph would be a start to his career nonetheless.

A firm hand stayed Maximus's toga flinging. "You're going to get hurt." Kaeso had removed his tunic. Sweat glistened on his heaving chest. "Please, master, return to the chariot."

"No! We must save everything." Maximus swiped away sweat blurring his eyes and started for the nearest flame. From the corner of his eye he noticed his servant fighting alongside him and he was encouraged to fight harder. Soon people came from every direction, water sloshing from the jugs they carried. Their liquid offerings were like spitting in the face of an angry god. Billowing black clouds whooshed toward the sky and obscured the sun.

"Help!" A distant cry was but a kitten's mew above the building roar of flames, but it was a voice Maximus recognized immediately.

"Epolon!" Maximus sifted through the haze to locate his mentor. Perched atop thirty feet of scaffolding was his beloved teacher. Epolon clung to a corner of the heavy tapestry that was draped between a semicircle of twelve massive stone pillars. "Leave it, my friend!"

The wind shifted. The carnivorous blaze immediately switched its attention from the charred bones of flimsy set pieces and began eating its way to the scaffolding, devouring Maximus's hopes of saving the show. Horror seized him. The fire wasn't after the show. It was headed straight for his only hope for the future.

"Get down, Epolon!" His mentor could not hear him over the deafening march of hungry flames. "Get down!"

Maximus raised his forearm to shield his face. Intense heat singed the hair on his arms. He lowered his head, pulled the neck of his tunic over his nose, and charged toward Epolon. He was halfway between the stage lip and the scaffolding when two giant hands grabbed his shoulders. "Go back, master!"

"Not without Epolon!" He pointed to the man frantically working to free the stage curtains. "We must save my instructor!"

"I'll get him." Kaeso ensnared Maximus under the arms and began dragging him toward the lip of the stage despite the pummeling Maximus gave him with his fists. Once they reached the edge of the stage, Kaeso gave him a big push and sent him flying into the musicians' pit.

Tumbling head over heels, Maximus landed on the stone floor with a jarring thud. The impact knocked the breath from his dis-

tressed lungs. He scrambled to his feet and climbed the wall between the pit and the audience seats. Coughing smoke and soot,
he clawed at his watery eyes. From his front-row seat, the tragedy
played out only fifty feet from him.

"Kaeso, no!"

At the back of the stage Kaeso had reached the scaffolding.
Flames chased his servant's assent up the wooden crossbeams.
He'd just climbed aboard the plank platform where Epolon held
tightly to the curtain when something exploded. Maximus's hands
flew to his face as a demon-eyed head of seething flames rose high
above the two men.

The cloud of fire rained down its wrath at the exact moment
greedy flames ignited the scaffolding beneath his mentor's feet. Orange and yellow tongues climbed up the wooden support beams
and licked Kaeso's boots. The frightened director jumped for the
heavy tapestry. With the skill of a circus performer, Epolon managed to snag two handfuls. He held on with one hand and motioned for Kaeso to join him. But they both knew the fabric from
which Epolon hung could support only one. Kaeso was stranded,
sandwiched between fire from above and fire from below.

"Kaeso, I'm coming!" Maximus raced for the side entrance,
rage pumping strength into his legs. When he was less than fifteen
feet from the stage the scaffolding collapsed. He stood frozen,
watching his servant plunge into the roiling flames, like a lobster
the gods had dropped into a boiling pot. "Kaeso!" Maximus released a scream so painful he doubled over and vomited.

"Help!" Epolon's shrieks drew Maximus immediately upright.

Through his tears he could see his wiry director, still clutching
handfuls of fabric and hanging suspended over the incinerated
stage. Epolon began to kick the air as if he were a bird trying to
take flight. Swinging back and forth, he kicked harder and harder,
aiming for the next pillar. For a brief, hopeful moment it looked as

if Epolon would reach his goal and from there be able to shinny down to safety.

Suddenly the foundations beneath the stage groaned. A cracking snap echoed against the stone seating dug into the hillside. The pillar from which Epolon hung swayed, a little unsteadily at first, then grew more and more wobbly.

Maximus could tell the teetering stone longed to be free of the added weight. He had to get Epolon out of there. Maximus took a step forward, tripped over the hem of his tunic, and fell flat on his face. Before he could get to his feet, the pillar from which Epolon swung crashed to the stage. Epolon plunged into the hissing flames with an animalistic scream. Maximus managed to right himself just as the force of Epolon's rapid descent jerked the fabric attached to the next pillar. The adjoining marbled post fell to the stage in a thundering boom. One by one each pillar toppled. Within seconds the entire structure had crumbled into a pile of kindling sticks. Sparks flew fifty feet high and showered burning ash upon the staircase where Maximus stood helpless.

When he realized he'd not been buried alive, he started beating at the sparks burning holes in his flesh. He staggered back to the chariot, covered in the ashes of everything he held dear.

His theater. His mentor. His loyal servant. His dreams.

The inconsolable wailing of Maximus could be heard far beyond the cheap seats.

40

L ISBETH KEPT ONE HAND tightly attached to the back of Pontius's tunic and one hand grasping Tappo's muscular arm for fear of losing them in the thickening smoke. What was burning? Surely she hadn't missed her own mother's execution. "Hurry!" she screamed above the roar of the increasing panic in the streets.

Both men were struggling to clear a path through eddies of smoke obstructing their view and the frantic citizens trying to exit the clogged alleyway. Her hope of finding Maggie or her parents in this chaos was disappearing along with the fresh air.

As people pushed past her screeching "Fire!" she'd reach out and ask, "Have you seen my daughter? She's blond and—" But they'd shake loose of her grip and hurriedly move on.

Ahead, officers had made a barrier with their shields and spears. "Back!" The crowd shrieked and surged away from the danger. Pontius and Tappo attempted to turn around but changed their minds after Lisbeth threw a fit.

"Back, plebs!" Soldier spears and shields were at the ready by the time they reached the end of the alley.

"My daughter," Lisbeth pleaded, not caring that her boldness put her in direct danger of the military's shortened tempers. "I've lost my daughter!"

"No one has come this way."

Lisbeth's building rage exploded. Her eyes locked on the line of shields raised in her face. "She has!" Her swollen knuckles pounded into the nearest shield with such force the soldier took a step back. "I know it."

"Stand down, woman," the soldier warned.

Tappo and Pontius had her by the arms, but Lisbeth thrust her body forward. "Let me pass!"

The soldier's blow landed hard on her forehead. A cracking sound rang in Lisbeth's ears. Gray wisps of smoke swirled the possibility that Maggie was lost to her forever.

AS LISBETH'S mental haze lifted, she realized she was laid out on a fine feather bed. Faces black with soot and eyes dark with concern stared down at her. Where was she and how long had she been incapacitated? The bitter taste of panic soured her tongue, but she couldn't remember where the fear came from.

"Pontius?" She needed to sit up, to extricate the smoke in her lungs, but the command never made it past the jumbled neurons fighting for order inside her head. It was all she could do to struggle for a deep breath.

"She's awake." Pontius's teeth were white against the gray of his ash-covered face.

"Give her a minute." The gravelly voice penetrating her grogginess was a voice of her recent memory, but she didn't have the energy to identify the speaker or pinpoint why his presence was so reassuring. The need to get up nagged her. She attempted to push herself up to . . . She couldn't remember what she needed to do.

"Maybe she's thirsty?" Tappo suggested.

"Sit her up slowly," the elderly voice directed. "Easy now."

Every fiber in her body rebelled against the rearranging. Her head weighed a ton and some evil little monster pounded a drum between her eyes. A cup appeared under her nose. The rising steam smelled medicinal. She cocked her head to shake loose of the nauseating odor and caught a glimpse of the man who belonged to the gnarled fingers wrapped around the cup. "Metras?"

"Little sips." His kind eyes encouraged her to cooperate.

Lisbeth obeyed and parted her lips.

"That's a good girl." The old man gently tilted the cup. A bitter mix of warm beer, fennel, sage, and something reminiscent of animal droppings lubricated her mouth and allowed her tongue to break free. "Go slow now."

Lisbeth swallowed, gasped, then launched into a coughing fit. When she finally caught the breath she'd been craving, she raised her head. "What happened?"

"She's going to be fine," Metras announced with a toothless smile. "Bring me the basin."

"I don't have time for this." Lisbeth waved him off and swung her feet toward the floor. Her off-kilter equilibrium spun her back onto the mattress. "I may need to rest for a minute longer."

"You need those wounds tended." Metras propped his cane against the bed, tied a towel around his waist, and dipped a clean cloth into the basin. "We'll start with the nasty gashes on your head. Looks like you've been on the south end of a northbound mule for the worst part of a week." Before she could protest, Metras began sopping up blood and rinsing dirt and debris from each knock she'd taken to the head. "Tappo, you and Pontius go on and see to our other patients. Send Tappo's wife to me. Lisbeth's going to need a woman's help." His face had deep tracks left by suffering and hard work. "Go ahead, Lisbeth. Close your eyes." His hands were careful and gentle, a sculptor repairing cracks on a rare piece of marble.

Lisbeth's heavy lids sanded her burning eyes. "What happened?"

"Shhhh," Metras said softly. "I'm going to press this bandage to that gash on your forehead. Might hurt a bit." She opened one eye enough to see he held a strip of muslin dripping with a sticky golden mixture. "Hold still." A sickly sweet smell passed her nose as he lifted the strip above her head.

"What is that?"

"Pure honey. Apparently Titus has been holding back. Saving this treat for a special occasion." Metras chuckled. "Good thing he thought you were special."

"Honey?" Her fingers traced the borders of the laceration while her cotton-stuffed brain worked to calculate the depth. "I probably need stitches."

"Sinew leaves a nasty scar." Metras returned her hand to her side. "Honey seals the wound and keeps out the infection." He pressed the bandage to her head and she moaned. "Quarry workers still call me when they need a wound tended." He rinsed his hands in the bowl, then shuffled to the end of the bed.

She felt his rough hand clasp her ankle. "What are you doing?"

"I can't tell if the blood on your foot came from your head injury or if we've got another problem. Afraid I'm going to have to take a look. I'll go easy." Metras untied the laces of her sandals and slipped them off. He lifted her foot for a closer inspection. "Thought I smelled infection. Your heel is rank. This didn't happen today." Gentle poking sent needles of pain up the back of her leg.

"I stepped on a pottery shard my first night back."

"Back from where?"

Another world? Another life? Another failed promise. "Uh, Maggie was sick. I took her to a special doctor. Remember?" Hot tears spilled onto Lisbeth's cheeks. "Has anyone seen her?"

Metras cast a questioning look at Tappo's wife, who had slipped into the room with her arms full of supplies. The beautiful woman with raven-colored hair shook her head sadly. A cute little girl followed after her.

Metras patted Lisbeth's leg. "Don't worry. We'll find Maggie." His gummy smile was strangely reassuring. "If we don't get this infection stopped you'll be in worse shape than Aspasius."

"Antibiotics," she mumbled. "In my bag."

"Shhhh. I think we have enough of that potion down you to help you sleep." Metras stroked the top of her foot. "Candia, you got an onion in that load of supplies you're toting?"

"And some garlic." Tappo's wife piled a fresh tunic, a wooden herb box, and a hairbrush on the bed. "Want me to make a poultice?"

"You peel the onion, I'll heat the rags." Metras hobbled over to the glowing coals in the small brazier. He crouched by a pot and began crumbling leaves and bark into the rising steam. Soon the room smelled like wet wool and the corned beef and cabbage the hospital cafeteria served on Tuesdays.

Lisbeth fought the warm, slushy feeling creeping through her veins. She searched her jagged memories for clues. What had happened and how had she ended up a patient in her own hospital? Losing the battle against whatever drug Metras had slipped into her drink, Lisbeth attempted to grab Candia's hand. "Must. Save. Maggie."

Candia's fingers found hers, then laid Lisbeth's hand upon her chest. "Sleep." Those same kind fingers gently grazed Lisbeth's eyelids and slid them shut.

Alone in empty darkness, Lisbeth lost her grip on the frayed edges of reality and plunged into the abyss.

41

B Y THE TIME MAGGIE felt steady on her feet, late afternoon shadows spilled in through the grotto's doorway. Leaving Barek to fight alone then falling apart the way she had was pretty pathetic, even for her. She couldn't undo what she'd done. All she could do was move forward.

She glanced around the underground graveyard. Jaddah's face was flush, and when her grandmother thought no one was looking she clutched her middle as if someone were twisting her insides into knots. If they stayed, Jaddah would soon join the countless dead buried in this place.

Maggie dusted herself off, then listened carefully. The earlier hustle of alarmed citizens and volunteer firefighters rushing about the streets outside the Tophet had subsided.

Tough as the task would be, seeing her grandparents safely tucked away in Barek's old shop had to be her first priority. Next, she'd find out what happened to Barek and Eggie. The keys to the iron shackles were still with Barek. Maggie couldn't do anything about the distinctive noise of the prison chains except pray the descending darkness would make it hard to pin down the source of the rattle. Maybe she could find some kind of hammer once they arrived at the shop and whack the cuffs off the way heroes in G-Pa's westerns did. If they ever made it to the shop.

And last on her very sketchy list, if Eggie hadn't found her mother, she'd track down her parents and beg their forgiveness.

"Let's go." Maggie helped her companions to their feet, then stuck her head out the back exit, the same opening in the cave she and Barek had used to escape the soldiers who'd chased them when she was a child. "Clear."

One by one they followed her out into the deepening twilight. Their bedraggled group wove through the leaning gravestones of the Tophet yard. Maggie checked over her shoulder every few seconds, although without her knife there wasn't much she could do if they were discovered. "Come on, everybody. We've got to get out of here."

The farther their little entourage traveled from the heart of the city, the slower her grandmother moved. G-Pa was doing his best to prod Jaddah forward, but each step was an effort. Maggie fell back and joined arms with her grandparents. "Lean on me." What if her grandmother's strength gave out before they reached the dye shop?

Darkness was settling fast over the city as Maggie led her frightened little group through the narrow, twisted streets lined with mounds of crushed seashells. The dye district stank worse than Mom's car had after what her family jokingly dubbed "the sand dollar incident." The summer of Maggie's tenth birthday she'd talked her mother and G-Pa into taking her to Galveston. She'd loved walking the beach and picking up sand dollars. She'd begged to bring her living treasures home. Mom said the fragile creatures would die in the hot car, but Maggie sneaked them aboard anyway. They weren't halfway back to Dallas when Maggie realized the price everyone, including the dead sand dollars, would pay for her disobedience.

Maggie put out her hand, indicating everyone should stop and keep quiet. "Hear that?" The rusty creak of metal and the scrap of wood brought a relieved smile to her face. "It's the wooden tooth." She led them toward the sound. "We're almost there, Jaddah."

A few more weary steps and they were standing outside the boarded-up windows of the dye shop. The labored breathing of her grandmother and the rapid pounding of Maggie's own heart were the only signs of life in the eerily silent rug and dye district. She did as Barek had instructed and checked to make sure they'd not been followed.

"Let me go first." Maggie moved toward the latch. Her hand froze midreach. The door was slightly ajar. She didn't want to go inside, but after today's very public trial, Jaddah's face might as well have been posted on Facebook. Everyone would recognize her. Even more important than securing a place to hide, her grandmother needed medical care.

Wishing once again that Barek hadn't taken her knife, Maggie picked up a stick. "Stand back," she mouthed. Hiking her flimsy club, she used her foot to push the plank open a couple more inches, hoping for a better look inside. Scents of rotten fish, wool, and abandonment rushed out to greet her. At the scuffle of feet too big to belong to a rat, she backed away from the door.

"Who's in there?" Adrenaline jangled her body. "Barek?"

The door opened slowly. Everything inside her screamed *Run!* But her feet had rooted to the ground and the club swayed over her head like a branch in a thunderstorm.

"Maggie?" Eggie stuck his head around and waved a cautious hand. "It's me."

"You scared me half to death." She still hadn't lowered her club. "Where have you been?"

"Me? What about you?" Eggie opened the door. "I've been here for hours."

"Do you have my mother?"

"By the time I made it back to the Forum, she was nowhere to be found."

Worry scampered over Maggie's skin. She lowered her stick and all of them stumbled into the dark room. "Barek's not here?"

"No. Isn't he with you?"

"We got separated." When Barek didn't show up at the Tophet, she'd refused to believe the worst. Instead, she'd told herself he'd decided it was safer to meet them at the rendezvous spot. But deep down she knew he'd never leave her to navigate this dangerous city on her own. Something wasn't right. "Is there any light?"

"Didn't want anyone to know I was here so I haven't moved around much," Eggie said.

"Well, I've got sick and wounded who can't be tended in the dark."

Their hands outstretched, everyone but Jaddah crashed about the shop in a terrifying game of blindman's buff. Maggie had never missed Barek more. If he were here he'd know exactly where to find the lights and what to do next. Kardide was the first to come up with a lamp. Tabari discovered a small jug of rancid oil and a flint in a cupboard. Iltani struck the flint, and a weak spark became a tiny flame that gobbled the dry wick. The place where Barek had grown up slowly materialized.

"Looks like Barek's family left in a hurry." Eggie plucked a blanket off a small bed and draped it over the boarded window to make sure no light escaped.

"They moved in with my father after his conversion." In the flicker of the oil lamp, Maggie could make out the remnants of Barek's past life.

Skeins of yarn, dusty and dry as everything in this city, hung from the rafters like a fading rainbow. In the corner near the only window, a loom was strung with a project that appeared to be more than halfway completed. Maggie ran her fingers over the tightly woven threads, wondering what it would have been like to have a closely knit family, one where everyone lived in the same century. The tapestry was an exquisite garden scene similar to the one hanging in her father's atrium. On the opposite side of the room, near a door that led to the alley, the limestone tiles beneath a huge copper vat were splattered with multiple colors.

Maggie closed her eyes, breathing in the scent of people who had lived and loved within these four simple walls. She could imagine Barek chasing his father's dogs around the dye vat and stubbing his chubby little toe on one of the wooden feet of his mother's loom. She could hear Ruth's laughter as she reached out for him and drew him onto her lap.

No wonder Barek wore such a scowl now. He must have been so happy here.

"Let's see if we can't find something to get these iron bracelets off these ladies." G-Pa's touch snapped her from her guilt-ridden fantasy.

Maggie went to the table beside the dye vat and retrieved a mallet and a piece of iron that looked kind of like a tent stake. "What about this?"

G-Pa smiled. "That's how they do it in Dodge."

Barek's father hadn't brewed his famous purple dye in this place in nearly three years. Yet various shades of deep violet still ringed the empty dye vat the way her mistakes ringed her heart.

If Maggie had stayed home today, as her mother had asked, guilt wouldn't be closing in, pressing against her chest and making it difficult to breathe. Jaddah was definitely not well. They had no food or water. Every soldier in town was looking for them. And worst of all, her parents and Barek could be dead in a gutter because of her. Hadn't the sand dollar episode taught her the danger of doing whatever she wanted? She longed to bust out the windows and suck in huge, cleansing gulps of fresh air.

Murex shells crunched beneath Maggie's feet as she jammed the tip of the iron stake into the lock on Kardide's wrist. "Hold your arm still." She hammered as if she were driving a stake for one of G-Pa's excavation grids. Breaking someone out of chains was a lot harder than it looked on TV.

It took a few solid hits to the stake before Kardide's cuff broke open and her chains fell to the floor and raised a cloud of dust. Everyone gave a muted cheer. Maggie did a little victory dance, waving the hammer above her head like a tomahawk. Maybe God could redeem her mess after all. She freed the rest of her grandmother's friends with renewed strength. They all set to work quietly righting stools, clearing tools from the table, and searching the cupboards and storage crocks for anything edible.

"Everyone stand back." Eggie gave the straw tick that had been on the small wooden bed frame a good shake. Spiders and dust flew everywhere. It took all of them to convince Maggie that it was safe for anyone to use the bed, let alone Jaddah, who seemed to be melting right before her eyes.

"We need water and a way to boil it," Kardide ordered, sweat dripping from beneath her blood-stained turban.

"You need a fresh bandage and a good rest yourself." Jaddah's deepened cough turned everyone's head. "Maggie, see if you can find some clean rags around here."

The uneasiness seeping into Maggie's bones wasn't worry about what they would eat or drink. It was how she was going to keep her grandmother alive. Not only did she lack the proper medications, she didn't even have the basics: Cool, clean water for sponge baths. Mild broth. And several gallons of the nasty rehydration drink Naomi pushed on everyone who had a fever. Maggie needed more than her mother's medical expertise; she needed her mother.

"We have no way to clean this woman's wounds unless I find a well," Eggie offered.

They all agreed the proconsul had probably added extra patrols. The risk of Eggie's being caught while moving around the city outweighed their thirst or injuries. Best if they waited until morning, when those who'd been denied running water were forced to trudge to the wells. Maggie found an old cloak in a trunk. Tomorrow she would disguise herself, hoist a water jug to her shoulders, and slip in the procession of women making their daily water runs. For now they should all try to get some rest.

Jaddah's friends made a pallet near the loom and curled up together.

Eggie, armed with a stained paddle he found in the dye vat, stationed himself by the door. "I'll take the first watch."

"Thanks." Maggie turned her attention to her grandparents.

G-Pa was sitting on the bed and doing his best to care for Jaddah. He looked old and tired as he concentrated on tending his wife's bloody knees. His trembling hands picked dirt and gravel from her wounds with the same care he'd used to soothe Maggie's cuts and bruises growing up. While he worked, he whispered assurances that eased Jaddah's breathing.

It had been so crazy these past few hours Maggie hadn't taken a moment to savor the sight of seeing her grandparents reunited in the same century. They'd waited so long to be together. They deserved better. She couldn't let her inability to help them ruin whatever time they had left.

"Tomorrow I'll figure out a way to get to my parents," she told her grandfather. "Mom will have medicine for Jaddah and she'll know what to do about that tube hanging out of Kardide's head."

Her grandfather pulled his attention from tending Jaddah's knees. "It's not safe for you to go alone."

He was right, of course. Maggie hadn't thought through the details. How would she navigate the city and find her parents? For all she knew, soldiers had taken her father prisoner and her mother had died from that blow to her head. Maggie's knees turned rubbery. She'd been so focused on saving her father, it never occurred to her she could lose her mother. She joined her grandfather on the bed.

Her grandmother reached for her hand. "You're as brave as your mother, Maggie." Tears spilled onto her rosy cheeks.

The constriction in Maggie's chest wasn't her normal anxiety from being trapped inside the small dye shop with no easy exit. It was the suffocating regret of her impulsive actions causing everything to fall apart. She'd felt it the first time she jumped into the portal after her mother. Then the night Ruth died because Maggie had gone in search of a doll. This time the squeeze to her conscience was ten times worse: her entire family was in danger because she'd come here to rescue her father without a plan.

She stroked her grandmother's trembling hand. "I don't think 'brave' is the word Mom would use to describe what I did today or any day."

Maggie's skirmishes with her mother usually weren't the knock-down, drag-out kind. Their disagreements were more civilized, always stopping far short of drawing blood. But that didn't mean they didn't manage to cause each other damage. Neither of them ever gained any ground, Maggie realized, because the truth of it was that she was not going to roll over, and her mother was never going to lift her iron fist or unlock her shackles.

Maggie had detected the familiar signs of war the first time she mentioned that she'd Googled her father and found out the truth.

"What do you mean, we're not going back to save my dad?" she'd argued. "They're going to cut off his head!"

"Don't you think I did everything I could to keep that from happening?" Mom had immediately shut down any more questions. The finality in her tone indicated the subject was closed.

Permanently.

Once Maggie learned the whole story about her dad she'd changed from the occasional strong-willed child to someone who couldn't leave the idea of time traveling alone. The rebellion growing inside her had blossomed into a raging inferno she couldn't douse if she'd wanted to. So she'd let the fight die down with her mother and secretly started counting the days until she turned eighteen. Somehow, some way, she was going to Africa. Once she got there, she wouldn't stop until she saved her father from his fate in the third century.

Funny, now all she could think about was how she was going to save her mother too.

Maggie kissed her grandmother's forehead, cringing at how fiery it felt beneath her lips. "Let me sit with her, G-Pa. You won't do her any good if you get run down."

His mouth gaped in a yawn. "I'm good."

"Liar, liar, pants on fire."

He looked at Jaddah. "And you thought you wouldn't recognize her." He kissed Jaddah's weak smile, then turned his attention back to Maggie. "You'll wake me if there's any change."

"I promise."

Her grandfather was too exhausted to keep up his arguments. He rolled off the bed, dropped to the floor, leaned his head against the wall, and closed his eyes.

Maggie checked the room one last time. If she weren't scared out of her wits, she'd rank spending the night with both of her grandparents under the same roof right next to having both of her parents in the same century. She blew out the lamp and slid down the wall beside her grandmother's bed. Every muscle in her body ached and her head hurt from the questions demanding more brainpower than she had available.

What if Barek didn't show up? She'd led everyone to an abandoned shop with no food or water. How was she going to keep them alive? She didn't know that Barek could come up with a solution, but it had been Barek's quick thinking years ago, when he cut through the Tophet carrying her and his mother's burial urn, that had saved them from being caught after curfew. At the very least, if Barek were here he'd know how to escape before they were discovered by the troops scouring every inch of the city.

Enough, she told herself. Her brain was so full of questions that adding one more worry would make it explode. Eyelids heavy, she let her head fall back against the bed. She'd just started to drift off to sleep when a noise outside the shop whiplashed her upright. She grabbed her stick and joined Eggie in a defensive stance at the door. Behind her, she could hear the others doing their best to silently surround Jaddah's bed.

Someone outside was fumbling with the latch. Her mother would have planned for a possible invasion—slid something in front of the door for protection. A barricade of furniture might not have stopped the army of Rome, but it would have at least slowed them. With the windows boarded over, they weren't even able to peek out so they'd have an idea of how many soldiers to expect.

The latch lifted. Maggie braced herself and poised her stick the way a Little Leaguer crouched over home plate would. The door creaked open. Someone stepped inside. She reared back and swung for the fence. The intruder groaned, doubled over, staggered into a stool, and then hit the floor with a thump.

"Drag him in," she told Eggie.

She and Eggie secured the intruder under the arms and hauled his limp body across the threshold. Kardide closed the door. Tabari lit the lamp.

"Maybe we should tie him up," Kardide offered.

"He doesn't look like he's going anywhere anytime soon." Maggie prodded the guy with her foot. When he didn't respond she bent down and rolled him over. "Oh. No."

42

EGGIE RIGHTED THE STOOL Barek had toppled when Maggie turned him into a foul ball. "Sorry, my good man." He dusted the seat with such skill no one would have ever guessed Eggie was third in line for the throne. He eased Barek onto the chair. "Are you hurt?"

Barek rubbed his stomach and scowled at Maggie. "I think she broke a few ribs." He was mad. But for now, she didn't care. Barek was safe. He was here. And having him close enough to touch settled her.

"I'm sorry." She dabbed at the gash Barek's fall into the stool had left on his head, pressing a little harder than necessary so he wouldn't be able to detect her tremble of relief that he had lived. "Where have you been?"

Barek stayed her hand. "Saving your backside." His gaze grabbed her and held on as tightly to her wrist. "I managed to get in a lick that dropped the redhead. Then two other soldiers started for me. I was outnumbered and underarmed. They would have taken me down and come for you."

"So you ran?" Maggie asked.

"I decided to provide a diversion. So I set out in the opposite direction of the Tophet." Barek drew a painful breath. "Didn't give that zealous soldier boy the slip until I reached the docks. Had to spend the afternoon holed up in the skiff I've borrowed a few times from the groom in Titus's stable."

"And a worthy vessel it is," Eggie added with a smile.

Maggie could feel her pulse beating against Barek's hold. "Do you think he's still looking for us?"

"He and every other soldier stationed on African soil. Not only did four condemned prisoners fail to arrive for their executions, someone burned down the theater."

"The theater?" Eggie's smile slid from his face. "I set some trash on fire at the back of the stage. You don't think it could have—"

Barek dropped Maggie's arm. "*You* burned down the theater?"

Eggie gave a confused half shrug. "I would never destroy such a thing of beauty on purpose. I promise."

"A fire?" Barek exploded. "During a drought? Have you lost your mind? It's a wonder the whole city didn't go up in flames."

"Why are you so upset? It's not like I burned down the theater on purpose." Eggie waved his hand over the bedraggled group gathered around the lamp's weak flame. "My diversion worked. All accounted for. Safe and sound."

"Fool!" Barek stood so quickly the stool toppled behind him. "That theater was the property of Rome, and Rome will make certain someone pays for its destruction."

"So the proconsul raises taxes." Eggie gave another unconcerned half shrug. "What's that to you? You and all those living off Titus Cicero pay nothing to Rome."

Barek grabbed him by the collar. "You have no idea what I've paid to Rome."

Eggie held up his palms in surrender. "It was an empty theater."

Barek shook his head and twisted Eggie's collar tighter. "I heard the soldiers saying a freedman and a slave died."

"Died?" Eggie's face went slack and his arms fell to his sides.

"Oh, no," Maggie said. "I didn't mean for anyone to die because of me."

"Me neither," Eggie said. "Not even plebs."

"My father was a pleb, you *vappa!*" Barek shouted. "Who do you think you are?"

"He's not scum!" Maggie pulled at Barek's arm. "Tell him, Eggie. Tell him who you really are."

Eggie's face had taken on the same crimson shade of his hair. "Publius Licinius Egnatius Marinianus," he spit out. "Third in line to the throne of Rome."

"What?" Barek let Eggie go, not because he didn't still want to hit him, but because the strength seemed to have drained from his shoulders. He took a step back. "No you're not."

"Yes he is," Maggie confirmed.

Barek's eyes grew wide. "You knew?"

Maggie's gaze darted to Eggie, who was rubbing his throat, and then to her grandfather. G-Pa had climbed back onto the bed with Jaddah and scooped her feverish body into his arms. She'd never seen her grandfather so worn. He couldn't help her get out of this situation.

Maggie drew herself up. "I knew."

"For how long?" Barek demanded.

"I made her promise not to tell." Eggie massaged his throat.

Barek's gaze continued to drill Maggie. "So you weren't going to tell me this cocky jerk pretending to be your new friend is the grandson of the man who wants to see us all dead?" The hurt in his voice was a spear to Maggie's heart.

"He can't go home," Maggie said.

Barek spun. "Why not?" He challenged Eggie. "Are you some kind of spy for your grandfather?"

"No." Eggie raised his chin. "I'm my grandfather's last choice for the throne."

Barek took a speechless step back.

Maggie touched his arm. "I'm sorry, Barek—"

"Keep your excuses." He pushed her away. "We're done."

"You promised my father you'd look out for me." Maggie knew she sounded exactly like that spoiled five-year-old he'd always detested. She shook off her embarrassment. "You know what? Forget it. I can look out for myself."

"Then we should all take cover." Barek stared at her, his eyes burning coals beneath his lowered brows. "I'll help you get to the well. And then I'm going to try to forget that I ever knew you."

"I'm not going."

"Yes you are."

"You can't make me."

"Wait." Eggie stepped between them. "I thought we decided it was safer to wait until morning to fetch water."

"Not for water." Maggie mentally grabbed for her careless words, desperate to take them back. She'd kept Eggie's secret. But now that she'd forced him to lay his identity on the table, she wasn't sure she could trust him to keep her true identity quiet. Best she could do was to try to cover her tracks. "I meant we don't know how far we'll have to go."

"Those wells are in the northwestern corner of the city," G-Pa said, coming to Maggie's rescue with the last of his energy. "We are in the far southern quadrant."

"Your grandfather is right." Barek's simmering eyes said he wasn't stepping in to bail her out. He was stepping in because he didn't trust Valerian's grandson to know about the time portal. "Your grandmother is in no condition to make it across town."

"Even if we were, we wouldn't go without Maggie and her mother," G-Pa said.

"What are you people talking about?" Eggie's confusion creased his forehead. "Wells are wells. There's probably water not a hundred paces from the shop door. If we need water, I'll go get it."

Barek and Maggie exchanged tense looks. Hopefully Barek would see that kicking the future emperor of Rome to the curb was risky. He possessed insider information. He knew the location of the new hospital, who was running it, and most important, who was financing the entire Christian movement. The twitch in Barek's jaw told Maggie he would keep this potential enemy close.

"She's not from here," Barek explained, giving her a glare that said *Follow my lead and don't you dare stir any more trouble.*

"I knew it." Eggie pumped his fist in the air. "She is a goddess fallen from the heavens, right? It was the eyes that gave her away." He was snapping his fingers, trying to nail down exactly what he knew. "No . . . no, it was the magic in her box, the pink one that captured our likenesses and my heart." He drew her hand to his lips. "Never fear, I shall take you to your magic well, my princess."

Barek snatched Maggie's hand free of Eggie's. "No you won't."

"If we cannot reach her magic well, then where shall we go?" Eggie's lips had left a blaze of heat on Maggie's hand. "For we will surely be discovered if we stay here."

She wanted to say she wasn't magic, but Barek's dirty look not only shut her down, it also caused her to withdraw her hand abruptly.

"We are close to the city wall," Barek said. "Before the sun rises I will see if a gate is unguarded or if the wall can be climbed."

"And then what?" Maggie asked.

"Cyprian has a summer home in the mountains." Jaddah wearily sat up to put an end to the bickering.

"Leave town?" New worries joined the wad churning in Maggie's stomach.

"Only until things calm down," Barek said.

Could Maggie leave her parents behind without letting them

know where she'd gone? Okay, she'd be the first to admit that she'd skipped out on college and left the country without saying a word. But that was different. Deep down, she'd known all along that with a couple of clicks on the computer her mother would know exactly where Maggie's share of the inheritance money had taken her. What Barek was suggesting—disappearing into the barbarian countryside in the middle of the night—would have the same traumatizing effect upon her mother as that night years ago when Jaddah disappeared through the time portal and left Mom without a mother. Mom would spend the rest of her life looking for all of them.

Her mother hovered way too much, but Maggie couldn't bear the thought of causing her inconsolable heartache. "We need food, water, and medicine for Jaddah before we can even consider such a trip," she said, hoping to stall the plan's momentum. "Maybe we should go back to Titus's to get a few supplies."

"Too risky," Barek said.

"On my way here, I skirted the soldiers billeted at the harbor. They eat well," Eggie said. "They had barrels of salted ham, venison, chicken, oysters. Crates of apples, honey, Celtic beer, and wine. We could get our supplies there."

"How?" Maggie asked.

"I could steal a ham. Maybe even a chicken," Eggie offered.

Maggie's mouth watered. "Don't forget the garum."

"Do either of you ever think past the end of your nose?" Barek dropped to the stool, his face pale. "Stealing a ham could very well cost one of us his life."

"Lighten up, Barek," Maggie said. "I was just teasing. Someone has to go."

"I'll go." Barek ran a hand through his dark mane. "Eggie doesn't know his way around."

"No one can connect my face to the riots," Eggie reasoned.

"You, on the other hand, have made an indelible mark on the minds of far too many soldiers today."

"He's right, Barek." Maggie pointed at the blood trickling from his arm. "Besides, you're hurt."

"Just a scratch." His attempt to return to his feet failed and he had to clamp a hand on her shoulder to steady himself. "I just need to rest a minute."

"You need to quit being such a stubborn jerk." Maggie tossed him the cloth she'd been using on his head.

"He could lead Maximus right to us."

"He could have done that a long time ago. But he didn't. He helped me save my grandparents, Barek. I owe him."

Barek threw up his hands. "If he brings destruction on our heads, that's on you."

Maggie looked at Eggie. He was leaning against the wall, arms crossed. Despite his calm exterior, she could see that the weight of people dying because of what he'd done tugged at the corner of his lip. His heart was probably beating a hole in his chest. He was wondering whether she'd bring up why he'd run away. Understanding passed between them. She wouldn't tell of Eggie's aversion to battle and he wouldn't betray the whereabouts of her family. "I'll take that bet," she said boldly.

Barek reluctantly supplied Eggie with specific instructions as to what to take from the military food stores and his opinion of the best way to avoid being detected. "Steal only enough supplies to get us down the road a few days," Barek said sternly. "And I don't care who you are—no more fires."

Eggie gave a solemn half bow, and then turned to Maggie. "And what special treat can I bring that will aid your grandmother's relief?"

"We'll have to ask her." Maggie gently roused her grandmother. "Jaddah, is there anything other than Mom's medicine that would make you feel better?"

"Honey and water. Maybe some basil, saffron, and black pepper to grind into an edible paste."

"Your wish is my command, dear lady." Eggie flashed Maggie a mischievous wink and raised his hood.

Barek growled low in his throat. "Don't take foolish chances."

"I've learned my lesson when it comes to fire, but I will remain bold when it comes to love." Eggie swept up Maggie's hand and kissed it soundly. "When I return, I expect to be rewarded properly."

Maggie rolled her eyes. "Stay alive."

Barek's lips grew taut, his eyes hard. He sent Eggie out into the night like Noah releasing the dove from the ark.

"He won't betray us," Maggie said. "I know it."

Barek snatched a blanket from the open chest. "What else do you know about Eggie that you're not telling me?"

43

T HE PROCONSUL HAS BEEN inconsolable." Maximus heard the soldier stationed outside his bedchamber arguing with whoever had dared to knock on his door. "He has issued strict orders to be left alone."

"He shall see me." Titus barged into the room with a force that brought Maximus's face out from behind his pillow. "What is the meaning of arresting Cyprianus Thascius?" Titus's roar shook the mosquito netting draped around the large ivory bed. "Have you not caused enough trouble for one day?"

"Someone burned my theater." Maximus had ordered the shutters bolted, for he could not bear looking at the blackened rubble. He swiped his hand across his nose. "Two very good men died."

"I'm sorry for your loss." Titus's fleeting sympathy was quickly replaced by the real reason he'd come. "You're fortunate this entire town did not go up in flames."

Maximus lifted his head, indignation straightening his spine. "If you want an apology from me, you won't get it."

"I want Cyprian granted the freedom accorded him in the codicil to the late proconsul's will." Titus shook his long finger and looked down his nose with the same accusing stare Hortensia used when she wished to threaten him. "That document clearly granted him a pardon and justified Cyprian's reinstatement as a

Roman citizen and a solicitor. You have no legal basis upon which to hold him."

Something inside Maximus snapped. A loud crack reminiscent of the one that sent the theater's pillars plummeting to the stage. A bitter brew of desolation and despair seeped from the fissure. He was the one who'd lost everything, not this monkey-faced frontier patrician. Kaeso was right, he *could* still fix this. But he wouldn't do it by issuing pardons. No, he would make a new path for himself— one where he would never again cower in fear. Maximus would make certain everyone feared *him*, including his mother-in-law. He would fix it so that whoever was responsible for this searing agony in his chest would feel the same pain.

Maximus threw back the mosquito netting and leaped from the bed so quickly Titus staggered back several steps. Now it was he who pointed a finger. "You dare to come into my palace and issue demands?" He drew his robe closed and cinched the sash. "Cyprianus Thascius is the leader of those professing heresy and burning my city."

"You don't know that it was Christians who set fire to the theater."

"Prove that it wasn't!" Maximus said. "Cyprian knew his rebels were plotting destruction and he did nothing to stop it."

"Christians are too busy caring for the sick to plot rebellion." Titus drew in a slow, angry breath. "Cyprian surrendered in a magnanimous effort to avert further bloodshed. His surrender is by no means an admission of any wrongdoing by the Christians. He is admired in this city. Free him and let him calm the masses . . . Christian or not."

Maximus strode to the bedside table. He snatched up the wanted poster he'd ripped from a post as he'd stormed from the empty arena. "I lost more than a fine servant and a theater in that fire. Those convicted of the murder of Aspasius have escaped into the smoke. I'll not let another felon go free."

"Why must Cyprian bear the blame for your military's ineptitude?"

"According to eyewitness reports, the women were stolen by a scruffy little group of Christians who ambushed my troops." He thrust the poster into Titus's sobered face. "Valerian wasn't lifting the persecution when he had Cyprian recalled. He was bringing that Christian traitor home for execution. To put an end to these rabble-rousers who refuse to bow to the gods of Rome. Do you think I do not know who Cyprianus Thascius really is? I will not let his Christians destroy Carthage."

"Yet you allow your troops to rape and pillage," Titus said. "You saw how all of Carthage supports Cyprianus Thascius. He is the only one who can restore order."

"As long as I am forced to live in this godforsaken rat hole, I shall be the one to whom everyone turns."

"And what is to become of Cyprian?"

Kaeso's exhortation to *fix this* once again rang in Maximus's ears, a clanging cymbal that would drive him mad if he did not silence it. Which he could not if every time he closed his eyes he saw his servant take his place in the flames. He must shift his focus to Epolon. More than a theater and a friend had perished today. His dreams of acquiring a skill that would forever liberate him from the clutches of his mother-in-law went up in smoke. Someone would have to pay for what had been done to him.

"Cyprian must die."

"The people will never support his death. Without the support of the people you have nothing. And without Cyprianus Thascius to reassure them as they struggle through this famine and plague, you will not have an end to this uprising."

"Then they will leave me no choice. I will flood the temples with candles and incense, call forth more troops, and summon the wrath of the gods."

44

MASS HYSTERIA AND LOOTING of the city had gone on through the night. The two guards now stationed outside Cyprian's former home had dragged him from the Forum, tossed him inside his villa, and locked the door. He'd stumbled about the atrium looking for a lamp. After stubbing his toe twice, he gave up, slid to the tile floor, and propped his forehead against his drawn knees.

What had happened to his family after he was arrested and escorted from the Forum? Had Barek kept Maggie safe? Had Lisbeth been reunited with his children? Had Magdalena been put to death in the arena? Had Lawrence died with her? Lisbeth would be crushed.

Distress and fear swirled in his empty belly. Was this the future Lisbeth had risked everything to prevent? Cyprian had tried to forget the dreams that had haunted his nights on that lonely beach during his exile—dreams of facing a horrible death. He didn't know why the visions had terrified him so. Everything that had happened since his conversion kept pointing to one hard truth: living as a Christ follower would cost him more than his mentor, Caecilianus, or his dear, sweet Ruth and their unborn child. He would also lose his wealth and position. So why was he surprised that he now found himself separated from his faithful deacon, Pontius, with no way of offering his wife and daughter protection?

With the Lord's help, Cyprian knew he could accept his fate. But he'd racked his brain trying to think of a way to get word to the church members and beg them to come to his family's defense.

"Lord, help me" rolled off his lips again and again.

WHEN CYPRIAN awoke hours later, he was stiff and sore from sitting on the floor. Pale rays of light filtered through the opening in the atrium's roof and illuminated a message of hate scribbled upon the tapestry Ruth had woven for his family years ago. He clambered to his feet. The marble heads of two toppled statues that had guarded his father's entry had rolled several feet away from their voluptuous bodies. Their vacant eyes stared at him.

Cyprian stepped around the stone heads and ran his fingers over the tapestry. Dried blood. He pulled his sleeve over the iron shackle chaffing his wrist, cuffed the hem with his fingers, and scrubbed at the stains with his forearm. Heat rose from the friction. He stepped back to look. His efforts had been pointless. Like so many things he'd touched, the story of God's love was ruined.

He dropped his arm and surveyed the atrium. The destruction went well beyond personal possessions. He was powerless. He was a condemned man. He was alone.

Cyprian fell to his knees. "Oh, God. Help me." His plea echoed off the stone walls. And then it was silent. He released a long, slow breath, then filled his lungs again, repeating the process several times until his thoughts had cleared.

His mind skipped to happier times, to the early days of Lisbeth's arrival. Cyprian had loved her from the moment his eyes beheld her standing for inspection upon the slave block. She was bruised from her tumble through the time portal and angry as a cornered animal, but the spark in her emerald eyes had immediately kindled a burning desire in him. Bringing her and her crazy medical practices into his home had changed his life, opened his heart to a world of new possibilities. He loved watching her glide through the halls of his home with her mother's strange medical instrument draped around her beautiful neck and her slender hands dispensing healing to broken bodies and souls.

His in particular.

Not only had she hauled Cyprian from the sea after a terrible ship explosion, on her second return to his world she'd also extricated him from the pit of his own despair. When he'd fought plagues and persecution alongside Lisbeth, he'd known a sense of purpose. Those were days he would treasure. Days that mattered. Days of loving and being loved.

The turmoil in his gut settled. His spirit was strangely peaceful.

Muted voices drifted into Cyprian's consciousness. He scrambled to his feet. The door opened and his friend Titus bustled in, a heavy bag slung over his shoulder. He slammed the door shut behind him.

"The world's gone mad, I tell you. Mad." He plopped the bag upon a table. "I've brought what few supplies Metras felt the hospital could spare. Plus a little something from my private stores." He pulled out a wine amphora embellished with a painted rural scape Maggie would have enjoyed re-creating. "Been aging this sweet white from Surrentine for five years." He offered a hopeful smile. "It must put a fire in your belly, for there is much to be done to beat these ridiculous charges against you."

"Give it to the sick." Cyprian pushed the sack away, far hungrier for something to sustain his heart. "What news do you have of Lisbeth and Maggie? Did they make it back to your villa?"

Titus's mouth tightened into a tortured line. "The reports are muddled because of the fire, but a few claimed to have seen a girl with white-blond hair and a young man with a small knife overtake the soldiers guarding Magdalena."

Cyprian's heart lifted for the first time since he'd been imprisoned in his own home. "Magdalena was not executed?"

"No."

"She's safe? In your care now?"

Titus began unloading bread and fruit in a definite stall. "Magdalena has . . . disappeared along with your daughter and Barek."

Cyprian's throat constricted with a strange combination of fear and pride. "Are you telling me my children may have been involved in aiding a sick old woman's evasion of the law?"

"Plus an old man and the three servants of Aspasius who were supposed to have been executed along with your sweet mother-in-law."

"Lisbeth must be sick with worry."

Titus set the jug on the table. "You may not have heard of the fire's destruction of the theater."

Cyprian shook his head, his mind grasping at possible reasons why his friend continued to avoid his questions about Lisbeth. None of them good. "I couldn't tell what was burning, but from the commotion I knew it was more than a bakery fire."

"Maximus is beside himself." Titus motioned toward an upended settee. "I've been on my feet all night." Together they righted the small couch, and Titus sank in a huff of weariness. "For reasons I cannot figure, the destruction of the theater has turned the proconsul from all reason." Titus pinched the bridge of his nose, as if what he had to say next pained him greatly. "My attempts to force Maximus to release you have proven fruitless."

"He can't blame me for the riot."

The immediate lowering of Titus's eyes indicated the answer was exactly as Cyprian had feared. "You and the Christians." Titus's face creased with worry and sadness. "Maximus believes the destruction can only be stopped by eliminating the leader of the Christians."

"And he believes me to be that leader?"

Titus eyed him. "Yes."

If Maximus had hoped to use him to extinguish the flames of rebellion licking at his door, he'd captured the wrong man. Starving people had nothing to chew on but discontent. During Cyprian's time of exile on the outskirts of the empire, he'd seen desperation press many good men to the wall. When men with nothing to lose were cornered, anything could happen.

"You could recant."

Cyprian sighed. "I cannot do that."

"No, I didn't think you would."

"Tell me of Lisbeth." Cyprian swallowed the knot in his throat. "If she were well, you could not have kept her from coming with you today."

The grave expression on Titus's face deepened. "I know she went in search of Maggie."

Now it was Cyprian who pinched the pain between his eyes. "That was my fault. I told her to get our daughter and go home."

"Tappo and Pontius wisely insisted on going with her. There was a skirmish between Lisbeth and some soldiers overwrought by the chaos of the fire."

Cyprian felt the last of his hope drain. "And?"

"She was hurt." Titus settled Cyprian back on the bench. "They managed to carry her back to the hospital. The church is doing what they can for her, but I won't lie to you . . . she is injured."

"How bad?"

"A blow to the head, but it is the infection in her foot that has us worried. She has fever."

Cyprian dropped to his knees. He should have let her tend her injury. Had his impatience to be with her again cost Lisbeth her life? His vision narrowed, the light growing dimmer. He lifted his chained wrists above his head. "God, do what you must to me, but please, spare Lisbeth."

Titus sat in silence, allowing Cyprian's grief to pour out. When he could cry no more, he felt a gentle hand on his shoulder. "There is another way."

Cyprian lowered his chains. "Another way?"

"Bella Rugia is only a day's journey inland."

"I don't understand."

Titus's eyes smoldered with a dark secret. "Rich men afraid of dying build contingency plans. Places of refuge should they ever need to make a hasty escape. Surely you have one?"

Cyprian shook his head.

"Your father most likely did. Perhaps at your country estate." Titus waved off Cyprian's shaking of his head. "Not to worry, my friend. You can use mine."

"Yours?"

"Years ago, I acquired a little-known subterranean wheat storage tunnel near my fields in Jendouba. Upon a closer inspection, I realized the maze of passages provided the perfect place to build a secret fortress." Titus inched in closer. "A small bribe to your guards, and you and your family could disappear until all of this nasty business blows over and Maximus calms down."

"But my family is scattered to the four winds."

"Put money in the right hands and I'm sure they can be found easily enough."

Cyprian drew back, surprised at how appealing he found this unexpected offer. Only a few moments ago he'd thought himself completely committed to dying for the cause of Christ. After all, when most of the church walked out with Felicissimus, he'd been the one to stay. He'd even stayed when he could have so easily flung himself down the well and followed his wife to the future—a future where Christians were free to worship the one God without fear.

Yet here he was, seriously considering how wonderful it would be to flee. To leave the responsibility of the fledgling church on someone else's shoulders. Did Cyprian not deserve the happiness that came from having his family under one roof? The joy of having his wife in his arms? His daughter close enough that he could stroke her beautiful hair, and his adopted son, Barek, sitting at his feet, learning the ways of truth?

Truth?

The word rang in his ears, piercing his soul as if the Lord himself had spoken directly to him. What truth would he teach his children or his church by running? Cyprian clasped Titus's shoulder. "My friend, thank you, but I won't hide again."

"A few weeks would give the riots time to die down and for the real culprits of the destruction to be rooted out. Then I could persuade the remaining senators of the merits of Christianity. If Maximus was outnumbered he would back down, I'm sure."

"Neither Maximus nor the senators will believe what they cannot see."

"I don't understand."

Cyprian had already traveled the treacherous road of deceit once, hiding from Aspasius for months. His cowardly actions had forced Ruth to bear the weight of the church upon her shoulders and nearly led to his own destruction. He had no intention of repeating those horrible mistakes. He was no saint and had never professed to be one. He was merely the conduit through which the Lord's agenda was to be accomplished.

"The court of public opinion will be changed the same way your opinion was changed." Cyprian saw understanding sweep the

face of Titus. "With the help of those who have repented and returned to the flock, you can continue dispensing medical help
from your home. It could make a real difference in this city," he explained. "My purpose was to rally and unify a fragmented church.
Perhaps yours is to see to it that the church becomes the hands and
feet of Christ. To ensure that the good works of the believers carry
the good news of our Savior far into the future."

"I am but a new believer. I have no holy purpose—"

Cyprian glanced at the soiled tapestry. He could not allow the
life-changing story of a Savior who'd come to redeem man die with
him. "Someday, in a land far beyond my reach and time, there will
be a little girl born. How will she hear of the story of salvation if it
dies with me? I want someone to tell her the same story Caecilianus told me those many days ago in the back of a small dye shop.
You are the man who will see it done."

"You want *me* to take your place?"

Cyprian shook his head. "Barek will take my place."

"The bishop's son? He's so . . ." Titus let his concern for Barek's
trustworthiness remain unsaid.

"You were thinking 'young, but up to the challenge.' Were you
not?"

He sighed. "Something like that."

"He'll need good counsel. And I know I can count on you."
Warm memories of sitting at the feet of Caecilianus wrapped
around the cold truth of what lay before Cyprian had thawed him
into awareness. *The dye shop.* Why hadn't he thought of it earlier?
He jumped to his feet. "I know where Barek took them."

"Where?"

"Where he felt the most comfortable: home."

"They are hiding in Caecilianus's dye shop?"

"I'm almost sure of it."

"I'll send Tappo and Pontius to fetch them immediately."

"Wait. If you inadvertently lead the soldiers to them, they could be trapped." Cyprian raked his hands through his hair. "Returning Magdalena to the hospital to aid in Lisbeth's recovery is the church's best hope."

"The healer is ill. She may not be much help."

"I know Magdalena. If she has breath, she'll rally to help her daughter."

"How do you propose we secure the services of the healer?"

"Station Pontius at the docks. Then spread word that the grain stores aboard the ships of Titus Cicero have been opened. All who are hungry can eat for free. Sooner or later, hunger will drive my family from their hiding place."

"There will be chaos."

"Exactly." Cyprian ignored Titus's obvious disapproval. "When you spot my family in the crowd, snatch them and take them and Lisbeth to Bella Rugia."

"Then you will come and join your family?"

Cyprian's slight shake of the head was an obvious disappointment to Titus. "I will endanger them no more."

"Then what?"

"I think the best way to avoid having my estate escheated to the crown is to liquidate my foreign holdings, land and estates neither Aspasius nor Valerian know anything about."

"If Valerian could figure a way to tax the nightly tossing of the chamber pots, I believe he'd do it."

"That's why I want you to handle the money, keep the transactions a secret. Use all the proceeds to help Barek continue the good works his father started in this place."

Titus's posture stiffened. "Don't ask this of me."

"It is not I who asks, but the Lord."

"And you?" Titus could not conceal his frustration. "What is to become of you?"

Cyprian clasped the hand of the man who'd been his enemy, grateful the Lord had blessed him with such a faithful friend. "Whatever the one God wills."

45

R UTH'S LOOM WAS EVERY bit as heavy as it was sturdy. By the time Maggie and Barek had dragged it to barricade the door, both were sweating.

"Maybe it won't keep the soldiers out, but it should at least slow them down." Maggie's attempts to patch up the hole in her relationship with Barek had been met with cold silence. She picked up a ball of fabric scraps she'd found in a trunk. "Let me have a look at your arm."

Barek waved her off. "You better get some sleep."

"I've had time to rest today. You haven't." She moved the stool over by the fire. "Sit."

His gaze swept the room. He'd already locked both doors and checked the shutters. Twice. The night air had become strangely cool so he'd stoked the brazier with wood chips and filled the lamp. Barek had gathered blankets and made her grandparents and their friends so comfortable they were already asleep. The look of resignation in his eyes told her he was out of excuses and could avoid the elephant in the room no longer. He would have to talk to her whether he wanted to or not. "My mother kept a jar of ointment in that cupboard."

Maggie went to the cupboard and found a little crock with a wooden cork. She popped it open. "Whew! This stuff stinks."

"It works." He sat with a wary sigh, watching her with naked suspicion. "But don't think applying a little salve heals our friend-ship."

"Nothing is ever that easy with you."

He grabbed her wrist. "Or you."

Maggie set the jar on the table and began to roll up his bloody sleeve. The fabric was stuck to a gash in his muscular arm. "This is going to hurt."

"I'll do it."

She batted his hand away. "Why is it always so hard for you to accept help?"

"Last time I accepted your help, I believe we ended up losing my mother's ashes and being pursued by soldiers." He'd done it again, managed to skewer her heart. "Forgive me if I'm not anxious to enlist your kind of 'help.'"

For two people who hadn't known each other long, they knew each other's tender places and the easiest ways to inflict pain. "Point taken." In the firelight Barek's face seemed older and very weary. "Look, I'm sorry. For everything. You're right. Sometimes I don't think ahead. But this time I did. I should have told you about Eggie, but I chose not to."

"Why would you think I wouldn't want to know we had an enemy living under our roof?"

"I was afraid."

"Of him?"

Maggie shook her head.

"Then that just leaves me!" Indignation had raised his voice. "I don't believe that."

She put a finger to her lips to remind him to keep it down. "I've never been afraid of you. But I *was* afraid you'd send Eggie home and frankly, I was willing to keep his secret because I know how it feels to be forced to go home when you don't want to."

"Why would I have sent him home?" he asked in a forced whisper.

"You're so determined to make it up to my father. To prove your loyalties to him and the church. How could you not send the grandson of the emperor packing?"

"Packing?"

"You know what I mean."

"No, I don't."

"Kick him out."

"What I did to Cyprian after all he'd done for my family was wrong." Barek flinched as she freed his sleeve from his oozing wound. "Sending Eggie home would do little to remove the stain of betrayal from my record."

"I understand guilt." The word hung in her throat. "Raging oxen stampede through my dreams almost every night."

For an instant, the same softness she'd seen in Barek's eyes the night he thought she was dying reappeared. "You were just a child." He reached for her hand. "I can't make the same excuse."

Electric silence surged between them. Her reflection shimmered in his dark eyes. In that brief instant, Maggie realized she wanted a place in his heart. Forever. Not as friends, but something far more serious.

Self-conscious about the heat flushing her cheeks and the possibility Barek might see the power his touch had upon her, Maggie slowly withdrew her hand. What was she thinking? She had no business falling in love with him. She was going home. If she had any hope of escaping with a smidgen of her heart, she couldn't let herself imagine what it would be like to stay here forever.

Maggie took a step back, smoothing the front of her tunic while her mind searched for a neutral topic, one that didn't involve undercurrents of attraction. "Mom never told me how your family met my father and came to live in his house."

"Your face is flushed."

"It's warm in here with everything locked up and the fire going."

He studied her with a disarming intensity. "You've never asked about my old life. Why do you want to know now?"

"You knew me as a child." Her hand fluttered toward the yarns dangling from the rafters. "Only fair I know you," Maggie said. "If you don't tell me, then I'll be forced to imagine you chasing your father's dogs around the dye vat and refusing to do your chores."

To her surprise, Barek didn't immediately pull the curtain that usually shut her out. Instead, his face took on a sadness she longed to kiss away. "I regret being so difficult, especially when my mother was pregnant with Cyprian's . . ." His voice trailed off.

Maggie held her breath, considering how many different ways she would have to say she was sorry before she finally felt as if he forgave her, when he suddenly let her off the hook and continued, "My parents were artists. Two of the best in the empire. Buyers of purple came from all over the world to purchase my father's yarns. My mother's tapestries hang in the halls of dignitaries and foreign kings. Cyprian started buying my mother's work shortly after my parents married. I remember his unannounced visits: he claimed he was in the neighborhood. My parents would smile as if they had no idea he had journeyed clear across town to see what new inventory they had created. But more than the tapestries, Cyprian wanted my father's stories."

"What kinds of stories?"

"Stories of the one God. Of how the one God made the world. How he raised a mighty nation out of a scrappy little group of misfits. But the stories Cyprian wanted to hear the most often were about the one God's Son. The Christ who came down from the heavens, walked the earth as a man, and rose again after Romans crucified him." Barek's eyes were locked upon the large dye vat, but he didn't seem to see his reflection in the pounded copper. He had the look of someone seeing the intricate details of bygone days with great fondness.

"Before long Cyprian was bringing others to hear my father's stories." A pleased grin lifted the corners of Barek's lips. "Sometimes the shop would be so crowded my father couldn't have stirred the people with his dye paddle." He paused and worked the lump from his throat. "But little did my parents know the days of happiness in this place were coming to an end."

The historical accounts Maggie had read mentioned Caecilianus and his involvement in her father's conversion, but she had no idea how their vastly different lives intersected beyond that. She had to know more. "What happened?"

The joy had drained from Barek's face. "Aspasius Paternus."

"The proconsul who sentenced my father to exile and executed yours?"

Barek nodded. "Aspasius declared Christianity illegal in this province, and anyone who traded with a Christian was subject to prosecution as well. Before long, no one but Cyprian would dare purchase work from the rebel maker of purple and his weaver wife. My father refused to worry, saying the one God would provide. Once their meager savings were gone, he gave in to my mother's pleadings and agreed to sell the shop. But no one would buy the business of a Christian. We had nothing left to eat and were on the verge of being evicted when Cyprian appeared at our door one day and said we were coming with him."

Chill bumps of pride prickled her spine. Maggie traced the tattoo on her wrist. "He said that?"

Barek nodded and lowered his chin. "We left everything behind, just walked out. On that day, a family of freedmen merchants became heirs of one of the wealthiest patricians in Carthage. Father was right: the one God had provided."

Neither of them spoke for fear even their breath could burst the bubble around this treasured memory. Maggie imagined her father sitting where she was, listening to the beautiful words of Caecilianus, and she pictured him happy, not stressed like he was now. She took a careful breath. "There's one more question I've never had the courage to ask."

Barek's eyes burned into hers. "Did your father love my mother when he married her?"

"I know he loved her. I mean, who couldn't help but love Ruth? She was wonderful. It's just that . . . I thought he loved *my* mother."

"Cyprian didn't think your mother was ever coming back."

"But he could have waited."

"For how long?"

"Forever."

Barek shook his head. "My mother and your father were two desperate people who thought it would be best for them and the church if they combined forces." He swallowed. "Your father was good to my mother, but he never stopped loving Lisbeth." Coals shifted in the brazier and a spark popped into the air and disappeared in a puff of smoke. "Your father was good to me. Protecting you is the only way I can ever make up for the pain my betrayal has caused him."

"Oh, Barek, I'm sure—"

He held up his palm, silencing her immediately. "Soldiers," he whispered, his body tensed. "Coming this way." He made it to his feet, doused the brazier fire with the lid, and spun both of them against the wall. "Don't move," he said into her ear and pulled her tight against his chest. Maggie fit so perfectly into the crook of his arm, she couldn't have moved if she'd wanted to. Which she didn't.

She could hear the muffled struggle of several pairs of metal-studded boots working to conquer the paved incline that led to the shop. The growing sounds indicated the soldiers were making steady progress. Maggie's heart thumped against her chest. She blinked back tears of terror and willed her eyes to speed their adjustment to the darkness.

G-Pa and Jaddah were still sleeping soundly, and thankfully her grandmother was not coughing. The rhythmic march of soldiers stopped outside the door. Muffled voices slipped through the cracks in the shutters. Someone shook the latch. When it remained locked, a discussion ensued as to whether they needed to fetch the battering ram to check the boarded-up businesses in the deserted dye district.

What would they do if the soldiers came in? Maggie saw that the same question plucked at a tiny muscle in Barek's set jaw. She and Barek working together couldn't muster enough manpower to get her grandparents and the three servants out the back door. Her small knife and the wooden dye paddle couldn't provide serious defenses. They were criminals who'd helped four convicts escape crucifixion. There would be no mercy.

The voices outside the door blurred in the swirl of blood racing from her heart to her head. Either Barek's hold was crushing the breath from her chest or she was experiencing the beginnings of a panic attack. "I can't—"

His lips came down hard on hers. Desperate to shut her up. Every muscle in her body strained against the demand. Her mind was ordering her to push away. *Breathe. You can't breathe.* The intensity of his kiss gradually changed from necessity to hungry desire. Every part of her body began to slide into the calmness at his center. She could think of nowhere safer.

Maggie had no idea of the exact moment the patrols decided the dye shop was deserted and moved on. When Barek's lips released her from their spell, the night was quiet. Her heart, however, was throwing a raucous party that she never wanted to end.

"I think they're gone." Barek's breathy whisper sounded as if he'd sprinted a marathon.

"But they could come back." She pulled him tight and kissed him again.

46

THE SMELL OF COOKING meat broke Barek free of the fierce grip of his dreams. He opened his eyes abruptly. The haunting sound of his mother's voice faded, but the words of her song, the offering of praise she always lifted to the Lord while her fingers worked their magic at the loom, floated in the mist of his thoughts. A soothing balm for the thirst deep in his soul. Above him, a rainbow of colors swayed ever so slightly.

Barek pushed up from the thin blanket spread on the stone floor. Why did every muscle in his body ache? Jagged realization snapped him alert. This roof no longer sheltered the home he'd known. The man and woman who'd raised him among the murex shells and downy twists of wool were dead. These four walls would not become the place where he'd raise his family. His father's deserted shop had become a hiding place for rats and frightened fugitives. And a poor hiding place at that. Without the security of his heritage, what kind of a life could he ever offer a girl like Maggie?

Why was he even considering a future with Maggie? The minute she had her family assembled, she would drop down the well and disappear from his life forever. And yet, try as he might, he could not push her from his mind. The little imp had always had the ability to needle his emotions. When had Maggie acquired the power to stir embers into flames? He should never have drawn her

into his arms and kissed her. Twice now. They'd been in danger before and he'd protected her purely out of his sense of duty. Why
did he feel he could run a man through if he tried to harm her
now? He needed a drink and something to eat. Something to remove the sweet taste of her from his lips. Barek drew his knees to
his chest and took in his surroundings.

Across the room, the three women who'd stuck closer than
shadows to Magdalena were all busy. One was helping Maggie's
grandfather mix herbs in his mother's bread bowl. The other two
were bent over the fire in the brazier. The steam rose from meat
Kardide tended in the skillet.

"Where's Maggie?" he asked, his throat dry.

"She and Eggie went for water," her grandfather said as he
lifted Magdalena to a sitting position.

"Without me?" Barek clambered hastily to his feet, a decision
he immediately regretted. The room was spinning and he felt a bit
off balance.

"You've got a pretty good knot on your head this morning,"
Kardide told him.

Barek looked down and someone had removed his sash and his
shoes. He blinked to bring everything into focus and aimed his gaze
at the door. "Maggie was supposed to wake me when Eggie returned."

Once he was certain the soldiers were gone for the night, before
he'd agreed to let Maggie take the first watch, he'd awakened her
grandfather. The three of them had managed to move his mother's
loom from the door just enough for someone to slip in and out.

"We tried waking you." Kardide flipped a piece of meat that resembled a tiny chicken wing. "Thunder would not have awakened
you."

The patrols had passed them by last night, but if they scoured
the city and turned up nothing, they would return to do a more
thorough inspection of the neighborhoods that bordered the city

walls. If Barek couldn't get their little entourage past the extra patrols policing the gates, it would be only a matter of time before he
and everyone he'd tried to save would be discovered.

"How long has she been gone?" he asked as he hurried to put
on his shoes.

"Long enough for this pigeon to cook."

"Something's wrong." Blood pounded in Barek's ears as he tied
his sash. "I'm going after them."

"I'll go with you," Lawrence offered.

"Someone has to stay to protect the women." But before Barek
could lace his shoes, Maggie burst in, tears streaming down her
cheeks.

"My father has been arrested! He's being held hostage at his
villa." She threw herself into his arms. "Oh, Barek, I have to find my
mother. She'll know what to do."

Her body was slight but strong up against him. Her hair still
smelled of smoke from the previous day's fire. "Slow down."

"A woman at the well said"—Maggie leaned back but kept her
arms wrapped around his waist—"the great solicitor of Carthage
has been put under house arrest." Terror suddenly froze her tears.
Her body went rigid. "What day is it?"

"Somewhere around Calends." Barek's heart quickened at the
growing alarm in Maggie's voice. "Why?"

She grabbed the front of his tunic. "What is Calends?"

Before Barek could explain the Roman calendar, Eggie inched
through the door. "Hope this was my last supply run. Nearly got
trampled out there." His arms were weighted with a full water jug.
"Right after Maggie heard about her father and took off, word hit
the well that the ships of Titus Cicero have opened their cargo
holds. There was a stampede toward the docks. Maybe we should
get in on the grain run before it's all gone." He placed the jug on a
table, then noticed the tension in the room. "What did I miss?"

"Is it September, Eggie?" Maggie demanded.

"Could be." Eggie's face looked puzzled, then he shrugged. "Last night was the new moon." He lifted a cup left on the table and blew out the dust. "So dark, I could hardly see my hand in front of my face. Were it not for the soldiers' cook fires I would not have found their camp. Don't worry, I didn't go near the flames."

Maggie let go of Barek and rushed to the table. "What does a new moon mean?"

"Calends." Eggie dipped the cup into the jug and helped himself to a big drink. "First of the month."

"What month?" Maggie was frantic. *"What month?"*

"Here. Cool down, my princess." Eggie offered her the refilled cup, but she pushed it away.

"What month?" Maggie demanded.

"I left Rome on the ides of August when the moon was full. Been here long enough it must be close to September by now."

She spun and found her grandfather. "I have only fourteen days." Maggie began to sink. "Maybe less."

Barek scooped her up and sat her upon the stool. "Fourteen days until what?"

Her grandfather left his post at his wife's sickbed and came rushing to his granddaughter's side. "Until Maximus kills Cyprianus Thascius." He stroked Maggie's hair from her face.

She sniffed. "G-Pa, we have to save my father."

"I don't know if he can be saved," her grandfather said gently. "Not without changing history."

"But right now my father's trial is in the future," Maggie argued. "We've got to try. What about Titus? He's rich and powerful. I know he'll help us if we ask."

"Even a senator can't stop an execution ordered by Maximus," Barek said.

"How do you know her father's trial will end in a death sentence?" Eggie still didn't understand Maggie's distress. "After the mess Maximus had on his hands after her grandmother's trial, he would be a fool to deny a pardon for the city's favorite solicitor."

Tension sizzled in the silence. Barek couldn't bear the worry shaking Maggie apart. He placed a protective hand upon her shoulder and confessed to Eggie, "She knows the future."

"How can she know the future?" Eggie's eyes darted between Maggie and her grandparents. "She *is* a goddess. I knew it."

"She knows the future because she comes from there." Barek could see Eggie's mind wrestling with the ludicrous idea. He still deliberated the impossibility of a child disappearing one day and returning the next a beautiful woman. In this, their common struggle bound them more than their competition for Maggie's love tore them apart.

"And in this future, do you know of me?" Eggie asked Maggie. She shook her head.

"Then you shall." Eggie straightened. "There *is* one man who can save your father." All eyes fastened on Eggie. "My grandfather."

"What are you talking about?" Barek asked.

"Valerian issued the order to murder Christians. As long as he is emperor he is the only one who can rescind the order."

"If your grandfather rescinds his order, it will change your history as well." Maggie's voice was barely more than a whisper.

"Make no mistake," Eggie said, "the only history my grandfather cares about is his own. If I agree to give him my devoted service, he'll do whatever I ask to ensure that his blood flows through the successor to his throne."

Eggie gave them no time to argue. "I remember when my grandfather was a great man, respected among the populace for his many good deeds. But then he fell under the influence of a man named Macrianus, the high priest of the Egyptian magi. When my father saw how Macrianus was turning the great Valerian from all he held true, he tried to warn my grandfather to be careful. But it was too late. Macrianus had already seduced the emperor with all kinds of sorcery."

Eggie began filling a burlap sack with a few of the food provisions he'd stolen from the soldiers. "There is only one power I know that will break the spell of Macrianus." He stopped and looked at Barek. "The power of your one God."

"But what if your grandfather refuses to see you?"

"I have seen your God's might demonstrated in the hands of your people. In the way they serve even those who are their enemies. It is a power stronger than that of the gods of my grandfather. If you pray that Valerian is feeling generous, he will be."

"Then we'll pray, won't we, Barek?" Maggie said.

Barek stared at him, both surprised and irritated. How dare Eggie make promises destined to break Maggie's heart? "There's not enough time to find your grandfather, have the edict rescinded, and get back here before Maximus executes Cyprian."

"If I leave on the next ship, a good tailwind will put me in Ostia in two to three days. Another half day afoot will put me at my grandfather's palace in Rome."

"But going home means you'd be giving up your freedom and dreams of becoming a sculptor," Maggie said. "Why would you do that?"

Eggie's fingers lightly brushed away Maggie's tears. "My love of beauty." The sleeve of his cloak fell to his elbow, once again revealing the mark of his royal bloodline, the destiny he'd risked his life to escape.

A lump formed in Barek's throat. "What if your grandfather is not in Rome?" he asked. "There is war on nearly every border."

"Then I shall inquire as to his whereabouts, secure one of his swiftest horses, and find him." Eggie's gaze surveyed the stunned disbelief on every person in the room. "My friends, if you wish to help, beg your one God for favorable winds and a calamity to delay the trial." To Maggie he said, "May the future speak as well of me as it will of your father."

Barek's urge to drive his fist into Eggie's smiling face vanished. The hope Eggie's promise brought to Maggie's eyes was something for which Barek was grateful. Of course Maggie should be delighted. Eggie was offering something he'd never have the influence to do.

"Your sacrifice is more than we deserve, Eggie." Barek's admission of gratitude was as much for Maggie's sake as his own. She may never love him as he'd grown to love her, but he couldn't bear it if Maggie thought him a stubborn fool who'd ruined their best chance of saving her father. "Our problems are not yours."

"My problems were not yours and yet you pulled me from the depths of my despair and restored me, body and soul." Eggie clapped Barek on the shoulder. "What kind of a man forgets that kind of sacrifice?"

47

MAGGIE PLACED HER PALM on her grandmother's forehead. Jaddah was much cooler and more alert than she'd been the day before. She'd even managed to hold down some chicken broth. "Guess those were some powerful herbs Eggie stole from the soldiers." She kissed Jaddah's cheek. "Are you sure you'll be okay?" She and Barek had decided to go with Eggie to the docks in case they needed to create some kind of diversion that would allow him to stow aboard the first boat lifting anchor. No fires. And then they would go on to find Maggie's mother.

Jaddah clasped her hand. "Your mother needs you now, more than ever."

"Not so sure about that."

"Don't underestimate Lisbeth's ability to forgive." Jaddah's voice was thick with tears. "When she found out I'd chosen to stay, it was hard for her. But she managed to forgive me. That's how I know if you have anything to be forgiven of, she's already done it." She squeezed Maggie's hand. "Your only crime is growing up." Jaddah brought Maggie's hand to her cracked lips. "Because your mother loves you, she'll let you become your own woman when the time is right. Whether she can bear it or not."

Maggie couldn't pretend that she didn't want to believe her grandmother's words. Lugging around the shame of the many tragedies her actions had caused was exhausting. To be free of the guilt would be more than she deserved.

But she didn't want to be free of her mother.

Not really.

Maggie wanted them to be friends the way Mom and Jaddah were now. While they didn't have medicine in common, it had been eye opening helping her mom tend Quinta and her grandson. The experience had given Maggie a peek into the heart of a woman she'd always wanted to be like. Jaddah was right. Her mother was a woman with a huge capacity for love.

In preparation for their trip to the docks, Barek checked the food and water supplies for those staying behind. He showed Tabari and Iltani his mother's secret stash of extra oil and wicks for the lamps. He snuck out the back and restocked a bin with bits of wood for the brazier. Maggie followed Jaddah's instructions and changed the bandage on Kardide's head. G-Pa and Kardide promised to barricade the door immediately after they left.

Maggie withdrew her phone and asked her grandfather to take a picture of her standing between Barek and Eggie. Then she snapped a picture of her grandmother and grandfather together. "So Mom won't worry," she said, although deep down she knew the picture was for her. In case something happened and she couldn't get back to them.

The moment the sun set, Maggie slid the phone in with the manumission papers she kept in her pocket. Her heart beating fast, she kissed her grandparents and then joined Barek and Eggie to set off for the docks. Barek's prediction of added patrols proved correct. Fortunately, his knowledge of the back alleys of Carthage kept them from detection. When they reached the harbor, lit torches flickered above the huge crowds crying out for food and pressing toward a large grain freighter.

Maggie grabbed Eggie's arm. "Maybe you shouldn't go."

"My ride's waiting." Eggie pointed out an imperial freighter anchored fifty yards away from the nearest pier. "See that ship sitting low in the water? It's full of grain. If those sailors know what's good for them, they'll lift anchor and hightail it to Rome before this mob swamps them too." Eggie kissed her hand and winked at Barek. "I'll be back before either of you have time to miss me."

The wind whipping off the water sliced through Maggie's cheap tunic and reminded her how little time she had left. She didn't need a calendar to know fall was swooping in with a vengeance and it had brought the wrath of Rome to Carthage. She moved to the protection of one of the large concrete pillars, waiting in the shadows while Barek and Eggie pushed off in the homemade skiff hidden in a secret slip by Titus's stable hands.

"Godspeed, Eggie," she whispered.

Eggie was smooth and daring. Barek was cautious and bristly as a dried-out toothbrush. And yet they'd become an odd little family, the three of them, hiding in the deserted dye shop, foraging for food and supplies under cover of darkness. Everyone doing what he or she could to protect the fugitives and nurse Jaddah back to health. Maggie couldn't bear the thought of facing the days ahead without either man.

A commotion around the docked grain freighter drew Maggie from her worries. People pushed and shoved, fighting with the last of their strength to gain a place in line. She spotted a scarecrow of a man exiting the ship with a little sack of grain held close to his chest. He elbowed his way past those accosting him on the gangplank. But the moment the poor man set foot on the dock, a gang of starving vultures descended and tore his sack from his clutches. The bag ripped open and grain spewed into the air. Fifty people dived for the grains raining down upon the warped planks. Stones from a slingshot flew through the air and hit the man in the head.

He staggered backward, his body teetering hopelessly on the edge of the pier.

Maggie bolted toward the man who'd been robbed. She heard her named called above the din of people scrapping like dogs over a bone. Had she not been so stinking mad she would have been more alert. She would have known it was not Barek who called her and she would have pretended not to hear. But she couldn't help herself. She stopped and turned, searching for the one who knew her. A cloak swept over her head and strong arms locked her arms to her sides.

"Come with me. Now."

48

MAXIMUS PEERED THROUGH A window high in his palace. Below, hysterical men with sticks in one hand and blazing torches in the other had left the smoldering theater ruins and blanketed the royal grounds. They shouted threats and obscenities. Maximus closed the shutter and dismissed his concern. He'd doubled his guard. If the residents of Carthage attempted to storm his doors, they would face the same fate as Cyprianus Thascius.

Maximus trudged down the stairs. All he had to do was hang on until the emperor granted his leave. He'd sent a sealed request to Valerian the morning after the fire. In it, he'd explained the chaos the Christians had caused and his plan for vengeance. He would do what he should have done when he first arrived and eliminate their leaders. He'd ordered his soldiers to tear this city apart until they found that murderous woman healer. After he nailed her to a cross, he'd execute the man who'd dared defend her.

Once Cyprianus Thascius was dead, there would be no one left to defend these heretics and troublemakers. Without someone to come to their legal rescue, the Christians would be forced to return to the passive, peace-loving citizens Titus Cicero claimed them to be.

Maximus tightened the sash of his robe. The thought of making someone pay for the hurt he had suffered gave him great pleasure. Once he had order restored, he was certain the emperor would be more than happy to grant his transfer back to Rome. There was still the problem of what to do about Hortensia. She would not be happy his term had been cut short.

In the atrium, the birds fluttered in their cages, protesting the unease they sensed in the province.

Maximus reached inside the golden cage and removed one of the multicolored birds. These foul creatures had pecked and cackled at him for the last time. He was a new man. His own man. The emperor would reward his performance in Africa.

In one swift, decisive move Maximus snapped the bird's blue-ringed neck, then tossed the limp creature at his feet. He hated Aspasius's pets almost as much as he hated his mother-in-law. With the emperor's gratitude behind him, Hortensia could not stop him from returning to Rome, secreting his wife in the middle of the night, and sailing to the edge of the earth.

Until then, Maximus would remain barricaded in his palace and entertain himself.

"My lord?" The voice belonged to one of guards he'd added to fortify his security detail.

"Not now." He stuck his hand back into the cage. Riled birds mocked him as they flew to the safety of the highest perches. "See what you've done?" He turned to see the red-faced soldier holding out a small scroll. "What is it? Speak, man."

The soldier stared at the dead bird at Maximus's feet. "An urgent message from Rome."

"Finally." Maximus slammed the cage door and yanked the scroll from the soldier's hand. "Wait for my reply." He ripped the waxy seal and began to read.

With his troops weakened by plague, Emperor Valerian
suffered a major defeat. He was taken prisoner by the

Persians and executed. Delay your departure until further notice.

> *Gallienus Augustus, the newly*
> *proclaimed emperor of Rome*

"NO!" MAXIMUS cursed and jammed his fist into the bars of the nearest cage. The birds fluttered in a frenzy. He was stuck here forever. Trapped like the frightened parrot he was. He no longer had the luxury of waiting until the healer was found to exact his revenge. If he was to acquire any satisfaction, he would have to act and act quickly. Squeezing the paper in his hands, he pondered his next move.

"You will tell no one of this, understand?" Maximus eyed the guard as he wadded the paper, opened the birdcage, and tossed it inside. "Bring the solicitor Cyprianus Thascius to me at once." He held up his hand. "No. Send two officers to remove him from his home. Insist they use discretion. Keep him in one of their houses for the night. Then once I have assembled the Senate, bring him to me quietly. I do not want the masses to disturb a moment of my pleasure."

49

THE NEXT TIME LISBETH emerged from a drug-induced sleep, the room smelled like an order of sizzling fajitas. She turned her head slowly to locate the source. Someone new had joined Metras in his mission to nurse her back to health.

Tonight it was Candia and Arria, the abandoned senator's wife. Arria had been no more than a frightened skeleton clutching a dead baby when Cyprian allowed her to trail in with the repentant church members. Now she crouched confidently by a small brazier. Her filthy silk stola had been replaced by a clean, simple woolen tunic. Her matted hair had been washed and combed. Her cheekbones no longer protruded like jagged cliffs. Still, the sprinkle of brown scabs across her porcelain face made it impossible to forget she'd only recently survived the plague. This woman frying onions was just barely well. She really should have been convalescing and recovering from her own losses. Instead, here she was, preparing another poultice for Lisbeth's foot.

Lisbeth's stomach rumbled. Not with hunger, but with the shame of having so quickly judged another.

"Are you thirsty?" Arria asked when she noticed Lisbeth was awake.

Lisbeth's tongue was stuck to the roof of her mouth, and her throat felt as if big scoops of ash had clogged her vocal cords, so she just nodded.

Arria brought her a cupful of something steaming with the stink of a dusty homecoming mum. "It's feverfew," she said in response to Lisbeth's wrinkled nose. She slid her hand beneath Lisbeth's shoulders and elevated her head slowly. "Metras says it will help purge the inflammation in your foot and ease the pain in your head."

"What does it matter?"

"You are more fortunate than most. There are many in this home who love you."

"Love? When the world can be lost in a blink of an eye, does anyone have the luxury of love?"

"That's all we have." Arria quickly lowered her eyes, but not before Lisbeth saw the woman was struggling with her own pain.

"I'm sorry." Lisbeth had spent her whole career repairing flesh. It was foolish to think her wounded soul could be so easily stitched together with kindness and a few leafy weeds crumbled into water. "My daughter and I parted on such caustic terms. What if . . ."

"You never see her again?"

Lisbeth nodded.

"The same kind people who helped me carry on will help you."

Tears took Lisbeth to a place words could not. Arria waited patiently. When Lisbeth had cried herself dry, the woman offered her a cloth for her nose and more of the steaming tea.

"This won't bring your daughter home, but it will help ease the pain." She lifted the cup to Lisbeth's lips and Lisbeth did her best to choke down a few sips of the third-century version of ibuprofen.

The senator's wife eased Lisbeth's head back to the pillow. "Do you think your stomach could handle some broth?"

Lisbeth nodded. "Why are you helping me?"

"I owe it to you."

"That's impossible. Until a few days ago, we'd never even met."

"When my little girl became ill, my husband was afraid she would infect the rest of our household. I begged for mercy but he turned us out. None of my wealthy friends would take us in. We had nowhere to go and when the end came for my baby, I couldn't leave my dead child on the streets for the wild dogs." Arria's watery eyes slid gratefully to Lisbeth. "I was lost. Without hope. Then the very man whom my husband had voted to exile took me in."

A cold shudder scampered up Lisbeth's spine. She couldn't speak. She could only stare at the contrite woman standing before her.

"My husband was there when Caecilianus was condemned to death. Everyone in this church loved the old bishop and his wife. And yet they bathed me and fed me when I could not care for myself." She swiped her wet cheek. "Were it not for the mercy extended by my enemies, I would be dead." Arria looked directly into Lisbeth's eyes. "I'm so sorry for my part in what was done to you and your family." She could barely continue. "What my husband and others in high places are saying about Christians is not true. They are kind and forgiving. Metras built a little box for my daughter and then he buried my Sophie beneath the palms in the corner of the garden." She dipped a cloth in the basin and began to gently wash Lisbeth's face. "I will never forget what it feels like to be forgiven."

Forgiven? The word fell softly upon Lisbeth, wrapping her in a cloak of warmth. Cold embers stirred. Recollections of kindnesses she did not deserve but had received on her first voyage into the third century. She'd dropped into this world alone, afraid, and so angry she'd been almost impossible to deal with. And yet Ruth and Caecilianus, enemies she thought at first, had been exceptionally patient and kind. Taking *her* in. Making her feel welcome. Even when the end came for Ruth, the amazing woman was thinking more about Lisbeth than she was herself. She had forgiven every hurtful word Lisbeth had hurled at her, calling her "friend" with her last breath.

As Lisbeth watched the senator's wife hold the clean muslin pouch while Candia carefully ladled in hot onions, she knew she was once again the recipient of undeserved kindnesses. After all, she was the one who'd condemned Cyprian's decision to forgive those who'd betrayed him, and yet those very same people were now risking their lives to save hers. How could she dare condemn this woman for her ill-informed decisions when her own had caused so much pain?

Candia reluctantly interrupted her pondering and gently removed the cooled poultice from Lisbeth's foot. "I think we're making progress. It's not nearly as red."

"It's much better, and I think my fever has broken." Lisbeth flexed her foot, surprised at what little pain remained. "Thank you." She reached for Arria's hand and looked at Candia. "Both of you." Maybe it was time she let someone share her burden. "Help me find my daughter."

Uncertain looks swiveled between Candia and the senator's wife. It was obvious neither of them wanted to upset her, but it was too late. She'd passed that point a couple of days ago.

Candia said softly, "My husband is looking for her. He will do his best to find her."

"Lie back," Arria said. "Rest."

"I can't rest."

"Give my husband a chance," Candia said.

"If they're not back within the hour, I'm going."

"If they don't return soon, we're both going," Candia said.

Lisbeth did as she was told. But her mind refused to turn off the questions. Where was Maggie? Titus had told Lisbeth that people were talking about a girl who had stolen the prisoners with the help of a young man. Titus was convinced Maggie and Barek had found some secret place to hide Lisbeth's parents until the riots calmed down. Lisbeth wasn't so sure.

Dread thick as atrial sludge coursed through her body. If Maggie was safe, surely she or Barek would have gotten word back to Titus. Lisbeth could only hope the silence meant Barek had taken Maggie and her grandparents to the well. *Oh, God. Let it be so.*

Titus bustled into the room, followed closely by Metras, who was leaning heavily upon his cane. "Can't it wait until she's stronger?" Metras huffed in his effort to keep up.

"No. It cannot." Titus came to Lisbeth's bedside. "Good. I see you're awake." He took her hand. "Are you feeling better, my dear?"

"Yes. Thank you, Titus. And thank you for all you've done for me."

He dismissed her appreciation with a wave of his hand. "I have news if you feel up to hearing it." His low, urgent voice caused her blood pressure to spike. Something was wrong.

"Is it Maggie?"

He shook his head. "I went to check on Cyprian." He pressed her shoulder. "Lie down. He is well."

She was too anxious to settle back on the pillows. "When can I see him?"

"He doesn't want you to risk coming to his villa, where he is being held under house arrest. Instead, he asks that I take his family to the country."

"How will he meet us there?" She sat forward. "Can you free him?"

"I'm afraid not."

Would Cyprian ever comprehend the danger he was in? "And leave him to face Maximus alone? I won't do it." Lisbeth flinched when the heat of the fresh poultice lightly touched her heel. "Besides, I'm not going anywhere without my daughter." She gritted her teeth as Candia wrapped the muslin tight.

"Your husband has devised a clever plan for your reunion with your loved ones." Titus told her of Maggie's suspected location and Cyprian's plan to release the grain stores to create a smoke screen. "I've sent Pontius and Tappo to carry it out. They are at the docks as we speak. With any luck, we should have your family safely rounded up within the hour."

Lisbeth made no effort to hide her relief. Barek would throw himself in front of a train for Maggie, and from the way Eggie looked at her daughter, Lisbeth suspected he'd do the same. They were clever young men if they'd managed to save her mother from the arena. If they had indeed made it to the safety of Barek's old home, she could only hope they'd hear about the grain and employ that same resourcefulness to return her daughter to her alive and well.

50

M AGGIE KICKED AGAINST THE two men hauling her away
from the free-for-all at the harbor. "Pontius, wait!"

Her father's best friend and a guy named Tappo ducked into
an empty warehouse and dropped Maggie to her feet. She flung off
the heavy cloak they'd used to subdue her, furious that so far neither of them had been willing to listen. "What's going on?"

Pontius motioned for her to keep it down. Tappo checked to
make sure they'd not been followed. Once he slid the heavy door
shut, he leaned over and rubbed his shins where she'd landed several successful blows. "You are to come with us."

"Where?"

"We don't have time."

"Time for what?" Her heart raced ahead. "Am I too late to save
my father?"

Pontius straightened. "Where are the others?"

"I tried to tell you." Maggie didn't care how disrespectful she
sounded, she was tired of never being heard. "Barek is taking
Eggie to catch a ship to Rome and my grandparents are at the dye
shop with—" The look on Pontius's face stopped her cold.
"What? Tell me."

"Why is Eggie going to Rome?"

"He's going for help."

Pontius spoke to Tappo. "Take Maggie with you. I'll go back for the boy and the healer." Pontius refused to tell her more than that her father was incarcerated and her mother suffered with a fever from an injury.

"Mom's sick? Where is she?"

Pontius's condescending pat was hardly reassuring, but for now she must cling to the fact that her father was still directing the actions of his followers and somewhere in the city her mother was still alive. That meant trusting Pontius and Tappo to deliver them all safely.

Maggie followed Tappo into the night. The abandoned streets leading away from the harbor bore evidence of someone's frustration. Not only had the stacked and rotting bodies been tossed about and trampled, but here and there smoke rose from smoldering piles of furniture and household goods. Ugly words condemning Rome had been painted on the stucco. If the mob at the grain ship had done this, what would they do once they realized most of the grain was sailing to the capital?

Maggie swallowed the bile rising in her throat. She knew what would happen next. When starvation sent the masses pounding on the doors of the nobility, Rome would blame the Christians.

A woman's screams echoed in the eerie silence. Tappo's massive arm pressed Maggie into the shadows. Up ahead, two soldiers with torches dragged a woman bound at the wrists from a shop. Her body bounced over the curb and landed with a thud on the cobblestones.

The redheaded soldier snagged the woman under the arm and lifted her to her feet. Her dress was shredded and bloody. "Bow toward the temple!" the soldier shouted in the woman's bruised face.

Maggie clasped her hand over her mouth to capture a gasp. This was the same soldier who'd chased her and Barek.

"Bow, dog!" The soldier smacked the woman hard.

The wild-eyed captive stumbled backward, caught her balance before falling, and then raised her bloody chin. "I will never bow to the gods of Rome."

"Are you a Christian?" he demanded. The blame had already started.

"I have been born again," she proclaimed without hesitation. "Go ahead, kill me. I will be raised in death."

"Fool!" The soldier raised his whip and brought the lash down hard across the woman's face. She fell to her knees.

"No!" Maggie broke free of Tappo and ran toward the woman. "Stop!"

The redhead wheeled. "There you are!" His whiplash curled around Maggie's wrist. One swift jerk and he had reeled Maggie in.

Tappo burst from the shadows and charged headfirst toward the redhead. "Let her go!"

Maggie watched in horror as the soldier noticed Tappo's angry approach. The soldier shoved her to the ground. In one well-trained movement, he spun, planted his feet, and drew his sword.

Maggie scrambled to her feet. "No, Tappo!"

"Run!" Tappo shouted. "Now!"

Maggie glanced at the soldier. The smile on his mouth had grown wide. She did as Tappo ordered and ran. She heard the plunge of the soldier's blade into Tappo's body. Tappo cried out. Maggie stopped and glanced over her shoulder. Tappo staggered, then fell back upon the pavers. The soldier put his foot on Tappo's chest and yanked the blade from his fallen body. Then he promptly turned and thrust his sword into the woman. The entire encounter had lasted less than twenty seconds.

The soldier withdrew his bloody sword and looked around for Maggie. Sweat dripped from his face. He spotted her standing in the middle of the street. "I've got something even better for you."

With a cough he sheathed his sword and swiped his eyes. He started for her but had to stop and catch his breath.

Maggie took advantage of his coughing fit and turned toward the hill where the patricians lived. She did not stop running until she burst through the door of the only man who could help her find her parents.

51

"Titus!"

The scream coming from the atrium of Titus's villa brought Lisbeth from her bed. Her bandaged foot did not slow her as she pushed past Candia and Arria. "Maggie!"

"Mom!" Maggie fell into her arms. "It was awful, Mom. Awful. I think I outran him, but I'm not sure."

"Outran who?"

"The redheaded soldier."

Titus immediately sent men to guard his front gate while Lisbeth led Maggie to her room.

"Tell me everything." Lisbeth held Maggie as the horrible story of Tappo's death poured out.

"I'm sorry, Mom. So sorry." Gut-wrenching sobs erupted from Maggie.

Lisbeth wrapped her arms tighter, as if her touch could purge the poison of shame and guilt forever from her daughter's heart. "I love you, Maggie."

"I shouldn't have come."

Lisbeth thought hard on how to counter this despair. She wanted to say something healing. Something Maggie could repeat and forever banish these regrets. "You came here because love never gives up."

Maggie hugged her back. "I'm glad you never gave up on me."

"I'll have to tell Candia about her husband."

"No. This is my fault. I'll tell her."

Lisbeth went to the door and asked people to squeeze into her room. Hushed and nervous, barely daring to exchange fearful glances, they listened as Maggie poured out the story of saving the emperor's grandson. When she told of Tappo's sacrificial death, horrified gasps sucked the air from the room. Candia, who'd been feeding her daughter stewed dates, slowly put down her spoon and drew her daughter into her lap. Throughout the rest of Maggie's careful and kind recitation, Tappo's wife remained stoic, probably in too much shock to absorb the fact that her life would never be the same.

Lisbeth surveyed the fearful faces. When the soldiers came, these people would scatter as quickly as they had when Felicissimus offered them his cheap writs. She couldn't let everything Cyprian had worked for fall apart. "Metras, assemble the church within these walls. Once I've slipped out, bar the doors."

Maggie swiped her nose. "Where are you going?"

"To your father."

"It's not safe and you can't run on that foot," Maggie argued.

"Sometimes a girl's gotta do what a girl's gotta do, right?" Lisbeth kissed Maggie's forehead. "The church needs him. We need him."

"You're not going without me," Maggie said.

"Or me!" Barek called over the crowd. The sea of people parted. In the doorway, Barek and Papa supported Mama between them. Behind them stood Iltani, Tabari, and Kardide.

"Barek!" Maggie flew to him. "You're safe."

"MAMA?" LISBETH hurried over to her mother, surprised at how little pain she felt in her foot. Metras and his crew had done a remarkable job. "When I saw you at the trial, I knew you hadn't had enough Cipro, but you look like the worst is over," she said between kisses and tears.

"Lots of honey water with a pinch of basil and saffron." Papa looked at Maggie. "And a good little nurse."

"Papa?" Lisbeth embraced them both. "I didn't think I would see either of you again."

"You wouldn't have were it not for that stubborn daughter of yours and this fine boy. Barek put his life in jeopardy to save ours on several occasions," Papa said.

Lisbeth turned to see Maggie and Barek wrapped in each other's arms. Her daughter's joy at this young man's return was more than happiness over the safety of a good friend. Something deeper had blossomed, and Lisbeth couldn't let herself think of how painful it was going to be to pull them apart when she took Maggie home. "Thank you, Barek."

Laurentius poked his head between Mama and Papa. "The whole family together at last."

"Almost," Lisbeth and Maggie said at the same time.

52

MAGGIE WATCHED HER MOTHER tuck a small dagger into the folds of her cloak with the skill of someone who went looking for a fight every day. Who was this woman with flint in her eyes, a steel backbone, and the ability to rally everyone to her side?

"Metras, where's my bag?" Mom's announcement that she would not allow Cyprian to surrender had mobilized every able-bodied person in Titus's home. "I could need medical supplies."

Looking at her mother now, Maggie saw the truth. Any woman who could put herself through two medical residencies, raise a child alone, and take on two third-century plagues armed with nothing but her wits and a few twenty-first-century meds was one tough lady. If anyone could save Cyprianus Thascius, it was Dr. Lisbeth Hastings.

Maggie raised her hood to cover the blush of shame heating her cheeks. Had she really been so self-absorbed that she'd never considered how hard falling into the third century had been on her mom?

"You still have that knife, Maggie?" her mom asked.

"No, I gave it to Barek."

"Arm yourself."

The weight on Maggie's chest suddenly lifted. She didn't have to save her father alone. Her mom loved him so much she was willing to die trying to change history. Maggie tucked one of the extra knives in with her cell phone and manumission papers. The first private moment that came along, she would let her mom know how proud she was to be her daughter.

"The plan is simple," her mother explained to the group who'd finished gathering anything they could use as a weapon. "Metras, you will stay with Mama and her friends. The hospital must be protected at all costs. Arria and Candia will help, along with two able-bodied men chosen by Barek, to stay behind. Papa, you'll stay as well."

"Oh, no." Papa grabbed the only weapon left, a large stick. "I'm going with you, Beetle Bug."

Mom argued for a few minutes, but when she saw G-Pa wouldn't give, she threw up her hands. "Fine. But I want all doors barricaded after the rest of us have exited." She didn't need to clarify their purpose. Everyone understood the mission.

The larger the contingency, the easier it would be to distract the guards long enough to give her an opportunity to get close to Cyprian, to convince him that he had supporters who would be sorely disappointed if he gave up. And his legal expertise was needed if they were going to delay his trial until the emperor's grandson returned. Either Eggie would arrive with news that a stay of execution had been granted from the throne or he would bring with him the full wrath of Rome.

While Barek and Pontius checked the streets for soldiers, Mom checked her medical supplies one more time.

"You and G-Pa are going to stick with me, kiddo." Her mother's reference to her former immature self no longer sent Maggie over the edge. She'd follow to the ends of the earth this woman who'd forgiven her everything. "I think it best if we divide into small groups and use different routes to meet again outside Cyprian's back gate."

Maggie and her mother held tightly to each other's hand, counted to two hundred, then stepped into the outer garden. They turned in the direction of her father's villa and stopped.

They stood face-to-face with the redheaded soldier and his bloody sword. "You're not getting away this time."

53

CYPRIAN SET HIS LAMP upon the floor. He would not be caught unprepared when the time came for his transport before the court. He pulled one of the heavy trunks from the storage closet and began to paw through the tunics he'd worn before his exile. Fine silks slipped through his fingers, but it was the crisp white linen that he secured in his grasp. The ample sleeves had been trimmed with an expensive band of threads woven and dyed to the deepest purple. His finger traced the exquisite work of Ruth and Caecilianus.

"Perfect." He slid the garment over his freshly washed body and immediately felt as if he'd been wrapped in a peaceful presence. He tied a gold sash about his waist and covered his burial clothes with a crimson cloak.

Next, he dug out a handkerchief to cover his eyes in his final moments. His courage went only so far. He would not embarrass his Lord by shying away from the executioner's blade. He tucked the cloth into his sash, then set out to complete one last chore.

The library door creaked against Cyprian's trembling hand. Traces of ink and parchment lingered in the air. Memories flickered in the lamplight. He'd experienced so many wonderful discoveries and conversations as he and his dear friend and mentor pored over the sacred scrolls. Bits and pieces of those treasured

Scriptures lay scattered about the carpets, destroyed by the hands of those who refused to believe. Cyprian squeezed back the sting of tears.

Some words on one of the larger scraps caught his attention: *Love will last forever.* He held the paper tightly and finished from memory the verse penned by Paul, "Even when the end comes." Warmth spread through his veins and fortified his bones. He folded the tiny piece of paper and tucked it inside his tunic. These were the words he would carry into his next life.

Cyprian set his lamp upon the desk and flipped a secret latch hidden behind one of the mahogany bookshelves. He reached into the cubby and retrieved a heavy bag of gold. He counted out twenty-five pieces, added the money to a pouch sewn into his sash, then returned the bag to its hiding place. If the Lord granted him opportunity, he would whisper the location of this treasure's whereabouts to the first trusted face he encountered upon his way to his death. If not, the Lord would provide for those left behind.

The insistent knock at his door came as no surprise. Cyprian backed away from his sanctuary.

Two high-ranking officers strode into his atrium. Chinstraps secured their transverse crested helmets. Their faces were unreadable.

"How can I help you, gentlemen?" Cyprian prayed the fear rising in this throat wouldn't taint his feigned cheerfulness.

An officer with a triangular face and a scruff of hair on his chin said, "You are to be moved to my house. From there, you will be taken to the Praetorium at first light to be tried before Galerius Maximus."

Cyprian allowed himself one last look at the home he'd filled with all sorts of people: Rich. Poor. Sick. Healthy. All of them had changed his life for the better, and he prayed that one day they could say the same about him.

He stepped over the severed head of his father's marble god and said, "Then let's get on with it." He raised his hood and walked boldly toward the unknown.

To his surprise, a legion of swords and shields did not await him. If he presented such a dangerous threat to the state, why was he guarded by only the two men who flanked him?

"Cyprian," someone called from the side garden.

"Pontius?"

Members of his little church waited in the shadows. His guards drew their swords, but when the commander saw there was no threat from a few ragged peasants, he ordered the other guard to sheath his weapon.

Pontius stepped forward. "Where are they taking you?"

Cyprian scanned the crowd drifting into the light. Relieved and disappointed that his wife and daughter were not among them, he said, "Where you, and anyone else who loves me, cannot follow." He clasped his friend's shoulder, desperate to say what must be said before it was too late. "Promise me you'll salvage what you can from my library." He hoped Pontius caught his meaning and would remember the money he kept stashed behind the bookshelves. "And promise me you'll see my family returned to safety."

Pontius nodded. "They should be here. We took separate paths."

"Find them, Pontius. Find them and take them home."

Cyprian surveyed the frightened faces awaiting his next move. He'd seen them bravely reach across the boundaries that had always separated patrician from pleb, join hands, and work together. Of one thing he was certain: these were his people and they loved him more than they feared the future. He longed to give them more than the gold from the sale of his foreign holdings or stashed in his library. He wished to bestow upon them the strength to continue, something they could hold on to when he was gone.

The Scripture resting near his heart came to mind. He held up his hands. "My friends, I have only one thing left to give, words that will carry me as I complete my journey. 'Love never gives up, never loses faith, is always hopeful, and endures through every circumstance. Love will last forever . . . even when the end comes.'" He lowered his hands. "Go and make disciples."

"Were those Christians?" the guard whispered to the commander.

"Who could know for certain in this darkness? Not I, and not you." The commander took Cyprian by the elbow. "Let's go."

Cyprian climbed into the waiting chariot. Flanked by the two officers, he did not look back as he rode into the night.

54

LISBETH POSITIONED HERSELF BETWEEN the soldier's blade and her daughter, her heart pounding against her chest.

"Going somewhere?" The redheaded soldier coughed as he jabbed his sword over Lisbeth's shoulder, pointing at Maggie. "You two will not escape me again."

"You have us confused with someone else." Maggie whipped around her mother. "We are freedmen." She pulled papers from her pocket and held them out. Parchments fluttered in her clutched hand. "Manumission receipts. All in order. Check them."

Lisbeth dared not let the soldier see how impressed she was with Maggie's quick thinking and preparation. "Go ahead. Check our papers."

"Manumission?" His laughter was cut off by another round of coughing. "I don't care if you're a slave or not, you'll burn on a cross for your part in the death of the proconsul and aiding the escape of his murderers."

Barek stepped out from behind Lisbeth. "Your fight is with me. Let the women go."

"You're the son of the pleb I saw beheaded." The soldier spit at Barek's feet. "No wonder you hide behind the skirt of a woman."

Barek lunged but Lisbeth pulled him back.

The soldier's hacking cough forced him to lower his head. His helmet fell off and rolled to Lisbeth's feet. When he rose she could see the sweat glistening on his forehead. He wiped droplets from his eyes. "We have a score to settle, scum."

"Not tonight. You're too sick." Lisbeth reached in her bag and came forward with her stethoscope extended. "I can hear the congestion in your lungs from here. You have the plague."

"Liar." The soldier waved his sword, his eyes wide with the horrifying possibility she was right. "Stand back."

"Already the rash is spreading to your face. From the flush of your cheeks I suspect you're burning up with fever. Soon you'll not have enough strength to rise out of bed let alone swing a sword." She didn't like the small voice whispering in her head, the one that said she was to help this boy, but she could not deny its demand. She was to take a risk. Lisbeth inclined her head toward the stack of bodies not ten feet from them. "Let me help you. I know you've heard the Christians have a healer."

He coughed and shook his head. "Christians are going to die."

"As we all do eventually. But we're the only ones who can help you now."

"You'd help an enemy?"

"Yes, even our enemies." She stepped toward him, her hand outstretched with the offer of her most prized possession, her mother's stethoscope.

"Lisbeth, don't." Barek tried to pull her back but Lisbeth wouldn't be deterred.

"Take this to the house of Titus," she said. "Tell the healer that Lisbeth sent you. She'll know what to do."

The soldier's face creased in distrust. "Why would you do this?"

"Because those I believed to be my enemies have cared for me."

He dropped his sword and the papers, snatched the stethoscope, and ran in the direction of Titus's villa.

"Let him go, Barek."

"But he could—"

"He won't." Lisbeth picked up the pieces of parchment. "Maggie, where in the world did you get manumission papers?"

"Googled them and had several sets printed in case I had to smuggle Jaddah out of Carthage."

"And all these years I thought you couldn't plan ahead." Lisbeth smiled and kissed Maggie's cheek. "Forgive me."

Hand in hand, they hurried toward Cyprian's villa. Cool pinpricks stung Lisbeth's skin: fall was here. She didn't have much time. How they would get past the guards at Cyprian's villa she didn't know.

When they arrived the place was deserted except for Pontius, who waited on the steps.

"Am I too late?" Icy-hot tingles pushed Lisbeth forward. "Where is he?"

Pontius waved his hands to slow her down. "They've taken him, but his trial is not until tomorrow."

"Take me to him."

"I promised I would take you to safety."

"Listen to me, Pontius. I haven't risked everything just to walk away now." Lisbeth grabbed his cloak. "Take me to my husband!"

The group reached the corner of Venus and Salus and found they could proceed no farther: a rather large crowd had surrounded the officer's residence. Only one soldier with a spear guarded the front door. Lisbeth recognized the believers who were clustered in the shadows, but the majority of the crowd had never darkened the door of a church service. Had they come to see a wealthy patrician humbled?

"Wait here," Lisbeth told Pontius.

He clasped her elbow. "I cannot."

"Then I guess whatever happens, we're all in this together."

"How are we going to get to Dad?" Maggie held Barek's hand tightly.

"By the grace of God."

As Lisbeth pushed her way into the crowd, someone recognized her. She turned to shield Maggie, but instead of being mobbed, it was as if the Red Sea parted. Lisbeth braced for an attack.

A man stepped forward and declared the great solicitor of Carthage a man worthy of praise. "My daughter belongs to his church. She's alive because of those in the house of Cyprianus Thascius. I promised her I would cast our idols into the street."

Murmurings of support rippled through the crowd. Her husband's good works had reached beyond the walls of his garden. Was the court of public opinion turning in favor of the Christians? That was exactly what happened in all the early church historical accounts she'd read. Romans had been so touched by the care and sacrifice of Christians during this third-century plague that there had been an outcry for the legalization of Christianity . . . but that didn't happen until *after* Cyprian's death. Lisbeth's chest constricted around her heart.

The crowd surged forward as Lisbeth and her little rescue party trudged the steps. Wind knifed through her thin tunic. Foreboding dimpled her flesh. "We've come to see Cyprianus Thascius," she announced to the guard.

"No one here by that name," the guard reported.

"He was injured during his arrest." Lisbeth produced her medical bag. "I'm here to tend his wounds."

His spear pointed at her throat. "Best move on, woman."

"Cyprian!" Lisbeth shouted above the growing murmurings behind her. "Cyprian! I'm here!"

The door swung open. A large man wearing the sleeveless woolen undertunic of a soldier and boots that laced to his knees filled the doorframe. His waist was free of the sword military guards usually holstered in their belts. His calm face indicated he was not the least bit concerned that he was unarmed and outnumbered.

Lisbeth knew better than to let herself hope this seasoned soldier would take pity on her, but hope was all she had. "We're here to see Cyprianus Thascius."

"I tried to get rid of her," the lone guard told his commander.

"It's all right, Flavius," the commander said. "Our new proconsul is a fool if he thinks the citizens of Carthage will not hear of his plans for their favorite son." He looked at Lisbeth. "I don't want trouble."

Lisbeth could feel the crowd growing as anxious as she. "Then let me pass."

To her surprise, the commander stepped aside. There stood her husband, adorned in his finest election toga, his hair combed, and his face remarkably peaceful despite the lash mark left by the redhead's whip.

The sight of him, alive and whole, instantly buoyed Lisbeth's spirits. "Cyprian!" She threw herself into his arms.

"My love." His embrace was over far too quickly. "Pontius, you should not have let them come." Before Lisbeth could accept the blame, Cyprian turned and hugged Maggie. "Thank God you're alive."

The commander waved them inside and closed the door. "Your friends must be hungry."

Lisbeth looked to Cyprian for an explanation. "Why is he being so kind?"

Cyprian smiled. "I've told him about the Christ."

"And I have believed." The commander lowered his voice. "But I don't know how long I can guarantee your safety."

"They won't be staying, Commander." Cyprian's gaze pleaded with Lisbeth to forgo argument.

"I'll give you a moment alone with your family." The commander donned his cape and helmet and indicated Pontius should go with him.

"We'll be all right," Lisbeth assured Pontius, then swallowed the fear creeping up her throat.

The crowd's unrest could be heard when the two men exited the front door. The commander was right: they didn't have much time.

MAGGIE BROKE the tense silence. "Eggie's gone to Rome." Tears slipped over her lashes. "To convince his grandfather to help you."

"I don't understand." Cyprian looked from Maggie to Lisbeth. "How can a stowaway's grandfather help me?"

"Eggie's the successor to the throne," Lisbeth said.

Cyprian's brows rose. "I'm sure there's more to this story."

"He's cocky and can really get on your nerves, but deep down he's a good guy," Maggie said. "And because of the kindnesses the church has shown him"—Maggie wiped at her cheeks—"he's going to tell Valerian about how wonderful Christians really are. How wonderful *you* are." Maggie was begging now. "That's why we're here. We *have* to delay your trial until Eggie can return with a new edict."

"There will not be a new edict, Maggie," Cyprian said gently. "War presses the empire on every border. Even if Valerian wanted to humor his grandson, the emperor needs capital to finance his armies. What better resource than the properties of people not given to war?" Cyprian pulled her close and kissed her forehead. "I can't allow this to continue. Someone has to stand up and say 'Enough.'"

"People do horrible things when they're scared," Maggie argued. "Giving up is one of them."

Cyprian took her by the shoulders. "More innocent people will die if Maximus does not consider the score settled. I cannot let that happen." Before Maggie could protest, Cyprian turned and placed his hands on Barek's shoulders.

"After your father's execution, I thought it was my duty to take the weakened believers by the scruff of the neck and bring them back in line. I made mistakes. Being hard on you was one of them." He released Barek and took a step back. "When your mother asked me to lead the church, we both knew my term as bishop was to last only until you were no longer a storm-whipped reed. I knew when you risked your life for mine in the alley you had become a man of strong conviction. A man not easily deterred. A man I trust with the future of the church."

"No, not me—I . . ." Barek stuttered.

Cyprian silenced him with a raised palm. "You'll become the leader your mother always thought you would be." Then Cyprian turned to Maggie.

"Maggie, I regret I won't see you marry"—he took Maggie's hand, and Maggie's gaze darted to Barek. Lisbeth's heart dropped. Her daughter was in love. Did Cyprian see it too? How could she ask Maggie to leave this world now?—"but you deserve to have a man who would die for you as I would for your mother. I'm counting on you to find that man."

"Daddy, please . . ."

Cyprian joined Maggie's hand to Barek's. "Promise me you'll take my daughter to safety." He kissed Barek's cheek. "I need a moment with Maggie's mother."

"I won't go!" Maggie cried.

"You will," Lisbeth said.

Disbelief scrolled into resignation on Maggie's face and for once she didn't argue. She pulled her phone from her pocket. "One picture, please?"

"Not now, Maggie," Lisbeth said.

"Now is all we've got, Mom."

Lisbeth folded her arms across her chest in an effort to keep her heart from breaking. "You're right."

Maggie showed Barek how to press the button on her phone. She waved Lisbeth over to stand next to Cyprian, then she squeezed between them. Their family together at last. The Christmas card photo Lisbeth had always dreamed of, minus the terrified stares.

Maggie looped her arms around Lisbeth's and Cyprian's waists. "On the count of three, everyone say 'Free.'"

The light flashed. Cyprian flinched. None of them made an effort to move.

Barek started to hand back the phone. "Maggie, are you all right?"

Cyprian pulled his daughter to him, but it was too late. When Maggie realized she was hugging her father for the last time, the sobbing became more than Lisbeth could bear. Cyprian reluctantly handed Maggie off to Barek, who wrapped his arm around her heaving shoulders and led her outside.

Lisbeth waited until they were alone before she allowed the acid flooding her esophagus to erupt. "Die for *me*? Don't make your decision to die about me."

"Lisbeth, you should know better than anyone that the future depends upon—"

"I know you have to do this, no matter the future. Dying a martyr's death is part of who you were meant to be." Her words choked to a whisper. "So why isn't this easy? I thought I could come here, get our daughter and my mother, and go home. End of story. And then I fell in love all over again. Not just with you, but with these people. I can't keep doing this and you can't avoid death forever."

Cyprian's Adam's apple rose and fell under her disappointed gaze. He had no words, no smooth oratorical explanation. He had only his conviction. From the set of his jaw Lisbeth could see he would never let faith go. And she couldn't help but love him all the more.

Cyprian moved toward her slowly. His fingers skimmed her arm from shoulder to wrist. Her involuntary shudder tightened the invisible tether between them. She could stomp her foot and try to shake free. It would do no good. They were bound, heart and soul. For better or worse.

"You're cold," Cyprian said softly. He lifted a scarlet cloak from the hook on the wall and wrapped her snugly against him. Encircled in the warmth of his musky scent, Lisbeth felt her resistance melt. She molded to his body, the one she'd always known had been created to fit perfectly against hers.

Cyprian buried his nose in her hair and inhaled deeply. "From the moment I saw you standing upon the slave block," he whispered, "I knew God had sent you here for a purpose."

Lisbeth lifted her chin. "To torment you?"

An attempt at a smile wrinkled the corners of his mouth. "To teach me how to love." His hands cupped her face. He lowered his lips to hers and whispered, "You never gave up on me."

His salty kiss proved Lisbeth and Maggie weren't the only ones who'd shed tears. She'd said good-bye before, but in the back of her mind there had always been that tiny seed of hope that they would somehow be reunited. This time it was different. This good-bye was final.

This time she would not be the one traveling into the unknown. Cyprian was the one being sent ahead. Not to the twenty-first century. But beyond the boundaries of time. Beyond even

Lisbeth's comprehension of the future. His decision would send him to a world neither of them knew, a world where those who dwelt with God were so happy that time no longer mattered. As enchanting as an eternity in heaven sounded, it was still a world she couldn't quite comprehend.

And from the quiver of his lip, Cyprian was as shattered as she at the prospect of not going together. Would they be able to find each other in this timeless place? Would they know that once upon a time they had loved each other despite all odds?

Lisbeth choked back tears. All she knew for certain was this: once Cyprian passed through death's portal, she could not press her hand to some long-forgotten image and follow him . . . not until the Lord opened the gate that separated them. Until then she would have only her memories.

"You're so beautiful." Cyprian's thumbs rubbed her wet cheeks. "I'll love you forever." His kiss, gentle at first, pressed harder. His hands slid slowly over her shoulder and down her back. His fingers anchored at her waist. As they grasped each other, she twined her fingers in his hair and shuttered the chants of the demanding crowd.

This was their last moment, the last time they would ever touch, and Lisbeth intended to savor every second with this man. A man who cringed at her sharp tongue but respected her quick mind. A man of impeccable honor, yet a soul so humble he was willing to forgive those who failed to live up to his standards. A man whose inner strength was as beautiful as his strong body.

Lisbeth banished despair and allowed the warmth of his arms to thaw the chill in her bones. The thumping of his heart against hers declared she had loved not a dream, but a real man.

Cyprian's hold tightened. "When it's over, take your family and go home."

But she couldn't . . . no, she wouldn't.

Tomorrow was September 14, 258.

Shortly after sunup, the man she loved, the man born to carry the weight of his calling all the way to the foot of the cross, would die.

Lisbeth laid a hand upon his chest and pushed away. "I've risked everything for you." Uncontrollable shudders shook tears over her lashes. "But I won't watch you die."

She kissed him hard, then fled, refusing to let him see her total meltdown. Because her tears would tell him what she could not.

She lacked the courage to wait for eternity.

55

ORNING RUMBLED IN WITH a distant clap of thunder and put an end to Cyprian's sleepless night. He rose from his mat and opened the window. A brisk, northerly wind carried the scent of rain and the hope that Carthage could somehow be washed clean.

Craning his neck, Cyprian searched the sliver of space between two tall buildings for one last glimpse of the sea. Black clouds swirling over blue water had churned the mix into a gray mist. Keeping his spirit from sinking into the fog would be a challenge.

In an effort to clear his mind for prayer, Cyprian dunked his hair in the washbasin. He raised his head and let the water trickle into the bowl. Using his flattened palms, he battled his wet curls into submission. The image of Lisbeth's disappointment, however, refused to be pushed aside. All night he'd wrestled with his decision to relinquish his family's hope in Eggie's persuasive powers. Maybe in Lisbeth's future world rulers listened when a sound case was made for mercy. But in this world, the world his God had called him to serve, there was only one way to make a point: unflinching sacrifice.

Lord, give me the strength. Not just to finish, but to finish well.

Cyprian was so deep in prayer when his host came to deliver the solemn news that the time had come he had to be shaken into awareness. He finger-combed his damp hair, donned his tunic, then reached for the letter he'd written when sleep would not come.

He handed the commander the note. "Could I trouble you to see this is delivered to . . ." He hesitated, for if his death did not accomplish its purpose he did not want anything he'd penned to bring retribution upon Lisbeth before she could reach the time portal, nor upon the church she would leave behind.

Understanding filled the officer's eyes. "I'll see it discreetly delivered into her hands."

Cyprian could express his gratitude with only a pained nod.

The multitude of people had grown throughout the night despite the commander's attempts to send them home. News of this gathering of support for Cyprian's release had prompted Maximus to issue a full cohort to march the prisoner from the Saturn quarter of the city to the Praetorium.

Cyprian passed through a living hall of spectators who lined the route and perched on gnarled tree branches. He scanned the crowd for one last glimpse of Lisbeth and Maggie, but their beautiful faces were missing from those staring at him now. Relieved, he set his eyes on the path before him.

Though the air was brisk, perspiration trickled down Cyprian's back as he climbed the steps of the Praetorium.

Two solemn-faced guards yanked open the heavy doors to the senatorial chamber. The stink of damp wool, smoking braziers, and condemnation assaulted him one last time.

56

"Aren't you going?" Maggie's hands trembled with strained hope as she held out a pair of shoes, an undertunic, and a beautiful gown she'd borrowed from Titus's wife. "Barek said he would take us."

Lisbeth stared at the tattoo on Maggie's wrist. *DAD.* She was willing to give her daughter space, even the opportunity to make her own mistakes. But this time she couldn't give her daughter what she wanted most: one more try at saving her father.

Lisbeth wrapped herself in Cyprian's cloak and crawled into the bed they'd shared under the eaves of Titus's villa. "I can't." She drew the hood over her head and breathed in her husband's scent in a desperate attempt to burn his essence into her memory.

"What do you mean you can't? I've seen you face down a Roman soldier and order him to turn himself over to a bunch of Christians for healing. If anybody can stop this, it's you." Maggie peeled back the cloak and drew closer until they were nose-to-nose. "You've wanted our family together your whole life. I can't believe you're going to stop now."

"What do you expect me to do, Maggie? Your father told us to go home."

"I don't know. Challenge Maximus to a duel. Cause a riot." Maggie paused. "Be there for Dad."

Lisbeth lowered the blanket and stared at her bossy daughter. "When did you get so grown up?"

Maggie offered her hand. "With God's help we'll get through this. No matter what happens. And we'll do it together." Maggie's eyes locked with hers, pleading for her to do something.

The terror squeezing Lisbeth's chest loosened a millimeter. She let out a long, exhausted sigh. "Give me five minutes."

Maggie tossed Lisbeth a washcloth and instructed her to scrub the tears from her face. "That's better." She dropped the soft linen undertunic over Lisbeth's head and wrapped her in the silk stola. "Cover your head with this scarf, just in case the redhead's friends are still looking for us."

According to Maggie, she'd helped her grandmother tend the soldier who'd chased them with such malicious intent, and she was pleased to report that this morning he was both contrite and on the mend. "But I've got to tell you, Mom, this loving your enemy stuff isn't easy."

"No, it is not." Lisbeth clasped Maggie's hand.

When they entered the atrium, Titus, Pontius, Candia, the senator's wife, Metras, and Papa were dressed and ready to go. "I can't let you risk your lives," Lisbeth told them.

"If a man falls alone, he's in trouble." Metras waved his cane. "You won't be alone."

Mama stepped forward, the stethoscope Lisbeth had given the soldier wrapped around her neck. "Laurentius and I will help my friends hold the fort."

"Mama, what if I can't stand it?"

Her mother kissed her cheek. "Sometimes in this life we are forced to part from those we love, but God never leaves us. He'll give you the strength for whatever comes."

The misty air was thick and oppressive with the threat of rain. Distant thunder rolled in closer and closer, as if heaven were sending an army to take on the injustices of Rome.

Had everything led up to this horrifying test of her love?

Lisbeth's first trip to Carthage had been one of accident and ignorance. It was only because of the kindness of the church that she had survived. Her second trip had been well planned. Relying on her knowledge of what had happened before and what was yet to come, Lisbeth had been certain her second journey would be different, that she could control the outcome. Yet she'd failed to factor in the possibility of Maggie making a sudden plunge into the portal and then contracting typhoid. If Barek hadn't stood in the gap and fought off the soldiers so she and Maggie could get away, they would have lost their lives.

Now here she was once again with her back against the wall. Only this time the world was in collapse. Was Lisbeth really going to insert herself into history armed with nothing but love and a ragtag little group who were no match for the swords of Rome?

Lord, help me.

Lisbeth and Maggie followed Barek, Titus, and Metras. Candia, Arria, Pontius, and Papa brought up the rear. Her little posse of friends fell in with the masses headed to the burned-out theater where it was rumored Cyprian had been taken after the kangaroo court condemned him in the Praetorium. According to Titus's sources, a guilty verdict had been issued in less than five minutes.

"Hurry, Mom." Maggie tugged on her sleeve. "Eggie could be inside."

"Maggie, don't—"

"Eggie's coming. I know he is."

For a split second, Lisbeth grabbed hold of Maggie's hope. The crowd jostled her, and she realized they'd lost sight of the rest of their party. She held firmly to Maggie's hand and pushed past the long lines of people making their way to the theater. After several reprimands and rude shoves sent them stumbling toward the back of the line, she spotted Metras.

"This way," the old man said.

Lisbeth and Maggie followed him through a small gap in the shrubbery that acted as a thorny hedge to keep any nonpaying customers from the entertainment. Scratched and bloody, they emerged at the top row of the theater's seating, so high above the orchestra pit that here the flames that had destroyed the stage and backdrop left only a few singe marks. From this vantage point, Lisbeth searched for Eggie. He was nowhere to be seen. Help would not come. Not from Eggie. Not from the proconsul's change of heart. Not from the Lord.

As Lisbeth's gaze settled on the blackened space where the elaborate stage had been, a gasp escaped her.

Cyprian waited in the center of the ash and rubble. Though his hands and feet were bound, he stood tall, unafraid, and ready to sacrifice his life for the cause of Christ. From the contented smile on his face, Lisbeth could see he knew his sentence had actually been cast long ago—on the day he happened into a little dye shop and met a man who told him the life-changing story of the one God.

His head slowly turned as he searched the crowd for someone . . . not just anyone . . . he searched for her.

Be there for him.

The dread that had gripped Lisbeth for so many years dissipated. Her purpose had never been to change Cyprian or his circumstances. Her purpose was to love him, and that she would do until her life came to an end. "Cyprian! I'm here." She jumped up and down, waving her arms. "Cyprian!"

A guard shoved him toward a soldier holding a long sword.

Lisbeth's shout did not carry over the din of a thousand clamoring spectators. "I'm sorry, my love." Her frantic hands slid from the sticky air and hung limply at her sides.

"Go to him!" Maggie pushed her forward. "Now!"

Her daughter's order snapped Lisbeth into action. "Stay with Metras. Do you hear me?" Lisbeth wiggled through anxious spectators, all of them cranky from a night of sleepless waiting. Darting left and right, she worked her way to the nearest aisle. She reached the top landing. The stairs were a river of people climbing to the cheap seats. Lisbeth rose to her tiptoes and craned to see the man she loved. She prayed that if she fastened her line of sight on his, her husband would somehow feel her love.

Cyprian's face did not reflect the night of mental torture he must have endured after her refusal to stand by his side. Instead, his eyes were peaceful, the corners of his lips lifted in a satisfied smile. She remembered the butterflies in her stomach the night of their wedding. Cyprian, who was just as frightened as she at the unknown outcome of their marriage, had displayed the same courage at the altar. His chin was lifted proudly. His bronzed shoulders were draped in a brilliant white toga. His air of absolute certainty was indisputable.

Fighting like a salmon swimming upstream, Lisbeth shoved toward her husband, forcing her voice to rise above the roar: "Wait!"

Cyprian's eyes locked with hers. He broke into a grateful smile. The clock she'd been fighting for years stopped ticking in her head. For a breathless moment it was just the two of them, hand in hand beneath the stars, their hearts entwined by a love so deep nothing could sever it.

"I love you," she mouthed.

He swallowed and rewarded her with a nod.

"Mom!" Maggie had caught up with her.

"Maggie, go back!" Lisbeth shouted, but her daughter shook her head and pointed across the arena.

Maximus had assumed his place in the royal box. "State your name, prisoner of Rome."

Lisbeth held her breath along with the spectators who had their eyes trained on the man standing among the ashes. She felt Maggie's fingers lace with hers. Lisbeth squeezed tightly. They held on to each other, neither of them breathing.

"Caecilianus Cyprianus Thascius."

"Are you the leader of the Christians?"

"I am a follower of Christ." His bold proclamation was followed by a distant rumble of thunder.

Maximus rose to his feet, as if elevating himself in the eyes of the populace. "As their ringleader, you shall pay for their heinous crimes against the state." The crowd erupted. "So that no one is seduced to follow your example, I order you beheaded."

Stunned silence blanketed the arena.

"Blessed be the one God!" Cyprian's whisper floated in the rising wind.

"Do you have one willing to stand with you and hold your patrician garments?"

"He does!" Barek shouted from somewhere in the bleachers. Everyone watched as the handsome young man sprinted down the steps. "I'll not only stand with him, I'll take his place."

"Barek, no!" Maggie screamed.

Barek arrived at the stage, his chest heaving. "My father was the rightful bishop of Carthage. As his heir and successor, it is I who should perish for any perceived wrongs committed by my people."

"I'll not let him do it." Cyprian clasped Barek's shoulders. "God has other plans for you. For Maggie."

Barek slowly backed down. His chest heaving, he held out his arms to accept Cyprian's garments. Maximus signaled for the execution to commence. Lisbeth pulled against Maggie's hold, desperately wishing she was worthy to take Cyprian's place.

Cyprian removed his toga, folded the garment neatly, and then handed it and a small pouch to Barek. "Pay my executioner his twenty-five-aurei fee."

Barek nodded, tears streaming from his eyes.

Cyprian raised his face and looked at Lisbeth. Peace had ironed the lines of defiance from his brow. A contented smile played at the corners of his lips. His eyes had been washed clear of all hate.

His lips began to move as he seemed to be coaxing sound from deep in his throat. A hushed whisper at first, his voice gained confidence and carried to the highest seat in the house: "Father, forgive them, for they know not what they do."

From proconsul to peasant, everyone heard his unflinching declaration. Cyprianus Thascius would sacrifice everything for the future. Lisbeth's included. She didn't deserve his gift any more than the world deserved what Christ had done at the cross. It was love so freely given it swelled her heart to bursting.

Cyprian folded his handkerchief and tied the cloth across his eyes. He knelt on one knee and then bowed before his executioner.

Grief drove Maggie to her knees.

Thunder boomed and summoned a mighty wind. Ashes rose from the rubble. Howling squalls crashed against the harbor walls.

In a flash of the sword . . . the moment Lisbeth had desperately tried to stop for nearly twenty years was over.

Cyprian was dead.

White-hot lightning ripped apart seething black clouds. Torrents of fresh warm rain poured forth and washed over Lisbeth as if heaven itself wept for what had just happened in this place.

Lisbeth stood with her face to the wind, her hands outstretched to God. Water slipped through her fingers and pounded her until she could stand no more. She joined Maggie on the ground and wrapped her in her arms. They clung to each other and wept.

Strong hands reached through the storm and gently lifted Maggie from Lisbeth's grasp. Lisbeth raised her head to see Maggie securely enfolded in Barek's arms.

Metras stood before her, the rain sliding down his nose. He offered Lisbeth his hand. "If one person falls . . ."

"A friend can help them stand," she said through rivulets streaming down her face.

Metras pulled Lisbeth to her feet. One by one, Christians surrounded her and carried her forward.

Epilogue

LISBETH SAT BESIDE HER father beneath the arches of the pergola where she and Cyprian had made love. Smoke rings from Papa's pipe drifted on the pink streaks of dawn. Maggie, Barek, Mama, and Laurentius splashed about in the harbor shallows. A breakfast of leeks rolled in curly cabbage leaves and swimming in olive oil steamed over the fire Papa had built for one last church picnic on the harbor walls. Once the sun had completely risen, Christians not on duty at the hospital would soon join them for a time of worship and prayer.

Since Eggie's return, things had changed for the followers of the one God. While the emperor's grandson had arrived a week too late to save Cyprian, the ill-fated timing of the news he brought was sobering. Valerian was dead. Eggie's father was the new emperor of Rome. Gallienus had been so impressed by what Eggie told him that he'd declared it illegal to persecute Christians. The church no longer had to meet in secret.

History or God's plan? Lisbeth wasn't sure there was a difference.

The new emperor had stripped Maximus of his title and ordered him to return to Rome. Tempting as it was to wish Maximus executed, Lisbeth was shocked and saddened when Titus told her the proconsul's body had been discovered swinging from the last standing column in the theater.

Lisbeth had agreed with Titus: Carthage was in good hands now that Eggie had assumed the office of proconsul.

Speaking of Titus, because of the land merchant's generosity Cyprian's house had been purchased from the state and remodeled to expand the church's ability to care for the sick. More beds meant more work, but under Lisbeth's direction the tireless efforts of Pontius, Metras, Candia, Arria, and even Quinta were beginning to put a dent in both disease outbreaks. Lisbeth's chest threatened to cave in upon her every time she thought of leaving this selfless team to fight this battle without her and Mama's expertise.

Clutching Maggie's cell phone, Lisbeth stared out at the water lapping the stone wall. Spring winds snapped the scarlet sails of the imperial freighters returning to Rome. They were loaded with only a portion of the grain stores from Titus Cicero's silos. Gallienus had ordered the rest left behind to feed the African provinces until the harvest. A new day was coming to Carthage.

So why did the rusty grind of lifting anchors and the shouts of restless sailors anxious to leave the stench of smoldering funeral pyres fill her with such dread? History had proven it was a river that would not stray from its banks. For now, the empire would survive. But would she?

Maggie's squeal drew Lisbeth's attention to the beach. "I can't believe you just did that." Her curls were wet from the water Barek had poured. "You know I'll get even." She chased him into deeper water, where he pulled her into his arms and then promptly dunked her. When she came up sputtering, Lisbeth couldn't help but remember the times she and Cyprian had flirted on this very same beach.

"See, Laurentius," Mama said, encouraging him to wade in past his knees. "You just spit the water out and everything is fine."

While Mama had spent these past few weeks acquiring the stamina necessary to withstand the rigors of time travel, Lisbeth had spent hours in the pool teaching Laurentius how to use nose plugs and hold his breath. She hated that her half brother was still terrified of water, but she didn't know what else to do. If they were all going home, then Laurentius would have to come too. She could only hope her promise of a shopping spree at an art supply store would eventually convince him to take the plunge into the well.

Papa's days had been consumed with scurrying from one historical site to the next, scribbling copious notes in his journal.

And then there was the church.

Cyprian's letter outlining the details of Barek's appointment as bishop had been delivered by the centurion the night of Cyprian's death. Titus had easily convinced Lisbeth her support would go a long way in helping the church make the leadership transition. Barek had been leaning against a shadowed pillar, pressing his back to the cold stone when Titus herded everyone into the garden. Without much fanfare, the land merchant announced Cyprian's wish for the son of Caecilianus to assume his father's place. Barek had straightened his back and stepped from the shadows, giving everyone full access to what little he had to offer. At one time Lisbeth would have doubted this boy could shuck his churlish attitude and take his father's place. But Barek had proved her wrong again and again, and the day he held her husband's toga and boldly offered himself in Cyprian's place, she knew Barek had become the man of his mother's dreams.

Lisbeth had prepared to oppose any dissenters. But there had been none. No hostile looks. No concerns voiced. No other candidates put forth.

The clapping had started in the back. One after another, hands went together in a show of support that traveled through the crowd. The church was also in good hands now.

So what was impeding Lisbeth's ability to pick a day for their trip through the time portal? Why was she stalling?

Maggie.

Lisbeth watched her daughter's graceful strokes slice through the water. The impetuous girl had become a disciplined young woman these past few weeks. It was as if she'd grown up right before Lisbeth's eyes. Maggie had suffered a great loss with Cyprian's death, but she seemed to put her pain second to Lisbeth's grief. In an ironic turning of the overprotective tables, Maggie had even offered to live at home and finish college in Dallas.

Maggie stumbled onto the sand. "Are you going to let a girl beat you?"

Barek was only two strokes behind her. "Don't think you've won." He chased her down the beach. They disappeared behind the lighthouse pillars, where Lisbeth guessed a few quick kisses would most likely be stolen.

Lisbeth's chest constricted. "Did I do enough, Papa?"

He took a long draw on his pipe, then gently laid his hand upon hers. "That's a question for the ages, Beetle Bug." He gave her fingers a squeeze. "The past is a desert wind." His lips formed a circle, and another smoke ring floated on the breeze. "It can rise very unexpectedly and bury every trace of beauty deep within the earth . . . deeper still in our hearts." They sat in silence, watching the tiny smoke ring expand as it drifted toward the sun. "But after finding your mother I know this: if you're not afraid to excavate the ugly layers, beauty can be discovered again." He turned and smiled. "Don't be afraid to dig deep. There is love yet to be discovered beneath these ashes." He kissed her cheek. "Now, if you'll excuse me, your mother promised Laurentius and me one last stroll through the Tophet."

Water filled the footprints Papa, Mama, and Laurentius left in the sand as they set out hand in hand.

Lisbeth wiped a tear from her cheek and powered on the phone. The battery bar was nearly empty. She went to the camera roll and quickly scrolled to the image of Cyprian, Maggie, and herself. She stared at the picture, comparing Maggie's features to Cyprian's, until it faded to black. She pressed the button again, but the power was gone. Without a way to charge the drained battery, the family she'd worked so hard to put together would be forever lost. Or was it?

The truth was a pill she could hardly swallow. To rewind the clock and return to the twenty-first century would be like pulling threads in the tapestry of her life. Which one was she willing to remove? Her mother's plunge through the time portal? Then she would never have known her father. What about her decision to study medicine? Lisbeth couldn't imagine another profession more suited to her than healing people. What about her father's summons to the Cave of the Swimmers? If Lisbeth hadn't fallen through the crack in time, she wouldn't have met the bravest man she'd ever known. If she hadn't fallen in love with Cyprianus Thascius and his people, her beautiful daughter would never have been born. And if Maggie hadn't painted that little swimmer family on Ruth's urn, Lisbeth might not have ever discovered the true meaning of *family*.

All her life she'd limited the term to those with the same DNA. Lisbeth believed her happiness was dependent upon her ability to assemble all of her blood relatives in the same time period. But in her quest to reunite those physically related, Lisbeth saw that her failure had brought her an entirely unexpected family. The care the church had given her these past few months had shown her the truth: family was more than blood. Anyone willing to love someone more than he loved himself was family. These people had been that selfless. Leaving them now would be like amputating a cherished body part.

Lisbeth's gaze drifted up the beach to where Barek and Maggie had just emerged from behind the pillars, their faces flush with love. Behind them came Metras, Quinta, Pontius, Candia, and Arria.

Lisbeth clutched the dead cell phone. Somewhere deep inside she'd always known that she would never grow old with the bishop of Carthage. And yet, despite everything she'd lost, she did not feel robbed. The moments she'd had with him had changed her life and given her a group of people who loved her. She would be forever grateful.

Lisbeth watched Maggie lean into Barek, the water swirling around their ankles. Their love was a tender seed, a new beginning destined to ensure that Cyprian's legacy of faith and generosity would live on.

"Mom?" Maggie's voice cut through the roar of the waves. "You okay? You seem a million miles away."

The question wasn't whether Lisbeth was finished with the past. The question was whether she was willing to believe God was directing her future.

Lisbeth smiled. "For the first time in my life, I know I'm exactly where I belong."

In the amber light of dawn the decision was made. Lisbeth walked toward her beautiful daughter and the handsome young man who was destined to become the next bishop of Carthage. She waded out to them, the phone in her outstretched hand. In one freeing move, she pulled back her arm and sent the last of her doubts sailing into the sea.

Their good deeds will never be forgotten.
—Psalm 112:9 NLT

Acknowledgments

A STORY IS ALWAYS BETTER when it is shared. I treasure the time you've taken to share this epic adventure with me.

I wrote this story for you. But I also wrote it for me.

A few years ago I felt betrayed by those in the church. Their hurtful actions changed my life forever. The injustice shook me to the core and dumped me out at a crossroads of faith. I had to make a decision: Give up on God's plan for the church. Or cling to the promise that His love endures through every circumstance.

While wrestling with my decision, I was also researching our hero, a third-century martyr who faced this very same dilemma. Cyprianus Thascius also found himself at the crossroads of faith. He didn't deserve the betrayal he suffered at the hands of his little church. He had options. He could have recanted or fled and left the church to fend for itself. But he didn't. His decision to stay and remain faithful to his calling cost him everything. Why did he choose the more perilous fork in the road?

Simple. Cyprianus Thascius believed in the power that comes from joining hands with God and with other believers.

So many people joined hands with me to bring me to a place of healing. Many of them worked to help me bring this story to readers, and I am forever grateful. The numerous works of early church scholars and historians sparked my imagination. Gary

Tucker helped me wade through Roman trial procedures. A young doctor tried to steer me away from having a character perform brain surgery with a tent stake, but when she saw the historical evidence for this procedure, she helped me drive the stake through the skull with the least amount of damage. The fabulous, hardworking team at Howard Books, especially my crackerjack editors, Jessica Wong and Katie Sandell, championed and polished. My ever-supportive husband, children, and tribe of writing friends cheered and celebrated. And a huge thank-you goes to my new online friend the Carthaginian Wanderer, who lives only eight miles from the fascinating ruins of Carthage. This brilliant young local whose hobby is passionately re-creating the lost art of making purple dye has enthusiastically become my eyes and ears into that ancient world.

So by now you've probably figured out I've chosen to continue on the path of faith. You see, when I joined hands with the perfect Christ I also became part of his imperfect human family. No longer can I walk this earth and ignore the plight of my fellow man. While I'm alive, there will be struggles and disappointments, but when I die I will go to a place not bound by the confines of time but a place of perfection. And I feel compelled to take as many with me as I can. My prayer is that you too will join hands with the Savior and those who love him and set a course for this timeless world.

Until we meet in eternity, I leave you with the words Cyprianus Thascius penned for his friend:

> *This seems a cheerful world, Donatus, when I view it from this fair garden, under the shadow of these vines. But if I climbed some great mountain and looked out over the wide lands, you know very well what I would see—brigands on the high roads, pirates on the seas; in the amphitheaters men murdered to please*

applauding crowds; under all roofs misery and selfishness. It is really a bad world, Donatus, an incredibly bad world. Yet in the midst of it I have found a quiet and holy people. They have discovered a joy which is a thousand times better than any pleasures of this sinful life. They are despised and persecuted, but they care not. They have overcome the world. These people, Donatus, are the Christians—and I am one of them.

—St. Cyprian, martyr for his Christian faith,
beheaded September 14, AD 258

VALLEY

of

DECISION

Lynne Gentry

Introduction

THIRTEEN YEARS AGO, LISBETH made an impossible decision: leave third-century Carthage and her husband, Cyprian, for good. She did it to protect her daughter, Maggie, and Lisbeth gathered the strength to move on with her life.

But Maggie is sick of being protected. In an act of teenage rebellion Maggie decides to do what her mother can't—secretly return to the third century on a quest to bring back her father, leaving Lisbeth no choice but to follow.

Topics and Questions for Discussion

1. If the propensity toward rebellion dwells in each of us, why are we so surprised when our children rebel? What is our greatest fear when their rebellion rears its ugly head? How do you deal with the rebellion of a child? Share ways you've dealt with your fears for their future. How do you know when to let them go?

2. When Magdalena is taken to the prison beneath the Hippodrome, she tells her friends, "Do not be afraid." Ironically, she is relieved when she discovers she and her friends are to be held in a dark tunnel. Tell about a time when you were rescued from a dark place, physically, emotionally, or spiritually.

3. In *Return to Exile*, fear struck hard. Cyprian felt his duty as bishop required him to take the splintered Christian community by the scruff of the neck and somehow bring the members back in line. In *Valley of Decision*, he adopts a new strategy. What was it? Discuss examples of how Cyprian's decision to forgive and love changed hearts (hint: Barek, Metras, Arria).

4. When Cyprian welcomed back church members who'd purchased certificates of libellus to save their own lives, Lisbeth was not happy. She didn't trust them and she didn't think they should be allowed to waltz back into the fold as if nothing had ever happened. Her disagreement with Cyprian's decision is patterned from actual third-century accounts of the church's fracturing during this severe persecution. Some church members who'd risked their lives to remain faithful refused to offer mercy to those who'd defected. What important issue does the unwillingness to forgive raise for the church? Is there a differ-

ence between love and discipline? Should people have to make amends for choices that hurt others?

5. Deadly virus outbreaks are frightening. Today, when an outbreak threatens to become an epidemic, the World Health Organization sends in a team of highly trained disease hunters known as epidemic intelligence service officers. These masked young physicians, nurses, and scientists run toward the disease while everyone else runs away. In the third century, the Christians had similar choices. They could have decided to flee, but the majority chose to stay. What do you think compelled them to make this decision? What would you have done?

6. Interestingly, these disease control specialists report the biggest hurdles they face in the field is not the virus, but poverty, misinformation, and fear. For example, the recent Ebola outbreak in West Africa was fueled by decades of civil war that devastated health care systems, ruined public health infrastructure, and left the population vulnerable to infection. How can a few WHO disease detectives undo this kind of damage? Name a time in recent history when misinformation caused irrational fear.

7. When everything erupted in Carthage, the chaos reminded me of the turmoil I battle in my own life. People running me over, confusion on which way to turn. If it weren't for hands extended in love, I could easily get lost in my circumstances. Has there been a time in your life when everything felt out of control? Who came along and helped you?

8. Decisions, even small ones, can alter our futures and change the course of our lives. In *Valley of Decision*, everyone has a decision to make. Lisbeth has to choose between going and stay-

ing. Maggie has to choose whether to forgive herself. Cyprian must choose to submit to or rebel against God's will. Barek chooses between accepting his destiny as leader or denying his calling. What past decisions would you undo? Share how past decisions are woven into the tapestry of your life. What decisions lie before you?

9. Throughout the series, Lisbeth's goal is to reunite her family. What does she discover about true family? Does your "family" reach beyond flesh and blood? If so, whom does it include? The people who love you and support you? Tell how someone unrelated physically came alongside you. Have you thanked them?

10. Maggie was determined to return to the past, no matter the risk. Name one twenty-first-century item you would be unable to live without. Do you have something in your past would you be willing to risk everything to change?

11. What do you think happens to Lisbeth and Maggie? Do you think they remain in Carthage forever or eventually return to the twenty-first century?

12. Do you see Maggie and Barek's relationship working? What obstacles would they face?

13. If you could meet one of the characters from the series, whom would you like to meet?

Enhance Your Book Club

1. One of the things that drew Lisbeth to the third century was their need for good medical care. She had the skills. Her change

came when she decided to use them. Every community has needs. Our neighborhoods. Our schools. Our churches. What would happen if each of us decided to use our skills to take on just one of those needs?

2. Today, people around the world are suffering for their faith. Some are being forced to leave their homes with nothing but the clothes on their backs. Others are in prison. Maybe you can't go to a foreign country and rescue them, but you can contact support organizations or missionaries, you can give, and you can pray. Choose to make a difference.

3. It's fun to explore other cultures. Why not invite your book club friends to wrap up in a sheet and come over for a Roman holiday feast? There are several suggestions and recipes on the Internet. I even have a Pinterest Board called Toga Party Ideas. http://www.pinterest.com/lynnegentry7/toga-party-ideas/. For my Roman party, I lit some candles and tossed the couch cushions on the floor. My friends sat around my coffee table and ate cheese, olives, an avocado and cucumber salad, a spicy chicken soup they spooned up with toasted garlic tortillas, and Roman cheesecakes drenched in honey for dessert. We played some Roman trivia games and talked story. It was wonderful.

A Conversation with Lynne Gentry

How does it feel to complete *The Carthage Chronicles Series*?
I feel like I have been on an epic journey. A personal journey of exploration and growth. This story had its roots in my own regrets. My desire to go back and make some different decisions. The paragraph I wrote about Lisbeth realizing that if she could change anything in her past,

it would be like pulling a thread in the tapestry of her life. With that thread missing (her daughter, for example) she would be a totally different person. In the end, she decides all of those threads have made her who she is. That's how I felt when I wrote the epilogue of Valley of Decision. I'm comfortable with who I am ... an imperfect person who loves God and I know God loves me ... even when I fail.

Why did you decide to set the book in Carthage?

The Roman era has always interested me. When I stumbled across a third-century plague that nearly destroyed the empire, I had to know more. The Plague of Cyprian acquired its name from Cyprianus Thascius, a wealthy lawyer from Carthage. Although the sickness spread throughout the empire before it was brought under control, it actually originated in Africa. So I didn't choose the setting; history did.

If you could go back in history, what time period would you visit?

I would love to return to the time of Christ and walk the same cobblestones and sandy beaches with him. I think my love of all things Roman came from sitting in Sunday school and listening to the stories about that intriguing part of the world.

Did you always know that Cyprian would have to die? Did you question saving him?

Yes and yes. I know readers love to see the hero and the heroine get together in the end. That I let Cyprian die will undoubtedly disappoint some of you. But this series is loosely based on historical truths, and one of those truths is that Cyprianus Thascius was a real man, a man who changed the world by his sacrificial actions. I so greatly admire the courage of this early Christian. To me, changing Cyprian's decision to die for the cause of Christ would have done more than change historical truths. It would have taken away from this martyr's actual sacrifice, and that just felt wrong. So I let history take its course.

Did you always know that Barek and Maggie would develop feelings for each other?

No. That was an accident. Maggie wasn't supposed to have traveled to the third century until this last book, but when she accompanied her mother to the Cave of the Swimmers in Book Two, the little stinker refused to stay behind. She raised her chin and jumped through the portal before I could stop her. But the moment Barek dropped down into the well and Maggie asked her mother why this mean boy was wearing a dress, I knew they were perfect for each other.

Which character was your favorite to develop in the series?

That's like asking me to pick my favorite child. I don't know that I can name one. Of course, Lisbeth is very dear to me. In a lot of ways, her spiritual growth represents my target goals. As she transitioned from a place of selfishness to selflessness, I thought, with God's help that may be possible for me. I also enjoyed the mother/daughter relationships among Magdalena, Lisbeth, and Maggie. I will miss having all of these women in my life on a daily basis.

What projects are you working on next?

Stories are always clamoring for my attention. My next series is but a nugget based on a very unique thing that happened in a dusty Middle Eastern town at the end of World War II. But I promise you, the stakes will be high, the adventures outlandish, the romance heart-melting, and in the end, the world will be changed for the better.

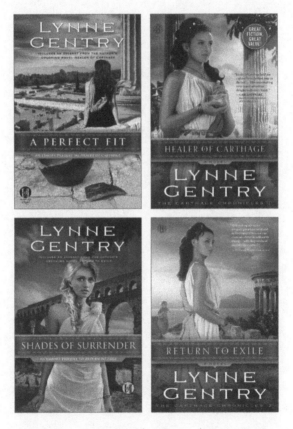